Books by Kasey Michaels

The Passion of an Angel
The Secrets of the Heart
The Illusions of Love
A Masquerade in the Moonlight
The Bride of the Unicorn
The Legacy of the Rose
The Homecoming

Published by POCKET BOOKS

Kasey Michaels

The Homecoming

POCKET BOOKS

New York   London   Toronto   Sydney   Tokyo   Singapore

This book is a work of fiction. Names, characters, places and incidents are products of the author's imagination or are used fictitiously. Any resemblance to actual events or locales or persons, living or dead, is entirely coincidental.

An *Original* Publication of POCKET BOOKS

POCKET BOOKS, a division of Simon & Schuster Inc.
1230 Avenue of the Americas, New York, NY 10020

Copyright © 1996 by Kathryn Seidick

ISBN: 0-671-50123-2

First Pocket Books printing April 1996

10 9 8 7 6 5 4 3 2 1

POCKET and colophon are registered trademarks of Simon & Schuster Inc.

Front cover illustration by Lena Levy

Printed in the U.S.A.

*To Constance Walker; friend,
cheerleader, and author.*

Special thanks to
Valerie C. Colas,
for both her invaluable research
and her willingness to share
that research with a fellow writer.

Dear Reader—

After dealing for so many years with the Regency period and elegant gentlemen and ladies of the *ton,* I've been asked by many why I've decided to uproot a few similarly sophisticated English creatures and plunk them down in 1763 Pennsylvania. I want to tell you why.

Have you ever ridden along a rural highway and looked deep into a stand of old trees, and thought—just for a moment—that you may have glimpsed a proud Native American silently running through those trees?

I have. Living in eastern Pennsylvania, once the home of the Lenni-Lenape, I probably couldn't avoid it. I grew up playing in the small woods behind my house, digging for arrowheads and imagining myself to be an Indian chief.

Eventually I grew up, but around me the physical reminders—except for those that were bulldozed to make way for shopping malls—remained, and the memories lingered.

Then, several years ago, I was asked to compile a history of my township, Whitehall, Pennsylvania. That history began with the Lenni-Lenape, or Original People, and they fascinated me. The colonists fascinated me. I began to see the Lenape, as well as the *shawanuk,* or White Fathers, who had settled in the area. They wouldn't leave me alone.

Over the years, I began to play the "what if" game all writers play. Slowly that game became my ruling passion. What if there was this wise Lenape brave . . . and what if he befriended a wealthy, mysterious English gentleman who had not so much emigrated to Pennsylvania as he had fled there . . . and what if that gentleman suddenly found himself saddled with this fiery Irish wife . . .

And thus were born Lokwelend, and Dominick Crown, and one Miss Bryna Cassidy.

I hope you enjoy their story.

The first man who, having fenced in a piece of land, said, "This is mine," and found people naïve enough to believe him, that man was the true founder of civil society.
—Jean-Jacques Rousseau

BOOK ONE

Planting the Seeds

*If you can look into the seeds
of time, and say which grain will grow
and which will not, speak.
— William Shakespeare*

Stranger in a strange country.
— *Sophocles*

CHAPTER 1

❧❧❧❧

New Eden, Colony of Pennsylvania
1763

"WHERE IS SHE?"

Dominick Crown had addressed this question to Alice Rudolph. She had entered the inn close on his heels, still slightly starry-eyed because Mr. Crown had actually helped her down from the wagon—treating her like a lady, and not just Truda Rudolph's unwanted cripple. Quick as she could, Alice pointed toward the corner, and a small table occupied by the lone female who had arrived at the inn last night.

Not that she had been dressed like a female when she'd arrived. Oh, no. As Alice had told Mr. Crown when her mama sent her to fetch him this morning, the female had shown up on the mail coach, dressed all in breeches and a heavy redingote, and with a muffler tied high round her mouth like it was still the dead of winter. She had been masquerading as a young lad, that's what she'd been doing—and carrying out her playacting fairly well until she'd heard all Alice's pa, Benjamin, had to tell her.

Then she had screamed like a mad thing, calling Benjamin a "damned liar" and a few other things Truda Rudolph

3

routinely called her husband but nobody else in New Eden had ever dared.

The female had cursed Benjamin Rudolph a blue streak, she had—until, of course, he'd cuffed her a good one on the ear with one of his hamlike hands. Then she hadn't said anything at all; not even after Alice's pa had picked her up from the floor, thrown her over his shoulder, and carried her upstairs. He'd dumped her on a bed, and then left it to Alice to undress the female's limp body and see that lovely white skin, those perfect legs—so unlike Alice's own—the lush beauty of the long, vibrant copper curls that had tumbled out from beneath the tricorn hat and bag wig that had previously concealed them.

No, Alice had not told Dominick Crown about any of that. And it wasn't as if she had to tell him, either, not now that the female was sitting right in front of him. Sitting there all queenlike in the prettiest gown Alice had ever seen, her long, fiery hair piled all in curls, her back as stiff and straight as a poker as she sipped tea and dared, with those strange, almost colorless eyes of hers, for any of the men in the common room to so much as blink at her.

"A rose among thorns, wouldn't you say, Alice? I can see that a rescue is very much in order, and I thank you again for apprising me of the situation," Dominick Crown said quietly, and Alice nodded furiously, not understanding half of what the Englishman said, then disappeared into the kitchens.

Dominick motioned to Benjamin Rudolph, who was in his usual position behind the small wooden bar, wordlessly commanding the man to bring him a pint. He then nodded to the half dozen men who sat all on one side of the tables jammed into the low-ceilinged room, their backs to the fire. They had obviously positioned their chairs the better to goggle at the strange female.

"Good morning to you, gentlemen," he said as he removed his dusty hat. He didn't care that his one-sided smile told them he had employed the title in jest, or that he was aware that at least two of the men, the Austrians, Traxell and Miller, spoke little English.

"Newton," he then added coldly, giving one particular man, Jonah Newton, a more personal reminder that he knew the tannery owner was only sitting in his chair, watching, rather than pursuing some greater vulgarity, because he had been warned that the damnable Dominick Crown was on his way to the inn.

Then, aware he had put off the inevitable as long as he could, Dominick started across the dirty wood floor. He halted, he sincerely hoped, a good fear-reducing four feet from the table where the young woman waited, her slim white hand holding the chipped, handleless cup poised halfway between saucer and mouth.

Good Christ, but she was beautiful! How long had it been since he'd been in the presence of a woman half so refined, one quarter so lovely? It seemed like a lifetime. In many ways, it was.

"Madam? Dominick Crown, at your service." Flourishing his worn, dusty hat in his right hand, and feeling more than slightly ludicrous, he made the young woman an elegant leg, the sort he had mastered in his youth but not had much reason to practice for nearly seven years, since his arrival in this fairly benighted community. "And you are Miss Cassidy, I presume?" he asked as he straightened once more, aware of both his rough clothing and her unsmiling refusal to extend her hand or in any other way return his greeting.

He didn't actually blame her. After all, Alice had found him already out in the fields, and he had pulled on his deerskin jacket, mounted his horse, and headed straightaway for the inn, choosing speed over respectability when told of the Cassidy woman's predicament. Leaving a gently bred female alone in Benjamin Rudolph's common room for any length of time was nothing short of an invitation to disaster, and he hadn't been of a mind to fatigue himself with having to bare-handedly beat anybody into flinders this morning.

The young woman's chin lifted a notch at his greeting, which was quite a remarkable feat, as she already held herself as high as a queen, for all that she was a mere scrap of a thing. When she finally spoke, her voice was cool, and cultured, and entirely devoid of either maidenly awe or mannerly respect. "Yes, Mr. Crown. I am Miss Cassidy. Miss Bryna Cassidy. The only question, sir, is how you presumed to know my name, as we have not been formally introduced."

Dominick motioned toward the empty chair across from her. At her slight nod, he sat himself down just as Rudolph slammed a mug of ale on the table.

"Pardon my informality, Miss Cassidy. But, as I doubt there is anyone save you and I in this small community who is actually aware of the niceties of social convention, we would have had a long wait for anyone to step forward and do the pretty. But, by way of explanation, Alice Rudolph informed me that you had introduced yourself here yesterday evening as being one Mr. Sean Cassidy. I merely took the chance that, although you are quite obviously an audacious fibber, you are not an extraordinarily inventive one. Although I would have laid down a goodly sum to have seen you in breeches."

The cup hit the saucer with an audible crack—if it had been constructed of anything less than the most crude pottery, it would have shattered into a thousand pieces. Bryna Cassidy leaned forward, her eyes narrowed in fury. "You insufferable dolt! Give me at least a modicum of credit, if you will. Or would you have had me travel here from Philadelphia, alone, without disguising myself in some way? I had thought to fashion a false wart for the end of my nose, but a score of warts and even a rash of running sores wouldn't be enough to dissuade animals like those leering hyenas over there."

Dominick spared a moment to glance over his shoulder at the leering hyenas, then smiled, spreading his hands wide to show that he, at least, was harmless. "I see your point. However, I wouldn't have condoned your traveling unaccompanied at all, Miss Cassidy, especially since you are aware of the less than desirable element running rampant here in the colonies. But then I am not in charge of your comings and goings. Now, had I been your father, I would have—"

He frowned, seeing the sudden sorrow in her oddly intriguing eyes, darkly lashed, yet curiously colorless in a way that had first seemed gray, then had flashed a clear, light green when she had defended her descent into breeches. "Yes, well, we'll leave that for the moment, shall we? I gather from Alice that you've already learned about the raid?"

She sat back against the rude wood of the chair, her posture still that of a gently bred female, but suddenly seeming so young, so small, so utterly vulnerable. He gave a slight cough and quickly took a drink of ale, wishing himself out of this conversation, out of this inn, and miles from what looked to be a further complication of his already complicated existence.

"Yes, Mr. Crown, I've heard. And in the bluntest of terms. My aunt and uncle, Daniel and Eileen Cassidy, were brutally murdered by savages not three months ago," she said quietly. "My young cousins, Joseph and Michael, are also dead. Hacked to death the same as Uncle Daniel and Aunt Eileen, I believe Mr. Rudolph said."

Her gaze was still steady, although he could see tears shining in her once more pale gray eyes, and her small, firm chin had begun to quiver. He felt instantly protective of her, which immediately made him angry, with her or with himself, he wasn't sure.

"Cousin Brighid," she continued doggedly, "just sixteen, and my dearest friend in all the world, has been taken by those savages, to be raped and abused. Yet not you, nor any one of those *gentlemen* over there, has so much as lifted a finger to try to rescue her in all these three months. And little Mary Catherine—" she hesitated, drawing in a long, shuddering breath "—only five years old—whom the innkeeper laughingly called the *dummy*—is with you. You, Mr. Crown, the grasping, greedy Englishman who barely hesitated an instant before taking claim to my uncle's beloved farm. History has ever been so, hasn't it? The English seeing

7

anything Irish and assuming it their God-given right to steal it."

"I'm sorry." Dominick winced even as he heard himself mouth those two woefully inadequate words. "Rudolph is an ass, if you'll excuse me for being frank. I wish you could have learned about your family some other way."

Her humorless smile blighted him. "Why? Would it have hurt less then, Mr. Crown? I think not. Quick and clean. That's the way to sever an arm; to break a heart. The captain of the *Eagle* took an unconscionable amount of time dithering about with meaningless sympathies and maddening inanities before at last informing me that my father had gotten himself roaring drunk and fallen overboard two nights before we docked in Philadelphia harbor. It took Captain Bishop nearly ten minutes to tell me what I knew in an instant, that I was about to disembark in a strange country, alone, with my only chance for sanity residing in the hope of somehow getting myself to the comfort of my father's brother Daniel."

She picked up her teacup once more, lifting it to her lips and taking a sip before closing her eyes for a moment, then opening them again, to look at him levelly. All the misery in the world was visible in those two eyes. She seemed to be holding herself so tightly, reining in her emotions with such determination, that if someone were to touch her, Dominick imagined she would shatter into a thousand small, pain-lashed pieces. "Thanks to Mr. Rudolph's bluntness," she ended quietly as she put down the teacup, "it took less than an instant to know that, with Uncle Daniel also gone, I am now even more alone than before. And I can assure you, sir, I hurt none the more or the less for Benjamin Rudolph's quick telling."

"Christ," Dominick swore quietly, turning in his chair to once more look over at Jonah Newton and the others. They were still just sitting there, grinning and staring, like bettors waiting for the cockfight to commence.

"See here, Miss Cassidy," he said, rising and holding out a hand to her. "If you don't mind, I think it might be best to continue this conversation at my estate. I give you my pledge as an English gentleman that you will be safe there. I'll see that Rudolph loads your luggage into the wagon, and I can tie my horse to the back. One of my staff will return the wagon later, not that I'm overly concerned on that head. At least then you can see Mary Catherine, and she can see you. Who knows? She might even talk to you."

Bryna looked at his hand for long moments, then placed hers in it and stood up, proving that his assessment of her size was correct, for she measured no taller than his shoulder. "My bags are already packed, Mr. Crown, and waiting, as I should like above all things to go to my baby cousin, Mary Catherine. And then, Mr. Crown, we will discuss mounting a rescue. Or did you think I would leave the baby and Brighid here with these barbarians when I return to Ireland?"

Dominick Crown wasn't all *that* huge. Tall, yes. Obviously strong. But not the total savage he had appeared to be when first he had entered the inn, raised his head after navigating his way beneath the low lintel, and skewered her with a single look.

He had still reminded her of an all-powerful giant as he'd crossed the room toward her, dressed so outlandishly, almost barbarously, in tan, ankle-length leggings gartered just below the knee. A ridiculous double-collared and fringed jacket, which looked as if it had been fashioned with a knife, was cinched at his waist by a multicolored sash, thus nearly concealing the pale blue and quite dirty homespun shirt that showed dark with sweat. He wasn't even wearing boots, but a sort of slipper made of some soft leather.

She had seen drawings of such attire in books she had read about the colonies before ever leaving Ireland, and knew Mr. Crown's ensemble to be constructed from the hides of some animal or other. Perhaps that of a deer? Yes. His clothing *was* barbarous.

But not nearly so barbarous as the man himself. His long, midnight black, unpowdered hair was tied at his nape with a thin strip of leather, a crude device that had not proved sufficient to keep several locks from escaping to hang down straight on either side of his deeply tanned, rather handsomely chiseled face. His eyes were just as black beneath straight, slashing brows, and although they seemed to laugh as he spoke, they revealed nothing of the man she now sat beside on the rough plank seat of the Rudolph wagon.

A man who seemed infinitely well suited physically to play the savage, that was Mr. Dominick Crown, for all his courtly bows and cultured English speech.

And if it hadn't been for that cultured English speech, and his promise to take her to Mary Catherine, Bryna would have declined his invitation. Not that the idea of remaining at the inn seemed any less dangerous than making her way, alone, through an endless forest that was probably knee-deep in bloodthirsty Indians.

Why had Uncle Daniel come here? Yes, life had been hard in Ireland, but surely not so terrible that he could have considered this desolate wilderness a near "paradise," as he had written in his letters to her father. And now this paradise had taken not only Uncle Daniel's dreams, but his very life—and the lives of his beloved family.

And for what? *For what?*

If this primitive wilderness was the "freedom" Uncle Daniel had spoken of, the "opportunity" he had chased with as much enthusiasm as her father pursued a winning streak at cards—well, she was having none of it! Her malleable English mother had followed wherever Bryna's loving but feckless father had led. Aunt Eileen and the children had followed where Uncle Daniel led.

But Bryna Cassidy had suffered enough at the whim of men and their dreams. From this day forward, she would direct her own steps, follow her own path. The very moment she had Brighid and Mary Catherine safely in hand, they could board ship in Philadelphia, leaving this tragic land and its cold memories behind them forever!

"I abhor this country," Bryna said feelingly as one of the wagon's wheels found an unusually deep rut in the dirt road and she was nearly pitched from the seat.

Dominick Crown turned his head and smiled at her,

showing her both his straight white teeth and the small lines that appeared next to his eyes. His smile made him look less a savage and more approachable—if she were idiot enough to be taken in by straight white teeth and laughing eyes. Which she wasn't. She might be her mother's daughter in many ways, but she was not the sort to trust her destiny in a handsome face.

"Abhor it, do you? Which, of course, Miss Cassidy, entirely explains your presence in it," he responded after a long moment in which she glared at him in what she knew to be real hatred directed toward both him in particular and the male of the species in general. He then once more turned his attention to the horses, who were showing a marked tendency to drift toward the side of the roadway, where clumps of tender spring grass seemed to wave an invitation to them.

"I was never to reside anywhere save the relatively civilized confines of Philadelphia, Mr. Crown," Bryna informed him coldly. She wished she didn't feel compelled to explain herself, her chin quivering only slightly as she remembered her father's promises, her father's unrealistic dreams and schemes, all of which centered on either the throw of the dice or the turn of a card.

"Papa suffered a few slight reverses of fortune in London during the past years, since my mother's death," she continued stiffly, not believing it a sin to lie in order to protect her father's memory. "Business reversals—unwise investments —you understand. In the end, we were forced to accept Uncle Daniel's kind offer that we reside in his home in Ireland, both before and after Uncle Daniel's family departed for the colonies last year. We remained in residence there until such time as we could sell the property and bring the proceeds here, where my uncle was to use them to patent the land he had traveled to England and claimed under a warrant granted to him from . . . from—"

"From Thomas Penn, no doubt," Dominick said, "son of William, and the most rascally, pernicious piece of mischief to have ever mastered the bending of laws to the benefit of his own deep pockets. He has a long legacy of deceit and dishonor in dealing with the Lenni-Lenape, the Indians native to this land, and the Lenni-Lenape, sadly, have equally long memories."

"The savages who murdered my family, you mean? You will, of course, excuse me if I do not find it necessary to demonstrate any sympathy toward them." Bryna looked off into the forest to both her right and left, once more nervously aware that the trees were so dense, the underbrush so thick, that it would be impossible to spot a band of attacking Indians until they were on top of the wagon. "You see, I doubt anything this Mr. Thomas Penn could have done warrants the slaughter of innocent women and children."

Dominick smiled again, the action carving slashing lines into his thin, chiseled cheeks. "Remind me to tell you of a little ruse of more than five and twenty years ago called the Walking Purchase, Miss Cassidy, the consequences of which, in large part, led to the massacre of your family. Then you will be more able to judge the depth of Thomas Penn's perfidious nature."

"Yet you are also a landowner, so obviously you deigned to deal with the man?"

He shrugged. "I wanted land, and the Penns were selling. Thomas is back in England these many years, old and fat and happy, I presume, and counting his money. I, thankfully, dealt directly with a Penn relative, and a far fairer man than Thomas. I met John Penn here, in Pennsylvania, when I patented my own land several years ago, and again when I patented your uncle's land. Your uncle's and that of two other properties adjoining mine and, as a result of the recent raids, suddenly without tenants."

"I see." Bryna's heart was pounding hurtfully in her chest, and her lips were stiff, so that she could barely force out her words. "How fortuitous for you, sir, that so many should die."

He was no longer smiling, and Bryna knew she had gone too far. "Yes indeed, Miss Cassidy," he said shortly, his precise English more clipped, more formal than before. "I took advantage of what could only be called a tragedy, knowing that my own property was spared an attack because I'd had the foresight to build myself a nearly impenetrable fortress, extending the hand of friendship to the natives while prudently arming myself as well."

"And prudent as well, you say? I vow, sir, I grow more impressed by the moment." Bryna shivered, so intense was her hatred for this man that her blood ran cold.

"Please, Miss Cassidy," he said, his tone relaxing slightly once more. "I suggest we cry friends for now, as what's done is done, and there is no recourse save to accept it. Now, as to what we have been discussing—well, I have developed an attachment to my scalp, nothing more. I am a colonist like all the others who have come here, perhaps better off financially, with the desire to grow an estate, a dynasty, here in this country. And the land in New Eden is good, the whole of it. Your uncle's in particular. Daniel was a hard worker, and more than half the acreage was already cleared and ready for planting. He hadn't had time to build a house, but the barn they built and lived in with their animals is still standing, if you wish to see it."

"Is it now? And you'd agree to take me there? Today? How terribly generous of you, I suppose." Bryna wondered why she was sitting so still in the wagon, her hands folded in her lap, when all she really wanted to do was turn on this arrogant, boastful man and draw her fingernails down his cheeks, scarring him for life with the evidence of her disgust.

Perhaps she was simply too hungry to marshal the energy to do more than snipe at him. She had been conserving her small store of funds as best she could, and that had meant her meals for the past few days had been both scanty and rare. The cup of tea she'd had at Rudolph's was all the nourishment she'd allowed herself in the past four and twenty hours. Her head pounded as a result of weeping most of the night, and it was all she could do not to lean against Dominick Crown's deerskin-clad shoulder and beg him for a hot meal and a soft bed.

"Mr. Crown? You haven't answered me. Will you take me there today?"

"Not today, Miss Cassidy, as I have work to do that cannot wait. Tomorrow, perhaps. Everything is, as I said, still intact, and I doubt that will change between today and tomorrow. The Indians would have set fire to the barn, you understand, but the troops stationed at Fort Deshler had rallied the local militia. They came out in force after seeing the smoke from the O'Reilly homestead, and probably frightened the attackers off, thank God, or else Mary Catherine would have been burned alive. As it was, I didn't discover her until the following day—tucked up under her parents' bed where Eileen must have placed her—wide-eyed and silent as a mummy. Which, unfortunately, she remains. I don't take pleasure in telling you any of this, but as you said it would be no easier for you to hear bad news slowly, I thought it best we get the worst of it over quickly, and before you meet with your cousin."

Oh God, oh God! Oh, sweet Jesus! Would he never shut up? With her gentle English mother four years in her grave, with her father's hot-blooded Irish temper springing to the forefront, and with her stomach crying out to be fed, Bryna at last turned to the man, knowing her sharp tongue remained her most dangerous weapon, and dropped into an obviously deliberate, broad Irish brogue. "Ack, sich a tale of wild wonder ye tell, sir, with yourself cast as saint and savior and the smartest of men! And is it proud of yourself you are then, Dominick Crown—crowing of your brilliance like a cock on his own dunghill, then hopping so swiftly into a dead man's boots?"

His grin was maddening. "Well, hello! And who would you be, ma'am? I was just now speaking with a most imperious young society miss who learned her prunes and prisms in her cradle, and who fairly reeked of respectability. Would you have any notion where's she flitted off to—leaving in her place a fiery-haired Irish termagant who drips sarcasm and vile accusations exactly as if she wasn't alone in a strange land, at the mercy of the man who did nothing more than look to increase his estate? While taking in that proud woman's young cousin, by the by, which wasn't all that easy a trick, considering the fact that I first had to teach her to keep from biting me each time I came within a yard of her. Would you perhaps care to see my scars?"

"I'd prefer to see the back of you as you walk out of my life." Bryna was furious with herself for having been so stupid as to show this man a side of herself her mother had striven for many a long year to eradicate. She had nothing in this life, nothing save her pride, her dignity. Now she had sacrificed even that for the sake of getting some of her own back at the one man in this terrible country who had offered her anything more than a leering grin or the back of his hand. "However, as I am grateful to you—after a fashion— I hereby apologize for my outburst. It was uncalled-for."

Dominick laughed out loud, and she pressed her teeth shut on another sharp retort. "God's teeth, but I'll bet that hurt!" he remarked, still laughing. "Very well, your apology is accepted, even though you didn't mean a word of it. And welcome back, Miss Cassidy—although I do believe you'd be wise to keep the fiery Bryna close at hand. She might be useful to frighten off the hyenas whenever you are in the village."

He gave the reins a quick flick, rousing the horses to a trot as he turned them off the dirt track and onto one that was not quite so narrow, and showed the effect of being carefully constructed rather than just carelessly hacked out of the forest. "We'll be at Pleasant Hill in a few minutes, in case you're interested."

"I care only to see my cousin, Mr. Crown. Other than that, we could be heading straight into blazes for all I will be impressed by anything you may have had a hand in building."

"Do you wish to know something interesting, Miss Cassidy?" Dominick prompted, just as the horses moved out of the overhanging trees and she espied a clear sweep of neatly scythed lawn and a softly rising hill topped by a large, three-storied Georgian mansion fit for London's finest neighborhood. "I'm beginning to think the wrong Cassidy is mute. Mary Catherine, as I remember her from my visits to

Daniel's homestead, had a most melodious voice. You, however, put me in mind of a carping fishwife, and I believe the world could only be improved by your vow of silence."

"Go to hell, Dominick Crown!" Bryna exploded, trying not to show any hint of admiration for the glorious house she had just seen peeking through the trees leading up the long drive.

"I already reside there, Miss Cassidy," he answered smoothly, pointing to his home. "Dubbing it Pleasant Hill is only my faint notion of a joke. And, Miss Bryna Cassidy, if you meant your vow to remain until your cousin Brighid is rescued from the savages who kidnapped her, and unless you harbor a wish to return to the inn, *you* will be residing here as well. Now, that's a thought to give a person pause, don't you agree?"

Bryna lifted her chin imperiously, not answering, for Dominick Crown had said it all, damn him, and there was nothing else to be said.

*There is no greater sorrow than
to be mindful of the happy time in misery.*
— *Dante*

CHAPTER 2

DOMINICK CALLED FOR THE BIG BROWN DOG TO FOLLOW HIM AS
he slammed out of the foyer and out of the house, intent on
heading for the large oak tree behind the building, and as far
from the tearful reunion as possible.

Bryna Cassidy had hopped down from the wagon un-
aided the moment he had brought the horses to a halt, the
hood of her deep blue cloak falling back to reveal her copper
curls. Holding her full skirts high above slim ankles, she had
then swiftly raced up the steps to the house, already calling
out her cousin's name.

She hadn't bothered to knock. She had simply thrown
open the large red door and run inside, past a startled
Lucretia—who had been walking through the foyer with
Mary Catherine—to scoop up the child and cover the five-
year-old's small, dimpled face with kisses. "It's all right,
Mary Kate," she had crooned, motherlike. "I'm here now,
love, and everything's going to be all right."

By the time Dominick had explained the situation to
Lucretia, Bryna and Mary Catherine Cassidy were col-

17

lapsed in each other's arms on the drawing room floor. Bryna's skirts formed a puddle of deepest blue against the flowered carpet, and the child's arms were wrapped tightly around her cousin's neck.

The two had been both sobbing and smiling, oblivious of their audience . . . and Dominick knew he had to take himself off before his memory was jogged, pulling him back to his own childhood and the world he had lost.

"Gilhooley! Leave off chasing that poor butterfly and come here to me," Dominick said, patting the ground beside him as he sat down. He leaned his back against the tree trunk, and the dog collapsed on the grass, laying his immense, flat head on his master's thigh and soulfully looking up at Dominick through huge brown eyes.

"We men are decidedly de trop at the house for the moment," Dominick told the animal. "And you'd better watch yourself while indoors from here on out, my mangy friend. You know what they say about being as nervous as a dog near an Irishman's boot. Well, Gilhooley, we've got ourselves saddled with yet another true Irish female at Pleasant Hill, so you might want to take those words to heart, as I doubt your name will be enough to save you."

Dominick sighed, as weary as if he'd put in a full day in the fields alongside the day laborers. He looked out over the sunlit acreage he had worked so hard to claim from the wilderness; the land that was his pride, his comfort, his challenge. With the addition of the Franklin, O'Reilly, and Cassidy homesteads, land he had so foolishly let slip through his fingers in the first place because he'd believed he could patent it at any time, he now owned more property than the Marquess of Playden held in Sussex.

More land, and better land. Fertile land. Rich farming land. Land that stretched to include acreage on either side of the river he used to ship his goods downstream to Philadelphia. Trees enough to keep his sawmill flourishing for decades. Water enough to sustain the cows and sheep he'd imported from England, and a natural spring of sweet, clear water running through a trough in the cellars of his fine house. There was even the stone quarry he'd already tapped in to in order to build that fine, handsome, eminently defendable house.

He had everything, all he'd vowed he would possess the day he'd taken ship in Dover over seven years ago, heading for the colonies. He'd landed first in Virginia, a land as fertile as New Eden, but there was no place for him there. Too many of the landed gentry journeyed back and forth to England, and someone would recognize him sooner or later. So he'd traveled north, taking with him his single servant and Lucretia, the slave he had purchased, then freed, succumbing to a hatred for human bondage he had not known he'd possessed until the day he'd seen Lucretia's former master beating her on the streets of a small Virginia town.

Philadelphia held its own large contingent of English. To Dominick, it was a city already too large for him to care for the notion of living within the strictures of a society that survived on rumor and innuendo and prejudgments.

So he had moved north once more, until he'd found the small colony of New Eden just sixty-five miles away, with its fair-sized village and its collection of Austrian, Swiss, Irish, and English settlers, none of whom had ever traveled in the first circles in London. None of whom would recognize either his face or his name.

And here he had stayed.

This was a new land, a raw, demanding, at times brutal land, but it held all the promise, and freedom, and hope for a better future that Dominick could have dreamed of when he'd been forced, he'd believed, to choose between his pride and the possibility of a hangman's noose.

Here, in America, his enemies were clearly defined, easily recognized. His challenges were equally clear: to take up the land, to learn it, to tame it, to nurture it, to grow with it. To build a new life, a better life, and to put the past behind him. Put the memories behind him.

He had been in New Eden for more than six years. Seven years had passed since he had left England. A lifetime since he had stared back at the Dover docks as he stood on deck, his hands gripping the rail until his knuckles turned white, straining for one last look at his mother's tear-wet face, watching England, his home, fading from sight . . .

"Master Dominick?"

Dominick flinched, aware that he had been so lost in his reverie that an entire platoon of militia could have come up on him, unheard. He looked up at his valet, his sole connection to his old life, his constant reminder that living in the midst of this undisciplined new land was no excuse to abandon the genteel conventions of the civilized world. "Lucas," he said, smiling. "Has the house fallen down? I can think of nothing else that would pry you from the safety of those stone walls these last three months or more."

"They'd be safer still if you'd say yes to keeping the ground-floor shutters locked shut," the servant said, pouting.

"And damned dark inside, you gloomy-gus," Dominick replied, pushing Gilhooley away as he stood up, to tower over the much shorter, slighter man. "Lokwelend assures me there is no danger anymore, that the raid was an isolated incident, and will most likely never be repeated. After all, New Eden is laughingly termed civilized, settled land. It's those to our west, on the frontier, who need to guard their hair. But enough of that. I suppose you're here to discuss Miss Bryna Cassidy? I suggest, at least for the moment, that we put her in the green room and attempt to pretend she doesn't exist."

Lucas sniffed, then pushed at the spectacles that had slipped down the bridge of his nose. "Miss Cassidy has already settled herself in Miss Mary's bedchamber. She also made it clear that it would not be in the best interests of— as she so rudely put it—my spindly-shanked self to naysay her. I have resigned myself to the situation."

Dominick gave a crack of laughter. "Pushy little thing, isn't she, and with a tongue that could slice cheese. Irish to the marrow, for all her obvious proper English schooling."

"Yes, she is fairly civilized, sir, I suppose. But only because her deceased mother was English landed gentry born and bred. Although—as Miss Cassidy put it—she considers this an accident of birth only, and no fault of her mother's. Does she know that your own mother is Irish, sir?"

"You two must have had a charming coze, probably just before she shut the bedchamber door on your foot. And the answer is no, Lucas. Although it will probably upset Miss Cassidy no end to know that we share a somewhat similar ancestry—considering her evident disdain for our English blood—we have not yet had time to exchange family trees. Which we won't until the time is right, unless you break into the port one fine evening and unhinge your tongue at both ends."

The valet-cum-butler stiffened, clearly affronted. "Have I ever betrayed you, sir?"

"No, Lucas, you haven't. Even though you, more than any, had cause to condemn me without a hearing. Forgive me for saying anything, even in jest. Now tell me more of this touching reunion between Miss Cassidy and her cousin. Did little Mary talk to her?"

Lucas shook his head. "She cried, she even whimpered a time or two, like a poor lost soul, but nothing else. I begin to despair that the sweet angel will ever recover her voice, sir, to tell you the truth. And, sir—are you really planning to mount a rescue of the sister, this Brighid person?"

"Miss Cassidy told you that, too, I'll assume," Dominick said, starting for the stables, where one of the staff had undoubtedly taken his horse. It was time he was back in the fields, working alongside the day laborers. They were good men, men he'd hired for the season, before they moved on to the West to start their own farms, but they needed direction. "And no, Lucas, I am not about to go haring off into the wilderness to effect a rescue. The militia are handling that, or they will, if they ever get enough of Rudolph's ale to screw up their courage to the sticking point. I have an estate to run, a crop to put in, acreage to clear, a grist mill to build—"

He took a deep breath, hating himself for the litany of excuses he had just uttered, then let it out in a rush.

"Lokwelend informed me that the girl has probably already been sold to one of the tribes passing through the area. She has also doubtless been moved beyond the mountains, perhaps as far as the Ohio, and is therefore untraceable. Or she's dead. To be honest, I rather hope for the latter, even if Lokwelend says Lenape slaves are for the most part well treated."

Lucas skipped along beside his master, taking two steps to Dominick's one in order to keep up. "You should call him Wayland, you know, with him being a Christian now, and not a godless heathen. He and his children, Peter and Cora. Sir," he added, his pale cheeks flushing an embarrassed scarlet at his own impudence.

Dominick turned to look at his servant. "Ah, to be a simple man, and live a simple life. How fortunate you are, Lucas, truly."

The servant halted in his tracks, his recently flushed fair English skin drained to parchment white. "Are you saying, sir, that Wayland is still a heathen, for all that the Moravians have converted him? That he only pretends to be what he is not?"

"Don't we all, Lucas?" Dominick answered, unexpectedly thinking not just of himself, but of Bryna Cassidy, who presented herself as a finely bred young lady of society, yet who had already showed him that her facade of sophistication was just that—and a much more fiery, intelligent woman simmered beneath that smooth, beautiful surface.

The servant sighed, lifting his thin shoulders, then letting them fall before saying, "Forgive me, sir. I am grown so accustomed to our new life that, at times, I cannot remember there ever was another, for either of us. I will say no more on that head, as it is a time we both wish to forget. You will, of course, be at table this evening?"

Dominick willingly let the subject slide. "I shouldn't miss it for worlds, Lucas. Have a tub waiting for me at five, if you will, as I would like to show both Pleasant Hill and my own sorry self to their best advantage this evening. It is best to begin as I plan to go on, wouldn't you say?"

"To go on? With Miss Cassidy, sir? Then she will be staying on indefinitely? I don't believe she sees herself as more than a temporary, and most unwilling, guest."

"Ah, Lucas, that's where you're wrong, except, perhaps, for that business about being unwilling. Miss Cassidy may not admit it, even to herself, but she has nowhere else to go, or the funds to get there, if I'm any judge. The question remaining, I fear, is not whether or not she is staying, but just what I am going to do with her."

"What am I going to do about that man?" Bryna mused out loud as she sat in the middle of the high, wide bed. Mary Catherine sat cross-legged in front of her, allowing her cousin to run silver-backed brushes through her soft, fiery red curls.

Bryna leaned forward and kissed her young cousin's cheek. "He has been good to you, Mary Kate, for which I am grateful. But it is one thing to take in the orphaned child whose land he has stolen for his own, and quite another to extend that charity to someone old enough to know him for the greedy, grasping creature that he is. Charity is cold, Mary Kate, most especially when it comes from the English. I know. And yet it's his charity we both need right now, damn his arrogant hide."

She continued to brush Mary Catherine's hair, even as the child shifted so that she was lying with her head in her cousin's lap, her thumb in her mouth, her huge, Ireland green eyes slowly closing as she drifted off to sleep.

How Bryna loved this little scrap, the last bit of family she had left in the world save her mother's family in Wimbledon, and a more pinch-mouthed, pinchpenny collection of thin-blooded Englishers she could not imagine.

She could picture herself showing up on their doorstep, a mute child and a damaged Brighid on either side of her, begging entry. There'd be a pope in Canterbury before she'd ever see the day her mother's family opened their arms and their pockets to any of them. "Lie in the bed you made, Felicia," her mother's father had pronounced the single time Bryna had seen her grandparents—during that unfortunate interlude when her papa had been installed in the Fleet for debt. No, Bryna would rather sleep under the hedgerows than ever apply to any of the Harringtons for so much as a crust of stale bread.

If she ever returned to England, that was. Which seemed highly unlikely, as she had no more than three pounds sixpence tied up in the handkerchief now stuck in the bottom drawer of the fine burled-wood cabinet in the corner of her cousin's bedchamber.

All her uncle Daniel's patent money, all of her own small dowry—and all the easy winnings her father had bragged he'd taken away from the table each night they were aboard the *Eagle*—lay on the bottom of the ocean with Sean Cassidy, leaving her with barely enough money to get herself to New Eden.

She had not a feather to fly with, and nowhere to fly to if she did. Not that she would take so much as one step back toward Philadelphia or aboard a ship heading to either Ireland or England without both Mary Catherine and Brighid by her side. And most certainly not before she searched out and confronted her ex-shipmate, one Renton Frey, which she would most certainly do, as soon as she found her feet. She had hoped for her uncle's help in the matter, but losing Uncle Daniel did not mean abandoning her self-imposed mission. It had only delayed it, that was all, while she was stuck here, cooling her heels in the back of beyond.

Which brought Bryna back to one Mr. Dominick Crown, and the glorious mansion that seemed so out of place in the midst of this benighted wilderness. What was he doing here, when he so obviously belonged in Surrey, or Sussex, riding his fields, entertaining the local squire and his comely daughters, tooling up to London for the Season, dressed all in satin and with his powdered wig on his head, before traveling to Scotland to fish for salmon?

He was nothing like Benjamin Rudolph, or any of the other ragtag ruffians she had encountered at the inn. He didn't belong in Philadelphia, with its tidy shopkeepers and newly wealthy bankers and ships' captains home after months at sea.

Even dressed so outlandishly, aping the appearance of the heathens she had, thankfully, not yet encountered, he fairly oozed London airs and sophistication. His house was totally English, furnished both lavishly and expensively in the best English style. His speech, his manner, were both impeccably English. Even his valet—and, pray, what need had the man of a valet?—was a pattern card of upper-servant hauteur and respectability.

Yet Dominick Crown was here, playing at lord of the manor in the midst of this savage, untamed land—just as if he had brought England with him and done his best to blend that age-old dignity with the raw, rough landscape of a new country. Blend with it, or conquer it.

Lace curtains and deerskin leggings. Fine English china such as she had eaten a woefully small snack from earlier, and heavy inside shutters meant to protect him in times of marauding heathens. Delicate rosewood furnishings, plush Oriental carpets, Chinese wallpapers, an enormous crystal chandelier in the foyer—and at least two long-barreled, fully loaded rifles and containers holding ball and powder positioned alongside every door and window in the house.

He, and his mansion, were studies in contradiction. Who was he? What was he about? And, most important, what was she to do with him?

Bryna carefully shifted Mary Catherine's warm, slumbering body fully onto the bedspread, then covered her with the oddly patterned wool blanket that lay folded at the bottom of the bed. She slid her bare feet toward the floor, then stood and walked to the window that overlooked the rear of the large house, pushing back the curtain.

She shook her head, frowning in confusion as she once more gazed out over the nearly three acres of neat English gardens and the carefully scythed wide sweep of lawn surrounding them. She instinctively knew none of these improvements could be considered a natural part of any farmer's priorities when struggling to establish a profitable holding in a new land. Her uncle Daniel had written of the daily labor to clear the land of tree stumps, of his notion of planting corn for the few animals he'd yet been able to purchase. There had been no mention of roses, or rosemary.

Standing here at the window, her toes curled into the deep carpeting, looking out at the immense sweep of garden and lawn, Bryna could not imagine that only three months previously her family had been butchered no more than a mile or so away, set upon by painted savages who wanted not their money or their belongings, but only their deaths.

"And now I am here," she said softly as she turned to smile at the sleeping child, speaking only to break the quiet. "On sufferance, surely, but I am here, and here, for the moment, I will stay. As much a captive of this land as Brighid, as much a prisoner of my fears as poor little Mary Catherine. But what will I do about Dominick Crown?"

She blinked back a tear, straightened her shoulders, and gazed out the window once more, knowing she must be the most shallow creature on all the earth to be wondering if dinner would be served soon, as the tea and cakes the serving woman, Lucretia, had brought to her had barely made a dent in her hunger.

How she longed for a heaped plate of potatoes and golden roasted onions arranged about a slab of thick, red meat. Every fiber of her being was screaming for meat. Fresh beef, not the salted pork she'd been served at sea. She was so hungry her head was pounding, her arms and legs all trembly inside. Her physical weakness made it difficult for her to concentrate on anything save restraining herself from taking up one of the rifles and racing off to the kitchens to demand a bite out of whatever it was that was filling the entire house with aromas that alternately teased and sickened her shrunken stomach.

She must be a terrible person indeed to be thinking of her stomach when her dear cousin Brighid was probably subsisting on roots and berries and living in a cave, but as it wouldn't do Brighid or Mary Catherine any good if their cousin should starve—

"Sweet Mother of Christ!" Bryna's hands flew to cover her mouth as her eyes grew wide at the sight of two dark-skinned savages appearing out of the trees at the bottom of the lawn. They were still more than three hundred yards from the house, but she could already see that they were nearly naked, the pair of them. Their long hair was pulled back and stuck with feathers, their glistening bodies bent nearly in half as, carrying long rifles, they ran straight for the house.

She didn't bother to hunt for her shoes. She completely forgot the fact that her hair was unbound and she was dressed only in her shift. She simply turned and bounded to the door and into the hallway, racing fast as she could down the winding staircase as she loudly called for Lucas and Lucretia.

She skidded to a halt in the foyer, taking in great gulps of air as her senses swam with her exertion. She struggled to get her bearings, then made her way to the back of the mansion. Somehow, she found herself in a dark-paneled study that boasted a door to the outside. Just as at every door, there were two immensely long-barreled rifles standing at the ready, propped against the wall.

"Lucretia! Lucas! We're under attack!" she shouted yet again, then sprang into action.

She snatched up one of the rifles, looked at it quickly to be sure that, although its long, thin barrel was unlike anything she had seen, the operation of the already loaded weapon was similar to that of the one her father had taught her to use to bring down game. Satisfied that she could handle the rifle, she then took a deep, steadying breath, clutched the weapon tightly against her breasts, and threw open the door.

The two savages were still coming toward the house. Both were still running up the long, slowly rising hill in that odd, crouched way, seeming to glide over the lawn a few inches above the ground. Their advance was as silent, and as swift, as the death that had come in the night to take her beloved mother from her.

Still calling out for help, Bryna moved outside the door, past the flat stone that served as a stepping-off point to the lawn. Heaving with all of her might, she shouldered the rifle, which was nearly a full foot taller than she, closed one eye, squinted as she looked down the long barrel, and locked the closest Indian in her sights.

She squeezed the trigger.

The next thing she knew she was sitting on the flat stone, her hands still gripping the rifle, her legs splayed out in front of her. Her ears rang, her right shoulder felt as if it had been broken, and she coughed as she raised her good hand to wave away the blue smoke that choked her lungs and smarted at her eyes.

"Dear Patrick and all the saints!" she exclaimed, shaking her head to clear it. Had she gotten one of them? She threw down the spent rifle and clumsily scrambled to her feet, knowing she could not spare so much as a moment to check on her success or failure, then turned to rush back into the house and snatch up the other weapon.

Only she never made it. Instead, her eyes still watering, making it difficult for her to see, Bryna ran smack into the broad chest of one Dominick Crown. He took hold of her upper arms—nearly bringing her to her knees with the pain that sliced through her right shoulder.

He shook her, hard. "Idiot woman! What in blazes are you about? Lokwelend!" he called out loudly. "Pematalli— are you all right?"

Bryna stilled within Dominick's crushing grip. She looked up at him, openmouthed, seeing him through the swirling haze of powder smoke and the sickening light-headedness caused by her hunger, and now intensified by her fear.

"You—you *know* them?" She peeked over her shoulder, seeing the two Indians who were now only a few yards away, one of them twirling the remnants of a feather in his hand as he smiled widely, his teeth showing a blinding white in his dark face. Until he got a good look at her, that was. Then, suddenly, his harsh, hawklike features smoothed, and he was at once incredibly sad.

"So, Crown, this is your woman, the one you spoke of earlier when we met in the forest? I had feared so," he pronounced in a low, guttural, yet easily understood voice.

Bryna became suddenly aware of her near undress, and her nearly fatal mistake.

For the savage spoke a clipped, precise English and, now that she could see him clearly, carried not only a rifle, but a brace of rabbits he must have been bringing to the mansion kitchens. Behind him, the younger Indian also held two rabbits, and was openly grinning in her direction. This was in contrast to the elder Indian, who continued to look at her as if she were somehow responsible for everything bad that had ever happened to mankind since Eve first presented Adam with a lovely red apple and suggested he might care for a wee nibble.

"You boasted that she possessed the heart of an eagle," the elder Indian continued, his dark eyes eloquent; not showing hate, or fear, or even derision, but somehow *aware*—as though he knew her, and accepted, had even expected, her presence. "You spoke the truth, my friend, just as I already knew it. For I have seen this woman in my dreams, and dreams do not lie."

Bryna stood very still within Dominick's arms, unwillingly grateful for his support, unable to breathe. The Indian stepped up to her, taking hold of a lock of her hair for a moment, then moved away from her again. "It is warm, this hair, and alive, like the embers of a banked fire. Pematalli, my son, look closely and learn. You see her hair; now see how her very eyes shine with light. These are the smoke-eyes of my dream."

The Indian smiled then, looking to Dominick, but even his smile was sad. "Smoke and flame. Your woman is the Bright Fire, Dominick Crown; come to conquer, as your fellow *Yankwis* came to conquer, as all the *shawanuk* have come to conquer, offering their hands and then snatching from us all that we hold dear. Take care how you deal with the Bright Fire, my friend, or this will end badly for you, I believe. Perhaps for all of us."

You roll my log,
and I will roll yours.
— Seneca

CHAPTER 3

DOMINICK ENTERED THE DRAWING ROOM JUST AS THE MANTEL clock chimed out the hour of six and headed directly for the drinks table to pour himself a glass of burgundy. He caught a glimpse of himself in the large, ornate Queen Anne mirror he'd had driven up from Philadelphia just last year, along with the immense dining table, chairs, and sideboards a fine Broad Street cabinetmaker had copied from a book of Chippendale designs Dominick had forwarded to him for just that purpose.

He appeared almost civilized this evening, Dominick decided, touching the foaming lace at his throat, then turning slightly sideways, to check the fit of the blue silk coat that reached nearly to his knees. It suited him well, this French-inspired *habit à la française,* a fitting complement to his finely embroidered velvet vest and the white kid breeches that buckled just at his knees. The wide lace at his cuffs, the pristine whiteness of his soft lawn shirt and jabot, the jewels that winked out from the lace at his throat and glinted on three of his long fingers—all combined to make him the compleat gentleman.

Or would have, if Dominick had allowed Lucas to powder his hair. It remained his servant's deepest shame that his master refused to either have his head shorn for a wig or powder his midnight-dark hair. The former, as Dominick had explained more than once, was ludicrous, as he had no use for *cadogans* or bagwigs when in his deerskins. The latter—powdering his own considerable head of hair, and then having Lucas brush it out again—was simply a waste of time.

When Pleasant Hill was complete, when Dominick had taken himself a wife, or when his mother was at last convinced to leave Sussex and take up residence, *that* would be the time for the full measure of pomp Lucas thirsted to exercise in his master's house. Which wasn't to say that Dominick was unaware that he had been a bit of a slacker of late. Lately he spent most of his time in those comfortable deerskins, taking a larger percentage of his meals out of doors with Lokwelend, falling into bed at night without first playing at the spinet in the music room, or opening a single book in his study.

Yes, he needed the softening influence of the refined, gentler sex here at Pleasant Hill. He'd known it for some time. Although he hadn't done anything concrete to remedy that lack. Nor could he, not without the risk of opening an old wound best left undisturbed.

What a happy coincidence that the woman fate had thrust at him today bore all the outer trappings of a well-educated English lady. And what a further unlooked-for pleasurable happenstance that appearances, pleasing as hers were, were rarely ever a reliable measuring stick, for there was much more to Bryna Cassidy than a background of fine English schooling.

The damnable little minx had nearly killed Lokwelend this afternoon! How his mother would have enjoyed seeing her in all her fire and Irish temper. Dominick then sobered, drinking down the burgundy in two quick gulps, remembering the look of naked hatred Bryna had thrown him as she had stomped past him into the house once Lokwelend had recited his party piece full of dark warnings. Hers had been a look that had told him his newly born hopes for their relationship did not hold a candle to her disdain for him and this country. Not that her quick, searing glare had done anything to discourage him from appreciating her slim waist and shapely ankles as she flounced out of the study.

He smiled now at the memory, which overshadowed Lokwelend's intriguing caveat that Bryna Cassidy could prove to be trouble for him, for all of them. It wasn't like Lokwelend to behave like an old woman, speaking of dreams that portended some terrible future. But then it had been Lokwelend who had been shot at, not him, and the man was entitled to some sort of comment. Saying Bryna could prove a disaster, however, was laying it on a little too thick and rare. After all, she was only one small woman. How much damage could she do?

"Excuse me, kind sir," he heard that one small woman chirp brightly from the doorway, so that he automatically turned to bow in her direction, "but have you perhaps seen one Mr. Dominick Crown? I have had the displeasure of meeting with him twice, earlier today, but can find him nowhere in evidence this evening. Perhaps you know him? A tall, rather dirty man, singularly uncouth, and dressed all in animal skins?"

The smile that had tickled at his lips a moment earlier grew into an unholy grin. Little devil! Try to get some of her own back, would she? How he enjoyed listening to the hint of Ireland that crept into her voice when she was angry. He had sat at Daniel Cassidy's table many a night, allowing Eileen Cassidy's Irish lilt to wash over him the way his mother's voice had done, bringing back pleasant memories of a life long since lost to him.

He walked over to Bryna, doing his best not to notice how lovely, if rather pale, she looked in her fashionable green-and-white-striped panniered gown, the green reflected once more in her strange, chameleonlike eyes. He only offered his arm to escort her to the couch, saying, "I suffer from a similar dilemma, madam. I had hoped to catch another glimpse of the petite, wild-eyed, barely clothed barbarian *I* had encountered earlier today. Her name, I believe, is Bright Fire, her occupation that of conqueror."

She let go of his arm and sat down all at once, so that her skirts billowed out around her. "I see that cloaking yourself with the outward trappings of a gentleman does nothing to curb your impudence, Mr. Crown. Are we to dine any time soon, or do you feel it imperative we amuse ourselves with inane talk for an hour, just as if we were in London, and you were about to preside over a dinner party? You do seem to delight in playing the gentleman—when you're not playing the barbarian, that is."

He poured her a glass of sherry and handed it to her before crossing to the fireplace, to lay his forearm on the mantel and take up a relaxed pose he was far from feeling. "Please accept my most profound apologies. I believe, Miss Cassidy, that we have gotten off to entirely the wrong start. Shall we begin again?"

"With the way we seem to be constantly at loggerheads, I would suppose arguing, apologizing, and then beginning again could conceivably become our only method of conversation." She took a sip of sherry, then put down the glass with, he noticed, a slight tremor of her fingers betraying her unease. "Oh, very well, Mr. Crown. As I, too, would like very much to put the events of this day behind me, I will agree with your plan. We shall have a civil discourse. May I suggest we begin with a more in-depth recitation of your version of how my uncle's land came to be in your possession and precisely how you plan to recompense my cousins for its loss?"

A good spanking wouldn't come amiss, Dominick thought, clenching his teeth. "If you wish, as I suppose you have come as close to being civil as you know how. I also suppose you would like me to begin at the beginning." She looked up at him, her expression bland, although he was sure she was dreading his explanation.

"That would be best, if I am ever to understand anything about this godforsaken country. I would also like to know, somewhere in your story, how and why you have come to befriend two of the savages that so brutally murdered my family," she said, as he hesitated, gauging how much he could say, how much truth she could handle.

He decided to take the long road, rather than the short, so that he could measure his words.

"Difficult as this will be for you to do, Miss Cassidy," he said at last, "I will ask you to place yourself, for a moment, in the shoes of these savages you have such good reason to hate. The Lenni-Lenape, or Original People, as they term themselves, were here first, much as we all tend to forget that small fact. They did not ask us to come to this land, and they certainly were unprepared for losing that land to the *shawanuk*, or white people, as they call us. Being Irish," he added, smiling, "I believe you might be better able to identify with the Lenape if you keep this fact in mind."

"You ask a lot, Mr. Crown," Bryna told him, once more picking up her glass. "But please—continue."

He inclined his head a fraction, acknowledging her words. "The Lenape and the first colonists coexisted rather well for many years, until Thomas Penn—you do remember that name, don't you?—decided that buying up the Lenape land parcel by parcel was taking much too long. Thus the Walking Purchase, in which Penn tricked the Indians into deeding him land along the Delaware River and extending as far north as a man could walk in one day and a half."

"I begin to think we will be dining unfashionably late, Mr. Crown."

"You need to hear this so that you may better understand, Miss Cassidy," he told her. "You see, Penn engaged the fastest walkers he could find. They succeeded not only in walking off land that extended into ancient Lenape hunting grounds, but Penn then drew a line at a right angle all the way to the river—covering an area not originally in the agreed-to area—and neatly doubling the land he now claimed."

"That doesn't seem fair," Bryna said, frowning. "But the Indians had agreed, hadn't they?"

"Precisely. And, although they knew they had been duped, they remained true to their end of the bargain. The very land this house is built on was a part of the Walking Purchase, which worked out rather nicely for me, but chagrined Lokwelend and his son and daughter no end when I first came to mark off the boundaries of my property."

"You let them stay, didn't you? Why?"

Dominick smiled. "It seemed easier than fighting them, I suppose. And I did feel more than a twinge of shame when I'd heard the full story of the Walking Purchase. I deeded them some land near the creek, where they had built a log house—much as Lokwelend protested that land cannot be either sold or given away by those who have never owned it in the first place—and gave them free run of all my property. Lokwelend, by the by, is Lenape for The Traveler, but he'd informed me he'd had enough of traveling and wished to remain here. He'd become a Christian, thanks to the Moravians that settled in Bethlehem—a rather lovely small town several miles to the east of this property—and wants his son and daughter to learn to live with the *shawanuk.* He has seen the future in a dream, or so he told me, and he believes the Lenape are doomed to extinction if they continue to either withdraw to make their stand beyond the mountains or in any way resist the power of the *shawanuk.*"

Bryna sniffed, raising her small chin. "Obviously many others of the Lenape disagree with Lokwelend, or else my family would still be alive."

"Do you enjoy being wrong, Miss Cassidy, that you are always so quick to leap to conclusions?" Dominick asked, leaving the fireplace and coming to stand in front of her. He caught a faint hint of jasmine in the air, and stepped back from the couch a pace, surprised by his immediate, gut-clenching reaction to this womanly perfume. "As an Englishman, as a human being," he went on quickly, "I am embarrassed to tell you what has been happening to those of the same mind as Lokwelend—those Lenape who believed they could continue to share this land with us, the people they so trustingly called their 'white fathers.' You see, we're a greedy bunch, and each year we took more and more of the Indian lands, until they found themselves with no place to hunt, no way to feed their families. We have made them dependent upon us, our goods, our knives, our rifles—and then we took those things from them, turning them away from our trading posts."

She frowned, causing small lines to appear across her smooth forehead. "Does Rudolph turn away the Indians?"

Dominick shook his head. "Not yet. He is, for the moment, content merely in fleecing them, charging them double for anything they buy. But the Lenape children are suffering, Miss Cassidy, and their way of life is dying. The Lenape are being called women by the other tribes, an insult to their honor, and otherwise ridiculed for their peaceful ways. That's why some of the tribes closest to the frontier began to fight back, refusing to leave the last of their land and, yes, attacking those who dared to claim it. The latest injustice is the murder of one of their chiefs, Teedyuscung, who was burned alive in his cabin because he dared to protest when even more Lenape land was taken from his tribe. It was only then that we were attacked by one of the avenging war parties, here in New Eden, and your family was killed. The Cassidys, the O'Reillys, the Franklins— they all paid the price of the *shawanuk's* lies and treachery. In short, they became innocent casualties of war."

"You call what happened a war? The Lenape make war against children? I'm sorry, Mr. Crown, but although your sad tale may evoke some pity within my heart for these people, it in no way justifies the murder of women and children. What does that have to do with war, or with honor?"

"How does hanging a ten-year-old boy in London, for the crime of stealing a loaf of bread, improve the honor of our interpretation of English justice, Miss Cassidy? How civilized do you believe *we* look to Lenape eyes?"

"Oh, God," Bryna said softly, lowering her head for long moments, then looking up at him, her eyes now the color of woodsmoke, and bright with tears. "I believe I've had enough of history for the moment, Mr. Crown. Tell me about my family, please. I want . . . no, I *need* to know how they died. Rudolph said the savages took their hair, which I don't fully understand. Did they suffer overmuch?"

Dominick shut his own eyes, as if Bryna might see the horror he had witnessed at both the O'Reilly and Cassidy farms reflected in their dark depths. The four Cassidys had been hacked to death with tomahawks, then scalped. It wasn't a pleasant thing, seeing a head that had been scraped to the bone between brow and crown. With no scalp to hold the rest of the skin in place, the victim's entire face slid downward, rendering that final expression of pain and fright into a movable mask of horror.

"I buried your family, Miss Cassidy," he said at last, steeling himself to look directly into her eyes. "I know where they were when they died, could see how they'd been surprised by their attackers, then quickly and almost painlessly dispatched. They barely had time to be afraid. With Lokwelend's help, with the help of his two children, I washed them and clothed them—and I buried them. I saw to it that a traveling priest blessed their graves not two months past. They're at peace now. Let them rest."

She nodded, then finished her sherry in a single swallow. "Thank you, Mr. Crown. I am in your debt, more now than ever. And I would appreciate your taking me to see their graves tomorrow, so that I might say my own farewells," she said simply, then added, "but I still cannot understand why no one has yet mounted a rescue of my cousin. Was Bridie the only captive?"

"The only one, yes. Lenape kill to avenge, and only so many as they have themselves lost. The rest are taken as slaves, or to be sold to other tribes—or even adopted, to replace dead family members. But there was still reason to believe another war party might attack, you must understand, so that none of the troops at Fort Deshler could have been spared to go off in search of a single female who might or might not still be alive."

"But that was three months ago. There's no danger now, is there? There couldn't be, or else you wouldn't have left your own front door unbolted and your shutters open while you were away, now would you? Why haven't you tried to rescue her?"

Dominick's jaw tightened. This woman saw too much; more than he wanted her to see. "I am not a member of the local militia, Miss Cassidy. I am a landowner, and my interests lie in that land."

Bryna shook her head, then looked up at him, her eyes narrowed, and nearly devoid of color. "No. Oh, no, Mr. Crown. That's not it. You simply don't care, do you? You have your land, yes, and this house. You have carved yourself a small slice of England within this wilderness, and you exist only for it as it exists only to please you. You're not a part of this land, this community. As a matter of fact, I believe those men at the inn actually hate you. I could see that this morning in the common room at Rudolph's. You are complete unto yourself, and uncaring of anything save your own concerns."

Dominick inclined his head slightly, as if the movement would allow Bryna's most recent insult to fly over his head without drawing blood. It didn't help. The dratted woman had an uncanny way of sending her verbal darts straight through the center of her target.

Maybe what he planned wasn't such a good idea after all. It remained, however, his only one, and as the alternative would be to put the dratted female out into the street, he really had no choice. No choice at all.

"You've been thinking about me, haven't you, Miss Cassidy? Why, you must have devoted most of the day to thoughts of me—apart, of course, from the moments you spent attempting to shoot down two of my dearest friends. I'm flattered."

"Don't be, Mr. Crown," he heard her continue as he looked at her, still liking what he saw, still impressed by both her beauty and her fire. "Five minutes' thought was more than ample to know who and what you are. My only question now is why you would deign to take Mary Catherine into your small, transplanted corner of England. Or do you simply plan to house and feed her on the chance a war party might someday be bold enough to attack your fortress, at which time you will push little Mary Catherine outside, sacrificing her to save your beloved property?"

"All right, Miss Cassidy," Dominick said quietly, angered at last by her accusations. "We'll have it your way. I'm a greedy, heartless bastard who boils babies for dinner. I consider myself better than my neighbors, I care only for land and money, and I am intent solely on myself and my plans to be the richest landowner not just in Pennsylvania, but in all of the colonies. And I have brought you here to Pleasant Hill, Miss Cassidy, not so that you could be with your cousin, not to remove you from the inn and the men who would at this very moment be drawing lots to see which of them would be first to bribe Rudolph for the key to your room tonight, but so that I might have the extreme displeasure of listening to you berate me at every turn. Or are you totally unaware of your delicate position, being a lone, unprotected, and unbelievably rude and ungrateful female in a strange, considerably uncivilized land?"

"Oh, God. I've been an idiot. I'm sorry—again. Please, Mr. Crown, forgive me." Bryna put her closed fist to her mouth and bit down on her knuckle. She looked small, and vulnerable, and increasingly pale. Almost ill. Perfectly positioned for what he was about to say, to propose.

He took a deep breath and let it out slowly. "Dominick," he then said gently, watching her closely for her reaction.

"What?" Her expression changed instantly from that of reluctant contrition to one of considerable anger. He was really beginning to enjoy watching her every emotion play out on her wonderfully beautiful face, in her unusual, vastly intriguing eyes.

"I'm saying, call me Dominick, Bryna," he said, pulling up a side chair and sitting down directly in front of her, his knees nearly touching hers. He looked at her levelly, letting her know he was serious, that his next words would be serious. "You have spent a part of your day thinking about me—five minutes, I believe you said? I have spent considerably more time thinking about you. About your situation, which, the moment Alice apprised me of it this morning, became *our* situation, especially when we add Mary Catherine's future into the equation. And I have come to a conclusion you will doubtless argue, but eventually concede is our only possible course of action. So, as I have deduced that the single answer to our dilemma is that the two of us marry in order that you might remain at Pleasant Hill with Mary Catherine, I believe the informality of first names between us is permitted."

"The Devil you say." The wonderfully Irish expression of shock and outright skepticism slipped from her mouth in a near whisper.

Dominick smiled, and responded in kind, unable to stop himself. "Aye, Bryna. The Devil I say." He watched, entranced, as another round of varying emotions danced across her easily read face. Shock first, then another quick bout of narrow-lidded anger, followed closely by a sly, fairly calculating look that told him she was not about to reject his coldly stated proposal out of hand. Her eyes, so very nearly transparent in repose, so flashing with hints of green fire when she was angered, or frightened, or close to tears, showed nearly colorless now as she mentally assessed her situation, his explanation of that situation, and the reasonable, if bizarre, solution he had just handed her.

"Why?" she asked at last, all business, and all Englishwoman, again. "I fully recognize my own predicament, but what reason do you have to propose marriage to a woman you don't know and do not particularly like? I can understand your need for a wife. I can imagine there is a paucity of gently bred females in this area. But wouldn't it be easier to find yourself a more suitable bride in Philadelphia, or send to London for some conformable milk-and-water puss? Why me? We'd murder each other in a fortnight."

Damn. He'd already deduced she was intelligent. He just hadn't counted on her being so very quick. "All I can say to that, Bryna, is why not the two of us? I've been contemplating marriage for some time, and today I have seen the benefits of our marriage. For you, for Mary Catherine—and for myself. Pleasant Hill is in need of a woman's softening touch. Listening to a woman play the spinet of an evening, watching her as she sits by the fire, embroidering on her tambour frame, would be pleasant, civilizing diversions. I also, frankly, need sons, to take over what I have begun here. I'm a busy man, and live a near solitary existence, and there are not many suitable females longing to bury themselves here, in New Eden, away from society. Yes, I could travel to Philadelphia and waste months wooing some ship captain's daughter, but it would save me a great deal of bother to have the matter settled both simply and expeditiously. You, Bryna Cassidy, are expedient. I'll be a gentleman and not add that you are also, from what I have so far deduced, desperate."

He took a deep breath, then finished: "Or would you rather I be a complete cad and lie to you—tell you that I stepped into Rudolph's common room this morning and immediately tumbled headlong into love?"

She looked at him assessingly, and he could almost hear the gears turning inside that lovely head of hers as she weighed her options. The color was back in her cheeks. Lokwelend's dream was wrong. Bryna Cassidy wasn't a conqueror at all. She was a survivor, pure and simple—one who had been dealt a hand few brave men would care to play—and she was not only going to play it out, but now that she knew he wanted their marriage, she was about to daringly up the ante.

"I've seen your house, the furnishings you must have paid dearly to have transported here from England or some distant city. I've seen your servants, eaten from the fine plate in your kitchens. Exactly how rich would you be, Dominick Crown?" she asked at last, and if he had not already seen the question coming, it would have surprised him to hear the cold calculation in her tone.

"Considerably more plump in the pocket than the three pounds six you have tied in a handkerchief and hidden in your chamber," Dominick returned smoothly, giving her back stare for stare, truth for unvarnished truth. "As I said, Bryna, you are rather desperate. Your feathers may be tolerably fine, but more than a few years out of fashion, and your wardrobe, once one gets past the four or five good gowns such as the one you wear to such advantage this evening, consists of little more than rags. And, while I admire the stylish red-heeled slippers now adorning your small feet, I can only imagine how uncomfortable it must be wearing the shoes you had on this morning—the ones with the paper tucked inside to shield you from the holes in the soles."

He sat back, awaiting the coming explosion.

"You had Lucretia rifle my belongings this afternoon while I slept?" Bryna exclaimed, not disappointing him with either her angry tone or her outraged expression. "You *are* a full-blooded bastard, aren't you, just as you said!"

"It was Lucas, actually," Dominick corrected, trying not to smile. He had her now, and they both knew it. Oh, she'd fight awhile longer, but he had already won, so he would allow her a small bout of righteous indignation. It seemed only fair.

"That spindly-shanked twit! I should have known." Bryna's icy gaze never left his face. "Did your spy also happen to catch the fact that these pearls around my neck are no more than fairly inferior paste? Or that my last good wig got wet during a storm aboard the *Eagle,* so that it now reeks of seawater, and that I have no funds to spare to buy powder for my own hair? Or that my late father's belongings, which I have brought with me from the *Eagle,* consist of three complete suits of clothing, a rather rakish-looking leather visor, a goodly supply of fine ivory dice, and three dozen sets of playing cards—while his money belt served only to help him on his way to the bottom of the ocean?"

"I've seen the dice and cards, yes. Tools of his trade, I'd imagined, when Lucas showed them to me," Dominick said, beginning to feel more than a little ashamed of himself. But he hadn't wished to make his offer just to be refused. He'd had to know that she had no recourse but to accept anything he suggested. His manservant's search of her belongings had convinced him Bryna couldn't afford to deny his proposal. Not unless she wanted to return to Rudolph's Inn and Stores, to make her living on her back.

"I detest you, Dominick Crown," Bryna slid in tonelessly. "I do hope you know that."

"Indeed, yes. But back to this matter of dice and cards—and leather visors. Those would be for the business your father planned to pursue in Philadelphia, wouldn't they? He had supposed to open a gaming house. Were you to act as his hostess? The air of cultured gentility would have doubtless gone down well with the Philadelphia pigeons your father planned to lull into well-liquored complacency, then pluck."

Bryna hopped up from her seat, nearly succeeding in tipping over Dominick's chair in her obvious rush to put as much distance between the two of them as she could without leaving the drawing room. It was either remove herself from his proximity, he supposed, or she would give in to the impulse to box his ears—which might be considered a trifle off-putting by the man who had just gifted her with a lifesaving proposal of marriage.

"My father," she intoned resolutely as she faced the fireplace, gripping the mantel with both hands, as if she might fall without its support, "would *never* have allowed either my mother or me inside a gaming hell, Mr. Crown, let alone use us to entice his guests. Never! We were kept totally separate from that side of his life. I was given years of schooling away from home—everything Papa could do to protect me—and I resent most strenuously your implication that Sean Cassidy was not an honorable man. You owe me an apology, sir, and I'll have it now or, by Patrick and all the saints, I'll have your liver on a spit!"

Christ, she had certainly told him! She wasn't gripping the mantel for support. She was doing it to keep from flying at him in her temper, and rending him limb from limb. "Allow me to offer my apologies," he said, being as solemn as his sudden, inexplicable good humor allowed.

She slowly turned around to face him, once more composed, and still the most beautiful thing he'd ever seen. "Accepted," she said, then she also smiled, making her even more lovely. "We will consider the subject of my father's profession closed, for now and all time. But it was, after all, your turn to take a second bite on your own words, don't you know. I'd as soon deny my Irish blood as to let an insult go by without getting a little of my own back. Now, with our insults and apologies hopefully behind us, at least for the moment—how deep in the pocket are you, *Dominick?*"

"Embarrassingly so, I fear," Dominick said easily as he stood up and replaced the side chair, still eyeing her carefully. "It's my curse, I suppose. Everything I touch seems to magically turn to money. Why?"

She walked behind one of the couches, trailing a fingertip along its intricately carved wooden back as she looked up at him through her thick, dark eyelashes. It was a good thing her father had not planned to put her at one of the tables, for she was about to play what she believed to be her ace, and it would take a blind man not to see the triumph in her face.

He wondered how much it was going to cost him, this impulsive marriage of his to the beautiful, available, half-English gentlewoman with the wit and scruples of a full-blooded Irish card sharp. "Then it would be simple enough for you, I'd imagine, to hire yourself some fine, strong, *brave* men to search out my cousin Brighid and rescue her from her captors?"

Her question took him aback. He had thought she wanted something for herself, some recompense for becoming, as he had so baldly stated, his bride. A diamond necklace. A personal maid brought here from Philadelphia. But her thoughts seemed all for her family. He was impressed. Truly impressed. "I imagine that could be arranged," he said, already deciding that he would approach Lokwelend and Pematalli with the mission. Lokwelend would probably leap at any chance to remove himself from the vicinity of the dangerous Bright Fire.

"Then I suggest you arrange it. Tomorrow will be soon enough." She walked around to the front of the couch, to stand face-to-face with him. "Now, as I'm truly longing for my dinner, shall we briefly discuss a few other conditions I wish your agreement on before I accept this marriage proposal? Papa would have insisted upon a substantial quarterly allowance, as well as a lump-sum settlement before the ceremony, I believe. I, being my father's daughter, hereby insist upon both. In writing, of course, and duly witnessed."

Her smile nearly blinded him, and he was once more impressed with her cool intelligence, her ability to negotiate when she should, by rights, be at his feet, thanking him for his offer.

Oh, yes, she was a downy one. And hard as nails. The sort that could find a way to turn a profit on the Devil himself. He found himself wishing—crazily, he knew—that she would bend, just a little, to prove to him she cared for more than money and her kidnapped cousin, that she had something other than totally practical feelings about their marriage. Which, he thought quickly, just proved that he had been years too long without the company of a gently bred, desirable woman.

"So your thoughts run straight to money, do they, Bryna? Plan on indulging in a spate of shopping at Rudolph's Inn and Stores, do you? I fear you will be sadly disappointed in the variety of his stock."

"You do have a talent for underestimation, don't you, Dominick," she said baldly, without inflection. "I have no intention to pad Benjamin Rudolph's pockets with my blunt. Oh, yes—have I mentioned that I fully expect you to include separate settlements for Mary Catherine and Bridie? To pay them for the land you took from them, you understand."

Money again! She cared for Mary Catherine, he was sure of it. She cared for her cousin Brighid. Did she consider what she was about to do as a sacrifice for their futures? He wished she would react in some other way than anger, than in demands for a share of his pocketbook. Where were the tears of this morning? Perhaps that had been the sham, and he was now seeing the real Bryna Cassidy for the first time. Was she totally mercenary?

And what did it matter? All he wanted was a wife, a woman to give him children, the prospect of which could very well be the perfect lure to finally bring his mother to

New Eden, to get her free of the cold bastard who was both her husband and his father. The fact that Bryna Cassidy was beautiful, desirable, could only be seen as a bonus. The fact that she was also very concerned with his fortune and her share of it was not so far out of the ordinary. What young lady, given her druthers, would willingly marry a poor man over a rich one?

"Well? Have we reached a sticking point? Are you going to allow a few pennies from your great, embarrassing wealth to stand in the way of this marriage you seem to desire? You owe my cousins, Dominick Crown. You *owe* them dearly."

Dominick knew, as he was sure Bryna did, that Daniel Cassidy wouldn't have had final claim to his land until the patent was paid—paid with funds she had told him were lying at the bottom of the Atlantic. But now was not the time to quibble. "It's agreed," he said shortly, extending his hand to seal the bargain.

Bryna quickly placed her hands behind her back, suddenly looking like a child attempting to hide a treat from a bully who wanted nothing more than to steal it from her. "Not yet, if you please. There is still one more thing, Mr. Crown."

"Dominick. You've used my name before this, Bryna, so I imagine you can continue to do so. Now, what final condition has that fertile Irish mind of yours concocted?"

Her eyes flashed emerald fire, betraying her delight in what she considered her impending moment of triumph. "I want to hear your assurance that ours, being a marriage of mutual convenience, will also be a marriage in name only for at least a year. Until we have gotten to know each other, accept each other. Otherwise, sir, I will take Mary Catherine and leave here with her this very night, even if we are both to perish before morning. And please, don't think I wouldn't do it. A year, Mr. Crown."

"Three months, Miss Cassidy, and not a day longer," Dominick replied immediately, refusing to alter his expression.

"Eight," she shot back just as rapidly, jutting out her chin.

"Six months, and that's the end of it," he said to conclude the debate, once more putting out his hand, allowing her another small victory, although he doubted it would take half that long to get her into his bed. "Six months is a reasonable enough request from a lady of sensibility. You have my word as an English gentleman."

One step at a time, he thought as Bryna hesitated a moment more, as if unsure that what she had gained was a victory, then carefully placed her hand in his. He raised that small hand to his lips, looking at her intently as he lingered over the kiss for only a single heartbeat more than was correct. *One small step at a time.*

It was after they had sealed their bargain that Dominick finally realized just how much it must have cost Bryna to act the confident deal maker. For only then did she betray herself, once she had taken back her hand and turned toward the couch, her chin high, her battle won.

And she did so by swaying where she stood, and then slowly, gracefully, soundlessly, slipping to the floor in a swoon.

When needs must, the devil drives.
— *Irish Saying*

CHAPTER 4

NEW EDEN TRULY WAS A BEAUTIFUL PLACE. GREEN AS IRELAND, save that the green was in the limitless expanse of trees that covered the distant, rolling hillsides, the faraway but visible mountains. The sky above New Eden seemed higher and wider than the sky over County Clare, an entirely separate thing from the gray, oppressive mass that hung low over the sooty rooftops and belching chimney pots of London.

It was clean here, the sky. Bluer than her favorite gown. The clouds, whiter than cotton batting. The birdsong, cheerier. The smell of the air, fresher. Newer.

And Bryna Cassidy hated every rock, every tall, nodding wildflower visible in the near distance, every blade of grass, every bird, every tree.

This land had stolen her family from her. Lured them with its false promise, taken them in and then murdered them, burying them below the rich, dark earth that had been a part of that promise, irrevocably wresting from them the freedom and liberty they'd so longed for. And the moment Bryna had Brighid safely back with her, she and her cousins would leave this cursed Eden, never looking back.

For three days Bryna had hidden in her bedchamber, the eerily quiet Mary Catherine close by her side. She had quite purposefully extended her supposed "illness," which had been nothing more than a mixture of grief and fright and anger and crushing hunger combining to weaken her to the point of fainting in front of the cold, demanding, manipulative Dominick Crown.

For three blissful days she had put off seeing that man again, content to remain safely hidden in her soft, sheltering bed, regaining her strength thanks to the mountains of food the friendly and marvelously attentive Lucretia brought to her.

For three days and nights Bryna had planned, and thought, and planned some more. She had silently congratulated herself on those plans, the seeds of which had been planted in her brain the moment Dominick Crown had proposed that a marriage take place between them.

She savored the beauty of those plans, the absolute perfection of them, deliberately ignoring the niggling feeling that they were both deceitful and, possibly, vaguely flawed. And while she had planned, she had silently thanked the opportunistic but arrogantly shortsighted man who had not only rescued her from one predicament, but had then gifted her with an avenue of escape from his unpalatable solution.

Now she was up and about once more, and none too soon, either, as it wouldn't do to get soft, and lazy, or even marginally content. She had bathed and dressed, then bathed and dressed Mary Catherine, and the two of them were now reclining on blankets spread on the lawn to the rear of the house, sitting at their ease in the shade, as ladies of leisure were wont to do on lovely spring mornings.

And all the time they had been there beneath the trees, munching on apples and watching the cotton-batting clouds move across the bluer-than-blue sky, Bryna was going over her plans, savoring their beauty.

She would delay the marriage for as long as possible. She

would demand that the search party, which had not set out three days ago as she had hoped, be on its way to rescue Brighid before she would even allow Dominick Crown to speak the word "marriage" again.

She would insist upon having a varied assortment of bride's clothes: an entire new wardrobe, undergarments, a suitable wedding gown, which she would design and sew herself . . . and, of course, there was the matter of a full two dozen fine linen handkerchiefs to be personally hand stitched and embroidered as her bridal present to her betrothed.

She would need new shoes, as Dominick Crown had been rude enough to mention that her footwear was sadly in need of replacement. And, naturally, Mary Catherine must have new clothing, for her few dresses had been Brighid's, cut down for her by her mother. Dominick Crown's ward, Bryna would point out to him when she faced him across the dinner table tonight, must surely be dressed more in line with her new station in life.

Oh, yes. She could conceivably drag out the time before her "marriage" for a month, possibly even two. That should be plenty of time for Brighid to be returned to New Eden.

In the meantime, Bryna knew she had to make the acquaintance of someone in the village—some able-bodied man who could transport her cousins and herself back to Philadelphia, where she would put the remainder of her plan into motion. It shouldn't be too difficult to find a man in New Eden willing to embarrass the high-and-mighty Dominick Crown. After all, she had seen the expressions on the faces of the men at Rudolph's Inn and Stores. Any one of them would suit her purpose, for the right price.

The right price. Bryna laced her fingers together in front of her face, tapping her index fingers against her pursed lips as she considered the matter of money. Dominick Crown was a rich man, but he wasn't a stupid one.

It was getting her hands on the money, the marriage settlement, that would probably prove to be the biggest sticking point.

She would most probably have to go through with the

wedding in order to see any of the blunt she'd demanded from him in that marriage settlement. She might even have to share a bed with the man, as she had not for a moment believed his promise that theirs would be a union in name only for the space of the next six months—which should, hopefully, be at least three months longer than her stay in New Eden.

For, if Dominick Crown was not a stupid man, Bryna Cassidy did not consider herself to be a stupid woman. He had been lying to her in order that she would agree to the marriage. Lying, in order to get what he wanted. Just as she had lied to get what she wanted.

Dominick Crown had built himself a fine estate here in New Eden. He had just—or so he thought—bought himself a convenient wife in order to begin growing his dynasty. A dynasty, Bryna supposed, that would include a clutch of strong sons to help enlarge the estate, to give a man reason to continue building and acquiring a legacy that his sons would carry on after he was gone. He might value her, but no more than he would a good broodmare who had unexpectedly dropped into his hands like a ripe plum, just at the time he decided he needed one. He'd no more wait six months to bed her than he would expect to grow crops without putting down seed.

She couldn't blame the man for wanting sons, for wishing that the fruit of all his hard work would be passed on to coming generations of Crowns. He might even be telling the truth in saying that their marriage would be a means of gaining himself some companionship out here, so far from the civilized city of Philadelphia. He might, at the bottom of it, be a good, decent man. He had taken in Mary Catherine. He had buried the Cassidys, and seen to it that their graves had been blessed. His servants seemed loyal. But then, Oliver Cromwell's manservant had probably held a fair opinion of his master.

Bryna looked down at the slumbering Mary Catherine, the quiet, staring child with the sad, century-old eyes that had seen entirely too much pain, and then lifted her chin, swallowing down on both her fears and her moment of guilt at what she planned to do—knowing that any sacrifice she might be forced to make was as nothing when compared to that child's loss.

She would give her body, but not her mind. Her word, but not her bond. And when that all-important money was in her pocket, when her cousins were safe at her side, she would walk away without a hint of remorse, knowing she had sacrificed little in comparison to what she had gained. She would then set the second half of her plan into motion, hiring herself yet another man to search out her ex-shipmate Renton Frey for her among the soldiers quartered in this place called Lancaster. And when this man had found Frey, she would demand that he bring her his head!

And, lastly, she would teach herself to forget how handsome Dominick Crown looked in his evening dress, how savage, how vitally alive, he appeared in his deerskins. How he intrigued her, even as she longed to see him as no more than a means to an end . . .

"Itah! Quatsch luppackhan?"

Bryna stifled the impulse to scream as she looked up to see that, without making a single alerting sound, the Indian Lokwelend had somehow come to be standing not three feet away from her. He was as tall as she remembered him. As imposing. As oddly regal. As curiously sad. And he smelled strongly of the bear grease he had rubbed all over his body.

"I'm sorry, I don't know your language," she said, shielding her eyes with her hand as she looked up into the sunlight that cast a golden glow around the Indian. It was difficult to look at him and not think of the monsters who had murdered her family. "But if you're angry that I shot at you the other day, I apologize. You must, however, understand my mistake."

"I said, *Itah.* Good be to you." Lokwelend inclined his head, his dark eyes hooded. *"N'schiweléndam,* Bright Fire. That is to say, it is Lokwelend who is sorry. You came to this place already sad, and the actions of my people increased that sadness. *Quatsch luppackhan?* This means, why are you crying? But your words have answered me. Your tears are for your dead family."

Bryna lifted her fingers to her cheeks, astounded to find them wet. "I—I hadn't realized . . ." She shook her head, unable to believe she might have been crying because of her coldhearted plan to use Dominick Crown to her own ends. But she couldn't have been crying for Dominick Crown, for a man who had everything in this world, while she had nothing. Yes, she had been crying for her family. For her dear, muddleheaded, overly confident father. But she wept not in sorrow, for that sort of weak grief served nothing and no one. If she cried, she cried out for retribution, for revenge! But the Indian couldn't know that. Just because he seemed to look through her, he couldn't possibly know what all was in her mind, her heart. Could he? She hastened into speech. "Yes, of course, Lokwelend, that is why I'm weeping. And I'm worried about my cousin. About Bridie. Did you know her before she was taken?"

Lokwelend grunted. "The *wusdóchqueu.* The young woman—Brighid. The one Dominick has asked us to find. I know her. She spoke kindly with my daughter, Kolachuisen, who is called Cora by her white fathers. Together, Kolachuisen and your cousin would walk along the riverbank, teaching each other, learning from each other. But your cousin is not the Bright Fire. She is the *nipawi qischuch,* the sun which gives light in the dark. She is the white fire of the night."

"Brighid is the moon? Yes, I think I understand why you would say that. Her fair skin—her dark hair, so like a midnight sky. That's very pretty, Lokwelend." Bryna wet her lips, feeling her heart beginning to pound hurtfully at this mention of her cousin even as she lost any lingering fear of the mahogany-skinned Indian who stood before her, his broad, gnarled hands grasping the long barrel of his rifle as he rested the stock against the ground. "I miss her very much, Lokwelend. Do you . . . do you think she's still alive? When do you leave? I asked Dominick to send someone four nights ago, and yet you're still here."

"You are as impatient as a bear breaking through the ice to catch up a fish. Our minds are already set for the search, Bright Fire, but preparations had to be made. We may have to do battle, and this we Lenape will not do until sacrifices have been made, until our minds and hearts are cleansed. On the dawn, my son, Pematalli, and I will travel west, beyond the mountains. We will find her."

We will find her. The simple words came as sweet music to Bryna's ears. She closed her eyes, sagging back against the tree trunk, not bothering to examine why she believed this man. "Oh, thank God!" She sat forward once more, watching as the Indian sank to his haunches beside the blanket and began to gently stroke Mary Catherine's soft burnished curls. "And you'll bring her back to me?"

Lokwelend held his hand still on the sleeping child's hair and looked at Bryna. Looked through her, all the way to her soul. "I have said it, Bright Fire. We will find her."

"Yes, I know, but—"

"The child does not speak," Lokwelend said, one long, brown fingertip lightly touching Mary Catherine's moist, pouting lower lip, then slowly trailing across her cheek. "Once she laughed, and Pematalli carried her high on his shoulders. Now she runs from Pematalli. She runs from Lokwelend. We miss her laughter. We miss her brothers. The price of war is too high, and it is our children who must pay it. Soon it will be my time to grieve. I have seen this in my dreams, even as I saw your coming to this place. You would do well, Bright Fire, to look to your own dreams, and discover what is most important to you."

Bryna turned her head, unable to meet Lokwelend's eyes. She wished him gone. Gone far from here, where he could no longer see into her soul.

He moved away from Mary Catherine and stood up once more, pulling a slim wooden cylinder from his belt. "The little bird must learn to sing again, even if she cannot speak. I have made this for her. It is my gift, although she will not take it from me. I ask you to give it to her once I am gone. Perhaps, when I have returned, the little bird will have found her new voice."

"Thank you," Bryna said, taking the flute and holding it in both her hands, her heart touched by the Indian's gift even as she hated the thought that anyone could believe a simple flute could take the place of Mary Catherine's voice. "This is very thoughtful of you. I hadn't realized . . ."

Lokwelend's smile was sad, and held secrets Bryna knew he did not trust her enough to share. "You have many years to travel, Bright Fire, until you know all there is to know. But we have made a beginning, have we not? Now Lokwelend will go, before the child wakes and shows his warrior's heart her fear, and he must carry that fear within him on his journey."

"Thank you again, Lokwelend. And . . . um . . . God-speed," Bryna added hesitantly, laying the flute in her lap and putting out her right hand to the Indian.

He took hold of her wrist, squeezing it, so that she felt she had no choice but to do likewise to his, the two of them holding firm for a long moment, gazing into each other's eyes. Bryna prayed her expression was one of calm, of trust, while the Indian's dark eyes revealed nothing, less than nothing.

"You are all I saw in my dream. All I longed for and feared. Do not hurt my friend, Bright Fire," Lokwelend said at last, preparing to move away, out of the shadow of the tree.

"Dominick?" Bryna smiled weakly, immediately guilty, knowing the Indian was speaking of her recent benefactor, the man she was scheming to use and then betray. "I don't understand what you mean. How could I possibly hurt him?"

"Hear yourself speak, Bright Fire, and listen to your words. You do not ask *why* you might wish to hurt him— but only *how* to achieve that hurt."

Bryna avoided the Indian's eyes, wishing the man were less observant. She was glad he was leaving Pleasant Hill, not just because he was going to search for Brighid, but because he saw too much, and could prove dangerous to her plans. "I'm confident, Lokwelend, that your friend is fully capable of withstanding any hurt a mere female might attempt to impart."

"Crown is a *sakímau,* a chief. He thinks like a chief, caring for all his people. He is strong, and fair, and just. But he holds many sorrows hidden in his heart. I ask that you do not add to those sorrows, Bright Fire, as my friend is just now learning to sing."

Bryna watched as Lokwelend moved away, refusing to dwell on his warning, then turned to look at the still-sleeping Mary Catherine. "We're going to get Bridie back, Mary Kate. I promise you. And by the time she is here, you'll be jabbering like a magpie. I don't know how I'm going to do it, but by God, I'll not have you reduced to tooting a flute to communicate. Not if it kills the both of us!"

The child roused slowly, possibly awakened by the loving fierceness of Bryna's tone. She smiled up at her cousin, pointing to the flute. Bryna returned her smile, saying, "Do you want this, Mary Kate? It's a flute. See?" She raised it to her lips and blew into the hollow instrument, wincing as a sharp, discordant sound issued from the other end.

Mary Catherine grinned, pulling herself up to her knees as she reached again for the flute, only to frown as Bryna quickly held it above her head. "Not until you ask nicely, Mary Kate," she told her. "Only then may you have it. Just one word, Mary Kate. Just say *please.*"

The child opened her mouth and Bryna held her breath, watching the cords of her cousin's slim throat working, trying not to wince as Mary Catherine screwed up her little face in the effort to push that single word past her unwilling tongue. After a few moments the child shook her head violently from side to side, then fell onto the blanket, to pound her clenched fists against the ground.

"Holy Mother," Bryna whispered, quickly gathering the child onto her lap and handing her the flute. "It's all right, darling. It's all right. Don't cry. We'll try again another time." She began rocking the sobbing child, who had clasped the flute tightly to her chest. "We'll try another time."

Dominick rode his large bay mare toward the village of New Eden, keeping to the rutted road that then moved south, toward Allen's Town, some twelve miles distant.

There, the packed-dirt road joined the much wider and more traveled King's Highway, which reached all the way to Philadelphia.

Allen's Town was a dozen years newer than New Eden. It would probably continue to prosper, becoming a center of commerce, while the village of New Eden would never do more than serve the neighboring farmers and the soldiers from nearby Fort Deshler.

New Eden's small size and limited potential pleased Dominick, who rarely traveled as far as either Allen's Town or Bethlehem, preferring to keep himself as far from civilization as possible without cutting himself off from the material benefits that civilization provided. Although one benefit he did not wish to hazard reaching for remained that of gaining introductions to suitable young women willing to sacrifice themselves to a life lived away from that civilization. Which was another reason he had given himself for proposing marriage to the conveniently desperate Bryna Cassidy.

Or at least that was what he kept telling himself.

As he passed beyond the small gristmill located on Indian Creek and entered into the outer reaches of the village, riding by Jonah Newton's tannery and Elijah Kester's smithy, Dominick wished only one thing for New Eden. The village needed the addition of an establishment that could rival Rudolph's Inn and Stores; offering an alternative to Benjamin and Truda Rudolph's unwelcoming manner and providing fairer treatment to the Lenape trading there.

Perhaps, Dominick thought, smiling, that should be his next project. Bryna would like that. She might even pass some of her time behind the counter, playing at shopkeeper, ordering in goods and serving the customers. It would give her something to occupy herself until the babies arrived. She was the sort who needed to keep herself busy, or else the Devil would be sure to set up a workshop inside her inventive brain.

Yes, he'd have to give the idea some thought, some serious thought.

Dominick turned the bay and guided the animal to a halt

in front of Rudolph's, tossing the reins to the small, barefoot boy who raced out to meet him. He dismounted from the crude, leather-blanketed saddle by swinging a deerskin-clad leg up and over the mare's head and landing on the packed dirt in a single graceful motion. He had nearly forgotten what it was like to ride atop an English saddle, and didn't regret the loss. Dominick regretted little in this world, preferring to concentrate on all he still had to gain.

Taking his Pennsylvania long rifle with him, Dominick mounted the two wide wooden steps to the single entrance that served Rudolph's establishment. He chose the corridor to the left once he'd entered, heading for the common room and a mug of ale before crossing to the other side of the building to place an order with Truda Rudolph.

He had to step back into the main entryway and wait as a single Lenape, a young buck he could not remember seeing in the area before now, staggered out of the common room, a brown bottle in his hand and clearly the worse for drink. He stopped just in front of Dominick, raised his head, then grinned with all the vacant cheerfulness of the blissfully intoxicated. He smelled of ale and bear grease and months in the forest beyond the Blue Mountains.

"N'achgieuchsu," the Indian said, grabbing Dominick's arm as if to steady himself.

"Yes, my friend, you are drunk. And considerably poorer, I have no doubt," Dominick told him, looking toward the bar and the rare beaver pelts an openly gleeful Benjamin Rudolph was just in the act of removing from the bar. *"Mattapewiwak nik schwannakwak."*

The Indian leaned forward to peer more closely at Dominick, then turned to glare at Rudolph for a long moment before looking once more to Dominick. His free hand moved to the knife tucked into his belt, then stilled, inches from the hilt, as his shoulders slumped in defeat. *"N'geptschat!"* He lifted his hand and poked an unsteady finger at Dominick's chest. *"Auween kháckey?"*

Dominick smiled sadly at the young brave's denunciation of himself as a fool, shook his head in the negative, then answered once more in the Indian's tongue. "You are not a fool, my friend. As to your question—no, I am not an Indian, or a man of any tribe save England. The firewater plays tricks with your eyes. I am Crown, the friend of Lokwelend. Do you know where I live?"

The Indian nodded, clearly not capable of much more than that.

"Go there, then, and wait for me. Take a sweat in my own sweathouse. Sleep safe tonight beneath the trees in my meadows. Then, tomorrow, we will talk of this trade you made with the *shawanuk*. But do not go to the house."

From somewhere inside of him, the Indian mustered up a wide grin. "I will take my woman and child, and I will do as the Crown says," he said in low, heavily accented English. "But we will not go near the Bright Fire. I wish not for the Bright Fire to make war on me as she did on the gray hair. I have only twenty summers. I have not so many feathers as he, and cannot lose them."

"Lokwelend's got a tongue that runs on wheels, for all he talks in riddles half the time," Dominick remarked ruefully as the Indian looked confused, then stumbled past Dominick and down the wooden steps. A young Lenape squaw waited for him there, her infant tied to a cradleboard on her back, a small sack of provisions at her feet. The Indian groaned and held up his hands to protect his aching head as the woman immediately began shrieking at him, slapping his shoulders and calling him names that made Dominick wince.

Taking a deep breath, and forcing down the worst of his anger at what had happened to the Lenape family, Dominick entered the dimly lit, low-ceilinged common room that stank of sweat and ale and rotten eggs.

Jonah Newton was seated at one of the tables, nursing a mug of ale, while three men Dominick recognized as trappers visiting in the village played at darts with a local farmer, their target a flat coil of rope nailed to the wall just beside the door to the kitchen area. A puffy-eyed, sullen-faced squaw sat wrapped in a blanket on the floor in the far corner. She had to be waiting for her man, who, from the comments being made by one of the trappers, had most probably wagered a tumble with the woman on the outcome of the game.

Dominick walked up to the small serving bar, placing his palms on the greasy surface. "Trying to start a war all by yourself, Rudolph?" he asked, inclining his head toward the beaver pelts.

"That'd be none of your concern, Crown," Rudolph shot back, opening a cupboard and quickly stuffing the pelts inside, then closing the door on the subject of his trading practices. "The savage was happy enough till you stuck your nose in. I saw that look he gave me, like he was hankering for my hair. What did you say to him?"

"Nothing much. I simply reminded him that the white man can be a rascally fellow. I do believe he agreed, and will agree even more once his blushing bride gets done taking a strip off his hide with her sharp tongue. I'll have a mug, if you don't mind."

There was the scrape of a chair being pushed back, and Jonah Newton came up to the bar. "Put Mr. Crown's drink on my bill, will you, Rudolph?"

Dominick looked at the tanner, seeing the gleam in the man's eye and knowing the fellow wanted something from him. "Many thanks, Newton. I do not recollect you ever being quite so generous. Perhaps you're unwell?" He picked up the mug Rudolph plunked down in front of him, took a deep swallow, then retired to an empty table nearest the single unshuttered window.

"Hey! I bought you that ale, Crown. The least you could do is sit and drink with me."

Dominick lifted one well-sculpted eyebrow as he looked at Newton, who was still standing at the bar, his florid face more flushed than usual. "I obviously thought otherwise, Newton, as I don't like you—which didn't mean I wasn't thirsty," he said, at once the urbane English gentleman, for all his deerskins and long, unbound black hair. "However, if I had known I should have to share my company with you, I would have declined the gift."

Then he shrugged, showing his indifference. "Oh, very

well. Why don't you slither on over here and tell me what you want. You do want something, don't you, Newton? Your sort always do."

If pride were clothing, Jonah Newton would have been standing in front of Dominick, naked as the day he was born. Grabbing up his own mug of ale, the smiling man quickly sat down across the table from Dominick, his watery blue eyes dancing in his head.

"I want to hear about the woman, Crown," he said, wetting his full lips with his tongue. "Was she good? Are you to be keeping her for yourself, or will we all get a poke at her now? She's a prime one, and no doubt. Thighs white as fresh cream, I'm thinking, and a cunt red as fire, if the hair on her head means anything. Nothing like Silky Wattson—the damn tattooed whore."

Dominick didn't remember rising, or tipping the table out of his way, or the sound of the two pewter mugs hitting the floor. All he knew was that he was holding Jonah Newton a full five inches off the floor, his two hands balled into fists as he gripped the man's jacket collar, his face no more than an inch away from the tanner's. "Smell hell yet, Newton?" he gritted out from between clenched teeth. "Or is that only your own weak piss, running down your leg?"

Newton grabbed on to Dominick's hands, tearing at them in an unsuccessful attempt to free himself. "Are you crazy? Put me down, you damn savage! Rudolph!"

The flash and loud report of a pistol and the sharp splintering of wood just beyond his head brought Dominick back to his senses. He gave Newton one last shake before slamming him to the floor and turning to face Rudolph, who was in the process of raising a second pistol.

"Won't have no fighting in here, Crown," the innkeeper warned, slowly lowering the weapon and backing up a pace as Dominick picked up his rifle and walked toward him, keeping one eye on the trappers, who had suspended play in order to watch the fun. "Jonah's one of m'best customers."

Dominick ran a hand through his hair, pushing its length away from his face as he struggled to keep from leaping over the bar and pounding Rudolph into a jelly. "And *I* am your best customer, God help me. But not for long, Rudolph, if you don't please me. Not for long."

The innkeeper smiled, showing the gap between his two front teeth as well as his sudden nervousness. "O'course, Mr. Crown, o'course! Truda was saying just the other day as how you'd be the heart and soul of our store. That's why you're here, ain't it? For another order? No reason to send all the way to Allen's Town, so I say. Truda will get you anything you want, Mr. Crown. And she won't be putting her thumb on the scales, neither."

There were times when Dominick missed England so much he could feel the ache deep in his belly. Missed the civilization. Missed the smooth, practiced deference of excellent shopkeepers. This was not one of those times, as he rather enjoyed watching the crude Rudolph squirm, hating his wealthy customer while coming close to groveling in order to keep his custom. He reached under his jacket and into his shirt pocket, pulling out a list of stores Lucas had requested, and threw it onto the bar. "I'll want Alice to deliver this tomorrow. Not you. Alice. Come within a mile of Pleasant Hill and I'll turn my dog on you."

"It'll be just as you say, though why anybody'd want that worthless Alice around sure beats me. Walks like she's got one foot in a hole, and lazy into the bargain. Cain't sell her, cain't marry her off, cain't do nothing with her at all."

Behind Dominick, Jonah Newton was clumsily regaining his feet, although he made no move to attack from the rear, which showed the tanner possessed at least a modicum of common sense. Which Dominick would have to indulge in now himself, if this incident with Newton meant anything.

Waiting until the farmer had gone and he could see Newton taking his place once more at the table he'd been sitting at earlier, Dominick said in a clear, carrying voice, "I didn't write it down, but I'd like you to have Alice pick three bolts of cloth for my affianced wife's gowns, if you please, Rudolph, as well as thread and ribbon and anything else she thinks necessary. Not your wife. Alice."

Newton made a strangled sound and pushed his way past

the three departing trappers in order to exit the building ahead of them in a rush. Which left Dominick to smile at Rudolph, who was standing stock-still, his mouth agape.

"Your—your wife, Mr. Crown?" the innkeeper asked, his gaze shifting to the doorway, as if he would like nothing better than to follow where the craven Newton had led. Then his eyes narrowed and his look turned crafty. "Would . . . would that be the, um, the lovely young woman who came to New Eden just the other day? O'course it would! Owes me a night's lodging, you know, not to mention all the food she ate. And the loving care my Truda gave her, too. I'll just be adding a small sum to your bill, Mr. Crown, seeing as how you're responsible for her now."

"You do that, Rudolph. Get all you can for as long as you can. Who holds the book?"

"The book?" Rudolph frowned, then brightened. "You'd be meaning the records book? Let me see—I think Henry Turner had it last, him wanting to write in about his missus's birthing. So you ain't going to Philadelphia for a proper wedding? Smart enough. Why wait, when the book is good enough for the rest of us?"

"Comforted as I am by your kind permission, Rudolph, I don't recall asking for it," Dominick said, looking to the Indian woman who still sat in the corner, sound asleep, her head fallen back against the wall. "It would appear those trappers left you a present, Rudolph. Doesn't she belong to one of them?"

"Not no more," the innkeeper answered. "They'll get themselves another convenient when they head back across the mountains." He scratched his forehead. "Newton was going to take her, but I guess he forgot. You want her? I can put her on your bill. Won't even charge you for the breed she's carrying."

"There are times, Rudolph, when I believe this village woefully misnamed. New Bedlam is closer to the truth of the thing. Make sure she is fed before Alice brings her to me tomorrow, understand?"

"Anything you say, Mr. Crown," the innkeeper called out

even as Dominick quit the room, the squaw forgotten, his mind already concentrated on getting the record book from Henry Turner—and then explaining its purpose to Bryna Cassidy.

He was fairly certain it would not be a well-received explanation.

*Death in itself is nothing; but
we fear to be we know not what,
we know not where.*
— *John Dryden*

CHAPTER 5

"IT WAS GOOD OF YOU TO DRIVE ME HERE," BRYNA SAID,
holding tight to Mary Catherine's hand as the wagon drew
closer to the small stone and wood barn she had first seen as
Dominick urged the team out of the trees and into the
clearing. "I had thought you were gone for the day, having
forgotten my request."

"I had to go into New Eden to order some supplies,"
Dominick told her as he pulled on the reins, halting the
team, then set the brake with his foot. "Lucas has given up
the job since the raids. Now he would rather starve than
take more than ten steps outside Pleasant Hill."

Bryna smiled, nodding, keeping her gaze concentrated on
the flowers in her lap. "So Lucretia has told me. Poor man.
He's as out of place here as a pullet in a lion's den. I only
wonder why he stays, when it is obvious he could have a fine
position in Philadelphia, or London."

"Yes, he reminds me of that fact almost daily. I'd like to
be on our way back to Pleasant Hill within the hour, if you

don't mind." Dominick alit from the wagon in a single, smooth movement, and Bryna found herself wishing he would stumble, or in some way show that he was not perfect in everything he did. Perfect, and self-assured, and so very much in control of himself and his surroundings, while she was in constant battle with her nerves, and started violently at every sound, expecting an attack at any moment.

"Mary Catherine, come to me, sweetheart," he said, holding out his arms to the child, who went to him without hesitation, so that he lifted her high into the air and whirled her around a single time before setting her gently on her feet. "Bryna?" he then asked, raising up his arms once more.

"Not yet, if you please. Mary Kate—say thank you to Mr. Crown."

"There's no need—"

"There most certainly is. There is *every* need," Bryna responded, cutting him off. "If she doesn't speak, it's because you've all made it so easy for her *not* to speak. Lucretia and Lucas anticipate her every need, waiting on her hand and foot as if she were some tongueless princess. How do any of you expect her to recover her voice if she isn't pushed into it? Well, no more, Mr. Dominick Crown. Not now that I am here. I will not allow it!"

Dominick's eyes narrowed, so that Bryna had to hold herself very stiffly in order not to turn away from his penetrating stare. "The world doesn't begin to turn in the morning until your feet touch the bedchamber floor, is that it, Bryna? It is you who makes the sun rise and the wind blow. So in control, and never, ever wrong. Is it by sheer force of will that you're going to get Mary Catherine to speak again?"

She lifted her chin a notch. "If necessary, yes," she answered tightly. "And what's wrong with that? Not that it's any of your concern."

"What's wrong, Bryna, is that one day you'll have to learn that you cannot mend everything, nor can you shout or bully the world into seeing that yours is the correct way. In short, you must learn when it is best to bend with the wind, and even accept the occasional defeat. For if you don't bend, Bryna, you will eventually break. This land will break you, break your very heart. And Mary Catherine, or Brighid, may break along with you. Shorter still," he ended with a smile, "is to say that you're very much the bossy, headstrong child, Bryna Cassidy, and in this rough land I've need of a woman for my wife."

"So you'll not force me to marry you now—vile, selfish child that I am? Now, there's a bleeding pity!" Bryna challenged, appalled to hear the betraying hint of disappointment in her voice and quickly telling herself that it was the possible loss of Dominick Crown's money that pained her, and not the loss of his nonexistent affections.

"Oh, I didn't say that, Bryna," he answered quietly. "I didn't say that." After a long moment, he bent to whisper in Mary Catherine's ear. The child hesitated a moment, then kissed his cheek before wandering off to pick a wildflower some distance away. "There. She thanked me well enough with her kiss," Dominick told Bryna, his own chin set in a firm line. "Now, would you like me to help you down from your perch of perfection?"

"I can manage, thank you," she told him stubbornly, vowing to leave this particular fight for another day before struggling down off the seat, nearly losing the flowers she had wrapped in the large white apron she'd donned over her gown. She looked at the barn, which seemed a woefully inappropriate home for her relatives. "This is where they lived? I—I can't imagine it."

"Imagine, then, cows and chickens in your drawing room," he said, motioning for her to precede him to the graves that were to the left of the barn, enclosed by a split-rail fence. "Animals and seed are the first considerations when starting a farm. Daniel had planned to start his house this summer, once he had planted his fields with the three sisters."

Bryna looked at him quizzically, their argument forgotten as her heart squeezed tight over the pain she felt upon seeing the grave sites. "The three sisters? I don't understand that, either. Sometimes I feel as if I have done more than travel to a new country. It is as if I have landed in an entire new universe, one that is most decidedly upside down."

Mary Catherine, who had presented Dominick with a wildflower and was now holding his hand, broke away, putting Lokwelend's flute to her mouth and blowing on it, producing sound, but no tune. She had played on the flute almost constantly since Bryna had presented it to her when she woke from her nap, her small fingers testing the half dozen variously sized holes as she alternately frowned and smiled at the different sounds she could produce.

Now, as Bryna looked to Dominick for an explanation of what he had said, the child danced in circles, her skirts flying around her ankles, tooting for all she was worth. Part little girl. Part village idiot. Bryna tensed once more, and silently vowed, once more, no matter what Dominick Crown said, that Mary Catherine would be speaking again within a fortnight.

"The three sisters, according to the Lenape," she heard Dominick explaining, "are corn, beans, and squash, and they form the backbone of Lenape crops. Lokwelend was to help Daniel with the planting. I admired your uncle for his willingness to learn, Bryna, and his acceptance that things are different here in Pennsylvania—that while we bring all that we know to a situation, there is still much we can learn."

"Uncle Daniel was always eager to learn new things about farming," Bryna said absently, ignoring the lesson he was trying to teach her. She still refused to look at the four neatly aligned crosses inside the fence, fighting the nearly uncontrollable impulse to flee the sight of this final evidence of her loss. "Would—would you please be so kind as to leave me alone for a few minutes?"

"Of course. There's something I need to get from the barn anyway."

"Thank you," Bryna said, wishing he would just go away. Go away, and stay away, leaving her here with her family, with her memories, and with her pain.

She stepped over a low section of fence and approached

the graves, trying not to see how much shorter in length two of the neatly mounded piles of dirt were than the other two. She needed no reminder that Joseph and Michael had been only eight and ten, that their small bodies lay just below her feet, their boyish smiles forever gone, their bright eyes closed to the future, their childish laughter never to be heard again.

Was there a Heaven? She'd always thought so. Was there a God? She'd always believed there was. But what God would allow the slaughter of these two perfect children? What greater glory had awaited them, that the loss of their young lives could be condoned as being God's will, a part of His infinite plan?

Faith was easy when life was easy. But today, as she stood here so very alone, feeling the warmth of the spring sun on her back, hearing the birdsong in the trees, and knowing that her family lay unseeing, unhearing, beneath the dirt? Knowing that her father lay beneath the deep, dark sea, gone to a grave not of his choosing, and years before his time? Right now faith was hard, and Bryna fought her anger, her outrage, as well as her grief.

Her chin began to wobble as tears stung her eyes and she took in a deep, shuddering gulp of air, trying to control the sobs that threatened to tear her apart. She could not cry. She would not cry. Not here, where Mary Catherine might see her. Where Dominick Crown might see her.

Kneeling between the two larger graves, Bryna placed some of her supply of flowers just in front of the two crosses, noticing as she did so that they each had something hanging from their crosspieces.

"Oh, sweet Jesus," she breathed quietly, reaching out to take hold of the rosary made of clear blue stones that hung from the cross to her right. "Mama gave that to you, didn't she, Aunt Eileen? It was Christmas, the year before Mama died. You cried when you unwrapped it, and immediately raced off to have Father Finnegan bless it before Mass. Then you found Bridie wearing it around her throat like a necklace, and you whipped at her tiny backside all the way up the stairs, not that you could catch her—calling her a godless little heathen while Uncle Daniel and Papa laughed and laughed . . ."

Her eyes awash in tears, so that it was difficult to see, Bryna turned to look at the cross marking her uncle's grave. His watch and fob had been wrapped around the crosspiece, where it glinted golden in the sunlight. She was reminded of how, long ago, Uncle Daniel had pulled her onto his lap and held the watch close by her ear, letting her listen to the even ticktock, ticktock, then slapped his knee in delight as the watch suddenly chimed out the hour, surprising Bryna into a small shriek of alarm.

So many memories . . .

She stood, then carefully stepped behind the crosses and knelt down between the boys' graves.

Joseph and Michael each had markers on their crosses, although she did not recognize either memento. One grave was decorated with a small ax, its wooden handle painted in bright colors and pierced by a thong of leather that had been slipped over the crosspiece. A small bow and a quiver holding a half dozen arrows had been suspended from the other cross. Instruments of war, of death, but miniaturized, as if fashioned more as toys than weapons.

Bryna's lips tightened into a thin line and she reached out to snatch up the weapons, only to have Dominick's voice stop her. "Pematalli made those for the boys," he told her as she looked up at him, barely able to see him through her tears. "There was blood on Michael's war ax when we found him. Two of Joseph's arrows lay on the ground some hundred yards from his body. Pematalli insisted their graves be marked with the weapons of Lenape warriors, not the colored blocks or spinning tops of children. Warriors are carried directly to the Great Spirit, who welcomes them with food and drink and a seat at the head of the table."

Grief died as anger won the battle for Bryna's emotions. "Warriors?" She raised her chin, her hands drawing into fists. "They weren't warriors, Dominick—they were babies. *Babies!* I hate this country! I hate the damnable savages who killed my family, and anyone who would think that children are the enemy. And I hate you! Oh, sweet Jesus, go away. Just go away and let me alone!"

He remained where he was, his face impassive. "I would, except that I think Mary Catherine needs you. She came into the barn behind me, but wandered off, through the small inner door leading into the living quarters. I found her under the bed, backed all the way against the wall and refusing to come out."

Bryna was on her feet before Dominick had finished speaking. Holding her skirts up above her ankles, she ran into the barn, calling Mary Catherine's name. She only halted once she had run in the direction of Dominick's pointing finger, through a small, open doorway, and inside what must have been the single, common room the family had shared.

She hadn't planned to go into the barn today, hadn't wanted to see where her relatives had lived, where Eileen, at least, probably perished while trying to defend her daughters. Now, looking at the scattered, broken furniture, the dark stains on the walls and rough wooden floor, she could only believe the barn should be burned to the ground, its ashes scattered to the four winds.

Swallowing down the bile that rose into her throat, Bryna fell to her knees just beside the stain that marred the floorboards next to the wide bed. She leaned down, lifted a corner of the stiff, rusty-tinged spread she remembered as being the once pristine white covering of her aunt's bed in County Clare, and peered into the space between the bed frame and the floor.

All she could see were the whites of Mary Catherine's unblinking eyes, and the white ruffle that topped her blue gown. The child had her back pressed hard against the wall, her hands crossed in front of her, holding tight to the flute, her knees drawn up against her chest.

"Mary Kate?" Bryna questioned softly, trying to keep the tremor out of her voice. "Have you got yourself a leprechaun under there with you, Mary Kate, him hiding with his pot o'gold, and you trying your best to relieve him of the lovely thing? And wouldn't that be a silly business? Why, everyone knows leprechauns only carry false gold when they're out to trick pretty little girls who would much rather be sitting in the shade, eating sugarplums and sipping sweet tea."

Mary Catherine didn't move. She didn't so much as blink, but only stared, as if caught up in a waking nightmare the horrors of which Bryna could only imagine. "Oh, those vile, vile wee creatures," Bryna continued, trying to keep her tone light. "How they delight in making your poor cousin break her back and dirty her nose, mucking around on the floor when she could be eating sugarplums—and feeding them to her darlin' Mary Kate. Come out now, darlin', and we'll trick that old leprechaun and leave him stuck here with his false gold, his breeches all dirty and his fine waistcoat stuck with spiderwebs."

Whether it was the promise of sugarplums or the threat of spiderwebs, Bryna didn't need to know, but she breathed a deep sigh of relief as Mary Catherine slowly began crawling out from beneath the heavy bed, not relinquishing her two-handed grip on the flute, her wide, dry-eyed gaze never leaving Bryna's face.

She reached under the wooden frame, to meet the child halfway, pulling her free of the bed and onto her lap. Bryna guided Mary Catherine's head against her breast to shield her eyes from the memory of what had happened here as the child began to cry, soundlessly, her entire small body shaking as Bryna held her tight, and rocked her, saying, "I know, darlin', I know. Oh, sweet Jesus, *aingeal,* I know . . ."

"She's got something in her hand," Dominick said, and Bryna looked up at him, wishing he weren't dressed in his Indian garb. He was so tall. How tall had he looked to Mary Catherine the day he had found her hiding beneath this same bed?

No wonder Mary Catherine had bit him, had scratched at him. Bryna herself was having trouble remembering that the Dominick Crown who stood beside her now was the same Dominick Crown she had seen in silks and pristine white linen, looking the complete English gentleman.

"What did you say?" she asked, finding it difficult to think.

Dominick went down on his haunches beside her. "I said, the child has something in her hand. See how her left hand grips the flute—with only two fingers wrapped around it?"

Bryna took hold of Mary Catherine's hand, carefully prying her fingers open, just to watch, uncomprehending, as a small ball suited for a pistol dropped to the floor and rolled to a stop at Dominick's foot.

"Damn," he breathed quietly, picking up the ball to examine it in the light. "This is one of mine—see, there's my mark, the *C* I had made a part of the mold. Now I understand. Eileen must have tried, but she just couldn't bring herself to do it."

"Bring herself to do what? Oh, never mind that for now. Let's get Mary Kate outside, and away from all this," Bryna said, hating her impulse to recoil from him when Dominick bent to touch her shoulders, helping her rise, Mary Catherine still in her arms. "Later, once we are back at Pleasant Hill, you can explain to me why seeing that pistol ball so upset you, and why this room has not been stripped of its belongings, but left as a constant, horrible reminder of what took place here."

Dominick was dressed for civilization again, having donned the outward trappings of a culture that seemed so alien outside the carefully constructed replica of English comfort that was Pleasant Hill.

He had washed himself free of the stink of Rudolph's Inn and Stores, scrubbed himself clean of the horror that remained inside the barn where he and Daniel Cassidy had often sat of an evening, drinking the wine Dominick would bring with him whenever Eileen Cassidy invited him to dine with her family.

But he could not rid himself of the memory of finding the bodies of Joseph and Michael sprawled on the ground a good fifty yards from that barn, their young blood staining the grass, a twist of brown paper filled with candies they had brought home with them from Rudolph's lying between them—sugared treats one of them had dropped in order to defend himself with a toy ax, or a miniature bow.

The glass of wine in Dominick's hand, his second of the evening, also could not rid him of the memory of the sight of Daniel Cassidy's body as he'd found it nearby the boys, his skull cracked so wide his brains had all but tumbled out. Nor would he ever forget the way he had found Eileen Cassidy, her body still in a kneeling position at the side of the bed, her rosary in the hand outflung over the blood-soaked spread, an unloaded pistol lying in her lap . . . her throat cut and her hair gone . . .

Why hadn't he burned the damn building, turned over all the earth that had been soaked with Cassidy blood? Why had he left everything as he had found it, only moving the animals to his own fields, only entering that terrible room long enough to gather the clothing needed to bury the family?

Was it sorrow? Was it his grief? Or was it guilt? Guilt that the Cassidys had died, that the O'Reillys had died. Guilt that Pleasant Hill, situated between the two farms, had been spared. Was that why he had taken Mary Catherine into his house after the raid? Because he had known beforehand that, if an attack were to come, it would be people like the Cassidys, like the O'Reillys, who would perish, while the fortress his money had built made him invulnerable to attack?

Oh, yes, he had tried to help the Cassidys when word had come that war parties might be in the area. He had advised them on how to defend themselves. But it hadn't been enough. He should have moved the six of them into Pleasant Hill until all possibility of danger was gone.

Dominick reached into his pocket, extracting the small ball imprinted with a *C,* marking it as his. He placed the ball on the flat of his palm, then squeezed his hand shut around it.

He had given this ball to Eileen Cassidy three full weeks before the raid, when news of a possible attack had first reached New Eden. It had been part of the gift of two of his own pistols and ample ammunition. He had told her how and when to use that "gift," avoiding her eyes as she had reached out to take the weapons from him, thanking him in a quiet, controlled voice.

And then he had mounted his fine bay mare and ridden back to Pleasant Hill, telling himself he had done all he could, all that was expected of him. Those three weeks had then passed, with no more word of war parties, and he had relaxed. They had all relaxed, and forgotten. Until the black smoke could be seen above the trees, coming from the direction of the O'Reilly farm . . .

No, Dominick hadn't cleaned out the room where the Cassidys had lived, where one of them had died. They had been his first real friends, the first white people he had trusted since coming to New Eden; the first he had allowed even marginally into his life. And he had failed them, failed them miserably. Like the graves, like Mary Catherine's quiet presence, that horrible room served as a reminder to him that there was more to life than his ambitions for Pleasant Hill.

"Mary Catherine is sleeping, finally."

Dominick kept his fingers closed around the pistol ball as he turned to watch Bryna enter the room. She was once more dressed in the gown she'd worn that first night, her beauty as obvious as the pain and anger in her remarkable eyes.

"Mary Catherine never tried to enter the living quarters before today. I'll have a new lock put on the door to the family side of the barn, to replace the one that was broken in the raid." He slipped the pistol ball back into his pocket before moving to pour Bryna a glass of sherry. "I should have cleaned out the remainder of their belongings sooner."

"On the contrary. They were my family, and it is my place to do whatever is necessary," she said flatly, taking the drink without thanking him. "Now, tell me about that pistol ball, if you please."

"Lucas will be announcing dinner shortly, Bryna," Dominick said, avoiding her question, and not bothering to remind her that she could not carry all of the world on her shoulders. He needed for her to face the realities of life here in New Eden, but the whole truth about her family would only cause her needless pain. "Perhaps later we might—"

"Perhaps we will talk about it now, Dominick. I don't know why, but I watched your face when you examined the ball, and I believe I should know why it disturbed you so. After all, wasn't it you who said I had to learn to accept the way things are here in New Eden? How can I do that if you won't tell me?"

"You're probably right," he admitted at last, waiting until she was seated before taking up position in front of the mantel, looking into the fire rather than at her. "You're a part of this country now, whether you like it or not, so you might as well learn what it means to live here. I told you that the ball had my mark on it, didn't I?"

"You did, yes. So what was it doing in my uncle's house? Or are munitions just another of your moneymaking indulgences?"

The flames danced in the fireplace, but Dominick couldn't feel their warmth. "Daniel had only a single rifle. As I explained to Eileen, in an emergency, one rifle would not be enough, not with the two girls, and Daniel might be caught outside, the rifle with him. So I loaned her a brace of pistols and taught her how to load them."

He turned away from the fire, hoping he had said enough.

Bryna shook her head. "I don't understand what you're trying to . . ." Her head shot up and she looked at Dominick, her eyes wide as she at last comprehended what he had told her. "Oh, sweet Mary! You gave her those pistols so that she could . . . she could . . . Oh, *no!*"

"I think she had time, Bryna," Dominick told her, sitting down beside her and taking one of her ice-cold hands in his. "Lokwelend believes the boys were surprised as they returned from Rudolph's, and Daniel ran outside to help them. He never made it more than thirty yards from the barn. Eileen could see all this from their single window. She had to know what she must do, had to have at least made an attempt to do it, or else I wouldn't have found the pistol in her lap, and Mary Catherine wouldn't have found the ball under the bed."

Bryna closed her eyes, allowing him to keep hold of her hand. "But Aunt Eileen couldn't bring herself to kill her own children, to reload and turn a pistol on herself? Could she, Dominick?"

He shook his head. "No, she couldn't. I didn't understand before, except to think she hadn't had the time—or at least that's what I kept trying to tell myself. But she did have the time. The rifle had been fired, probably by Brighid, because I found it inside the barn. There had been plenty of time. In the end, Eileen must have chosen to hide Mary Catherine under the bed, then positioned herself in front of it, probably in hopes the Indians wouldn't discover the child. I—I imagine she put up no defense, but just knelt there, reciting her Rosary, waiting for death."

"But not Bridie," Bryna said quietly, firm conviction in her voice. "Bridie would have fought. I know my cousin. She would have fought with everything that was in her."

"I agree. You saw the room. It is, as you said, exactly the way I found it that day. You saw the overturned chairs, the broken crockery, the obvious signs of a struggle." Dominick smiled sadly. "I imagine your cousin inflicted more than one or two injuries with that crockery before they finally subdued her. And, if she still lives, I doubt that she is making herself a well-behaved captive."

"Lokwelend promised he would find her." Bryna pulled her hand free of Dominick's, as if she had just realized that he had been touching her and she resented that touch very much. "I refuse to believe otherwise."

"Once more the world turns because Bryna Cassidy so orders it, and, she believes, *as* she orders it. I applaud your high hopes, but there's something you have to remember. The Brighid you knew—the young girl you last saw before she left Ireland—is lost forever. When Lokwelend brings her back, *if* Lokwelend brings her back, she will be very different."

Bryna put down her glass and stood up, beginning to pace the carpet in front of Dominick. "I saw a woman that morning at Rudolph's—before you came for me. She was slatternly, and dirty, and seemed half-mad. Her face . . .

her forehead and cheeks were covered with horrible tattoos."

"Silky Wattson," Dominick said, impressed yet again with Bryna's courage, for she seemed to know more than he'd had any intention of telling her, yet still persisted in her determination to have Brighid Cassidy returned to New Eden. "Did someone tell you about her?"

Bryna nodded. "Alice Rudolph explained it to me. The woman had been taken by the Indians, and tattooed in that way so that she wouldn't wish to return to her own people because of the shame of it. Yes, I know all about Silky Wattson. I know she was rescued by the militia against her own wishes, how her family turned her away, and how she now ekes out a living serving as whore to every heartless, randy wretch in this area."

She stopped pacing and turned to Dominick, that indomitable chin raised to an imperious level as she looked down at him. "Brighid's family *wants* her, Dominick. No matter how long it takes, no matter what trials she has been forced to endure, no matter her condition upon her return—I want her back. I *will* have her back!"

"You're quite a woman, Bryna Cassidy. Nothing touches you. Nothing deters you from the course you've set. Not death, not horror, not even common sense. You refuse to even think of defeat," Dominick said, rising as Lucas entered the room to announce that dinner was about to be served. "So very much the conquering Bright Fire Lokwelend has named you."

"Is that so terrible?"

"Not at all. I admire your courage in the face of adversity. Just as I had admired your family's courage, their determination."

"Thank you, Dominick," Bryna said, looking at him with, if not affection, slightly less animosity.

"You're welcome. And now that we've cried friends yet again, fool that I am, I'm going to tell you something that will most probably send you to spitting and clawing at me once more. But it can't be helped. Bryna, I've drawn up all the papers concerning the monetary settlements for our upcoming nuptials. I had been more than willing to go about this in a more leisurely fashion, but concern for your reputation adds a modicum of haste I cannot like. Therefore, I have decided that we will be married within the hour."

"I beg your pardon?"

"You do? Oh, I most seriously doubt that." Dominick smiled at her, admiring her control even as all the color drained out of her cheeks, then quickly pressed his advantage. "But I do have my reasons, Bryna. For one, if Brighid is returned to her family, I will be the head of that family, and it's important that everyone in New Eden knows she is under my protection. Secondly, I believe we will both rest better once we have all of this settled between us, don't you agree? Or are you having reservations about our plans?"

"Reservations? Hardly, Dominick, considering I am without alternatives, as you well know. I told you I would do it, and I will. But you're forgetting something. I had asked for a lump-sum settlement. I want that money in my hand, not merely some promises scribbled down on paper."

"And you shall have it. Before the ceremony."

"Again, your thoroughness astonishes me." Her shoulders relaxed slightly, even as she raised another protest. "However, I still find your haste unseemly. Surely there is no great rush? Why shouldn't we wait until Bridie is returned to New Eden, if her situation concerns you so? You also seem to forget that the conventions allow for a decent period of mourning before I should even consider marriage. In the meantime, I certainly could use some of that money to refurbish my wardrobe, and Mary Catherine's as well. I would be much happier if I were to have some funds of my own and not have to bother you for every small trifle I might need. Then perhaps in a month or two—"

Drat the woman! Dominick could not keep the sudden anger out of his voice. "I said, Bryna, that we will be married tonight. The matter is not open to further discussion." She clearly thought him a fool, and a gullible fool at that. Had she really believed he was so blind that he couldn't see through her plan to take his money, and her cousins, and desert him as soon as an opportunity presented itself?

Clearly she had.

"Again, Dominick, you show such heat!" Bryna smiled and batted her long, dark eyelashes a time or two, obviously trying out her feminine wiles on him, and just as obviously hating herself, and him, that she felt the need to do so. "I—I had hoped to wait until my bride's clothes were completed, so that I could appear at my best. And—and then there's the matter of my present to you. I had thought handkerchiefs . . . my mother taught me to sew a fine seam . . . and I want Bridie to attend me in the church, and . . ."

When her protests died away, Dominick waved an embarrassed-looking Lucas out of the room and went to the side table, where he had left the record book he'd retrieved from Henry Turner before returning to Pleasant Hill.

"There is no church in New Eden, Bryna, nor is there one in Allen's Town. Births, deaths, *and* marriages for the area are all recorded in this book. Lucretia and Lucas will listen to us recite our vows, and then we'll sign our names in the book. I believe it's called handfasting, and it's as close to a ceremony as we'll be before any minister or priest arrives here on his regular circuit next spring. We will have the ceremony then, at which point you may shower me with finely stitched handkerchiefs, if you like. But for now, Bryna, we'll sign our names in the record book. And we'll do it tonight, so that you don't have to hide in your chamber anymore to avoid me. Do you understand?"

"Oh, yes, I understand. I understand everything now. And you knew this. You knew this all along—all the time you were proposing this *marriage* of yours. You *knew* that there would be no priest, even as you said the word 'marriage' to me again tonight."

Bryna eyed the book in Dominick's hand as if it could turn into a hissing, coiling snake at any moment. "Well, I won't do it," she said flatly, backing up a pace. "You can't make me do it. Signing our names doesn't make for a marriage in the eyes of God."

"Perhaps not. But it does accomplish the deed in the eyes

of man, and I can't allow you to leave Pleasant Hill for so much as a drive into the village until you're under my protection. You live here now, Bryna. You've slept under my roof. In the minds of the sterling residents of New Eden, that means one of two things—either you are my wife, or you are my whore. I nearly had to horsewhip one man this morning to make him understand the difference, and I don't intend a repetition when next I go into New Eden. As my wife, you see, you will have their grudging respect. As my whore, it will be only a matter of time before someone discovers you alone and decides to sample you for himself, and I would be forced to murder one or several of the local gentlemen. Now do you understand?"

Dominick waited again, wishing he could look away from Bryna's expressive face, wishing he didn't want so badly to touch her, to bed her; wishing he were more the English gentleman than he was the near-savage this land, this time, had made him.

Needs must, when the Devil drives. Dominick heard his mother's words inside his head, remembering how she had said them as she pushed his father's full purse into her son's hands, then added a few pieces of her jewelry as her own parting gift, just as he was about to board ship.

Dominick needed Bryna. He needed her to help him build his dynasty, to make his a permanent mark upon this savage land. He needed her as his tool, to bear the sons that would entice his mother to leave England and come to him, to free her of the horror of her present life. He needed her to remind him that there was another world, a more civilized, gentle world out there somewhere, and that he could bring some of that world here, to Pleasant Hill.

And that was all right. He could marry her for those reasons and go to bed each night with his conscience clear.

What bothered Dominick, what had kept him from sleep these last nights and haunted his waking hours, was that he knew he not only needed Bryna Cassidy—he *wanted* her. He wanted her in his bed, not just his drawing room. He wanted her softness to help smooth the increasingly hard edges of his life. He wanted her beside him, warm and yielding, and with welcome in her eyes. He longed, day and night, to be warmed, even occasionally burned, by her "bright fire."

And so he waited, holding his breath, hating himself, until she finally answered him.

"Yes, well, it is only a book, isn't it? Hardly binding, except perhaps to the hyenas in the village. If it will make you happy, I can't understand why I've been making such a fuss. And there is still our bargain, if you recall. Six months, remember?"

"I remember."

"Good. Add a priest into that bargain, Dominick, if you please, and even if you don't. Now that you've made a change in our agreement, I see no reason why I should not have a new condition of my own. Don't bother to voice your agreement, for I'll simply shoot you if you don't hold to my terms."

She held out her hand so that he might offer her his arm as they went in to dinner. "Now—may we please eat first, Dominick? I'd really much rather not *handfast* on an empty stomach."

My tongue swore,
but my mind was still unpledged.
— Euripides

CHAPTER 6

❦

BRYNA HELD UP THE SMALL BRACE OF CANDLES, THE BETTER TO
inspect the tall, black japanned clock that stood in a corner
of the foyer, beneath the wide, curved arc of the stairs. She
recognized the colored portraits of George III and Queen
Charlotte that embellished the front of the case, but had
only been told by Lucas that afternoon that the third
portrait was of William Pitt, the prime minister who was so
favored by all the American colonists.

Not that she cared overmuch, because she didn't. But
thinking about how much the piece must have cost, and
how difficult it must have been to have it transported here
over the rough country roads, kept her mind from wandering back to the strange, informal "ceremony" that had taken
place in the drawing room that night after dinner.

She reached out her right hand, the one she had placed in
Dominick Crown's strong, callused one only a few hours
earlier, and with a single fingertip traced the intricate wood
carving that surrounded the portrait of the queen. Charlotte

was said to be very much enamored of her Farmer George. That was probably a good thing, Bryna thought consideringly, as it was a queen's duty to bear her husband as many children as possible. Being in love certainly had to make those necessary visits to the marriage bed more palatable.

Bryna pulled back her hand, closing it into a fist. What was she thinking! Dominick Crown would be making no trips to her bed. There was no need for love because there would be no lovemaking, and no children. Why, there hadn't even been a real marriage. Reciting a few empty vows in front of servants, and signing one's name beside a man's in a book marked more with Xs by illiterate laborers wishing to record the birth of yet another child—well, that meant nothing. Less than nothing.

She was *not* married. Words did not make a marriage. Signing her name did not make a marriage. She didn't even have a ring, for goodness' sakes! And having Dominick Crown lift her hand to his lips, turning that hand at the last moment so that his wedding kiss had been pressed into her palm? Well, that hadn't made for much of anything except a flash of anger on her part, which had nearly ended with her slapping his silly, grinning face!

Bryna opened her hand now and looked at it, almost as if it were alien to her, faintly surprised to see that her palm was unmarked. It should be red, and blistered, for all the heat Dominick's kiss had generated, for the way that heat had quickly raced up her arm in a fiery tingle she'd tried to ignore but could not.

And he'd known that she had experienced that unexpectedly pleasant reaction to his kiss. His smile had told her that, silently crowed it over her. Then he had quickly sobered, released her hand, and turned to thank Lucas and Lucretia before he quit the room, saying something about having pressing estate business to attend to in his study.

The devil he did! He had left the room because he had accomplished all he'd intended to accomplish. He'd bought himself a wife, and Bryna had the small, heavy velvet pouch in her bedchamber to prove it. He'd bought her, paid for her just as if he'd purchased a slave, or a fine English tall clock. Just one more addition to Pleasant Hill, the estate he had told her was his private hell, yet showed all the signs of being most deliberately made into a bucolic paradise here in the wilds of the colony of Pennsylvania.

If only she knew why he had chosen her. She had used him, would continue to use him, and if she couldn't get herself and her cousins away from this place quickly, he would be sure to use her. There would be no marriage in name only—not for long. Not if that kiss had anything to say in the matter.

Bryna jumped nearly out of her skin when the clock suddenly struck out the hour of one, hot wax from the candleholder spilling over onto her fingers.

"Silly gooseberry," she reprimanded herself quietly, transferring the candleholder to her right hand so that she could suck on her singed knuckle. "The man's been abed for hours, thank all the saints. If he didn't wake when the clock chimed at midnight, he most certainly won't wake now."

That was another reason she hated Dominick Crown. How dare he go to bed, go to sleep, when she felt as if she would never sleep again? She had all but raced up the stairs after he'd gone to his study, leaping into her nightrail and then quickly sliding into bed beside the sleeping Mary Catherine.

And there she had stayed, wide-eyed and apprehensive, unbelieving of his promise that theirs would be a marriage in name only, waiting for the knock on the door, dreading the summons to remove herself to the large bedchamber at the far end of the hall.

That summons had never come.

Only Dominick's firm footsteps had disturbed the quiet as he had mounted the stairs and passed just in front of her door, his pace never slowing as he made his way to his own room.

Only the sound of the tall clock chiming out the time every half hour had marked the passage of the hours, until Bryna could no longer stand being trapped in her chamber beside the sleeping child, trapped inside her own thoughts.

She had taken up her candleholder and gone downstairs, vaguely considering stuffing up the clockworks with her good shawl. Which was above everything stupid. Which just proved that she had succumbed to a bout of maidenly nerves.

Which made her think that she had moved a family of bats into her belfry—because she was actually feeling vaguely disappointed that Dominick Crown had *not* come scratching at her door, asking her to accompany him to his bed.

And now here she was, standing in the middle of the foyer, petulant as a child denied a treat sure to make her sick, sucking on her stinging knuckle, staring at a portrait of Queen Charlotte and envying her reported happiness. Perhaps she was her mother's child, after all. Perhaps she had been fashioned purely to be at the mercy of a man's whims, a man's schemes, a man's handsome, appealing appearance.

"Ha! And the day you find yourself believin' that, Bryna Maureen Cassidy," she told herself fiercely, "will sure an' enough be the day hens crow and pigs cackle!" She picked up her skirts and stomped none too quietly toward the back of the house, and Dominick's study, and the decanter of wine she was sure to find there.

The study was dark, as dark as the rest of the ground floor of the house, which had been closed up for the night, all those heavy wooden shutters bolted tight against the demons Lucas feared could come sneaking out of the trees to murder them in their beds. Bryna, however, was no longer quite so fearful of Indian attack, not when the greatest, the most immediate, threat to her security slept upstairs, locked inside the house with her.

She put down the candleholder after using it to light three more tapers in the room. She crossed to the side table to pour herself a full glass of wine, not caring if it wasn't seemly for a woman to drink alone, or to drink spirits at all if the glass hadn't been offered to her by a gentleman. Replacing the heavy crystal stopper with a smidgen more force than was actually necessary, she then retired to the large leather chair behind the desk and plunked herself down, intent on drinking herself into oblivion, or at least partway there. Far enough, in any case, that she would no longer remember the feel of Dominick Crown's lips upon her palm.

Determination etched on her features, she sat back against the soft leather, her fiery curls tumbling halfway down her back, her bare feet dangling a good four inches above the floor. She took a deep sip of the ruby liquid. And then she took another. And, after a few moments had passed, another . . .

Drinking alone had its drawbacks, Bryna discovered less than ten minutes later as she sat forward, put down the empty glass, propped her elbows on the desktop, sighed deeply, and looked around the room, more than slightly bored with her own company.

An idle mind might be the Devil's own workshop, but a troubled mind can find its way into more than twice the mischief in an effort to escape thought. Bryna, urged on by her own mind's soft whispers that told her she was now, in Dominick Crown's mind at least, the mistress of Pleasant Hill, decided that—as mistress of that house—she was entitled to do a small inventory of its contents.

Beginning—and wasn't it handy that she should be sitting right there at the time—with a thorough inventory of the contents of Dominick Crown's desk. Though, of course, first she'd need another glass of wine. Inventorying, as anyone would probably vouch for her if there had been anyone about for her to apply to for their opinion in the matter, was thirsty work.

Armed with a second full glass, Bryna began opening and closing drawers without touching anything because the dratted man was entirely too neat in his habits and would probably be able to tell if she so much as *breathed* a single piece of paper out of place.

Finally, in the wide center drawer, she located what she had been looking for—a large ledger book. "Hello, hello. Come to Bryna, you sweet, darlin' thing," she crooned, pulling out the book and opening it on the desktop. She moved one of the candleholders closer, the better to read the long columns of figures that went on page after page.

As she read, drawing a fingertip down the columns detailing the purchase of stock, the selling of lumber, the acquisition of goods from Philadelphia and beyond, Bryna—being not only her mother's but also her father's child—could get a quick sense of Dominick's worth.

And he was worth a great deal.

Only one entry, repeated monthly, puzzled her. It showed that a draft made on a bank in Philadelphia was routinely sent to a solicitor in Folkestone.

What on earth did that mean? Who was this English solicitor? Why would Dominick be sending him money, and a considerable amount of money, at that? Absently Bryna touched her fingertip to her tongue, then turned to the next page of the ledger, realizing too late that she had left a faint, wine-tinged smudge on the clean paper.

"Oh, damn and blast!" she exclaimed, using her father's favorite expression of chagrin as she rubbed at the smudge. "Time for bed, Bryna-girl," she told herself guiltily.

She opened the desk drawer once more, ready to slip the ledger back in its resting place, then hesitated. There was a folded but unsealed and not yet addressed sheet of writing paper sitting there, in the center of the drawer, just begging her to take it out and read what was written on it.

Was this the "estate business" Dominick had been working on this evening?

"You shouldn't, Bryna. You really, really shouldn't," she admonished herself sternly before, feeling slightly muzzy-headed from the wine, she gave in to impulse. Then she shrugged. "In for a penny . . ." she murmured, smiling. Replacing the ledger, she extracted the heavy vellum sheet and spread it open beside the candleholder, her lips moving as she read the bold, masculine scrawl:

Dearest Mother,
  Something momentous has happened since last I wrote, something you have long hoped for me. I have

*married. Bryna is a most delightful creature, Mother,
just the sort of well-bred, conformable young lady you
would have for me, and I am, indeed, the happiest of
men.*

*As chance would have it, my bride is the cousin of
young Mary Catherine, whom I wrote to you about just
recently. Now, more than ever, Pleasant Hill cries out to
you, Mother, as I cry out to you, longing for your
presence. It is a good life, here at Pleasant Hill, but a
sometimes lonely one. Bryna, and Mary Catherine as
well, would be, I am assured, much comforted by the
presence of another gentlewoman such as yourself.*

*You have denied me until now, dear Mother, telling
me again and again of your vows, your duty. I beg you
put those considerations to one side and think of, if not
your son or your own happiness, your new daughter,
who is alone and friendless in a strange country.*

*As always, Mother, I remind you of the funds in
Folkestone that are at your disposal, as well as of my
great, unwavering love for you.*

Dominick had scrawled his name at the bottom of the
single sheet, almost hurriedly, as if he had written the letter,
then read it over in haste before signing. Her hands trembling, Bryna refolded the sheet and slipped it into the
drawer. Dominick's obvious sense of urgency, his longing
for his mother, had touched her more than she cared to
acknowledge.

Bryna stood up and moved away from the desk, taking
her wineglass with her as she seated herself on the leather
couch placed beneath one of the shuttered windows. Now
she knew. She knew why he sent funds to that Folkestone
solicitor. And she finally understood Dominick's greatest
reason for wanting their marriage. Yes, he had wanted a
wife in order to build a dynasty; but he also had planned to
use her to lure his mother here from England.

Why?

And what a clutch of crammers he had told that woman
in order to have her come to him! All those lovely words

about his new bride. Delightful, was she? And well-bred? Conformable? Oh, yes, and then there was the fattest fib of all—that he was the happiest of men!

The *vilest* of men, that's what he was! Vile, and dishonest, and devious, and misleading, and . . . and . . .

"Papa would have adored him," Bryna ended aloud, taking another sip of wine as she curled up on the soft leather, tucking her bare feet beneath the hem of her dressing gown. "And, when I think on it, so far I have been the only one to have realized any clear benefits from our bargain. I have a dry roof over my head, Mary Kate safely with me, and Bridie soon to be rescued. I have a full purse, which will come in most handily when I leave here and go Renton Frey hunting."

She rubbed at the tip of her nose, which had gone unaccountably numb. "All Dominick has," she continued consideringly, her mind working, but in circles, "is the hope his newest lure will help bring his mother to him, to the house he has built here. He doesn't care a jot for me—just as long as she comes. I have no need to fear the marriage bed, not anymore. The 'happiest of men' wouldn't dare frightening his conformable bride away before his mother was safely aboard ship and heading for Pleasant Hill."

How much better she felt now, her heart lighter, freed of the last of her guilt—even if she knew she should be wondering why Dominick wanted his mother with him so badly, and why the woman should be thinking of her own happiness.

Bryna decided that she hadn't duped anyone; she had just entered into a bargain. A business proposition. Nothing more. With more than one hidden motive, on both sides. She rested her arm on the side of the couch and laid her head against the crook of her elbow. "A fine bargain all around, Papa," she said, yawning widely. "Everyone wins, and no one gets hurt. Yes, you would have approved. I only wonder," she ended, her voice slurring slightly as her eyelids drooped closed, "why he didn't tell me about his mother in the first place . . ."

* * *

Another night was over, once again ending a full hour before dawn, when Dominick, after sleeping badly if at all, finally rose from his bed. His empty bed.

Only this morning, this dark, sunless morning, was slightly different. This morning Dominick Crown was a married man, for all the good it had done him. His bed was still empty, and only his mind was full of the small, willful, fiery-haired creature who was now his *un*willing wife.

Moving around in his familiar chamber without need of candlelight, Dominick sluiced his upper body with cold water from the basin Lucas had left for him. He felt his cheek and decided that, having shaved a second time yesterday, in preparation for his "wedding," he could dispense with that particular nicety for the moment.

He dressed in the dark, stepping into his deerskins and gartering them below the knees with thin strips of rawhide. He slipped into his well-worn moccasins and a clean shirt, tying his comfortable deerskin jacket at the waist with a colorful sash Kolachuisen had woven for him, then tied back his long black hair with another length of rawhide.

He headed for the servants' stairs at the back of the house, intent on gathering up the letter to his mother and taking it into New Eden in time to go out with the mail coach that would stop there the following day. If he left immediately, he'd still be back at Pleasant Hill before Lokwelend and Pematalli set out on their bound-to-be-fruitless search for Brighid Cassidy.

How long would they be gone? A month? Two? Possibly three. At least as long as it would take for his letter to reach Playden Court. Bryna wouldn't attempt to leave until he had some sort of final word about her cousin. And if Brighid was so unlucky as to still be alive, Bryna would soon see the sense in remaining under his protection here at Pleasant Hill, where her cousin would be safe from those who would blame her for being so foolish as to have survived her time in a Lenape camp.

Yes, Bryna Cassidy Crown wasn't going anywhere, not that she was doing him much good here at Pleasant Hill right now, thanks to his promise to keep theirs a marriage in name only, for at least a little while. But she'd be good company for his mother, when she finally arrived—and escaped the prison of her own loveless marriage to a cruel, heartless man. To free her, just as she had helped to free him; that was Dominick's fondest wish.

He could only pray he might find a way to sleep nights, knowing that his virgin bride was just down the hallway—and hope his powers of seduction outstripped her determination to avoid his bed.

Dominick stopped inside the kitchen long enough to open the heavy wooden shutters on the half-light before dawn. He sliced himself a crusty piece of day-old bread that would keep his belly from protesting too loudly for another hour, before crossing the hall and entering his private study.

It was easier to open one pair of shutters than it was to bother with a candle, and once he'd let a little of the predawn light into the room, he turned toward the desk, to retrieve the letter he had written his mother the previous evening. He turned, and then he stopped in his tracks, the piece of bread hanging from his mouth the way Gilhooley would hold a rabbit in his jaws, staring at the sight of his new bride as she slept on the couch across the room.

"Wrrahta?" he mumbled in reaction, then took the bread from his mouth and repeated, "What the—?" Then he said nothing at all, but just stood there, staring.

She was curled into a tight little ball of femininity, her long white dressing gown spread out over her so that only the tips of her toes were exposed. Her fiery hair hung loose, cascading over her shoulders. Her features were as pure and finely formed as any Greek statue, her mouth soft and moist as she slept on, unaware of his presence.

Christ, but she was beautiful.

"And probably drunk," he told himself quietly, seeing the empty wineglass that lay in her lap, then shooting a measuring glance toward the level of deep red liquid that remained in the crystal decanter. "An intriguing reaction to finding oneself suddenly married, and one I probably should have considered myself."

He opened the desk drawer, never taking his eyes off

Bryna, and sat down in preparation of addressing and sealing the letter before . . . before what? Before leaving his wife here, sound asleep, and riding into New Eden? Before leaving the letter on his desk and picking up his sleeping wife and carrying her to his bed? To their bed?

No, it would be better if he got that thought straight out of his head, at least for now. It wouldn't do to push Bryna, especially when he considered the way she handled a Pennsylvania long rifle. Smiling at his own weak joke, he put the letter back into the drawer, deciding to give it over to Alice Rudolph when she arrived at Pleasant Hill. Then he crossed to the couch, sitting down beside his wife and removing the wineglass from her slack fingers.

Unable to resist the impulse, he then reached out and touched her unbound hair, silently agreeing with Lokwelend's conclusion that it felt warm, and alive.

He wanted to bury his face in that warmth.

His hand strayed to her cheek, a single finger running along its smooth contours, touching the corner of her mouth before trailing down the side of her exposed throat, to the white satin ribbon that held her dressing gown secure, her more intimate charms concealed.

How long had it been since he'd touched a beautiful woman? How long since he'd even desired one? He'd led a near monk's existence here at Pleasant Hill, declining both the dubious charms of the sadly unfortunate Silky Wattson and the release to be found in the willing arms of many of the Lenape maidens who passed through the area. Only on his twice-yearly trips to Philadelphia had he sought out the company of women. Talented women, experienced women. Women he bought for the night, as he'd purchase a fine bottle of wine or a good meal.

Desire cut through him now as Bryna moaned softly in her sleep, screwing up her features almost comically as, undoubtedly uncomfortable and instinctively seeking warmth, she moved toward him. She sighed in obvious pleasure as she laid her head in the crook of his shoulder, then snuggled close against him, her hand at his waist, cuddling like a kitten curling up on a soft pillow.

Dominick sat there, feeling stupid, feeling more than stupid; feeling the tortures of the damned, feeling her hand slip lower in her sleep, until it rested, quite innocently, on his rapidly heating manhood.

His reaction was anything but innocent, and if he didn't do something soon, something very English and very gentlemanly, he was going to regret it for the rest of his life. Probably even more than he would regret *not* doing it, he thought with a small, wry smile.

Although he'd be damned if he'd move her hand.

"Bryna," he said quietly, leaning down to whisper her name against her hair, breathing in her sweet jasmine scent. "Bryna, you might want to wake up now."

"Go'way," she mumbled, snuggling even closer, so that he could feel her left breast easing against his rib cage, the curve of her hip pressing against his thigh, her hand settling more firmly in his lap . . .

"For the love of—Bryna. Bryna!"

She stirred again, waking slowly, the hand that burned in his lap beginning to move, to investigate, to kill him with a sweet agony no man should be forced to endure. And then she stopped, and her entire body stiffened.

"Dominick?" Her voice was small, and confused, and faintly slurred. She raised her head and opened her eyes, her bewitching gray-green eyes, and he watched as they filled with confusion, turning nearly transparent as she struggled to understand what was happening and how she had come to be lying in his arms. Her hand moved once more, exploring the landscape that was his lap, as if she were attempting to get her bearings. *"Dominick?"*

He stifled a laugh that became a near groan. "That would be correct, madam. It is most definitely I. And it's a damn good thing we're married, or I'd think you to be a decidedly forward female."

"Sweet Mary and all the saints!" She was on her feet in an instant, leaving him sitting there alone and gasping for breath, for she'd used a most delicate part of his lower anatomy as a pushing-off point for her quick departure from the couch. "How dare you!"

Dominick sat forward, dropping his face into his hands, his gut in a knot. "I wonder that myself, Bryna," he said slowly, then rose to his feet, looking down at her flushed cheeks. "Did you have a good night's rest?"

She raised a hand to her forehead, avoiding his eyes. "Yes—no! I mean, I-I never intended . . . that is, I had only . . . and then I closed my eyes, only for a moment, and . . . Oh, my *head!* And I'm so thirsty! My father was right, a wet night leads to a dry morning."

"I'd suggest a hair from the dog that bit you, but I suppose you aren't interested in beginning your day with another glass of wine."

"I'd much rather begin it by picking up one of those rifles and shooting off your ear," she answered grumpily, pulling her dressing gown more closely around her.

"Yes, that was going to be my second choice, also." He crossed to the desk and sat down on the chair behind it— gingerly, for he was a man in pain—and opened the drawer. *Go away, damn it,* he told her silently. *Don't just stand there, looking every inch the Bright Fire Lokwelend has named you. Don't you know how much I want to touch you?*

"I suppose you're expecting some sort of explanation?" Bryna asked, although her words sounded more like an accusation.

"Not really," Dominick answered, closing his hand around the stick of sealing wax, sure the heat from that hand would melt it into a puddle.

"I-I couldn't sleep, that's all. It occurred to me that a small glass of wine might not come amiss, and not wanting to bother Lucretia, I just, um, I just—"

"I don't care." He looked up at her, every fiber of his body crying out for ease. "Do you understand that, Bryna? I simply do not care. I do, however, find myself wondering why it is that I am always stumbling over you in a state of near undress, and why that state of undress does not seem to bother you in the slightest. Has some new fashion of flaunting oneself *déshabillé* become the all rage in London? I have been rather out of touch with current fashion, you understand."

The slamming of the study door reverberated throughout the entire downstairs, nearly drowning out Dominick's heartfelt "Thank God!" before, at last alone in his study, he decided that a glass of wine might go very well with an early breakfast of day-old bread and sexual frustration.

A glass of wine, and perhaps a brisk walk to the stream and a cold bath.

Necessity brings him here,
not pleasure.
— Dante

CHAPTER 7

❦

THE SUN WAS CLIMBING TOWARD NOON BEFORE DOMINICK returned to the house. He'd had a busy morning. He'd started out with a visit to Lokwelend's lodge, only to have Cora, his daughter, inform him that Pematalli and his father had set out before dawn to begin their search for Brighid Cassidy.

Cora, or Kolachuisen, as Dominick still thought of her, had offered him a late breakfast of corn cakes, and the two had engaged in a cryptic conversation about the folly of trying to recapture "the bird that has already flown beyond the mountains." Never did she refer to Brighid by name, as Lenapes believed mentioning the names of the dead only served to keep grief alive.

It was, Dominick knew, a true measure of Lokwelend's love for his "white father" that he had agreed to go beyond the mountains in a search of the "bird" that, in the hearts and minds of Lokwelend and his children, no longer existed.

97

Or it's a measure of Lokwelend's respect for the wrath of the Bright Fire, Dominick had considered ruefully, although he was not foolish enough to say the words aloud, even when Kolachuisen had asked Dominick when she could meet the Bright Fire her father had first seen in his dream.

"As soon as I can convince her not to shoot at any innocent Lenape she sees," Dominick had told her.

Kolachuisen had giggled like the innocent girl she was, then solemnly promised to keep her distance until her friend Crown had tamed his new wife.

Believing Kolachuisen's promise to have effectively banned her from Pleasant Hill for the next decade, at the very least, Dominick had then taken his leave in order to visit with the brave he'd last seen at Rudolph's.

The Indian family had set up a rude camp in the East Meadow, but were clearly eager to be on their way west again, which they would not do until they had properly thanked Dominick for his hospitality.

And that's when the situation had become dangerous. Once he had pressed a small purse into the brave's hand to atone for Rudolph's near robbery of the man's beaver pelts, Dominick had spent the next quarter hour politely explaining why he had to decline an offer of the squaw's "favor" in return for his largesse.

To simply turn down the Indian's gift would be rude, and could end with the loss of his hair, so Dominick, calling on his knowledge of the Lenape, had made a great business about his new *Yankwi* bride and her fearsome temper. He'd wrung his hands and loudly belabored the fact that she would probably turn him out of his home if he were to share any blanket save her own.

Playing to the Lenape love of the absurd, he had even rolled on the grass, holding up his hands as if to protect himself from his wife's fierce blows. He bemoaned his sad fate as his audience gaped at this white father who had been brought so low, before they joined in the joke, laughing so heartily at his predicament that Dominick was convinced he'd soon be known all over the colony as Bright Fire's squaw.

Whipped Dog, Dominick thought now as he climbed the hill to the gardens, and the trade entrance to the house. *That's what I'll be called. Or Shiwapi—Shriveled Man. And I owe it all to my dear wife.*

His dear wife. The beautiful, willful, enticing, distracting, wholly infuriating woman he could not sleep, drink, or work out of his brain for more than a moment. How had he come to this pass?

"Because you're stupid, Dominick Crown, that's how," he muttered, pushing his windblown hair out of his eyes as he berated himself for what he had done. And how quickly he had done it.

He should have forestalled his marriage at least until he'd received his mother's answer to his plea that she come to Pleasant Hill to help him with Mary Catherine. Communication back and forth between the colonies and England was so slow, so erratic, that she may have already taken ship, for all he knew. His difficulty in finding a suitable bride notwithstanding, his marriage may have been totally unnecessary.

He should have lied. He should have taken his idea of having a wife being the ultimate lure, and used it by simply *telling* his mother he'd married. Then, when his mother arrived, he could have told her that his unfaithful and unsuitable wife had run off with a traveling tinker. He hadn't really *had* to marry Bryna Cassidy.

"You definitely need more sleep," Dominick told himself as he plucked a few stray blades of grass from his jacket sleeve, remnants of his playacting and reminders of just how low he had sunk in less than a week. "Or a keeper," he ended, sighing. "Because now you're talking to yourself, which has got to be nearly half again as crazy as believing you could have looked at Bryna Cassidy, this intriguing, infuriating woman-child the fates dropped into your hands like a ripe plum, and then let her walk out of your life."

The sound of wagon wheels on the drive brought Dominick back to an awareness of his surroundings, and reminded him why he was at the house, rather than in the fields with his tenant farmers, taking care of estate business.

His tenants were good men, most of them family men, but they needed direction, just like their counterparts at Playden Court. But, unlike in England, his tenants never stayed long, most of them moving out into the raw territory beyond the mountains as soon as possible, to claim and tame their own land. He might entice another family to stay at Pleasant Hill until at least the end of the growing season, if he rid the Cassidy barn of the horror that lingered there. Someone new to the area, who wouldn't shrink at living where so many had died.

"Just another one of the problems I don't want to think about at the moment," Dominick muttered. "Which certainly doesn't explain why I'm here, rather than out in the fields."

But he knew why. He wanted to be on hand to personally present his wife with the material for new gowns for both Mary Catherine and herself, and then enjoy the frustrated look on her face when she realized she had to thank him for his gift. As revenge for the humiliation he had suffered this morning, it wasn't all that satisfying. However, for the moment, he would take his pleasure where he found it.

"Good morning, Alice," Dominick announced cheerfully as he approached the wagon, taking one of the horses' heads as the girl gave a last haul on the reins and set the brake. "You might want to go into the kitchens to visit with Lucretia while I unload the wagon. And I'll have a letter for you to take back to New Eden with you, if you would."

"Yes, sir, Mr. Crown," Alice responded quickly, climbing down from the wagon and clumsily bobbing him a quick curtsy. She shied away from him like a frightened animal, averting her face as she tugged her shawl farther forward over her forehead, all but hiding her face from him. "I'll just be doin' that right now, sir. Thank you, sir."

What the devil? Had he grown two heads overnight, that Alice suddenly seemed so fearful of him? He'd always thought the girl liked him. Or was he being suspicious for no reason, and just now noticing, thanks to his wife, that females were, for the most part, highly unpredictable, unfathomable creatures?

"Wait a moment, Alice, if you would, please," he called after the girl. "I already see that something is amiss with my order. Where is the Indian woman?"

"I can't say, sir," Alice mumbled quickly, staring at her toes. "Pa says I dares not."

"Damn," Dominick swore quietly, replacing the sack of flour he'd already hoisted onto his shoulder. He walked over to stand directly in front of the young girl, hating that she flinched at his approach, as if he might hit her. "I'm not going to like this, am I, Alice?"

"No, sir," she said, twisting the ends of her shawl in her hands as she shifted from foot to foot, the action only accentuating her obvious limp. "Not a whit, sir, seein' as how you don't like that there Jonah Newton above half. But Pa says you're not God Almighty, even if you act like you are, and he says that as it was only a worthless Indian cow anyways, and you've already got yourself a prime piece, you shouldn't be so selfish as to not share. Not that you could anyways, not no more. Sir."

Dominick was surprised. First, that Rudolph had dared to defy his wishes, and secondly, at the length of Alice's speech. He couldn't remember her ever being quite so talkative before—although he rarely saw her away from Rudolph's, and out from under the thumbs of her domineering parents. Having those two carping bullies in the vicinity would be enough to goad a town crier into taking on a vow of silence. "And why would that be, Alice? What has happened to the Indian woman?"

"She's dead, Mr. Crown," Alice blurted out quickly, raising her head to look fully at Dominick, the shawl slipping to her shoulders so that, at last, he could see her face. "I'm that sorry, sir. I tried to help. I truly did."

Alice abruptly clapped her hands to her mouth, obviously realizing she'd said much more than her pa had wanted her to say, leaving Dominick to look at the livid bruise on her cheek, her cracked, bloody lip, and her badly swollen and blackened eye.

Dominick felt his jaw tighten. "Damn them. May God damn them all to hell."

Alice uttered a small, hiccuping sob and quickly drew the shawl about her head once more.

Dominick wanted to hit somebody. Anybody. Hit him hard. But he couldn't let Alice see the full extent of his fury; she was already frightened half out of her mind. "Forgive me, Alice," he said soothingly. "And of course you tried to help. I can certainly see that. Whatever happened, it was *not* your fault. Will you please tell me about the Indian woman?"

The girl took a deep breath, as if that would help her come to a decision, then let it out slowly, nodding her head. "Yes, sir. I'll tell you. It was last night. She didn't want to go with Newton when he come back for her, I'm thinkin', seein' how drunk he was and all, and mad as a scorched hen, and cursin' you for an interferin' bastard when Pa said she was yours. Sorry, sir, but that's what Mr. Newton said."

"Ah, yes, Alice, that's our Jonah Newton, straight down to the ground. Sophisticated, urbane, and wonderfully articulate." Dominick's rage simmered just below the surface as he waited for Alice to finish her story.

She frowned, obviously not able to understand. "He was bein' mean, real mean, and he started slappin' and pokin' at the Indian because she wouldn't go with him. I tried to stop him, Mr. Crown, sir, I really did. Especially when she fell down, and that blanket she was all hunched up in slipped off her, and Mr. Newton saw her belly and said he wanted that dirty breed outta her before he used her. He started in on kickin' her then. He kicked her and kicked her and kicked her, and I tried to grab his arm and pull him away—but then Ma, she . . . she . . ."

The girl was sobbing now, so that he could barely understand her. "Truda hit you?" Dominick thought of Benjamin Rudolph's wife, remembered her imposing height, her barrel of a body, and her way of verbally belittling Alice. He should have realized that physical violence wasn't beyond the woman. Not when both Truda and Benjamin Rudolph were so open in their disappointment in having a cripple for a daughter. "Your *mother* did that to your face?"

Alice nodded, using trembling fingertips to rub at her wet cheeks, her dripping nose. "Yes, sir. She kinda likes hittin' me, I think. Even when Pa doesn't tell her to. And now the Indian's dead, sir. Somethin' must have happened when Mr. Newton kicked her that last time, 'cause she started screamin' and screamin', and holdin' her belly, and then there was blood everywheres, and Ma made them throw her outside and—Mr. Crown? Where are you goin', Mr. Crown? Wait! Please, sir—don't do nothin'. They'll know it was me who told you, and Pa will be mad as fire."

Alice halted just outside the door, to sob in fear as Dominick burst into the kitchens, calling out, "Lucas! Lucretia? Come here—*now!*" He waited impatiently, pacing the floor, his fists clenched, his anger and frustration doubling and redoubling, until the two servants entered the kitchen at a dead run, asking if a war party had been sighted in the area.

Bryna was right behind them, a pistol already in her hand, her fiery hair a wild tangle around her shoulders. She was clad only in her shift, unconsciously advertising the fact that she had slept most of the morning and her husband had disturbed her in the act of dressing for the day.

"Dominick? We're not under attack, are we? No, of course not, or you wouldn't just be standing there looking ready to throttle anyone who said 'boo' to you." She placed the pistol on the table and brushed past the servants, to come straight up to him and lay a hand on his arm. "Dominick? What's wrong?"

He looked down at her, not really thinking of her as his wife, but seeing only that she was a woman. Soft, small, vulnerable. A defenseless being. Like Alice. Like his mother. Like the Lenape woman who didn't even have a name. Like Polly Rosebud. Poor, helpless Polly Rosebud, haunting his past. And every one of them so very unlike the Truda Rudolphs of this world, the Benjamin Rudolphs and Jonah Newtons and Giles Crowns of this world.

Dominick felt the fire of the rage he had been trying so hard to keep under control flaring to new, yet remembered heights, an anger he hadn't felt for seven long years. Shaking him to his core. Making him blind to anything save the need to do something—to do anything that would put a halt to the still clear visions, the nagging guilt that lingered inside his head because he hadn't been able to do anything at all for his mother, for Polly Rosebud.

"Alice Rudolph is waiting outside," he told Lucas, shaking off his memories. "I want you and Lucretia to take care of her for me. Feed her. Get her a bath. Find her some clean clothes. And for God's sake, do something about her face."

"Her face?" Bryna tugged on his arm, refusing to let him leave, so that he had to forcibly remove her fingers from their grip on his deerskin sleeve. "What's wrong with Alice's face? It's Rudolph, isn't it? My God, if that animal hit her— wait! I'm going with you!"

"The devil you are." Dominick shook off her hand once more and went back outside to where Alice waited, crying softly into her apron. He took hold of the young girl's shoulders. "Listen to me, Alice," he said intensely, his insides coiling up tight and hard as he bent down so that he could look deeply into her terrified eyes, seeing again the extent of the damage to her face.

Her sobs subsided slightly.

Damn. Did the child have to look at him as if he could solve all the world's problems? He couldn't even solve his own. "Alice, your father promised me the Indian woman. He didn't deliver on that promise, so I'm taking you in her place. I'll pay him for the privilege, because that's the only language your father understands, but from now on, and for as long as you wish it, your home is here, at Pleasant Hill. Lucretia has been asking me to find someone to help her with her work, and I think you'd do just fine. You could even assist my wife with Mary Catherine. Would that be all right with you?"

As Alice looked up at him, slack-jawed, and with something dangerously close to adoration in her expression, Bryna approached and gathered the girl against her shoulder. "I'm sure Alice is so overcome by the prospect that she can't find the words to thank you just yet," she told him quietly. She then turned Alice over to Lucretia's capable hands and followed after Dominick as he headed toward the barn.

"Although I," she continued, skipping to keep up with his long strides, "who am rarely speechless, will most probably eventually require some sort of explanation about your purchase of an Indian woman—when you get around to it, that is. In the meantime, what do you plan to do to Rudolph? Something suitably brutal, I most sincerely hope."

"To Rudolph? I'm not going to do anything to him, damn his eyes. Not yet. But when I act, I'll be sure Truda is no less affected than her husband. For now, I'm going to take my whip to a hyena named Jonah Newton, because he's not worth my fists."

"Newton?" That seemed to stop Bryna in her tracks. "I remember him. Well, damn me for a tinker! What did he do, not that it matters? Slice him one for me, while you're at it, all right, even if I don't know what he's done. And I wouldn't be at all upset if you loosened a few of his teeth."

His anger banked for the moment, but not abated, he stopped, smiled at Bryna, and said, "I'll be sure to do that. And then, my dear, underclothed wife, when I return, I may just take a moment to ask why it matters to you that I may have bought myself another woman."

He wasn't surprised that she didn't follow him all the way to the barn, but only looked down at her nearly transparent shift, mumbled something entirely unladylike, then turned on her heels and ran back to the house.

Bryna sat on the front steps of the big stone house, her chin in her hands as she stared almost unblinkingly at the place where the drive disappeared into the tree line, trying to wish Dominick into view so that she could know he was all right.

Which really made her angry, because she didn't want to care about the dratted man. She didn't want to worry about him, and if he had accomplished what he'd set out to do, or if he'd been overcome and beaten into a pulp by Benjamin Rudolph and that leering hyena, Jonah Newton.

Who did Dominick Crown think he was—some all-powerful avenging angel out to right all the wrongs of the world? He was only one man, and not a man well beloved by his neighbors, if Bryna was any judge in the matter. He was arrogant, and overbearing, and entirely too autocratic. He'd made no secret of the fact that he despised those men who'd been at Rudolph's the day he whisked her here to Pleasant Hill.

Didn't he realize that he was living in a raw, savage land? A place where being a wealthy English gentleman meant less than nothing, and if anything, his fortune and demeanor made him a target for envy and hatred?

He certainly dressed the part of someone who had accepted the differences between life in a backward colony and that of the cultured society of London. Whenever, that was, he wasn't rigged out in his fashionable clothes, presiding at his mahogany dining table, eating from fine china and sipping from a crystal goblet.

It was as if he were two separate men: the English gentleman farmer, and the near savage who had taken on not only the outward appearance but also the care and protection of the Lenni-Lenape. How strange that he had found friendship with the Indians, but not with his neighbors. Did he enjoy placing himself in the role of acting champion to the downtrodden? And if so, why?

For a man who told her she had to learn to accept that she could not change the world to fit her notions of it, that she should be more tolerant of Mary Catherine's inability to speak, of Brighid's capture by the Lenape, he certainly went out of his way to impress his own beliefs, his own code of conduct, on the less than civilized residents of New Eden.

Which, now that she'd had time to hear what had happened to the Indian woman, and had recalled Dominick's foolhardy reaction to this horrible crime, only proved to her that she could never, ever tell him about Renton Frey. For, much as Dominick might condemn her for her own temper, he had just proved himself not above a few angry reactions of his own.

Oh, no. She could never tell Dominick about her suspicions about Renton Frey. If she did, he'd make a lie of his warnings to her about learning to live with things she could not possibly change and go haring after the man himself. Which she could not allow—why, she didn't even want to consider—for that might mean that she was beginning to develop feelings for this handfast-husband of hers.

Oh, why couldn't she just get Brighid back and be on her way? Every day she waited, cooling her heels here at Pleasant Hill, very possibly moved Renton Frey just that much farther away from her.

Bryna bent her head and began rubbing at her temples, attempting to massage away the headache that persisted behind her eyes. She would never drink again, not ever! It didn't solve anything. And having to deal with a day that included mopping up after one of Dominick's rescues while fighting the less than lovely aftereffects of a night of imbibing certainly did not make for a pleasant experience.

And that was another thing, Bryna thought gloomily, pulling a face. Dominick certainly did seem to have a penchant for "rescuing" people. First Mary Catherine, then herself, and now an Indian family, a squaw, and poor, frightened Alice Rudolph. Lucas, indirectly, had told her about the Indian family as he had lamented the fact that his master had once more brought savages onto their land. It had been a gratefully Dominick-adoring Alice who, between sobs, had supplied her with the remaining facts pertaining to that poor woman whose death he was just now out to avenge.

Bryna knew she should probably be extremely proud of her husband—if she could consider him as her husband, which she sincerely wished she didn't have to keep reminding herself he most certainly was *not*. She also didn't want to think of him as kind, or charitable. And she most definitely didn't want to consider him as any sort of avenging angel. That was entirely too frightening.

But above anything else, Bryna wished she weren't sitting here with Gilhooley drooling at her feet, waiting for

Dominick to return from New Eden, hoping and praying he was all right, and feeling so damned proud of him that she could burst!

"Waiting on the master, are you, madam? He should be along any time now, if he found Newton at Rudolph's, which is where the man usually is all the day long."

Bryna turned to see Lucas standing on the top step, his hand raised to his brow as he peered in the direction of the tree line in order to keep the sun's glare away from his spectacles. She really wished he wouldn't insist on addressing her as "madam," but he seemed uncomfortable with anything less than total formality. "Are you worried about Mr. Crown, Lucas?" she asked. "He shouldn't have gone alone, you know. And please, sit down. It's difficult to have any conversation while having to stretch my neck in order to see you."

"As you require, madam." The servant produced a large white handkerchief and spread it on the step before splitting his coattails and positioning his skinny backside on the square, his posture so straight and dignified that Bryna had to stifle a giggle. Dominick might daily trade his consequence for deerskins, but Lucas was entirely the upper-class servant, full of rules and regulations—and himself. Hopefully he was also imbued with that most wonderful failing of all household staff: a penchant for gossiping about his master.

"Mr. Crown is a wonderful man, isn't he, Lucas?" she offered first, smiling as if she had suddenly come to the conclusion that Dominick hung out the sun each morning. "So generous, so giving. Yet I've seen such great sadness in him," she ended mournfully, "most especially when he speaks of his mother."

Bryna averted her eyes once that crammer was past her lips, for Dominick had most certainly not spoken to her about the mother he longed to have join him here at Pleasant Hill. But Lucas wasn't to know that, now was he, just as he wasn't to know that she was a snoop and a liar and was about to see how far her fibs could take her. She believed she had made a good beginning by mentioning the mother. As her papa had always told her, only a fool goes out to fish without taking along some prime bait. She had dangled Dominick's mother in front of the servant, and now she held her breath, her expression sad and concerned, praying he'd bite.

"She's a fine woman," Lucas said after a moment's reflection during which Bryna could feel his eyes boring into her, measuring her sincerity. "It near killed Mr. Crown to leave her behind with the—that is, with her husband. She's very unhappy there, you know, no matter how she says she isn't. But she has her duty, and her vows, or so she said when she refused to take ship with us. Seven years, madam. Seven long years, and he still hopes she'll come."

"He could visit her, couldn't he, Lucas?" Bryna purposely kept her voice low, her question short, so that she could feed him more line without his realizing he'd already gotten the hook stuck firmly in his mouth.

"No, madam, he can't, not after all that's gone on. His life is here now," Lucas said, shifting his position on the hard slab, but Bryna didn't believe it was because he was physically uncomfortable. He knew something. He'd known it for seven years. That was a long time to keep a secret. And that need for secrecy was killing him.

"No, of course he can't, can he? I knew that, Lucas, in my heart of hearts, but I had hoped—" she said now, sighing as she laid a sympathetic hand on the servant's sleeve, and a bit more soothing blarney on his ears. "Poor Dominick. And poor you, as you so obviously would be happier back in England. That's so unfair!"

"Oh, no, madam, no! Master Dominick would never keep me here if I wanted to return to England. But I couldn't leave him, madam. I just couldn't. Not now, after all these years, and most especially not in the beginning, when he couldn't have gone back without getting himself locked—"

Lucas shut his jaws with an audible snap, and looked to Bryna. His eyes begged her to ask him another question, to give him a hint that Dominick had already told her everything, so that he could comment on it, so they could commiserate together on whatever vagaries of fate had brought Dominick, brought them all, to this pass.

Employing her own quick mind, Bryna gathered up what little she now knew and leapt to a conclusion she hoped would get the man talking again. "Yes. How awful it would have been to be arrested."

"He told you that, madam? I can't believe he told you that!"

Bryna shrugged expressively, her heart pounding, her mouth very deliberately shut. Papa had told her the best cardplayers knew when to keep mum, allowing their opponents to assume whatever it was they wished to believe. Besides, she didn't believe her nerves were up to another outright lie. Not when she was reeling from the bits of truth she had just gained. Dominick Crown, her *husband,* was some sort of criminal?

No wonder he stayed to himself. No wonder he rarely traveled beyond New Eden. No wonder he numbered his friends among the Lenape, and did not seek out other English settlers or the English officers of the militia. And no wonder he had rushed her into marriage, and not traveled to Philadelphia or London to find himself a more suitable bride.

"But he didn't do it. Not really."

Not really? What on earth did that mean? Bryna turned to Lucas, not having to feign the look of hope she was sure was written on her often too expressive face. "Oh, yes! Of course he didn't do it. He couldn't possibly have done it." *What was "it"?* she longed to scream the question, even if she had to shake the answer out of Lucas. *How dangerous was this man she had married?*

"It's true enough that he thought he did, but he didn't. Even if I wish he had," Lucas added, confusing her all the more. "But he didn't do the rest of it."

The rest of it? There was more? Bryna's lips were numb, preventing her from speaking. She found herself hard-pressed to believe she was still sitting here, on Dominick

Crown's front steps, listening to Lucas's confusing statements, when she should be gathering up Mary Catherine and running away from Pleasant Hill just as fast as her legs would carry her. Only her legs were numb, too. She couldn't feel anything other than the rapid, hurtful beating of her heart. "I-I'm sure Mr. Crown is totally blameless in . . . in *everything*," she said at last.

"That's how I see it, madam," Lucas said matter-of-factly, rising to his feet and then bending to help her up, which was a good thing, for she doubted she was capable of standing alone. "Master Dominick would never have been the one who hurt poor, dear Polly. He just couldn't have, no matter that Master Giles found that jacket button right there, in her room. And then, after the rest of it, he didn't have any choice but to go, and I went with him, seeing as how there was no reason anymore for me to stay. Master Giles is an evil, selfish man."

Bryna didn't know where to look, what to say, although her mind was filled with questions. Who were Master Giles and Polly? And what was this about a button? What else could she ask without revealing that she really didn't know anything?

Fortunately, or unfortunately, she belatedly realized that Lucas had risen because Dominick was riding up the long drive, back from his mission in New Eden. Gilhooley had already heaved his great bulk erect and was running across the lawn, barking a welcome. One quick, assessing glance told her that her husband appeared none the worse for his horsewhipping of Jonah Newton.

Had Dominick beaten the man because he loathed what Jonah Newton had done? Had he been vicariously "beating" the unknown person who had "hurt" the unknown Polly? Or had he been trying to somehow atone for his own crime? And what was his crime? Nothing Lucas had said made any sense!

"I believe Mary Catherine needs me," Bryna told Lucas quickly. "Please tell Mr. Crown that I will see him later, at dinner." She then lifted her skirts and quickly bolted into the house, not stopping until she was in her bedchamber, breathing hard from her exertion, her back pressed against the locked door.

"And that will teach you to be nosy, Bryna Maureen Cassidy," she berated herself as she closed her eyes, her stomach queasy, her senses swimming. "Would you be after asking any more questions any time soon, or do you think you've done enough harm to yourself for now?"

Therefore, don't you be gentle
to your wife either. Don't tell her
everything you know, but tell her one thing
and keep another hidden.
— *Homer*

CHAPTER 8

❧❧❧

"AH, THERE YOU ARE, DOMINICK, LOOKING SO TERRIBLY COM-posed, so terribly *English* again. So sorry to not have sought you out earlier and inquired as to what transpired in New Eden, but I've been otherwise occupied with Mary Catherine all day, and couldn't tear myself away until now. You appear unmarked by your encounter with Newton. And the hyena isn't dead, I imagine, or else Lucas would be packing by now, to help you make good your escape before the militia comes for you."

"Jonah Newton, or the hyena, as you so aptly describe him, my dear wife, is not even wounded," Dominick told her, having risen as she had first entered the drawing room, looking lovely, and for once—probably just because she simply enjoyed the novelty of it—fully dressed.

She tilted her head to one side, eyeing him archly, and rather disappointedly, he thought, just as if she'd really hoped that he would have brought her Newton's head on a stick. "What happened? Did you have a change of heart? Perhaps even cry friends and share a pint with the man?"

"Hardly. I arrived at Rudolph's just to learn that Newton had already taken to his heels, having told his long-suffering wife he had pressing business in Philadelphia. As she runs the tannery without him anyway, I doubt that anyone in the community—save Rudolph, who must enjoy Newton's custom—will even notice his absence. Would you care for a glass of wine?"

Bryna remained where she was standing, just inside the doorway. "No, thank you, Dominick. I've rather decided to give any sort of spirits a rather wide berth for some time. So why were you so long, if Newton had already done a flit?"

What was going on? Bryna wouldn't meet his eyes. She wouldn't come near him. Her entire demeanor screamed of her unwillingness to be in the same room, perhaps the same universe, as he. Only her mouth remained as it had been: frank and blunt and thoroughly without artifice. She had come into the drawing room with a mind loaded down with questions, her body only a reluctant partner in her curiosity.

Maybe he *had* grown another head overnight, and only the fairer sex could see it. Lucas certainly hadn't said anything when he had tried, yet again unsuccessfully, to powder his master's hair, and surely the man would have noticed if there had been two unpowdered heads tripping down to dinner.

"I had to see to the burial of the Indian woman," he told her tersely, throwing back the last of his wine and heading for the drinks table to refill his glass. "And then, of course, I had to meet with Rudolph, and listen to Truda lamenting the loss of her *beloved* daughter, who was a good girl, really she was, except that Truda had been nurturing a snake at her bosom all these years if her sweet, biddable, hardworking Alice was really, truly leaving her poor, lonely mother."

"Cost you a fair amount in the end, I imagine," Bryna said, smiling slightly as she finally came fully into the room to take up a seat on the couch, her full panniered skirts spread around her like a pale green moat she was warning him not to cross.

"I'd have paid double just to shut her up, actually," Dominick said, staying where he was, sensing that if he so much as hinted that he might want to share the couch with her, she'd bolt. Or brain him with the fireplace poker. "And I'll see it all back, and more, when I open my own inn and stores in the building I commissioned this afternoon."

Finally she looked straight into his eyes, her own bright with amusement, and perhaps a small amount of genuine admiration. "Well, Dominick Crown, if you don't beat the Devil himself for roguery! You said your revenge would touch both Rudolphs, and it will. If I were to rethink that glass of wine, I'd raise a toast to your devious mind and deep pockets. Congratulations!"

Dominick inclined his head slightly, acknowledging her compliment, then watched as she withdrew again, folding her hands in her lap and lowering her gaze. "Call me a fool, wife," he said, trying to keep his voice light, "but I suspect there's something more weighty on your mind than the possible decline and fall of the Rudolphs. Would it be that you're still wondering why I should have bought myself an Indian woman? Not that a little jealousy in one's wife is unwanted, or unappreciated, I might add."

Her head shot up in an instant, proving to him, even before she spoke, that he had taken another wrong step. "Don't flatter yourself!" she told him, bristling. "It would please me immeasurably if you imported an entire harem."

"Again, forgive me." He decided a change of subject was in order. "Is Alice settled in? I brought her belongings back with me, the whole of them wrapped up in a single old blanket, and gave them to Lucretia. Perhaps you can spare a bolt of material to make up a new gown for her? There should still be ample for you and Mary Catherine, and if not, it would be a simple matter to purchase more."

Bryna rose and walked to one of the windows, keeping her back to him as she looked out over the still sun-washed lawn. "Lucretia is already making progress in that direction. But if you are reminding me that I have not as yet thanked you for your thoughtfulness in providing for me, for all of us, then I should say that I am, of course, most humbly grateful for your—"

"Would you *stop?*" Dominick carefully unclenched his hands, which had somehow drawn up into fists just as Bryna turned to look at him, her expression maddeningly blank. "I'm sorry, Bryna. It has been, one way and another, a rather trying day. For both of us, I'd imagine, which is probably why we're throwing brickbats at each other. Almost like the first day we met, don't you think?"

"I do my best not to think of that day at all, Dominick," she said stiffly, "for that was the day I learned the full extent of my loss, and the measure of my dependence upon your charity. Perhaps I will have that glass of wine now, *husband,* to assist in washing down yet another bite of the humble pie you go to such pains to remind me is to be my diet from now on."

She was being deliberately obtuse, and quite pointedly provocative, as if she wanted nothing more than for him to lose his temper with her so that she could storm out of the room, away from him. Did she really think he would be so disgusted with her that he'd throw her out? Her, and Mary Catherine, and the fat purse he'd given her the night of their marriage? What did she plan to do? Take up residence at Rudolph's, waiting for Lokwelend to bring Brighid Cassidy to her, so that they could then use even more of his money to book passage on the first ship leaving from the Philadelphia docks?

Possibly . . . if his fairly personal remarks of this morning had frightened her into thinking that he might decide to demand his husbandly rights, even after telling her that he wouldn't. But not probably . . . especially since Lucas had already informed him earlier this evening that his bride had just this afternoon moved herself into a new bedchamber, and her first sign of occupancy had been to place a loaded pistol beneath her pillow. If he made a move to enter her bedchamber, she'd much more probably simply blow a hole through his forehead, and have done with it.

No, something else was bothering her, frightening her. Something, obviously, about him. Something that had made her both belligerent and skittish at the same time. Something that had her shying away from him even as she took his every word and twisted it around to make him appear in a bad light—almost as if she had discovered one flaw in him somewhere and was examining him for more. And he'd be damned if he knew why. "Bryna, I think we should—"

"Dominick, this is ridiculous! I—"

"Dinner is served, sir."

Dominick looked at Bryna, whose shoulders were just then sagging in what looked to be a mix of relief and exasperation. He walked over to her, taking her hand. "Later, Lucas. My wife and I are just now going for a stroll in the gardens. Come along, wife."

"Dominick!" Bryna protested. "We can't just—"

"I was still the master of this house, last I checked, and *yes*, we can." He then pulled her past Lucas, who began prudently cleaning his spectacles with a handkerchief he'd extracted from his pocket.

Bryna continued to drag her feet, holding up her skirts and tugging away from him as he all but pulled her out of the room and down the wide hallway. "Oh, really? And what if I don't want to take a *stroll* in your bloody gardens, Master Crown? What if I'm hungry? What if I'm positively starving—near to fainting with that hunger?"

"Then I suppose," Dominick said as he opened the door that led across the lawn to the gardens, "I shall then simply have to catch you as you fall. Unlike the other night, when you were so inconsiderate as not to tell me you planned a forward pitch onto the floor."

"That's *not* amusing!" Bryna retorted, fairly breathless from their rather inelegant dash through the house to the rear door located in the study. Either that, or her nervousness had stolen her breath from her. As long as her condition would not render her speechless in the next few minutes, Dominick really didn't care what the reason was behind it.

And all her breath had not fled her, for Bryna opened her mouth yet again just as he propelled her through the doorway and out onto the grass, to say, "Did you hear me, Dominick? I said, you are not amusing. *I* am not amused!"

"Well, then, that is fortunate, isn't it, wife, as I am not attempting to entertain you." He continued to all but drag her across the expanse of lawn that was necessary to keep the house clear of enemy-sheltering shrubberies, and struck out on the main, center stone path of the gardens. He halted after a few more moments, took hold of her shoulders, and backed her toward a wooden bench, then applied enough pressure so that her knees buckled, and she sat down with a jolt. "I am questioning you."

Bryna lifted a hand to push an errant curl away from her forehead. "Ah, I see. This is to be an inquisition, is it? But where are the rack, the thumbscrews? And what is the subject? We must have a subject. No—don't say anything, Dominick. Allow me to guess the nature of your curiosity. We already know that its depth is enough to make you behave like a boor and a bully. What can it be? What bothers you? My ingratitude after your largesse? My inability to hide the fact that I very much resent being in your debt? My continuing, simmering anger that you have forced me into marriage with you in exchange for a roof over my head and the rescue of my cousin?"

"You forgot to mention my exemplary care of your other cousin, Mary Catherine," Dominick pointed out, sitting down beside her. "But we'll save all of that for another time, as I have come to enjoy your rather unique way of turning any hint of thanks into an accusation. What I wish to know now, wife, is why you're so bound and determined to goad me into an argument this evening. Not that any save a discerning man would detect the difference between your usual prickly self and the determined belligerence you entered the drawing room wearing draped around your shoulders like a mantle of thorns meant to keep me away."

"I don't have the faintest notion of what you're talking about," Bryna said, looking at him straight on, and quite obviously lying through her teeth. Dominick was privately amazed at how well he had come to be able to read this woman's face, her tone, her every small gesture. And what he saw now, hiding in those lovely woodsmoke eyes, was belligerence, yes—but fear, as well. But fear of what? Fear of *him?*

"Did I frighten you this morning, Bryna?" he asked quietly, taking her hand from her lap and holding it gently, as he would Mary Catherine's. "I was very angry when Alice told me what happened to the Indian woman, and to Alice as well, but I shouldn't have lost my temper and told you I was going to horsewhip Newton. Is that it? Is that what has you upset? Because I promise you, Bryna, no matter how angry I would ever become, I'd never harm a woman. Never. I'd never harm you."

She was silent for long moments, so that Dominick was sure he had stumbled upon the correct explanation for her behavior since coming into the drawing room. He had seen her earlier, standing with Lucas on the front steps of the house, as if she had been waiting for him, perhaps even worrying for him, but she had disappeared before he drew his horse to a halt. At the time, he'd thought she'd been embarrassed to be found out as having cared one way or another how he'd fared in New Eden.

But now he believed differently. She had been concerned for him, yes, but her new fear of him had sent her running from him once she was sure he was unharmed.

And what else had he expected? Her congratulations? A welcoming embrace for the warrior safely returned from the hunt? A declaration of suddenly realized affection?

Just as he was about to give up hope that she'd tell him what was on her mind, she squeezed his hand, so that he turned to look at her questioningly. "I believe you," Bryna said, her voice so low he had to strain to hear her. "You'd never hurt a woman. I'm not quite sure why I believe that, but I do." She took a deep breath, which she released on an equally quiet sigh, then ended, "Tell me about Polly, Dominick. Please."

"Damn you, Lucas," he swore softly, closing his eyes as all the pieces fell into place, and he knew for certain why

Bryna had been trying to distance herself from him. She *had* been afraid of him, just not for the reason he'd suspected. She was probably still more than a little afraid of him, except that she wasn't the sort to run from her fear, but to confront it head-on.

"Don't blame Lucas, please," Bryna said quickly, shifting on the wooden bench so that she was almost facing him, taking his hand, and her hand, and resting the two of them in her lap. "It's all my fault, because I tricked him into thinking I know more about you than I do. Which is ridiculous, when you think about it, because I know absolutely nothing, do I, other than that you seem to collect strays much the way my father collected young pigeons eager to be plucked. But now that I know more than I should know, and very much less than I need to know now that I do know at least something, I really think I need to know the rest. Dominick? Does that make any sense at all?"

He doubted she even realized she was holding his hand, let alone that she was stroking it with her soft fingertips, reaching out to comfort him in a purely feminine, oddly soothing, and yet curiously arousing way. And he did owe her some sort of explanation, now that she had admitted to knowing some convoluted "something." After all, she was his wife now, if only in name, and she resided under his roof. Her cousin resided under his roof. She deserved to know that she had not come to be married to some sort of monster who would hurt her as Polly had been hurt.

But that was all she needed to know, at least for now.

"Polly Rosebud was a maid in my father's employ," he began simply, choosing his words with care. "She was a simple, quite lovely girl, and had just become betrothed to Deems, our family butler. They were very much in love. Very much. My mother had given them a section of the third floor of our home to use as their quarters, and Polly spent a lot of her time up there, getting it ready for occupancy."

Dominick closed his eyes for a moment, reluctantly remembering the house, remembering his parents, remembering his brother, Giles—and most of all, remembering that terrible summer day their lifelong uneasy truce had exploded in all their faces.

"One morning Polly didn't answer my mother's summons, and she sent me to the third floor to look for her," Dominick continued, staring out over the land that was now his in this country that was now his. But he saw only the small bedroom tucked under the eaves of his father's house, and the sight that had met his eyes when he'd opened the door to Polly's room. "Damn," he said quietly, shaking his head to clear the vision from his brain.

Bryna took up the story for him, proving to him that she knew some things, but not everything. "But she was dead when you got there, wasn't she? Someone had killed her. And you were blamed because one of your coat buttons was found in her room. Lucas told me about the button, and I'm assuming it was yours. But he also said you gave your word that you hadn't done it, and he believed you. He's a good friend, isn't he, Dominick—to have left England with you and come here to Pleasant Hill?"

Dominick looked at Bryna, her lovely face pale, her eyes as colorless as a morning mist and awash with tears. "Lucas is a better friend than you know, Bryna," he told her. "You see, he worked as butler for my family. We called him Deems then, although we left that particular formality behind us in England. He is Lucas Deems, and young Polly was to be his wife. And nobody killed her, Bryna, not really. Somebody had, however, attacked her, torn her clothes from her, and raped her. As I said, she was a simple country girl. I imagine she felt she couldn't face Lucas with the truth of what she thought to be her shame—so she hanged herself."

"Sweet Mother of God," Bryna whispered softly, then laid her head against Dominick's shoulder. "Poor Lucas. Poor Polly Rosebud." She pulled away and looked up into Dominick's face. "And poor you, Dominick, to be falsely accused, to have your own family believe you to be capable of such a hideous crime."

"In all fairness, the evidence against me was damning," Dominick told her, becoming more aware of her by the moment, more aware of her closeness, her scent, her sympathy, and her willingness to believe in him. "I had scratches on my forearms and chest from rescuing a calf from a briar the day before, and the button my brother Giles found in her room had come from my blue jacket. From that moment on, I was guilty, with no way of proving my innocence."

Bryna nodded her head, her eyes narrowing thoughtfully, and just a smidgen nastily, if he was any judge. "So then, Giles is your brother, and he's the one who produced both the button and the jacket? Lucas mentioned Giles's name to me. That was a rather convenient discovery, don't you think? Did anyone think to check Giles for scratches?"

Dominick threw back his head and laughed, delighted by his wife's sudden vehemence on his behalf. "My dear brother, made to strip to the waist, as I was, in front of my mother, to prove his innocence? Hardly, Bryna. Our father simply handed me an ultimatum—leave the country within twenty-four hours in order to spare my mother the embarrassment of a public trial for my crime against Polly, or he and Giles would personally deliver me to the local gaol."

"So you left. Without putting up a fight? How very noble of you."

"Don't sound so disappointed, Bryna," Dominick said, lifting her hand to his lips in a gesture that held much more than mere thanks for her belief in him, for her anger against what had happened to him. "My father was—is—a very influential man, and he refused to champion me. I may be innocent, but innocent men have been convicted before. I could have been transported, or even hanged, neither prospect appealing to me overmuch. In the end, I had no other choice. So yes, I left, but not until I discovered who had hurt Polly badly enough that she took her own life."

"It was your brother, wasn't it? It was Giles. It has to have been him, for the way he was so ready to place the blame on you."

Dominick reached out to take hold of a lock of Bryna's hair, slowly twisting it around his forefinger, fascinated by its warmth, the way the hair clung to his finger, curling against his skin. "Yes, Bryna. He did it. Dear, dear brother Giles," he murmured softly, yet still hearing the anger in his own voice.

He could feel her gaze on his face, trying desperately to read his expression. "You killed him, didn't you? It was Giles who raped Polly, and you killed him for it, then fled the country. That's why you're here, stuck in the back of beyond. That's why you don't go to Philadelphia, or back to England. Not just because of Polly, but because someone might recognize you and have you arrested for killing your own brother. I'm right, Dominick, aren't I?"

"Partially." Dominick stood up, his hands folded across his waist as he looked out toward the slowly setting sun, and Bryna rose as well. "I confronted Giles that same night, while I was still half-convinced to stay and defend myself, and he admitted his guilt to me. He rather gloated about what he'd done, to tell you the truth, explaining how Polly had enticed him into her quarters, then refused him what he wanted. He was lying about that, of course, but I didn't care. And all he cared about was how brilliantly it was all working out for him. Polly was dead, unable to accuse him, and his despised half brother was leaving the country. He was all but preening."

"Half brother? Oh, I didn't know that."

Dominick smiled down at her. "Next time you're pulling information out of Lucas, you might want to consider those thumbscrews," he suggested.

"Don't change the subject. I want to know more about Giles, about your half brother. He hated you so much. Why? What were his reasons?"

Dominick began to pace back and forth in front of the bench. "I don't know, Bryna. Because I'm younger, stronger, and was better at games than he was when we went into the village? Because his mother was dead and my mother was alive? Because gambling debts hadn't forced me into a wildly unhappy marriage? I don't really care why anymore, frankly, although I spent a good portion of my childhood trying to please him as well as my father, whose marriage to my mother had also been for money. All I know is that I hit

Giles that night, as he stood there, enjoying his victory. He fell against a corner of the fireplace, and he didn't get up. Our father came in and started shouting that I carried the mark of Cain upon my forehead, and had killed my own brother. It was all very theatrical. My mother rode with me to the docks while my father stayed locked in the drawing room with Giles. Lucas and I left England on the morning tide."

Dominick turned to look at Bryna, to see her gnawing on her full bottom lip, her face a study in concentration. She looked up at him after a moment, spreading her hands helplessly, then stood up to face him. "What do you want me to say, Dominick? That I believe you? I do. Do I blame you? On the contrary, I applaud you. Except for one thing. Lucas mentioned your half brother, and if I can recall his words correctly, Giles is still very much alive."

Dominick chuckled self-deprecatingly. "And therein lies the rub, although I didn't learn the truth for nearly two years, when my mother's first letter at last reached me here at Pleasant Hill. Giles's head was harder than it appeared, and the bastard had recovered fully. But I had raped an innocent girl, attempted to murder my only brother, and— just to prove my guilt once and for all—then fled the country, not that anyone else knew that. And they don't know. Not yet."

"Not yet?" Bryna repeated. "Then you aren't really a fugitive?"

"No, I'm not. My mother wrote that Polly's death was reported to be the result of a fall down the servant stairs. However, if I were to go home, my father, who undoubtedly knows what Giles did—and is also aware that *I* know what Giles did—would not hesitate to go to the local officials, admit that he had lied about the circumstances of Polly's death, and name me as her attacker. Giles, you understand, must be protected at all costs, which makes me a danger to them both."

She shook her head. "No, Dominick, I don't understand. Why does your father favor him so? You're both his sons."

Dominick smiled sheepishly, almost eager to see Bryna's

reaction as he said, "Because Giles is of good English stock—blond, refined, and magnificently lazy—and I am nothing more than the oversized, dirt-loving, gollumpus son of the inferior Irishwoman my father married for her fortune. I believe the very sight of me curls dear Papa's toes."

He waited a moment for his information to register with her, then lifted his arms to defend himself when she pushed both her hands hard against his chest, exclaiming, "You're *Irish?* How dare you hide something so wonderful, as if you're ashamed of your own blood?"

She pushed at him again and again as she spoke, and he allowed her to back him toward the bench with each new assault. "Teasing me, baiting me, letting me call you a bloody Englisher—when you've just as much Irish blood as I have. So, is it shamed you are, Dominick Crown? Shamed of your own blood, your own mother?"

"Stop it, Bryna, before you push me all the way into New Eden!" He grabbed at her wrists, sure she was about to do her best to beat him into a jelly. She was like quicksilver, her moods changing so swiftly, he could barely keep up with her. It couldn't have taken her more than three heartbeats to go from pity for her poor mistreated husband into a raging fury at the dratted man who had buried his Irish heritage like a secret shame. "I would have told you eventually, as it's no small pride to me to have Irish blood. I even wondered why you never questioned the fact that I'd named my dog Gilhooley. But you were enjoying yourself so much, hating my inferior English heritage, that I didn't want to spoil your fun."

She went very still, looking at him intensely, then rubbed at her wrists when he let go of her, hopeful that she no longer wanted to hit him. "You've got a mass of secrets inside that dark Irish head of yours, don't you, Dominick Crown? But now, at last, I understand. My mother's family hated the ground my Irish father trod on, and wouldn't have lifted a finger to help him if he were facing the gallows. We have much in common, don't we?"

"Yes, Bryna, we do," he answered, taking her hand once more and pulling her back down onto the bench beside him.

"Although, if I had pointed that out to you at once, you probably would have hated me for it."

Her smile touched her eyes, turning them a soft, smoky green. "Loathed you, actually," she admitted. "And I probably wouldn't have believed you, either. Tell me about your mother, Dominick. Would I like her?"

"You would. You even remind me of her a little, although you're really nothing alike. My mother is tall, her hair as dark as mine. She sings as she talks, her voice full of that soft County Clare lilt that Eileen Cassidy used when speaking to her children." His smile faded. "My father quite openly dislikes her, in much the same way he very openly dislikes me, but she won't leave him because of her marriage vows."

"And you haven't seen her in seven years," Bryna said quietly, squeezing his hand. "All because you don't know what your father and Giles might do if you go back—although I'm willing to wager you're more concerned about how any punishment of you would affect your mother. Is there no chance that she might visit you one day?"

"I want to believe she will. I've even stooped to using you and Mary Catherine as lures. However, Bryna, you're right. If you harbor any notions of ever returning to England with your husband by your side, I suggest you forget them. As long as the threat of arrest hangs over my head, my life is here, and nowhere else. As is yours, if you'll stay."

"If—*if* I stay? I don't understand. What do you mean?"

Dominick took both her hands in his, feeling them tremble as she sought to hide her sudden nervousness. "I mean, wife, that I know you plan to wait for Brighid's return, and then get yourself shed of New Eden, and your unwanted husband, just as quickly as possible. You're an inventive schemer, my dear, but quite transparent. I am right, aren't I? I've told you the truth now, Bryna, and I expect the same from you."

"You're not being fair, you know," she told him, pouting. "I mean, first you act the selfless guardian, the hero, the avenger, then you tell me your sad tale about your past, about your mother, and then, just when I'm feeling extremely sorry for you—and guilty about the way I've treated you and thought about you—you go and ask me to tell you the truth. I don't consider that in the least sporting, Dominick. Really, I don't. Not when you hold all the aces and I'm scraping the bottom of my barrel of tricks to search out a workable lie."

Dominick grinned, knowing he had won, at least for the moment. "I know. I'm a rotter, through and through. But now that you're feeling sorry for me, and while you're so impressed with my better qualities—will you please stay? I won't make any demands on you. Not unless or until you tell me otherwise. I promise."

"That's very good, Dominick. Press your advantage as long as you have it. Papa would have applauded you." She continued to look at him steadily, then finally nodded her head. "All right, I admit it. I had planned to leave, just as soon as Brighid is returned to me. But you do know what you've done by telling me the truth, don't you? You've given me the power to destroy you, husband, while I could remain here at Pleasant Hill, enjoying all your lovely money. Why, with one word to Newton or any of those other hyenas, you'd be clapped in irons and sent back to England to stand trial, and your father and Giles wouldn't lift a finger to do more than denounce you."

"The thought had occurred to me, yes, even if, until my own family accuses me, in the eyes of the world I am nothing more than an ungrateful runaway son. But you're my wife, and I owed you the truth."

"Although you waited until after that ridiculous ceremony to share it with me," Bryna pointed out, the ghost of a smile hovering at the corners of her mouth. "And you wouldn't have told me at all, I imagine, if Lucas hadn't slipped when I . . ."

Something came and went in Bryna's eyes as her voice trailed away, and Dominick put a finger under her chin, lifting her face to his. "Yes, Lucas slipped, after holding in my secret for seven long years. That is odd. But you gave him a small push, didn't you, Bryna? Would you mind telling me how that happened? And why?"

Her smile was dazzling. "I'd rather not, actually. A woman has to have some small secrets, don't you agree? And a trusting husband wouldn't apply to his servant for answers, because that would only muddy waters that have finally cleared. So, all in all, I would imagine that this discussion is over. My, I'm famished! Now that we have everything settled, don't you think it's time we sat down to supper? I believe Lucretia is serving venison done up in a stew, which I have come to greatly enjoy."

"In a moment, Bryna," Dominick said, gently placing his hands on her shoulders, drawing her closer. "You still haven't said that you'll stay."

Her smile wavered as she searched his eyes for an explanation, her own eyes wide and faintly frightened. "No. I haven't, have I?" she asked quietly as she nervously wet her lips.

"Perhaps this might help to persuade you," Dominick said, tilting his head slightly as he slanted his mouth against hers, gathering her completely into his arms, aware of how small, how very fragile, she was beneath her veneer of prickly independence. Her arms were slack at her sides as he kept his kiss light, tentative, and unthreatening.

He longed to deepen the contact, longed for her arms to come up and circle his shoulders, giving him some indication that she was enjoying his kiss. His heart pounded. His body, so long denied, roused. He wanted. He needed. *Hold me,* he begged silently. *Let me hold you. Let me feel you.*

She didn't move. She didn't fight him, but she didn't welcome him either. She just sat there, accepting his kiss. "I'm sorry, Bryna," he said, pulling away. "I shouldn't have done that."

She lifted her chin slightly, staring deeply into his eyes, her own wet once more with unshed tears. "No, Dominick. You shouldn't have done that. You shouldn't try to make me forget what is most important to me, and the promise I have made to myself. Shall we go in to dinner now? Lucas will be beside himself, fearful the food will grow cold."

Dominick stood up, offering Bryna his hand so that she, too, could rise. He didn't know what she was talking about, and he knew he would learn no more tonight. He could only wait, and try to be patient, until she trusted him enough to confide in him. He tucked her arm through his and turned for the door to the study. "May I at least have your word that you won't run away before Brighid is returned?" he asked, hating himself for having to know. "Now that you know I'm not a thief or a murderer, that is?"

"Glad as I am to know you are not a murderer, Dominick," she said, her smile small but real, "you are still a bit of a rascal, I think. But then, so am I, perhaps with a promise or two of my own to keep. So I can't make any more promises right now and tell you that I'll stay. We both know I was fibbing when I agreed I would, don't we? I will, however, agree not to go looking for any more secrets. I gave myself a most uncomfortable afternoon after digging around to find the few I already know."

Dominick thought of his last remaining secret, the one that would either delight or infuriate her, and decided to be happy with Bryna's decision, believing that, in time, she would see the wisdom in remaining at Pleasant Hill. She might even begin to trust him enough to tell her about this "promise" of hers. "Shall I make a similar vow, or have you no secrets of your own?"

She looked away, affecting an interest in a large black crow that was strutting on the grass. "I have no secrets, Dominick. Only my promises to myself. Promises born only of suspicions, none of them concerning you or able to be solved by you. And I will deal with them, someday, in my own time and my own way. For now, I cannot look past getting Brighid back. I simply can't."

Then, her mood changing yet again, she smiled up at him, saying, "I do so adore that you're Irish, Dominick. I believe I'll understand you much better now."

"And this pleases you?" he asked as they entered the study and moved toward the dining room. "Should it please me, as well?"

"Oh, I don't think so, Dominick," she told him, her expression so wickedly delighted that he longed to kiss her again. "I don't think so at all."

129

BOOK TWO

A Bitter Harvest

The haft of the arrow had been feathered with one of the eagle's own plumes. We often give our enemies the means of our own destruction.
— *Aesop*

Time cancels young pain.
— *Euripides*

CHAPTER 9

"DANCE, MARY KATE! THAT'S IT—*dance!*" BRYNA CALLED out as her young cousin spun in circles on the grass, the ever-present flute to her mouth while Bryna clapped and Alice sang another chorus of "Now Is the Month of Maying," Lucas Deems joining in with his pleasing tenor for each *"fa-la-la-la-la-la."*

Lucretia, who didn't know the words to the old song, but who looked darkly handsome in her new day gown, clapped her hands in time as she stood next to the small table Bryna had begged Lucas to bring outside earlier for their impromptu alfresco meal.

Scrambling to her feet, Bryna joined in the dance, holding her skirts out to one side as she did her best not to dislodge the daisy chain of sweet clover flowers that adorned her fiery curls. Mary Catherine, Alice, and Lucretia also had daisy chains on their heads, for there had been no sense in making only a single crown, not when all four of the Pleasant Hill May queens could share in the honor.

Sparing a moment to take the flute from Mary Catherine, as it wouldn't do to have the child fall with the instrument between her lips, Bryna grabbed up her cousin's hands and together they danced, whirling round and round, going faster with each *"fa-la-la-la-la-la,"* until at last they tumbled to the ground in a heap, clutching each other and laughing in their glee.

They still had their moments of struggle, the tug-of-war Bryna and her young cousin indulged in sometimes when the child pointed to something she wanted and Bryna refused to give it to her unless she asked for it. And each of these confrontations still ended with the child in tears and Bryna hugging her and promising not to "push" her. Until the next time, that was. Bryna did not accept defeat easily, and the battle for Mary Catherine's voice was definitely one she intended to win.

But the return of Mary Catherine's easy melodic laughter was a recent gift from God. If it was the only "joyful noise" the child ever made, Bryna would still consider it a small miracle, but only one in a month generously littered with small miracles.

Once she and Dominick had struck their truce, Bryna had been able to relax somewhat. She no longer felt the need to be on guard every moment for fear of putting a step wrong, in terror of saying something, or doing something, that would betray her plan to use him, then leave him.

For he had told her he knew she might leave. And, trading an honest moment from him for a bit of honesty of her own, she had warned him that she might.

Even if she no longer wanted to go.

Mary Catherine was happy here. Brighid would feel safer here on the estate, behind the thick stone walls of Pleasant Hill, a haven where she could be out of sight of those who would either pity her or ridicule her for her horrible experience with the Lenape.

And, Bryna had concluded, only a wee bit smugly, Dominick Crown needed her here.

Not that he had made so much as a single gesture toward moving their relationship forward. Not since that single unexpected kiss. She still often wondered why she had allowed his embrace; wondered more often why she had not returned it.

For it had felt so good to have strong male arms around her. Protective arms. Sheltering arms. Mary Catherine's childish hugs were sweet, yes, but Bryna was the elder in that relationship, the adult, the rock the child could cling to.

Bryna longed for a rock as well, someone to watch over her, to make *her* feel safe. In less than a twinkling of an eye her father had been taken from her. In another twinkling, she had learned that the remainder of her family were dead, or damaged, or missing.

She had assumed guardianship of Mary Catherine because she loved the child and because she was now the last Cassidy and therefore had no choice but to do the "adult" thing.

She had beaten down her tears, for tears never solved anything. She had accepted the mantle of responsibility Dame Fate had hung around her neck like a millstone, and with that mantle, all of its attendant problems. She had done what she could, what she dared, and what she hoped was right, up to and including pledging herself to a man she did not know.

But none of this had been easy. Deliberately deceiving Dominick hadn't been easy. Allowing herself to be held, however, believing herself to be wanted, possibly needed, *had* been easy. Almost too easy.

Falling in love with her rock, her refuge, the man who had shown that, for all his own problems, he could be counted on to be there, be strong for her, and for everyone at Pleasant Hill, could prove easiest of all.

And most difficult.

Dominick Crown remained an enigma to Bryna, for all his heartbreaking confession of the series of tragedies that had brought him to Pleasant Hill. Was Dominick Crown even her husband's real name, or had he changed it upon coming to the colonies, to protect himself from detection? That seemed possible, because he still hadn't known that his brother had survived his fall against the fireplace. Except that the man seemed too comfortable with the name to not have been born with it, and grown with it. He wasn't a coward. He had taken himself off, begun building a new life, but he wasn't hiding. If anyone really wanted to find him, he was here, waiting.

Dominick Crown was a good man. An honest man. A caring, compassionate man. With a cold, terrible temper. Bryna still shivered when she remembered the dark, forbidding look on her husband's face the day Alice had come to them, the hard steel in his voice as he had announced that he would horsewhip Jonah Newton. He hadn't threatened. He hadn't shouted or blustered. He had simply stated his intentions, then gone off to do what he felt needed doing. Much the way he had struck down his half brother, without thought to the consequences, of the possible damage it might do *him*. Which was just another reason she could not confide in him.

Dominick was like the big black dog her uncle Daniel had once owned, a proud, handsome animal that walked through the world quietly, without complaint, without bluster or fanfare. Joseph and Michael had ridden that dog as if he were their own personal pony, and never been nipped or growled at as they tugged on the animal's ears or stepped on its tail. But when young Michael had been backed into a blind alleyway by two of the village bullies one summer day, that quiet dog hadn't wasted time barking. Without warning, with nothing more than a single low growl, he'd simply *bit*.

Dominick was being quiet now, and had been for the past month. He donned his deerskins every day and went out into the fields, working himself nearly into exhaustion pulling out tree stumps and clearing brush from yet another field he planned to put into production, supervising the construction of both the Crown Inn and Stores in New Eden and the gristmill he planned for his own use.

Every evening Bryna met him in the drawing room a half hour before Lucas called them in to dinner. Looking the complete English gentleman in his fine clothes, he always inquired about her day, treated her with deference, and then disappeared directly after the meal, usually apologizing that estate business awaited him in his study.

He hadn't kissed her again, not even her hand. He hadn't touched her except to offer her his arm as they went in to dinner. He hadn't suggested another stroll in the gardens.

And Bryna often heard him, well after midnight, pacing the floorboards in his study.

He was, in short, being true to his promise not to push her, not to hurry her into any more of a commitment than she chose to give him. In fact, Bryna had more than once considered bashing him on the head for his polite forbearance, for provoking his anger might also serve to unleash his passion and she could feel his embrace once more.

Knowing that this was not really a rational or even safe reaction to his exemplary behavior, she had, instead, poured all of her energies into—as her maternal grandparents had advised her mother—making the most of the bed she had found herself lying on.

Her virgin's bed.

Always a good housekeeper, she had sat Lucas, Lucretia, and Alice down for a long, amicable chat. They had divided their duties according to each person's ability and inclination. Lucretia would remain in charge of the kitchen, with Bryna overseeing the menus and, when it became necessary again, the procurement of foodstuffs and other goods in New Eden, as Lucas still steadfastly refused to leave the estate.

Lucas, Bryna gratefully agreed, would be in charge of polishing the silver, caring for the wine cellar, and handling the light, everyday dusting and straightening of the rooms; Alice would take over the duties of maid each morning, the care of Mary Catherine each afternoon and early evening.

In the end, Mary Catherine had altered that plan slightly. The child preferred Lucretia's company whenever that woman was baking. But she gravitated to the gardens in the afternoon, where Bryna could usually be found, down on her hands and knees, methodically ridding the enormous kitchen garden of weeds or just mucking about in the dirt, edging flower beds, transplanting young shoots, and generally enjoying the feel of the cool, rich earth under her fingers.

There were more than enough chores in a house the size of Pleasant Hill to employ the services of at least two more maids, which would be easily accomplished in England. But Pleasant Hill was not in England, and domestic help was not readily available in such an isolated area. So Lucas and Lucretia and Alice and Bryna did the best they could, not standing on ceremony or position when the butter churn waited or a mattress needed turning.

And Bryna was enjoying herself. For more than anything, she loved life, loved being alive, and she could not keep herself buried in the hurts of the past. Over the course of these last four healing weeks she had slowly come to begin accepting those terrible tragedies that had befallen her family and herself, and then very consciously decided to look to the future.

She had carried vase after vase of spring flowers into every room of the house. She had pitched in with a will, helping Lucas and Lucretia wash all the windows, ridding them of a winter of grime. She had scrubbed and rubbed and rearranged, cleaning out the corners of her mind at the same time she cleaned the cupboards; sweeping away sorrows as she swept the wide planked floors; banishing her anger to the attics along with the heavy velvet window draperies that kept out the spring sunshine.

She had come to grips. Accepted. As women have always learned to accept. And endure. And, hopefully, she had allowed her heart to heal somewhat, moving her on to a place where happiness could find her.

And all that while, Bryna had noticed, the man who had written to his mother that he was the "happiest of men" seemed to grow more solemn every day, unwilling, or unable, to find a single thing to smile about in his so serious, so solitary world.

Indeed, only last night he had refused, politely, to take part in Bryna's proposed Queen of the May celebration, insisting that he was needed at the sawmill. This was a whacking clanker if Bryna ever heard one, because if nothing else had happened in the past month to please him, he had at least hired Jacob Berringer, an estate manager who, having heard of the glory that was Pleasant Hill, had traveled all the way from Philadelphia to apply for the position.

Disappointed but undaunted, Bryna had gone on with her party plans without Dominick, bullying Lucas into joining in the fun, with a Maypole being the only missing element in their celebration. A Maypole, and the presence of her husband.

Yes, over the course of the last four weeks Bryna had found a new rhythm in her life, a reason for rising each morning, a mission that got her through each new day, and the horrors of the near past had begun to fade. Even her promise to herself, to search out Renton Frey and confront him with her suspicions, then punish him, had moved to the back of her mind. And that bothered her. Because she still did have a promise to keep. A promise that did not include involving Dominick in any new danger. Because that wouldn't be fair. The man had done enough, more than enough. This was her fight.

Now, lying on her back on the sweet-smelling grass, Mary Catherine's small head on her lap, Bryna dismissed all thoughts of her husband and her problems and begged Alice to sing them another song.

"You've such a beautiful voice, Alice," she told the girl.

Alice blushed prettily at the compliment and pushed back a stray wisp of dark blond hair. She then folded her hands in her lap, collecting her thoughts before she began to sing.

An angel's voice, that's what Bryna privately thought as the girl, her healed face a study in innocence, began to sing, her voice as pure and clear as the holy sister's in the small church in County Clare. *God never takes that He gives something else in return,* or so Bryna remembered her mother explaining the matter when she had asked her why some people were blind, or deaf, or lame. If Alice's limp was her cross, her voice was her sacred gift.

"When I was a bach'lor I lived all alone and worked at the weaver's trade," Alice began softly, the early afternoon

sunshine suddenly colored a somber gold as the slightly risqué yet deeply moving lover's lament poured from the innocent young girl. Her artless treatment of the lyric made each word more poignant than suggestive. *"I wooed her in the wintertime and in the summer too, and the only only thing I did that was wrong was to keep her from the foggy foggy dew."*

Bryna felt a sudden, unexpected catch in her throat as Dominick suddenly appeared as if out of nowhere. His long black hair hung freely around his face, making him look younger, even more appealing. His deerskins flattered his tall, muscular frame as he leaned slightly against the up-turned rifle planted on the ground in front of him and sang the second chorus:

> *"One night she came to my bedside*
> *When I lay fast asleep.*
> *She laid her head upon my bed*
> *And she began to weep.*
> *She sighed, she cried, she damn near died,*
> *She said what shall I do?*
> *So I hauled her into bed and I covered up her head*
> *Just to keep her from the foggy foggy dew."*

Alice looked up at him and smiled, her heart in her eyes as, together, they sang the final verse telling of love lost. Their voices blended in a beauty and sorrow that tore at Bryna's heart:

> *"O I am a bach'lor and I live with my son*
> *And we work at the weaver's trade,*
> *And every single time that I look into his eyes*
> *He reminds me of that fair young maid.*
> *He reminds me of the wintertime*
> *And of the summer too,*
> *And of the many many times that I held her in my arms*
> *Just to keep her from the foggy foggy dew."*

Lucas removed his spectacles, wiped at his tear-filled eyes with a large white handkerchief he had pulled from his pocket, and then noisily blew his nose before mumbling an excuse having to do with polishing doorknobs and heading for the house.

Lucretia scooped up the napping Mary Catherine and gave a quick inclination of her head toward Alice, who hastily followed the cook toward the path leading to the kitchen. Their departure left Bryna and Dominick quite alone, with only the echo of the song to bridge the silence between them.

"Was the party over, or did I scare them away with my caterwauling, do you think?" Dominick asked, leaning his rifle against a tree trunk before dropping to his haunches beside Bryna and lifting a hand to the daisy chain in her hair.

"Don't come begging to me for compliments, Dominick Crown. You'd charm the birds out of the trees with that voice of yours, and well you know it," Bryna replied quickly, nervously snatching the daisy chain from her head and tossing it away. "As it is, Alice is more than halfway in love with you."

He looked toward the house, clearly puzzled. "Alice? But she's just a child."

Bryna held out her hand, so that Dominick was forced to help her to her feet. "She's nearly sixteen, Dominick, only about two years younger than I."

"Two years obviously makes quite a difference in a young lady's judgment, however," Dominick said, drawing her arm through his as he retrieved his rifle and guided her toward the house, "for you are not so easily infatuated with my charm. Perhaps I should sing to you again? Or would you settle for getting your shawl and bonnet, so that I might take you into New Eden for the afternoon?"

"You'd take me to the village?" Bryna was so immediately enthused that she dismissed Dominick's teasing without bothering to wonder if he was being even the least bit serious about her seeming lack of "infatuation." She looked at him owlishly. "Why? You haven't invited me before. In fact, I was beginning to think I would never again step foot off Pleasant Hill land."

Dominick's smile, such a rare phenomenon this past month, nearly rendered her breathless. "The locals have had time to understand that you are my wife. I believe it's safe to take a stroll down the village streets before subjecting ourselves to a visit to Benjamin and Truda Rudolph's sterling, yet soon to be defunct, establishment. They have no idea of the nature of the building now under construction, by the way, and I'd like to keep it our small secret until the building is complete and our stock arrives. Otherwise, I imagine I'd be forced to get used to either gravel mixed with my sugar or traveling all the way to Allen's Town or Bethlehem for provisions."

Bryna took up her shawl and bonnet from the row of wooden pegs just inside a small recess in the front hallway: "If you're asking for me to dub my mummer—as my dear papa used to say when he wished me to remain quiet about something in front of my mother—I should imagine I can accommodate you. As long as I get to be there the day you have the sign telling of *Crown's Inn and Stores* hung from the front of the building."

Dominick waited while Bryna tied her bonnet strings, then helped her with her soft white woolen shawl. "Why, Mrs. Crown, I'm shocked! A lesser man might even think you plan to revel in the Rudolphs' coming financial misfortune."

"And you're not going to enjoy it? To quote my papa yet again, Mr. Crown, 'Thy complexion is black, says the raven,'" Bryna teased, skipping out the front door ahead of her husband, more than ready for her trip to New Eden, and delighted beyond all understanding at the notion of being alone with her husband for an entire afternoon.

He'd have to get himself a coach. No. A small closed carriage, which would suit Bryna even better. The wagon was good enough for trips into New Eden, especially when he needed its sturdy wooden bed to transport seed and flour and other goods, but Bryna deserved better. He couldn't imagine why he hadn't thought of it before now.

His few trips to Philadelphia had been easily accomplished on horseback, and he planned to hire a coach to bring his mother to Pleasant Hill when she made the journey across the Atlantic. But he couldn't ask Bryna to ride all the way to the metropolis on the unyielding plank seat of this wagon. And he most certainly couldn't leave her behind, or there'd be the very devil to pay. If he had learned little of his wife, he had learned that she was not the sort to meekly wave good-bye as he went off for a month in the civilized world that was Philadelphia.

"I want to stop first at Henry Turner's," Dominick told Bryna impulsively as they reached the outskirts of the small village. "He's a wheelwright of sorts, although he swore he was a premier coach maker back in Lincolnshire. I want to offer him a commission."

Bryna sliced an amused look at Dominick. "You want him to build you a coach? For this pitiful road? I hope Henry Turner has learned how to spring a coach body, or else the thing would be shaken into splinters within a mile. Or is a new roadway to be yet another of your projects? Perhaps even a turnpike, with a toll booth? What would you charge the great mass of travelers who would make use of that turnpike? Why, if you were to charge a penny per person, I imagine you could collect a solid shilling a year."

"I can see that you have little faith that New Eden will become a center of civilization any time soon," Dominick said, looking at her closely as she smiled up at him, her features tilted toward the sunlight. That sunlight turned the curls around her face to liquid fire, highlighted her glowing, faintly freckled skin, and transformed her laughing eyes into twin pools of sparkling mercury. Sweet Christ! The urge to kiss her was nearly overwhelming. How long would he be forced to live this monk's existence? Why was he cursed with being an honorable man?

"That's true, Dominick," she told him. "But it's also all right, as you've already promised that Allen's Town is growing at a fair clip, so that we aren't completely isolated. I rather enjoy the country life, if I could only convince Lucas that there will be no more marauding war parties in the area. Especially now that you've told us that more soldiers are soon expected at Fort Deshler."

"Yes, within the month, if the stories are to be believed." Dominick shook his head. "To be honest, I'd rather the additional troops stayed away. The local volunteer militia and our few regular soldiers are protection enough, to my mind, and quartering additional military in the area only calls attention to us."

Bryna laid her hand on his arm. "Then you still think it possible that there could be more raids? I thought we were safe. My God, Dominick——"

He lifted her hand to his lips, instantly sorry that he had voiced his thoughts aloud, then quickly released her hand as she seemed to freeze, as if caught between finding his touch unsettling or simply annoying. "We're safe enough at Pleasant Hill, Bryna. As long as Lokwelend and his children are on our land, I doubt anyone would think to attack us. I've gone to great lengths to make friends with all the local Lenape, because I genuinely like them, and because I intend to end my life in my own bed at a venerable old age, with all my hair intact."

He saw the pain of the memory of her relatives' fate cloud her eyes and added softly, "I promise you, no matter what might happen, you're in no danger."

"How could I ever have missed the fact that you're Irish when you so smoothly spout blarney like that? I'm almost ready to believe you," Bryna said, her smile tremulous as she faced forward once more, avoiding his eyes. "Do, er, do you know the identity of the soldiers who will be quartered at Fort Deshler?"

He shook his head, allowing her slight change of subject. "No. There has been no word as to what company is coming, or who will be in charge. Why? Do you number many English soldiers among your acquaintances?" he ended teasingly.

She licked her upper lip, a sure sign she was about to lie to him. "I met a few on the *Eagle*, during our passage. I-I had only wondered if they might be among those being sent here to New Eden." She turned to him, smiling, although her eyes remained unreadable. No. That wasn't true. She wasn't totally unreadable, for he could see a trace of fear in those beautiful eyes, and a quick flash of pain. "That's all, truly. Would that be Mr. Turner's shop just ahead?"

Dominick knew there was more to Bryna's unease than just not wishing to encounter fellow passengers from the *Eagle* who might remind her of her father's fatal accident. Had something else happened aboard ship? Something other than her father's tumble overboard? But he allowed the subject to be changed once more—although he knew that someday, someday soon, he was going to have to sit Bryna down and explain that she had to stop thinking like a sharp trying to keep his hole card hidden from the rest of the players at the table. Especially when she had no more chance of concealing her emotions than she did of concealing her beauty.

"Yes, that's Turner's," he said affably. "I'll ask you to stay in the wagon, if you don't mind. Henry Turner has a tendency to fall into a bottle from time to time, and I want to make sure he's sober before I try to talk to him."

Bryna nodded, then fell silent as he guided the horses into a small, packed-dirt area just outside a barnlike building sporting a large wagon wheel hanging from its face, advertising Henry Turner's occupation. Dominick set the brake and climbed down from the wagon, setting off for the barn just as Turner's young wife, April, came out, carrying her infant daughter.

He introduced Bryna to the woman, then spent the next quarter hour with Henry Turner, the majority of that time listening to the man's effusive thanks for the commission as well as his repeated promises to build the most impressive equipage New Eden had ever seen. Considering the fact that New Eden had yet to see more than the infrequent stops of the mail coach, Dominick decided to believe in the man's sincerity, if not his ability.

By the time he had come back to the wagon, April Turner and his wife appeared to be bosom chums. Bryna was holding the Turner infant, softly cooing to the child as she rocked back and forth on the wagon seat, causing Dominick to stop a moment and watch, taking note of the strange, warm feeling suddenly apparent in the pit of his stomach.

Bryna looked so natural with a child in her arms. She was wonderful with Mary Catherine. There was no reason to believe she wouldn't be a marvelous mother. Loving. Gentle, yet stern, teaching them their prayers and their sums and the difference between right and wrong. Nurturing them, raising them up to be exemplary men and women. Strong sons to be his legacy. Daughters fashioned in their mother's image.

Pleasant Hill had been his penance, his salvation, his purgatory, his sanctuary. It was the island of safety he had built for himself and for his mother, where he had hoped she could one day share his exile and escape her intolerable unhappiness.

But now it was more, so much more.

Now, when he closed his eyes, all he could see was Bryna. Bryna sitting at the foot of his carefully selected dining room table. Bryna in his study, curled into a small ball on his couch, sound asleep. Bryna in his drawing room, sipping from a glass of wine, asking intelligent questions while he told her about his day. Bryna's flowers brightening every corner, her own sweet scent filling the air, her laughter ringing throughout the house, her vitality breathing new life into every nook and cranny of his world.

Except for one room. One great, lonely chamber. Pleasant Hill was still a house, not a home.

How long? How long before Bryna came to him and told him she would not leave, would never leave? How long before she showed him some sign that she was ready to make theirs a real marriage? How long before he grew impatient for her to come to him and made some stupid mistake, perhaps scaring her away forever?

Dominick shook his head, exasperated with himself for allowing thoughts that could only disturb him to cloud these past weeks, this otherwise sunshine-filled day. He was like a sulky child, and he had to remember what he had, and not pine for what he still lacked. He had purposely decided on this outing, purposely decided to be cheerful.

After all, he and Bryna were friends; becoming better friends. Time would take care of the rest, if he could just be patient. Time. Was that all he did? All he had done for the past long, lonely seven years? Wait for time? Time to heal. Time to forget. Time had been his enemy for so long; it was difficult to think of it as his friend.

Bryna looked up and saw him, calling out, "Dominick! Come see this sweet angel. Isn't she dear? I can remember when Mary Catherine was an infant, but I had forgotten just how small babies are. Look at these fingers, Dominick. Did you ever see anything quite so perfect, so beautiful?"

"She is beautiful, Bryna," Dominick agreed sincerely as he climbed onto the wagon seat, deliberately avoiding the warm, melting look in his wife's eyes. "Thank you, Mrs. Turner, for entertaining my bride. We'll be sure to visit more often, so that she might indulge herself in playing with the baby, as she is so enthralled."

"Oh, Dominick, don't tease! What woman wouldn't want to hold a baby?"

"You'll be having babies of your own one day, Mrs. Crown," April Turner said, taking back the child and then stepping away from the wagon as Dominick took up the reins and released the brake. "Billie Kester, Elijah's wife, serves as midwife, you know. She was wonderful kind to me when little Henrietta was borned, even with her bein' a breech."

"Babies? Oh, yes. Yes, of course, April, thank you," Bryna said, and Dominick called out a quick farewell to April Turner and started the wagon rolling toward New Eden once more, avoiding his wife's eyes to give her time to recover from her embarrassed blush.

"I wish Turner had built his works closer to New Eden," he said after a minute during which he reminded himself that many, many women had given birth with only a midwife present, and the fact that there was no doctor closer than Bethlehem should not upset him. "He needed to be beside the water, to run his wheels, but he's still isolated, for all that the house is on the road. April is often alone here when Turner passes out on one of Rudolph's tables after a night of drinking."

"Still thinking about those war parties you tell me won't strike here again, aren't you? Please, don't. You can't take care of the entire world, Dominick," Bryna told him, patting his hand. "Not even if you want to. Henry Turner is April's husband. She and their child are his responsibility. Just as my aunt Eileen and the boys were Uncle Daniel's responsibility. If nothing else, I've figured out that fact this past month. Everyone in this life makes choices, and must live with the consequences of those choices. Or die with them."

"And is that what you're doing, Bryna? Living with your choices? Or still deciding what they will be?" Dominick asked. He was oblivious to the fact that they were now in New Eden, the widely spaced straggle of homes and shops lining the single main roadway appearing closer together until they came to the small, solid block of Rudolph's, Elijah Kester's smithy, the shoemaker's, the butcher's, and a half dozen other small stores that served the wide-flung community of farmers and trappers.

Bryna removed her hand from his. "You think entirely too much, Dominick Crown. Now, is that Jonah Newton I see just this moment racing up the steps to Rudolph's after glancing this way and espying you, looking as if his pants are on fire and he's trying to outrun them? Or have we been speaking of two different hyenas? I only saw him twice, when I first arrived here, and cannot be sure."

Dominick was more than willing to drop the subject and followed Bryna's lead. He turned in time to see Newton disappear into Rudolph's. "So he's back, and me without my horsewhip. I still have a score to settle with the man, but it will wait for another day. God knows, he'll give me provocation enough to go after him sooner or later. Now, are you still as eager to visit Truda Rudolph's side of the establishment, or would you rather I take you home and return tomorrow on my own to pick up supplies?"

THE HOMECOMING

His wife's smile was devilish, and highly attractive. "What? And miss the chance to deal the man the cut direct? I should never forgive myself. Now set the brake, Mr. Crown, and help your wife to the ground. She is about to make her presence known to everyone in New Eden— giving out with her 'how do you do's'—and she hopes more than a few of the residents choke on them!"

Doing as he was told, for he was a husband now, and a good husband—a *smart* husband—did not cross his wife when she was about to take her first social plunge, Dominick then followed along behind Bryna as she lifted her skirts a modest two inches above the dusty ground and mounted the steps to meet, greet, and snub her public.

Once inside the building, she turned to her right, elegantly swept into Truda Rudolph's domain, and declared, "Good day, Truda. You may or may not remember me. I am Mrs. Crown."

The innkeeper's wife continued to measure grain onto a scale, not bothering to look up at her customer. "So? Don't you go all high and mighty on me. I'm no servant girl, like that silly Alice, damn her ungrateful eyes. Mrs. Crown, is it? Ha! What's that to me?"

Dominick opened his mouth to protect his wife, but closed it again quickly, feeling almost stupid, for he should have known his Bright Fire knew how to singe Truda Rudolph's feathers.

"What does my being Mrs. Dominick Crown mean to you? Why, *Truda,* I think that should be apparent," Bryna fairly cooed in quite precise drawing room English as she picked up a corner of a bolt of calico linen, then let it fall, wiping her hands together as if disgusted with its inferior quality. "Oh, very well. I'll explain the obvious, but just this once. As Mrs. Dominick Crown, I am now in charge of purchasing the extensive amount of provisions necessary for Pleasant Hill. The *prodigious* amount of provisions. Despite both my husband's agreement to transport me to Allen's Town, and my extreme distaste for the way you have treated your daughter, I have decided to give you a chance to show yourself capable of filling my needs and worthy of my custom. Step sprightly now, Truda, and prove to me that my confidence is not misplaced."

"Yes, ma'am, Mrs. Crown!" Truda Rudolph blustered, wiping her hands on her filthy apron and then bobbing Bryna a curtsy. "I even got some new flower seeds in this week, got 'em all the way from Philadelphia, thinking how nice they'd be up at Pleasant Hill. Just let me run in back and fetch them."

With Truda momentarily out of the room, Dominick leaned close and whispered into Bryna's ear, "I am hard-pressed, Mrs. Crown, not to stay and applaud this sterling performance. However, I'm off to the taproom for a pint, too embarrassed for Truda to stay here and watch as she licks your boots."

"Do that, Dominick. I won't need you for a half hour, by which time I believe I'll be bored with my revenge," Bryna told him quietly. "Your choice may be a horsewhip, but I prefer to punish in other ways. And by inches. Beat Alice, will she! I think I see a few pewter pots on the highest shelf I'll need Truda to fetch me to examine, one at a time, before I decide not to purchase any of them," she ended, then quickly moved away, calling to Truda Rudolph to bring her a chair, so that she might examine a basket of loose ribbon at her leisure.

Jonah Newton had already bolted from the inn before a softly chuckling Dominick could cross to the taproom, which was probably a good thing, he decided, as he was in entirely too good a mood to ruin his day beating the tanner into a pulp.

Picking up the mug Benjamin Rudolph poured for him, he crossed to the single unshuttered window and looked through the grimy panes, taking no notice of the dusty roadway beyond as he thought about his wife.

Still very much the teasing, self-indulgent child, she was also very much a woman. It would take time for the headstrong Bryna to fully come to terms with what had happened to her, how she had come to be married and living across a wide ocean from all she had ever known.

But she was making a prodigiously successful beginning, and he would be content to wait. Wait for her sorrow to lessen, for her fears and anger to wane, and for the day she looked at her life and saw that she needed him as much as he was beginning to need her—so that when, at last, they came together, they would come together as equals.

Yes, he was content to wait. He had gotten very good at waiting.

Give me today, and take tomorrow.
— *Anonymous*

CHAPTER 10

"VIOLA TRICOLOR, DIANTHUS, GLOBE AMARANTH—EVEN IF IT IS a bit weedy. And caraway, fennel, dill, basil, marjoram, savory. Some we already have, I know, but I simply couldn't resist. You don't mind, do you?"

"The gardens are nearly three acres large, Bryna," Dominick reminded her, watching as she leaned over the seat and replaced the small brown seed packets she had pulled out of one of the many sacks he had loaded into the wagon. "I'm sure you'll find space for every seed you've bought and a dozen more varieties. As long as you're happy."

"Thank you, Dominick." As the wagon moved along the rutted roadway, Bryna pressed her head against his shoulder for a moment, a probably impulsive, definitely unexpected, and oddly pleasing sort of gesture he believed married couples shared as an everyday occurrence, although it was all very new to him. Certainly he didn't have any memories of seeing his parents appearing so in harmony with each other. Or was he reading too much into a simple, friendly action, no more than the open affection Bryna would show with anyone? Hadn't she just hugged Lucas last week for finding her favorite trowel for her? "I know I'm a goose, to be so excited by a few seeds," she told him. "But I can't help myself. I just adore making things grow."

Dominick realized something suddenly, and it brought a twisted smile to his lips. Bryna, knowingly or unknowingly, was punishing him by inches, as she had done Truda Rudolph. But she was punishing him with small pleasures, budding dreams, flowering hopes. The brush of her hand on his arm as they passed each other in the hallways of Pleasant Hill. Her gaze meeting his for just a moment too long as they said their good-nights. The way she had of noticing his favorite dishes and making sure they were prepared just the way he liked them.

Was she sending him silent signals? Attempting, without words, to tell him she was ready to become his wife in more than name? Or was he a desperate, pitiful creature, pinning his hopes on gossamer, a fabric too thin and fragile to do more than cloud his usually clear vision?

"So, Mrs. Crown," he asked, trying to keep his voice light, "all in all, I would imagine you enjoyed your first official visit into New Eden?" Dominick teased now as Bryna reached back into another sack and pulled out a small doll dressed in red calico, its hair fashioned of bright yellow yarn.

"Yes. All in all, Mr. Crown, it was a thoroughly delicious experience," she answered, hugging the doll to her as she had earlier hugged April Turner's baby against her. "And I thank both you and your deep pockets for allowing me to indulge myself to the top of my bent."

She held the doll away from her at arm's length, tilting her head as she inspected the small figure. "Do you think Mary Kate will like this?"

Dominick eyed the doll warily. "I'm not much of a judge, you know, as my own early years were littered with toy soldiers and rather jolly miniature weapons of war and mayhem. I only wonder if you'll give it up to the child when you get home, as you seem fairly well attached to the thing yourself. You will promise me you won't fight over it?"

"Beast!" Bryna exclaimed, stuffing the doll back into the sack. Then she laughed, a light, carefree laugh that held no hint of the sorrows she'd been living with since her arrival in New Eden. "But you've found me out, I suppose. I'm a terrible baby. I've already planned a lovely tea party for tomorrow. Just Mary Kate, Alice, Lucretia, Miss Arabella Thistlewaite, and me, sitting outside in the shade, sipping pretend tea and nibbling on imaginary biscuits. Why, we might even make mud pies, if Lucretia doesn't disapprove."

"Miss Arabella Thistlewaite being the young lady with the rather odd yellow hair, I'd imagine," Dominick said, joining in her silliness as he turned the horses onto the private drive that led to Pleasant Hill. "Will I be paying for her come-out in a few years, or do you believe we can marry her off to one of the kitchen brooms without more than a small haggle over a settlement?"

Bryna smiled at his joke, as he'd hoped she would, then suddenly sobered, and Dominick thought he had said something to upset her. *Damn! Have I stupidly spoiled our outing by reminding her of our own marriage? And just when things were going so well! When will I learn to keep my mouth shut until I measure my words?* "Bryna? What's wrong?"

"Nothing, I hope," she said quietly, placing a hand on his arm again. This time the gesture wasn't friendly, but protective. "Who is that, Dominick? Up there, just in front of the house? I thought you were the only person around here who dressed like that."

He peered up the hill at the large black stallion and smaller packhorse on the drive—and the London exquisite who stood, arms akimbo, on the top step of the wide front porch, looking in his direction.

"Giles?" Dominick breathed softly, his chest tight, his blood running cold. With a quick, fatalistic rush, he felt his new world of hoped-for happiness crashing down around his ears. Then he relaxed, but only slightly. "No, it can't be Giles. My God! I don't believe it—*Philip!*"

"Who?" Bryna asked, leaning forward on the wagon seat, as if this slightly closer inspection would make it easier for her to identify the stranger. "Can—can he hurt you, Dominick?"

"Giles's son? No, of course not." Dominick shook his head, still disbelieving what his eyes told him to be true. "He's hardly more than a boy, and my half nephew into the bargain. I haven't seen him since he was just barely into his teens. But what the devil is he doing here?"

"I imagine you'll have to ask him that yourself, Dominick, as we can't just turn this wagon around and head back into New Eden until he goes away. Perhaps he has good news?" Bryna told him, slipping her hand into his and squeezing it reassuringly. "I'll just allow you to introduce me, and then go find Gilhooley, in case the news isn't good and we decide to help the gentleman on his way back to where he came from."

Dominick laughed, which eased his tension even more, although not enough to make him genuinely happy to see his half nephew—who looked so much like his father, so much like Dominick's father, entirely too much like both the men whom he'd hoped never to see again. Blond, trim, handsome. So unlike their dark, half-Irish relative. "You could fetch a rifle with you as well, Bright Fire, except Philip has no feathers for you to aim at, does he?"

"A real gentleman wouldn't constantly remind a lady of her every niggling faux pas, you know," Bryna groused, pouting comically as Dominick drew the wagon to a halt. "It's not like I *hit* the fellow, after all."

He squeezed her hand one last time before hopping down from the wagon, calling out, "Philip! It is you, isn't it? And you're all grown-up! What in God's name dragged you to this isolated backwater? And how did you get past me on the road?"

"Dominick? Christ on a crutch—*Dominick!*" Philip bounded down the steps and launched himself at his half uncle, pounding him on the back as they embraced each other. "I thought you were a wild Indian. What are you rigged out for, anyway, a masquerade? I feel dashed underdressed, in comparison. My God, if his bloody lordship could see you now, he'd—"

"Just keep your mouth shut and follow my lead, nephew, and I won't have to murder you," Dominick quickly whispered into Philip's ear, returning the young man's embrace. "I'm busy building myself a house of cards with the young lady behind me, and you could bring it all down before I have a chance to shore up the foundation. So, for now, I am Dominick Crown, and you are Philip Crown, no more, no less. Understand?"

"No, I don't," Philip answered just as quietly as he stood back, looking Dominick up and down, touching at the fringe that hung from the sleeve of his uncle's deerskin jacket. "However, as I'm tired and thirsty and more hungry than I can tell you, and Deems refuses to allow me across the threshold, I suppose I shall be an obedient sort and do as you say. Now," he added, carefully keeping his voice low enough so that Bryna couldn't hear him, "are you going to introduce me to that absolutely gorgeous young creature just now glowering at me as if I am the Devil incarnate, or must I first swear a blood oath as to my willingness to lie for you?"

"I can't believe you're married," Philip began enthusiastically as he and Dominick walked around to the back of the house, toward the gardens, putting them out of earshot of anyone inside the building. "Poor Grandfather. The old bastard will be fairly put out, you know. I think he plans to sell you off to the highest bidder, now that my grandfather Goldsmith cocked up his toes this past year and left all of his blunt to me, just in time for me to celebrate the birthday that heralded my independence from my dear papa's guardianship. He got nothing, you understand, and all Mother receives is a small allowance, only large enough to keep her in cats and gin. As for Lilith—well, my dear sister seems to have found that lying on her back in London makes it quite easy for her to rise covered in diamonds. She does, however, manage to be discreet enough to avoid the label of either courtesan or whore. She beds titles, you see, not men—or so she says."

Dominick kept his hands clenched together behind his back, drinking in this rapid-fire summary of the seven years since he had last been in England. His mother's infrequent letters spoke more of the flowers she had planted and news of her best friends, the Crown servants. "Doesn't Giles have something to say about Lilith's actions?" he asked, not really caring all that much about his niece, whom he had caught, at the age of fifteen, gaily lifting her skirts for one of the stable hands.

"Papa? Care about Lilith?" Philip laughed without mirth. "You forget, dear Uncle. Lilith is the reason he had to service his wife again, in order to get himself an heir to go with all the moneylender's money that came along with his Jewess bride. Besides, Lilith is dark, much like Mother, although she's quite beautiful, if I must say so myself. But to our father, my dear sister is a Jewess, to the tips of her night black hair, and little more than an embarrassment. He wouldn't care if she leapt into the Thames with a whacking great boulder strapped to her ankle. In fact, I'm surprised he hasn't attempted to have her boosted over the embankment."

"Suddenly Giles seems uncomfortably close," Dominick said, shaking his head.

"Yet still an ocean away, thank God. But so much for Lilith. I, on the other hand, am now Papa's fair-haired lad both literally and figuratively, and he cannot do enough for me. Which has yet to serve to prod me into releasing my hold on so much as a bent penny of my lovely inheritance. That's partly why I'm here, truth to tell. To have a little adventure, to see you, of course, and to get as far as I can from the dratted man's incessant entreaties for money, which only echo those of his father. I thought you said someone would bring us a drink out here, Dominick. I'm more than parched, you know."

Dominick smiled sadly, thinking of his strange family.

"Lucas will bring something shortly. You know, Philip, I was fully grown and here, at Pleasant Hill, before I realized that all families are not like ours. Bryna's aunt and uncle, who were killed in an Indian raid, were wonderful parents. Simple. Loving. Much like my mother. Is she well? You haven't yet mentioned her. Have you brought me a letter from her?"

Dominick walked on for a few more paces before realizing that Philip was standing stock-still on the pathway. He turned, a question in his eyes, to see his half nephew's suddenly white face. A chill ran through his body as he moistened his lips. "Philip? What is it? What's wrong?"

Philip's fingers curled inward until his hands were two white-knuckled clenched fists. "Damn him," he gritted out. "How could he let me come here like this, without first telling me? Is there no end to the evil of that man!"

Dominick tried to swallow, but now his entire mouth had gone dry. "What man, Philip? Giles? Or my father?"

"Grandfather," Philip spat, as if the respectful title tasted vile on his tongue. "He *knew*. And still he wanted me to tell you all is forgiven and ask you to come back. All is forgiven? Isn't that a joke!" He looked off into the distance, as if seeking help in the trees, trying to discover some way of saying the words Dominick felt sure he didn't want to hear. He turned back to his uncle, his expression bleak. "Christ, Dominick—I don't know what to say."

The months of unaccustomed silence had now been explained. His mothers last few letters hadn't been lost. They'd never been written. "My mother's dead, Philip. Isn't she?"

The younger man closed his eyes and simply nodded.

"When? How?" *Don't tell me,* Dominick screamed silently. *Don't tell me, and then it won't be true. I can't bear it to be true. Don't tell me I'll never see her again.*

Philip ran a hand through his hair, a single lock falling forward onto his forehead, making him look very young, and more than slightly distraught. "Early last winter—" he said quietly, then hurried on, as if he wanted to get the rest of it over with quickly. "She . . . she hadn't been well, but I suppose you knew that? Something about her lungs. I was there, Dominick. I sat with her, I spoke with her—she was at peace, really. With her life, her God. And she wrote you a final letter, telling you how she loved you, how you weren't to grieve."

The young man shook his head. "You never got that letter, did you? Grandfather took it from her maid the morning . . . the morning she died. *Damn him!* Why, Dominick? Why would he do that? Out of pure meanness?"

Dominick started to speak, then had to clear his throat, for no words would come, although an idea snapped to the front of his mind. "The money. I sent Mother money every month, through a solicitor. He must have found out about it. Maybe she mentioned it in her last letter to me? That's why he didn't tell me, didn't forward the letter. He wouldn't have wanted her allowance to stop, which it would, the moment I . . . the moment I . . ."

Dominick didn't want to think anymore. He couldn't think anymore.

Philip laid a hand on his uncle's shoulder. "Are you going to be all right? Would . . . would you want to be alone for a while?"

Dominick, his head down, had drawn his right hand up into a fist and was roughly beating the side of it rhythmically, repeatedly, against his pursed lips. He didn't know why. He just did it, kept doing it. Beating back the screams, he supposed. The anger. The tears. At Philip's question, though, he nodded, saying, "Yes. I would like to be alone for a few minutes. If you don't mind?"

Giving Dominick's shoulder one last, bracing squeeze, Philip turned and headed toward the house.

Leaving Dominick alone. Once again. Alone.

Bryna paced back and forth in the kitchens in between trips to the window, looking out to see if Dominick and his half nephew were still standing together at the bottom of the garden, well out of earshot, if not out of sight.

The two men, true studies in contrast, both in their

coloring and their clothing, had been walking together, and talking together, for nearly ten minutes, ever since Dominick's quick, almost brusque, introductions, after which he had sent her off to fetch Lucas to drive the wagon around to the back of the house to be unloaded.

She was well aware that she wasn't wanted, not right now. After their gains of the past month, and most especially after their truly wonderful interlude earlier in the day, everything had come crashing down again. She had been relegated once more to the status of onlooker, kept from all but the fringes of Dominick Crown's obviously troubled life.

Why did Philip Crown have to show up at this particular moment? Why not tomorrow, or next week, or next year? With the amount of time it took to cross the Atlantic, and the difficult trip from Philadelphia, how had he managed to arrive at *precisely* the most inopportune moment possible?

"Are you trying to tell me something, Lord?" Bryna asked, grimacing up at the ceiling. "Attempting to remind me that I still have places to go, and a promise to keep? If so, I hope You won't mind overmuch if I tell You that I believe You are being an exceedingly poor sport about allowing me some small happiness, truly I do!"

"Miss Bryna? You sayin' sumthin' to that there God of yours?" Lucretia asked, halting in the act of popping a tray of muffins into the small bread oven built into the brick wall of the large fieldstone fireplace. "'Cause iffen you're sayin' sumthin' to the fella, I'm thinkin' you might be lookin' to have yourself struck down by lightnin' bolts or some such. Parson Tweed, down in Caroline, he was always talkin' of such terrible things when I was servin' Massa Hervey in the parlor come Sunday. Your God is chock-full of such stuff—fire and brinestone, and the like."

"That's brimstone, Lucretia, and I assure you, my God—*our* God—is a most forgiving sort. The fact that Master Hervey still breathes is more than sufficient to show God's forgiveness, if half you've told me about the man is to be believed."

Bryna made another trip over to the window, just to see

that Dominick and Philip were still deeply engrossed in speech, as if they planned to make up for a seven-year absence from each other's company in a single conversation. Except now Dominick's shoulders seemed slightly bowed, his head hanging forward, as if what he was hearing had little to do with gossip or good news.

"I can't *stand* much more of this, Lucretia," Bryna announced heatedly, allowing the white muslin curtain to fall back into place before all but throwing herself into a nearby chair. "I feel like a child who has been sent to her room without dinner. I'm the man's wife, for pity's sake! I should be sitting in the drawing room, pouring tea, *sharing* in whatever Philip is telling him."

"You'll be hearin' it all, sooner or later, Miss Bryna," Lucretia said soothingly, patting her mistress's shoulder before picking up a sack of sugar in preparation for measuring it out into earthenware jars with secure lids meant to keep away dampness and sweet-toothed vermin. She pushed the curtain back and looked out the window every few seconds as she worked. "Tell me about Mr. Philip, if you please, ma'am. I'd have to be stealin' a look through Lucas's spectacles to see him good for myself from so far away."

Bryna sighed, propping an elbow on the tabletop and resting her chin in her hand. "He's very young, very handsome. In a blond, blue-eyed, English sort of way. As tall as Dominick, almost, and dressed in the first fashions, I suppose, although he looked a little the worse for road dust as he made an elegant leg and bowed over my hand. You'd think he was just in from a canter in some London park, and not traveling through the wilds of Pennsylvania. But then, that's the British for you. Except for Dominick, I doubt there is an Englishman in the world who doesn't believe England travels with him on his back everywhere he goes."

Lucretia nodded. "Lucas was fair put out when Mr. Philip got here, demanding to be let inside so that Lucas could help him off with his boots. Seems he's been usin' a bootjack ever since Philadelphia, 'cause his man wouldn't come with him after hearin' about the raids. Lucas says Mr.

Philip will have a long time waitin' for him to help him with his boots. Or to have any help in shavin' his blond fuzzy self, if Lucas has anythin' to say about the thing."

"Yes, Lucas doesn't seem to like him much, does he?" Bryna commented, not really needing an answer. Lucas couldn't like Philip Crown. Couldn't like any reminder of Giles Crown, who had admitted to raping Polly Rosebud, and who still walked the earth a free man. "Mr. Crown mistook Mr. Philip for the young man's father, Giles, when he first saw him. I imagine they must look as alike as peas in a pod. It's difficult to believe there is any relationship at all between my husband and Mr. Philip, let alone a blood relationship. What an odd family. I look forward to having a private chat with the man."

"Then you'd best get yourself up and out of here, Miss Bryna," Lucretia said, pushing the curtain closed once more, "'cause young Mr. Philip is headin' this way. Well, lookee here. Mr. Crown is takin' hisself off into the trees, lickety-split, just like he was headin' to Lokwelend's, which he can't be, seein' as how Lokwelend isn't about anywheres, and Kolachuisen took herself off to visit a spell with some of them Lenape down to Bethlehem a ways."

Bryna scrambled to her feet. "They've gone separate ways? Damn! Philip must have said something to upset Dominick." She quickly patted down her hair and smoothed her gown even as she ran for the door, intent on cornering Philip Crown and finding out what he had said to her husband.

Not bothering to gather up either a shawl or her bonnet, she raced out of the house and across the first expanse of lawn. She ran straight down the center path of the huge garden, never stopping to catch her breath until she was within twenty yards of their unwelcome visitor, who was wearing a much more solemn expression than the first time she'd seen him.

"I thought he knew. Christ! I thought he knew!" Philip said as he approached, his handsome face a study in anguish as he reached out his hand, which Bryna, unexpectedly feeling sorry for the young man, took in her own. "I can't believe my grandfather didn't write to tell him. It has been nearly six months. All this time he's been writing letters . . . hoping—and the bastard never told him."

"Your grandfather never told Dominick what, Philip? *What?*" Bryna squeezed his hand hard in both of hers for a moment before releasing it, then hugged her arms close against her. Her heart was pounding, making her chest hurt, so that it became difficult to speak. But she knew. Before Philip said another word, she knew. "It's Dominick's mother, isn't it, Philip? She . . . she's dead."

The young man winced and turned his head up and away, rubbing hard at the back of his neck as he avoided Bryna's eyes.

"Oh, no. *Dominick.* Oh, sweet Jesus!" Not stopping to consider her actions, Bryna picked up her skirts, brushing past Philip as she ran down the path, past the neat rows of herbs and flowers and hedge and fruit trees. She exploded out onto the sloping lawn again, her lungs near to bursting before, feeling as if she were running in waist-deep water that kept her moving slowly, so damnably slowly, she plunged blindly into the dense shadows beneath the tall trees.

She hadn't gone more than twenty yards when she tripped over something small and solid, and pitched, face forward, onto the ground, all her breath knocked out of her. "Damn. Damn and blast!" she swore when she could catch her breath, then scrambled to her feet, pulling burrs off her skirt and twigs from her unbound hair. She wiped at her cheeks before realizing that her palms were smeared with flecks of green moss and dark smudges of damp earth, and swore again, feeling every inch an idiot.

"Dominick? Dominick!" she called out, trying to get her bearings. Bryna began to notice a distinct chill in the middle of the otherwise warm spring day, a chill that came as a result of the absence of sunlight beneath the tight canopy of trees. No wonder the Lenape could sneak up on their victims so easily! Once inside this cover of trees, it would be difficult to spot an elephant at five paces.

She set off again, her pace slowed to a skipping trot as she stepped over rocks and fallen tree trunks and low-growing plants, doing her best to keep to the narrow, nearly invisible path that must lead to the small creek and Lokwelend's encampment.

High in the trees, birds disturbed by both her calling voice and her clumsy, crashing progress through the underbrush called out warnings to their mates and took to the wing. The commotion must also have startled a sleeping owl who immediately took umbrage, his single, piercing screech setting off a ripple of movement on the ground as mice and other small creatures headed for their burrows.

After no more than a minute—a minute that seemed longer than any hour—Bryna turned around in a full circle, amazed to realize that she had lost all sense of direction after her fall. She was unable to see anything except trees, trees, and more trees, when she knew the sloping lawns and gardens of Pleasant Hill were no more than two hundred yards to her right . . . no, to her left . . . no, behind her.

"Dominick? *Dominick!*" She felt like such a fool. Such a stupid fool! He didn't need this, on top of everything else— that his silly, stupid wife would go charging into the trees and get herself lost! She wanted to help him, not be the cause of any more trouble, any more pain.

"Stop it, Bryna!" she demanded of herself, wiping her streaming eyes with the backs of her hands, hardly aware that she was crying. Crying for Dominick, for his mother, who had died without her son by her side to comfort her; crying for herself, because she felt so helpless, so useless, so powerless.

She took several long, deep breaths, willing her emotions back under control even as she offered up a silent prayer to the Virgin for guidance. Then she set off again, this time at a deliberately slow walk, heading toward what appeared to be a small patch of sunlight, hoping she was going in the correct direction.

"Thank you!" she whispered fervently a few moments later as she walked into the edge of a small, nearly circular clearing to see Dominick sitting on a large tree trunk, his elbows on his knees, his head buried in his hands. She stood very still for long moments, suddenly not sure that she should be here at all, for this man was clearly grieving, and grieving was a private thing. A solitary thing. A singular thing, different for all people.

He wasn't crying. He wasn't yelling, or cursing, or tearing at his hair. He was simply sitting. Quiet. Unmoving. Oblivious to his surroundings, to her presence, to the world at large. And his very detachment made her feel like an interfering wretch come to view his grief like some ghoul at a stranger's wake—so that she would have turned around and left him in peace.

If she only knew her way home.

A woman's husband is her home, Bryna Cassidy; never forget that, a small voice whispered inside her brain, and she remembered her mother saying the words as she explained why she had never left Bryna's father, even when his wild dreams and wilder schemes had tested her love to its limits, and beyond.

But he's not my husband, Bryna's mind objected. *Not really. He is a stranger to me, as I'm a stranger to him. I don't know how to comfort him. What to say. What to do. But he's breaking my heart, sitting there so quietly. So alone. So very alone.*

Slowly, moving quietly so as not to startle this man who was her husband in the eyes of man, and perhaps also in her heart, Bryna eased out of the shadow and into the dusty spillways of sunlight that filtered down through the tall oak trees, not stopping until she was close beside him.

She knelt on the damp ground, her skirts flowing around her, and pressed her cheek against his deerskin-clad thigh, her eyes open, yet unseeing, blurred by her tears.

And there she stayed. Not saying a word. Barely touching him. Waiting. Hoping to absorb some of his pain; take a portion of his hurt away from him if she could.

It was all she could think to do.

How long they remained that way, she would never know. A few minutes. An hour. A lifetime. Both their lifetimes, which had seen too many losses, too much death. Until she felt his hand on her hair. Until that hand began to stroke her unbound curls. Until his long, strong, yet slender fingers tangled in those warm, fiery curls.

Until, finally, he took hold of her shoulders and held her steady as he slipped to his own knees, facing her, his arms tight around her even as she raised hers to embrace him, reliving her own pain at having lost her father, her family.

And there these two silent people remained . . . kneeling face-to-face, their bodies close together. Washed in sunlight in the midst of all the beloved shades from their separate pasts. Their heads buried against each other's shoulders, both silently reliving the pain of their separate losses while comforting each other. Their hearts beating separately, yet as one. Their communication limited to touch, still eloquent beyond words.

Until Dominick let her go at last. He raised her to her feet, guided her back to the path that would lead her to Pleasant Hill, then turned and walked away into the trees. All without really looking at her, and all without saying a word.

There is no animal more invincible than a woman,
nor fire either, nor any wildcat so ruthless.
— Aristophanes

CHAPTER 11

ALL HIS LIFE, DOMINICK HAD THOUGHT HE KNEW WHAT HE
wanted. To be a good son to his parents. To have a home of
his own. A wife. Children. To be a fair employer, considerate and caring of his fellow man. A loyal subject of his king.
And to leave the world a little better than he had found it.
To be remembered.

His father had rejected him as inferior goods the day he
was born, and had continued to reject him every day after
that, no matter how hard Dominick tried to please him.

His adored mother was dead.

He lived a continent away from the land he had loved, the
country he had cherished, the king he had respected.

For the past seven years, he had contented himself by
doing what he could, by working toward that vision of what
he still hoped to have, laying the foundation for the day the
walls of Pleasant Hill would hold more than dreams of the
future and remembrances of the past.

And then, after those seven years of hoping, of planning,

of preparing, he had glimpsed what could be the beginnings of a new life with Bryna and been presented with a soul-crushing sorrow, both in the space of a single day. In one single day. Bryna had begun to open to him, shyly, tentatively, yet almost teasingly. And his mother had left him, slipping away silently, for always and forever.

For now, and for the past four days, Dominick's conflicting feelings of hopefulness and sorrow had warred with each other, serving to cancel each other out, leaving him curiously without feelings. Numb. Detached.

And alone.

He sat cross-legged on the ground beside the small cooking fire he'd built for himself in front of Lokwelend's log house. Acting automatically, he turned the makeshift spit that held the rabbit he had taken from one of the Indian's snares earlier that morning, wishing the aroma of the cooking meat would set off some answering hunger in his gut.

His memories of the past four days were vague, as unable to grasp as the swirling smoke from the spitting fire. But he was slowly finding some peace inside himself. His days and nights of solitude here at the small Lenape encampment had not been wasted. His separation from Playden Court was now complete. There was nothing there for him now, not really; there had been nothing for him there the moment Erin Roarke Crown had breathed her last, his name on her lips, if Philip was to be believed.

Dominick had always known she wouldn't come to him. Deep in his heart, he'd always known. His mother had raised him to be loyal, to be steadfast, even when presented with his father's indifference, his half brother's open derision. She had loved her son, but her greatest allegiance had been to her church, and the sacred marriage vows she had made.

And she had probably died still hoping to please the handsome, ruthless man who had coveted nothing more than her money, and used her solely for that money, and for the son she had given him. The disposable, dirt-loving, dark-haired gollumpus of a son who would become important only if the first son, the heir, allowed his recklessness and his wild nature to lead him to an early death. Philip's birth, when Dominick was not quite eight years old, had moved that disposable son even lower in his father's budget of "necessary things."

Yet now, according to Philip, Dominick's father wanted him home. All was "forgiven." The trifling matters of Polly Rosebud's death, of Giles's beating, were no longer important, and long forgotten. Dominick's father, it seemed, had finally discovered a use for his Irish-farmer son who had gone to the colonies and become a rich man. He needed his level head, his ability to draw the best from the tenants on the estate, his firm hand on the reins of what money was left in the Crown coffers. Oh, yes. His father wanted him home—now that he had a use for him; a use for his money.

Dominick closed his eyes, remembering Playden Court as he had last seen it. Fertile, flourishing, and all of it, he knew, thanks to his management and in spite of his father's disinterest, his half brother's neglect. He had been only one and twenty, as old as Philip was now, when he had sailed for Virginia. Yet it seemed as if three lifetimes had passed in those seven years, and Playden Court and its inhabitants were nothing more than dim memories.

What memories they were . . . and what pitiful realities Philip's words had told him they had become.

His once proud father had been brought so low as to send his grandson to plead assistance from his formerly unwanted, afterthought son.

Giles, once the toast of the racier neighborhoods of London, was now confined to the estate, once more a prisoner of his debt.

Myra, Giles's hated wife, who still lived in her rooms, remained soaked in her beloved gin, surrounded by a dozen or more of her equally adored orange-striped cats.

Then there was Lilith, Philip's senior by less than a year, and Giles's deep disappointment and failure, having been forced back into his marriage bed on orders from his father.

Yes, Lilith, the darkly beautiful but saber-tongued girl, was now living a life as wild in its way as her father's had once been, gleefully heaping shame on her family name.

Playden Court, that once proud estate, had been reduced to a heavily mortgaged shell, its fields lying fallow, most of its tenants gone.

And lastly, there was his mother, Erin Roarke Crown, lying alone in the cold mausoleum, forever a member of a long, not very illustrious line of Crowns.

Go back? Go back to what? He'd have to be mad. More than mad.

Dominick wished it could be different. He wished his mother had lived to see the woman he had married, the children he hoped to father, the future he had begun to carve out here, in the midst of a wilderness. He couldn't change the past, and he had chosen his present just as much as it had chosen him. The time had come to say good-bye to the past . . . and move on. The time had come to go to Bryna, confront her with his feelings, demand that she tell him about this promise she had made, and make her see that nothing in either of their pasts was as important as the future they could have together.

In short, the time had come for him to stop sitting here like the gollumpus Giles had always called him; sighing and moping, and—

Dominick looked up, suddenly aware of a noise somewhere in the near distance, then frowned at the sight that met his eyes.

"There you are, Dominick! Hope you don't mind the intrusion. Bryna and I were heading out for a little morning stroll earlier, and I thought it might be amusing to see how real savages live. You don't mind, do you?"

Dominick shook his head at the unexpected sight of his half nephew and his wife standing, arm in arm, at the edge of the clearing. Philip was smiling brightly, just as if he hadn't been left cooling his heels at Pleasant Hill these past four days, while Bryna avoided her husband's eyes, choosing instead to visually inspect the toe of one shoe as if viewing it for the first time. He hadn't seen her since guiding her to the path leading to the gardens and then disappearing back into the trees, to hide himself away at Lokwelend's cabin, and he was well aware of the awkwardness of this moment.

Was she embarrassed to look at him after the odd, quiet intimacy they had shared? Was she afraid to take the next logical step that he knew, that they both had to know, loomed before them? Or was she carefully keeping her fiery Irish temper in check, longing to do nothing less than tear a strip off his hide for having left her alone for four days while he wallowed here in his misery?

Dominick didn't really care. It was enough that she was here. Although he was fairly sure he had been right the third time, and she was mad as a wet hen, barely able to contain her fury as she had come here today, probably dragging a reluctant Philip with her, prepared to outflank her absent husband. Lord help any soldiers under her command if she were a general, for she knew no other order save "Attack!"

Dominick rose to his feet slowly, laying down the spit, the rabbit already forgotten. His spirit, and other appetites, were coming to the fore, making him feel surprisingly human, and happy, again. "This isn't Vauxhall Gardens, Philip, and I doubt Lokwelend would appreciate my giving you a tour," he said, running a hand through his long hair, painfully aware that, while his half nephew was dressed in relaxed country clothes, he was still clad in his deerskins, unshaven, and looking much the worse for his four days and nights in the log house. "And you'll have to learn to carry a rifle with you when you go adventuring, unless you think you can talk your way out of a confrontation with a wild animal—or some wandering Indian brave who just might take a liking to that blond mane of yours."

"Uh-oh, prickly this morning, are we? I told you so, dear Aunt." Philip turned to Bryna, who was now looking at Dominick in a way that made swallowing difficult, her smile small and yet faintly triumphant, her quicksilver eyes flashing a warning that he'd best be on his good behavior with his half nephew or she would fillet him. "Are you quite sure you want to be left alone with the fellow? I mean, the least I could do is to extract the thorn from his paw before heading back the way I came, following that trail of bent branches you insisted upon."

"Go away, Philip," Bryna said softly, probably not aware that Dominick could hear her quite clearly across the crisp morning air. "Otherwise I shall tell Alice that you are not half the god she foolishly believes you to be, knowing how you lap up female adoration. I shall set Mary Kate on you tomorrow at dawn, to serenade you with her flute. And then, once I have your attention, I'll really get nasty."

Philip's smile was young and slightly besotted, for it would take a blinder man than Dominick not to notice that the fellow had already tumbled halfway into love with the beautiful, desirable Bryna Cassidy Crown.

"Very well. I know when I'm beaten. Here, Dominick!" he called out, stepping forward a few paces and tossing a large burlap sack in his half uncle's direction. Dominick nearly missed as it flew toward him, belatedly catching at it with one hand and then quickly dropping it at his side. "But if you ask me, the only natural way to bathe is in a hot tub beside a hotter fire. Shall we see you in time for luncheon? Never mind. I'll tell Deems not to wait."

With a tip of his hat, Philip turned and melted back into the trees, whistling as he went.

"Bathe?" Dominick repeated blankly, looking to Bryna as she approached, a study in contained fury. God, but she was beautiful. And how he wanted her.

"Bathe, Dominick," Bryna bit out shortly, then brushed past him to kneel in front of the burlap sack and tug it open, and dump out a clean set of deerskins and various other personal items belonging to him. "Lucas packed this for you—tooth powder, soap, your brushes, a razor. He said, and I quote, 'It's one thing for him to be out there, but to be out there without tooth powder is a true, bleeding pity.' It's a shame Lucretia didn't think to stuff a freshly baked biscuit or two in here, however, for that rabbit looks atrocious. Half-burnt, half-raw."

She stood up once more, the sunlight setting small fires in her hair, her smoky eyes assessing him, her expression reminiscent of the one his childhood nanny had employed just before she grabbed him and forcibly scrubbed behind his ears. "There you are, Dominick. All the creature comforts one small sack can bring you," she said, turning away. "I'll be going now."

"No! Stay!"

It was only when Bryna halted, then whirled back to face him, that Dominick realized he had spoken—and that she had been daring him to speak. "Why?" she questioned him, her eyes narrowed, her chin set at a belligerent angle. "Certainly not because you need me. You don't need me. You don't need anybody. You're complete unto yourself—you and your bloody secrets. Aren't you, *my lord!*"

Dominick felt a quick flash of temper, so that his next words were issued through clenched teeth. "Bloody Christ! I should have known Philip couldn't keep his mouth shut." He put his hands on Bryna's shoulders and pressed down, so that her knees buckled and she was forced to sit on the hard ground beside the fire. "Stay here and finish cooking that damned rabbit while I go make myself presentable," he warned fiercely. "Then we'll talk. Move, and I'll chase you down and probably spank you." *Or kiss you,* he added mentally, sure she'd bolt completely if he said those words out loud.

She only nodded and reached for the spit, all her own temper seemingly gone, probably replaced by the reluctant knowledge that she had pushed as far as she could. Now she would simply sit back and wait for his temper to cool—at which time she would, if he knew this woman at all, lash out at him again.

He angrily repacked the sack, snatched it up, and walked around to the side of the log house, toward the creek that was still wrapped in morning mist. He didn't stop until he was sure he was out of sight of the campfire, then quickly stripped, located the bar of soap and his razor, and plunged waist-deep into the clear, cold, rushing water.

In less than ten minutes he was clean, the last four days washed from his body the way his solitude and reflections had helped to cleanse his mind of most of his regret. He looked toward the other side of the creek, and to the woods beyond the bank, and took deep breaths of the fresh air scented with pine and oak and hints of smoky rabbit. His stomach rumbled with hunger.

"Feeling more the thing now, are you, *my lord?*"

"What the devil—?" Dominick spun around quickly, nearly losing his balance on the soft, muddy creek bottom, to see Bryna standing on the bank, both his discarded deerskins and his clean clothing piled at her feet. He had known that she wouldn't stay quiet and controlled for long, but he had never considered that she might be so impetuous as to confront him here—like this! "Bryna, what in hell do you think you're doing?"

"And is it just a wee bit cold, you'd be, *my lord?*" she asked, pointedly ignoring his question. Before he could answer she continued in her deliberate, rather cheeky Irish brogue: "With any luck, *my lord,* you'll catch yourself a most terrible fever, at which time you just might ramble during your delirium, telling me what I want to know. It would be a fine day, that, wouldn't it? But I don't believe I'll be content to wait and hope. It's getting my answers now, I'll be, and that's a fact."

"Bryna—" he began warningly, only to have her cut him off again.

"The rabbit's done, and smells fairly delicious, although it will taste better hot rather than cold, I'm thinking. But first, *my lord,* I do believe we'll have us a small Inquisition. You do recall the word, I've no doubt. But no racks. No thumbscrews. I have my own torture devised, and it is far more humane than either of those things."

She picked up the leggings he had been wearing and held them in front of her. "It's telling me your father's name, you'll be, Dominick Crown, if you've a brain inside that black Irish head of yours," she ordered, pushing her hair out of her face as the breeze danced by, ruffling her skirts and sending a shiver down over Dominick's wet, bare shoulders. "Ah, so you *are* cold, aren't you? You'd better answer me, or you'll soon be shivering like a dog in a wet sack."

He deliberately lowered his voice, sure that she would

back down if she thought he was really angry, which he was, now that he thought about it. "I refuse to play games with you, Bryna."

"Is that so, *my lord?* But that's all right, as it only takes one to play this game," she answered brightly—then sent his leggings winging into the creek. He looked at the leggings, and then at her, watching as she calmly bent and picked up his shirt. "Shall we be trying this again? Much as I pressed him, after his single slip, Philip refused to tell me anything of real interest. So now I'm asking you. Who is your father? And, most importantly—who are you, Dominick Crown? Who are you, *really?*"

"I'm a man whose temper is on a very short leash, Bryna, and a man in no mood for being teased," he told her, taking a single step in her direction. Then he halted, belatedly realizing that the sight of his naked, fairly aroused body might do more than rid his virgin wife of her bravado. It might frighten her into retreating from him again, so that they'd have to start all over, from the beginning. And that, he decided, was out of the question!

"In no mood, is it? Prove it!" she taunted, and the shirt followed where the leggings had led, floating on top of the water like sea foam as the current caught at them both, dragging them off downstream. Both pieces of clothing were soon caught up on a tree branch that had fallen half into the water, and Dominick made a quick mental note to retrieve the dratted things later. But not now. For now, he had something much more important to occupy his attention.

"Bryna, I didn't tell you who I really am because it wasn't important at the time. It still isn't, not really. I've gotten so used to being Dominick Crown, colonist, that I've nearly forgotten I was ever anyone else, whether my father had ever openly accused me and anyone was looking for me or not. Which they aren't and won't be, by the way, in case you wanted to ask that as well. And I was going to tell you, just as I told you that I'm half-Irish. Eventually. I simply didn't want Philip to tell you. Do you understand? Bryna?"

She picked up his clean shirt. She was punishing him. Killing him. By inches.

"Bryna, I'm warning you—"

The shirt floated out over the edge of the bank and landed in the water a good five feet in front of him, even as she dropped her deliberate Irish brogue. "I don't want to know in your *own good time,* Dominick. I want to know *now.* So, once more, my lord—and with the full knowledge that the next article of clothing will be your last pair of leggings— who *are* you?"

"I am your bloody damn husband," Dominick gritted out from between clenched teeth, walking toward her, stopping only when the water level reached just below his navel. "I am also the man who is going to turn you over his knee and blister your round bottom if you send those leggings for a swim."

"Spank me, would you? Is that so? That's twice I've heard that threat in as many minutes. How dare you? After what you've put me through these last four days? The many levels of hell I've visited, worrying about you? The long nights I've spent awake, pacing the floors and watching out the windows, wondering if you were well, or hungry, or dying of a broken heart? And then, to find out that you've still been keeping secrets from me! *Spank* me? Why, you—you . . . you stupid, stubborn *googeen!* By God, Dominick Crown— I dare you to try!"

Still holding the leggings in her hand, Bryna charged straight into the creek. Her full skirts immediately billowed out behind her as her beautiful features screwed up comically and she began to cry. So obviously angry was she that she was quite oblivious to the fact that she was getting soaking wet.

Her mother may have been an English lady, but there was nothing even remotely cool and English about Bryna's temper. It was quick and hot and entirely Irish. Dominick braced himself for attack. He caught her wrists just as her waterlogged skirts were about to drag her down, pulling her close against him. She released her hold on the leggings as she struggled against him, doing her best, it seemed, to beat him into flinders—or drown the pair of them.

"Stop it, Bryna!" he called out as he gave her a quick

shake. "For the love of Heaven, stop it! I'm sorry! Do you hear me? I'm *sorry!*"

"Of course you're sorry—now that I'm about to murder you!" she shouted at him, still struggling. "You let me watch you all these weeks. You let me believe I had come to know you—know who you are, what you are. You let me even go so far as to begin caring for you, which I never wanted to do. Now I've spent most of the last four days crying for you, feeling sorry for you, my heart breaking for you! And all that time—all that time—you've been *lying* to me! Damn you, Dominick Crown, I've been a fool! How *dare* you make me into a fool?"

"Would you *shut up!*" Dominick was aware he was shouting, but it was the only way he knew to get through Bryna's anger and gain her full attention. "Do you think you're the only one who's been suffering? Watching you this last month as you took my house and made it your own? Listening to you sing as you work in the gardens? Dying inside when you take a bite of Lucretia's pies and close your eyes in ecstasy? Jesus, Bryna—you've been driving me *crazy!*"

She stilled in his close, if defensive embrace, looking up at him with those damnable eyes of hers. Eyes swimming in tears and widened in surprise and dawning comprehension of what he had been shouting loud enough for Philip to hear all the way back at Pleasant Hill.

He let go of one of her hands in order to shove his fingers through his wet hair, dragging it back from his face, never taking his eyes off her. And then, hardly knowing why, his anger drained away, leaving him smiling. "We're both googeens, Bryna. Stubborn Irish idiots."

She put out her hand, not to hit him, but to stroke his bare chest, sending a shiver through his body that had nothing to do with the fact that he was completely naked and standing in cold water. He drew her other hand onto his shoulder before releasing it, then slid his arms around her waist.

Neither of them said a word. The only sounds were of the birds winging high above them and the gurgle of the water as it continued its course downstream, to where most of Dominick's wardrobe floated on the surface, caught in the branches of the downed tree. They were both waist-deep in the water, Bryna's booted feet planted on his bare toes, probably to help her keep her balance.

If the sun were to come crashing down beside them, they would not have noticed.

Without closing his eyes, Dominick leaned forward, pressing a short, gentle kiss against Bryna's slightly parted lips, then withdrew slightly, awaiting her reaction. She blinked, once, and then sighed audibly, still obviously trying to catch her breath after her exertions. But she didn't move away. And she didn't hit him.

So he kissed her again, still watching her face, still watching her watch him. Until she closed her eyes. Until she sighed sweetly, into his mouth. Until her hand came up to cup the back of his head.

He broke the kiss, not without personal pain, and waited again. Waited for he knew not what, until Bryna grabbed at both of his ears, pulling his head back down toward her once more, saying, "You bloody fool—what took you so long?"

The material of her skirts plastered itself against his legs, making it difficult for him to walk, even as he lifted her high in his arms and made for the grassy bank. Although the quick, hot kisses she pressed against his throat, his bare chest, may have had a lot more to do with his inability to navigate clearly than any less intoxicating impediment.

"This is insane," he breathed softly as they lay together on the bank, his legs still partially in the water. "Totally insane," he said again as he worked to release the buttons and laces trapping Bryna inside her dripping gown, her sopping petticoats, her stiff panniers.

"You're right, Dominick," Bryna told him in a slightly breathless voice, lifting her hips to assist him in his crusade to relieve her of her clothing as rapidly as possible. She took a quick, teasing nip at his shoulder. "We—we ought to stop this right now, go home, and—and inventory the linens closet."

"You talk too much," he ground out huskily, fitting a leg between hers, effectively pinning her to the ground with his greater weight. He touched her cheek with his fingertips, then ran his hand down her body, sliding it around one soft, full breast before capturing the already firm nipple in his mouth.

He couldn't wait. He couldn't go slowly. The heat was too much. Was building too quickly. For him. For her. For them both.

Her satisfied moan became a whimper of surprised delight as he moved his hand again, drifting lower, over her flat stomach, before seeking out the buried treasure at the juncture of her thighs. He found her warm, and moist, and open to his touch. Ready for him. Eager. Untutored, yet so innately passionate in her loving, as she was passionate in all aspects of her life.

He stroked her, learning her innermost secrets with his fingers, caressing her sensitive nipple with his tongue. He felt her begin to arch against him, her breathing becoming more rapid, ragged. He kept on loving her, stroking her, ministering to her, even as her hands fluttered onto his shoulders, even after the last of her gentleness left her and her rounded fingernails dug into his flesh just before she cried out her pleasure.

Please don't let me hurt her too much. Please let her remember only the pleasure. His brain screamed the words as he soothed Bryna, as she reached up to drag him down on top of her, holding him against her with a strength he never knew she possessed, sobbing in her ecstasy.

Without a word, because there were no words, he pulled himself free of her grasp and moved himself lower, oblivious to the cool water lapping at his knees, and began worshiping her body with his mouth. Her stomach. The sweep of her hip. Her inner thighs. And then, as she suddenly lay so very still, so very quiet, he pressed the most intimate kiss against her, using his lips, his tongue, to set off another maelstrom of passion that once more turned Bryna into his Bright Fire, into a white-hot flame that burned him in her intensity.

Only then did he enter her, moving past that last physical barrier swiftly, before she could realize what was happening and tense against him.

She lifted herself to him once more, wordlessly telling him that she was not frightened, that she was ready for him. He raised himself up on his hands, looking down into her face as he began to move, fell into that age-old rhythm that blocked everything else from his mind, from his heart.

She was offering him a healing, and he was taking it. Taking it with both hands. And he was giving. Giving her passion, giving her a momentary release from all her own pain, all her own loss.

For now, for this moment, they were one.

He refused to think about any moments after that. He couldn't. Not when she was looking up at him with so much wonder in her eyes, a blaze of discovery that humbled him as much as it frightened him.

And then she made a sound, a soft, mewling sound, and he felt her body clenching around him, branding him with her heat. With tears nearly blinding him, with his doubts pushed to the deepest regions of his mind, he filled her with his own heat, claiming her as his own Bright Fire, for now and forever.

Bryna's heavy cotton petticoats billowed like white flags as they hung from the poles outside Lokwelend's log house, drying in the sun. Her gown, made of much thinner stuff, was already dry, and she was once more dressed as she had been when she arrived at the Lenape encampment—although her hem dragged in the dirt as she walked, barefoot, to where Dominick sprawled with his back against a fat log, grinning at her like a very young, very naughty boy.

"I'll be able to wear them soon," she said, dropping to her knees beside him. "And stop looking so smug, if you please. How was I to know you always keep a spare set of deerskins at Lokwelend's in case you chose to spend the night?"

"Lucas knew," Dominick said, watching her out of the corners of his eyes as she took in what he'd said, and digested it. "I do believe the man tricked you into thinking I needed you to bring me fresh clothing. Which either means he likes you very much and wants you to reign as mistress of Pleasant Hill forever, or he wants me to come back so that I can throw Philip out on his ear."

Bryna moved to lay herself against his side, sighing as she made herself comfortable, like a kitten curling up for a nap. "It also might mean that he was worried about you, you know. Now, are you going to tell me more of your life in England, or am I going to have to spend the rest of the day thinking up new ways of badgering you into sharing the information with me?"

"If your badgering would be anything like the sort you tried to such great effect this morning, Mrs. Crown, I might consider keeping my secrets until you worm them out of me one by one. After all, I may be a naturally secretive sort, but I'm not stupid."

The sudden stiffening of her body as she sat up once more and the quick flush of color that ran into her cheeks told him without words that, for all of their intimacy of the previous hour, she was not ready for such frank speech.

"I suppose it's time I answered a few of your questions, isn't it?" he asked after a moment, feeling a change of subject might serve to relax her once more.

She nodded her agreement, but remained seated close by him, no longer touching him. "Are you ashamed of your family, Dominick?" she asked at last, her tone solemn as she reached out to wrap a bit of fringe from his jacket around her index finger. "I understand why you didn't want to advertise your presence in the colonies at first, when you still believed you had killed Giles, but I've come to believe you also wanted to forget who you really are, and forget your family as well."

Dominick took a deep breath and let it out slowly. "I'm not ashamed of them, but I also didn't want you to think you should be feeling sorry for me. Your father had a gaming hell in London, didn't he, Bryna? A gaming hell most probably patronized by the wilder young bucks and inveterate gamblers among the *ton?*"

She looked at him in obvious confusion. "Papa mentioned more than a few names, if that's what you mean. He would much rather have catered to a more respectable clientele, but money was money, or so he said. I spent more than one night locked inside my chamber after my mother died, forbidden to so much as peek down the stairs. Why?"

"I thought so. And, that being the case, do you remember your father ever mentioning the Earl of Ashford?"

Bryna abruptly let go of the fringe, her eyes growing wide. "Good God, Dominick! *Ashford?* Papa would have forbade him the house, but he was afraid the man would have brought some of his Mohock friends to burn us down. He's vile and mean and thoroughly dangerous. But he couldn't be your father!"

"No, Bryna, he couldn't."

"Oh, good," she said, obviously relieved, moving close against him once more. "I shouldn't like to number him among my relatives, either."

"I said he couldn't be my father, Bryna. But he could be and is my half brother. Giles Crown. Dear Giles—Earl of Ashford, and firstborn son of Philip James Crown, Marquess of Playden." Once he had said the words, brought the identify of his father and brother into the open, Dominick felt a great weight lift from his shoulders. He discovered the idea of talking about Playden Court had become easier, and he began to tell Bryna about his life as it had been spent growing up without a father's love, with his half brother's animosity—and only his mother to bring any sort of gentleness into his life.

With Bryna nestled, silent, by his side, with the snap of linen blowing in the breeze, and the sound of birdsong all around them, Dominick at last told her the full story of the Crown family. He held nothing back, reciting it as he would have recapped a play he had seen but not actually taken part in, beginning where he had to—with his father, the Third Marquess of Playden.

"My father is a true reflection of the society into which he was born," he began slowly, "destined to one day rule over Playden Court, which is the Crown family's holding in

Sussex. He was a dutiful son, I suppose. He dutifully married the bride of his father's choosing, and she just as dutifully produced a male heir, my brother, Giles. All very ordinary. All very proper. Until Germain died, and my spendthrift father ran out of money."

Bryna twisted slightly in his arms, looking up at him. "So he married your mother—for her money."

"When Giles was in his early teens and already away at school, yes. Giles came home—he was sent down for the term for cheating, I believe—and he hated her on sight, and hated her even more when I was born. My mother was only sixteen when she married, and a very beautiful woman. I imagine my father couldn't resist her, even though he was constantly belittling her for her Irish ways, her Irish speech, her gentleness, her innocence. He made it abundantly clear in every way he could that she was an embarrassment to him and his ancient name. But he always desired her," Dominick added quietly, almost to himself, "at least until her health began to fail. After that, he had no use for her at all. I tried to make her happy. I really tried . . ."

"She always loved you, Dominick," Bryna said, placing her hand on his chest. "You must know that."

Dominick reached out to touch Bryna's hair, feeling its inner warmth against his palm. "I do know that," he said, then felt his lips twitch in a wry smile. "Just as I know that Giles couldn't stand the sight of me. If my mother hadn't kept a close watch, I imagine Giles would have dumped me into the pond when I was an infant—just to see if I could float. As I grew, and whenever he was home, he seemed to take great joy in tripping me as I walked by, or ruining my lesson papers with a carelessly tipped-over inkwell, or making sport of my long, gangly legs and fairly clumsy way. I really was a bit of a gollumpus for a long time, you know, looking much like Gilhooley did until he grew into his paws. Although Giles finally stopped teasing me the day I overheard him saying something about my mother. It took three footmen to pull me off him. I don't believe he ever forgave me for that, or for finally growing bigger and stronger than he."

"No, you're not like our silly Gilhooley. You're like Uncle Daniel's dog. No bark—just bite," Bryna said softly, then shook her head when Dominick looked at her questioningly. "Never mind. Tell me the rest of it—as I'm sure there's more."

"There's not much more to tell, and I'm afraid I've gotten ahead of myself, so I'll go back and explain. You see, I only went off to school for a few short years, as it was made clear to me that I had been born to work the land, to take care of the estate while Giles was off in London, doing his best to gamble himself into debtors' prison. It was probably a good plan, as I did love the estate, and Giles had always found farming a total bore. But to go back a few years—when Giles was only eighteen or so he had married Myra Goldsmith, the daughter of a moneylender in the City, in exchange for canceling his considerable debts. Our father, needless to say, was not pleased, although he was quick to take control of Myra's very generous dowry, and he ordered Giles home to Pleasant Court."

"So Giles did what his father had done," Bryna remarked, sighing. "And was Myra as unwanted as your mother?"

"Most definitely, perhaps even more so. She felt she and her father had been tricked into believing she'd have a place in polite society, only to end up stuck deep in the country. When Giles refused to allow her to return to London, she took to her rooms. And to the gin he taught her to enjoy. Later, even before Lilith—Philip's older sister—was born, Myra had added a devotion to orange-striped cats to her short list of favorite things."

"Not much company for your mother, was she?"

"Myra's not much company for anyone. I don't think I saw her above three or four times a year, to be truthful about the thing. And she truly hates Giles, whose visits to the marriage bed in order to conceive an heir contained— as Myra told my mother one day when I happened to be nearby—all the joy of being strapped to the rack and impaled by a fireplace poker. I do know she was relieved when Philip was born, so that Giles returned to London, leaving her alone with her gin and her cats."

"Oh, dear," Bryna murmured.

"Yes, Bryna—oh, dear! Ours was not precisely a happy home. I devoted myself to the land, and Giles stayed in London, only finding his way to Playden Court about twice a year. The last time he came home, however, was because he had fallen afoul of the moneylenders again. By this time Myra's father had seen enough, and refused to help him. Giles was at Playden Court for three months, hiding from his creditors—three very long, unhappy months during which we did our best to avoid each other. And then—well, that's when I found Polly Rosebud. You already know the rest."

"And now Philip has come to tell you that your father wants you home," Bryna said, wiping away a tear with a corner of her skirt as Dominick looked toward the horizon. "Don't go, Dominick. You don't owe the man anything, least of all your loyalty. That was a story. A sad story of sad people and a time that's over. It's all in the past now, Dominick. The past."

He longed to agree with her. But could he? With Philip here? With his father asking him to return to Playden Court? How could he turn his back on all his mother had taught him of loyalty? Unless his loyalties were now here, with this land, with the woman who sat so close beside him, her hand trustingly in his.

"And you, Bryna?" he asked, measuring his words carefully, knowing that their earlier intimacy had been a spontaneous action on both their parts. They had exchanged no words of love, but only a deep and almost frightening passion. "Is your past behind you? Are you ready to look to the future, without sorrow, without regrets? Are you ready to at last commit to a future here, with me?"

She was silent for long moments, moments during which Dominick found himself holding his breath, awaiting her answer, then shook her head. "I can't answer that, Dominick, because I don't honestly know. My father—well, nothing will bring him back to me, will it? A reasonable person would just forget and move on, wouldn't she?"

Dominick levered himself away from her, to look at her face more fully. He thought he understood what she meant, but wanted to be sure. "I don't understand. Your father? What do you regret, Bryna? Not being able to say good-bye to him before he died?"

Her gaze slid away, so that she seemed to be concentrating on the tree line, as he had done earlier. "Yes. Yes, of course. Only that."

He put a finger under her chin, guiding her face halfway toward his, although she still avoided meeting his eyes. "I thought we were done with secrets, Bryna. Are we back to talking about this promise of yours? I thought that now, after this morning, we had put all that behind us. Won't you tell me about this promise of yours? Let me help you?"

He waited for her answer, trying to be patient, then suddenly found himself alone as she pushed away his hand and leapt to her feet, only to stand stock-still, her hands drawn into tight fists. "What is it?" he asked, turning about and scrambling to his own feet in time to see Lokwelend and Pematalli come into the clearing.

Brighid Cassidy was not with them.

*How dreadful knowledge of the truth can be
when there's no help in truth!*
—Sophocles

CHAPTER 12

❧

"Itah!" LOKWELEND CALLED OUT AS HE WALKED ACROSS THE clearing, one hand raised in greeting.

Dominick took hold of Bryna's arm, gently restraining her as she tried to rush toward the newcomers. "And good be to you as well, Lokwelend."

She shook off his hand but stayed where she was, almost afraid to move, her heart pounding so hard she couldn't breathe. "Never mind about greetings! Where is Brighid? Ask him, Dominick! Where is Brighid? Did he find her? Did he leave her at Pleasant Hill before coming here? Oh, *God,* Dominick! *Where is she?"*

"I don't know, Bryna, not yet. The Lenape aren't quite as straightforward as all that," Dominick told her quietly, putting his hand on top of hers and giving it a warning squeeze. "First things first. There are certain ceremonies. Do you understand?"

"No! No, I don't understand!" Bryna was trembling now, her anxiousness to hear about Brighid warring with her reluctance to hear bad news. She had hoped for so long,

187

prayed every night. She had been sure, so *sure,* that Brighid would be returned to her. To do anything else would be accepting defeat, and Bryna did not understand that word, refused to understand that word.

"Bryna, please. You've waited this long. Surely another few minutes aren't going to make a difference?"

She glared at her husband, who showed no signs of altering this Lenape "ceremony" to placate his wife. "Oh, go ahead!" she exclaimed at last, wrapping her arms tightly across her waist as she looked to Lokwelend, who was still keeping his distance, his features impassive, as if waiting for a fractious child to be sent to her room before approaching so that the adults could speak without interruption. She wanted to leap at him, shake his information from him. But she didn't. Dominick was right. There were probably certain rituals involved somewhere—although she had never been one for standing on formality when she wanted to know something. "Just hurry. Please."

Dominick stepped forward a single pace and inclined his head slightly, saying, "I thank the Great Spirit, that he has preserved our lives to this time of our happily meeting again."

Lokwelend stood very straight and tall, his dark eyes solemn, the gray in his long black hair seeming more pronounced than it had been when last she'd seen him. "You speak the truth. It is through the favor of the great and good Spirit that we are permitted to meet."

Dominick spoke again, although Bryna heard him only as if from a distance as she rocked back and forth on her heels, trying to suppress a frustrated scream.

"I am pleased the Great Spirit has granted you both a safe return. Your daughter, Kolachuisen, is with her friends, visiting the Moravians, but I am here to greet you. You will rest, and refresh yourselves. I shall draw the thorns out of your feet and legs, grease your stiffened joints with oil, and wipe the sweat off your bodies."

Behind her husband, having dropped down to sit on the ground once more because she was afraid her trembling legs wouldn't hold her erect, Bryna rolled her eyes heavenward.

She had passed beyond anger now, thoroughly disgusted with the entire affair. There could be no less pomp and ceremony—and useless speech—at Court, when foreign dignitaries came to pay a call upon the king.

Lokwelend came closer, although his son remained at a distance, his expression grim. "The Bright Fire is impatient, my friend," the older Indian said, extending a hand to Bryna, "as is her nature. I do not mind her."

"Thank you, Lokwelend," she said, quickly taking the hand he offered and rising to her feet once more. She stood beside Dominick, throwing him a blighting smile, silently telling him that he was being silly, spouting all this gibberish about thorns and sweat and great spirits. "Now, Lokwelend, if you'll just tell me—"

Lokwelend dropped Bryna's hand and turned back to Dominick, dismissing her without another word. Her smile disappeared along with what remained of her composure, and she felt tears gathering behind her eyes. Obviously, she thought, the Indian had meant "I do not *consider* her," and felt no reason to pay attention to anything she said.

Knowing that any further interruption would only delay things even more, she bit her tongue again, both literally and figuratively, blinked back her tears, and did her best to remain quiet. But it wasn't easy. It was the most difficult thing she had ever done.

"The sky is overcast with dark, blustering clouds," Lokwelend was telling Dominick, his words meaning nothing to Bryna, as if the man were speaking in some sort of Lenape code only her husband was privy to. "A black cloud has arisen yonder, to the west, with another here, and a third to the south. They draw toward each other. The path to the west that was open, I fear, will soon be shut up."

"There will be a war?" Dominick took Bryna's hand in his and gave it another squeeze, but this time she didn't need his caution not to speak. Her throat had grown so dry, she couldn't have said a word. A war? There was going to be a war? Bryna closed her eyes and thought of Mary Kate, of Alice, of little Henrietta Turner and her mother. She thought of her uncle Daniel, her aunt Eileen, of Joseph and

Michael—all of them dead, all of them victims of the last "dark cloud" to pass through New Eden.

Pematalli stepped forward, his handsome young features sharp, and ominously harsh. "Enough! These evil *shawanuk!* They rape our women. They slaughter our children! They bring disease and death with them wherever they walk. They defile our land. All of them! All of *you!* You whites will never be content. You want nothing but to destroy the last of us. Make us disappear forever. *Geptschátschik*—fools! You want to make slaves of my people, but we will not be your slaves. So you kill us. You walk through our lands with your Bible in your left hand, but do not put down the rifle in your right. I am done with you! I am done with all of you!"

Pematalli spit on the ground at Dominick's feet, then turned to face his father, his low, guttural voice still full of loathing. "And you, old man. *Gepschat!* Fool! I have brought you safely back to your squaw house, but I am done with you as well! They have made you nothing but a woman, and not a warrior at all. You would give my sister over to her murderers. You have let them call her Cora, have let me be called Peter. I am not Peter! I am Pematalli! *N'dellennówi*—I am a man! *Lennápe n'hackey*—I am of the Original People! I will not stay and let them kill me. I will not stay and watch you die! I will take Kolachuisen and go!"

Lokwelend held out his hand to his son, taking his arm. "You talk of fools, my son. It is a foolish man, Pematalli, who thinks so little and talks so much."

"Lennápe n'hackey!" Pematalli repeated proudly. He shook himself free of his father's grasp, turned, and strode toward the log house, ignoring his father's further warning that he should remember their long-ago promise never to raise arms against their white fathers.

Bryna stepped even closer to Dominick, pressing against his side, not knowing what would happen next, but worried that Lokwelend's offer to search for Brighid might have cost him his son. Whatever the two Indians had seen in their travels over the mountains, whatever they had heard, Pematalli was no longer the smiling, carefree young man he had been when first she met him. And she hadn't been wrong. Lokwelend did look older. Older, and sadder, and heartsore.

Pematalli burst from the log house, a large sack in his right hand, his long rifle slung over his back, his chest crisscrossed with straps holding a powder horn and a quiver filled with arrows. His bow was in his left hand, and he had a hatchet and a knife tucked into his belt. He was a one-man war party, a human advertisement for mayhem and death, and neither Lokwelend nor Dominick did anything to stop him as he loped off toward the woods. The young Indian stopped only long enough to turn, punch his left hand holding the longbow toward the sky, and shout again, *"N'dellennówi! Lennápe n'hackey!"*

And then he was gone, and Lokwelend suddenly looked older than time, his proud shoulders hunched in defeat, in sorrow.

"It is true," he said after a moment. "My dream is true, and now it begins. The Bright Fire has come, and now we will be conquered. Our time on this land becomes shorter every day. Even Pematalli sees it now. He has gone to the west and looked into the eyes of the children as they lay starving. He has seen the women butchered in their burned fields, the strong men weeping as they blacken their faces in mourning, as they string their bows and shape their arrows, and prepare to die as warriors. As I feared, it will end badly for us. It will end badly for my son, for Pematalli."

Bryna had heard enough, seen enough. Her Irish blood stirred, pulsing a swift, sudden anger throughout her system, replacing her fears for Brighid, her sympathy for the old Indian. "That's ridiculous!" Pushing away Dominick's restraining hand, she walked straight up to Lokwelend, not stopping until she was directly in front of him. "Here, old man! Touch my hair. It's not fire. It's only hair! And my eyes are not smoke—they're simply eyes. Eyes that have just now watched you let your son go off to find your daughter and take her to join some horrible war party, so that he can lead a band of wild savages back here to murder us all."

"My son would not allow anyone at Pleasant Hill to be

harmed. It is none of your concern, Bright Fire, and not of your making. You are the herald, as is spoken of in your holy book. But you brought what will come along with you when you set foot on the shore. We will not speak of this again. We can only wait, and watch as it happens," the Indian told her, reaching into the pouch at his waist and extracting a small, tightly folded scrap of paper. "Here. The Night Fire asked me to bring this to you."

"The Night . . . Brighid? You saw Brighid? Then she's not dead? Oh, thank God—I thought she was dead! I thought you didn't know how to tell me!" Bryna snatched the paper from Lokwelend's hand, her fingers shaking so violently, she ended by passing the paper to Dominick in fear she'd rip the thing while trying to unfold it. "I can't believe you saw her, and didn't bring her back with you! How could you see her, and then leave her?"

Bryna was torn between elation that her cousin was still alive, and once more longing to beat at Lokwelend's chest with her closed fists in frustration over his calm appearance, his impassive voice, his ability to hold on to each small piece of information until her nerves were shredded by the waiting. "What did she say to you? How does she look? Have they hurt her? Oh, God—I'll kill them all if they've hurt her! Where is she? How many days distance from here? How many men will it take to free her? Lokwelend—for the love of Heaven, I can't stand this any longer. *Talk* to me!"

"She's not coming back, Bryna," Dominick said quietly from behind her, and Bryna whirled about to confront him. She felt like a shuttlecock being hit this way and that, beaten back and forth between the two men. And she was as ready to attack her husband for his words as she was prepared to assault Lokwelend for his silence.

She accepted the unfolded paper with trembling fingers, recognizing it as a page from a prayer book, and read the finely scripted message saying, "Brighid Eileen Cassidy, Her Book, 1759 A.D.," before turning the page over and seeing the message Brighid had written to her.

Sniffing, and wiping at tears that clouded her vision, Bryna read the words aloud: "'Sweet Cousin—I thank God for you. I thank God to know that Mary Kate is alive and safe with you, even while I grieve for Ma and Da and the boys. Lokwelend has promised he will tell you the rest, as we are leaving now and there is no time. As you love me, please do not try to find me. We each make our own choices, cousin, and I have chosen to remain with my new family, who need me with them.'" Bryna's voice broke as she read the last of the note, "'Your loving cousin . . . Bridie.'"

Bryna crumpled the page in her hand, unable to accept the message her cousin had sent her, unwilling to believe Brighid had been sincere in her words. Unwilling to believe her own new happiness could be so short-lived. She looked to Lokwelend, willing him to speak.

"We found the Night Fire in a small Lenape camp to the north of a mighty *Yankwi* structure called Fort Pitt, just before they moved on to the west, to a place I do not know," Lokwelend said as Bryna pressed her hands to her mouth, attempting to stifle her sobs. "She remembers nothing of the raid, the Great One having clouded her mind to save her spirit. It was left for me to tell her the fate of her family. This saddened her greatly even as she thanks your God that the little one was spared. For herself, she remembers only that she was sold by her captors, and taken in by her new family to replace a daughter lost to the smallpox. She has therefore been content, and is well treated. Her life here is over, and best forgotten. She has taken a new life, a new family. She is strong now, a woman, and knows many things. Do as she says, Bright Fire. Learn from her, and be happy for her."

"Lokwelend's right, Bryna, sorry as I am to have it end this way," Dominick said, placing his arm around her shoulders. "You knew she'd never be the same girl you remember. If Brighid is content—"

"Madness!" The word exploded from Bryna as she threw up her hands and backed away from Dominick, unwilling to have him touch her, to contaminate her with his calm, rational speech. "Complete and utter madness! I can't believe you agree with him, Dominick! Brighid's lying— can't you see that? She knew they'd kill her, and probably

Lokwelend and Pematalli as well, if she tried to leave with them. These people killed her mother and father—her brothers! She can't feel anything but hatred for them. And fear! I'm supposed to believe she *chose* this? To *live* with wild savages? To spend her entire life away from her own people? To someday be a squaw? To bear half-breed children, raise them to be like Pematalli, and then send them off to kill her own countrymen? Don't tell me you *believe* this madness, or I'll think you mad as well!"

She whirled around to face the old Indian, her eyes flashing naked hatred. "And you! How could you have left her? What sort of man are you, to lose a son without so much as the blink of an eye to show how you feel? Is it any wonder you turned your back on the defenseless woman you were hired to save? Pematalli was right. You're nothing but a bloody coward!"

Bryna's head snapped to one side from the force of Dominick's open-handed slap. She stumbled to the ground more in shock and surprise than from the pain of the blow, her fiery, tumbled curls falling forward over her tear-wet face, so that when she looked up at her husband her smoky green eyes smoldered through a tangled veil of living flame.

She was, although she didn't know it, a vision of all that Lokwelend said he had seen in his dream. In her anger, her fear, her frustration, her overwhelming despair, she was, for that moment, the Bright Fire.

Dominick dropped to his knees beside her. "Bryna, I'm so sorry. I promised I'd never hurt you, and now . . . oh, Christ—" Dominick said, rubbing a hand across his eyes, and suddenly looking nearly as old and tired as Lokwelend. "Damn it, Bryna, when will you learn that things don't happen just because you want them to? If we're to have any sort of a life here, any sort of life together, you have to learn to accept that you can't always win. The world does not turn on your orders."

"I don't want the world. I want Bridie back," she heard herself answer, barely able to recognize her own voice; the pain in it, the sorrow, the devastating agony it reflected of this new loss, this final blow that had proved to be one too many sorrows for her to accept. "Is that so difficult to understand? I want her back! Oh, sweet Jesus, Dominick—I just want her *home!*"

"And to heal my memories for me. And to force Mary Catherine to speak again. And to keep some ridiculous promise that threatens to keep us apart. What else, Bryna? Do you plan to move the entire world to your order through the sheer force of your iron-hard will?" Dominick asked her, reaching toward her as if to help her rise. "I need you to do more than that, Bryna, and less," he said, his voice now soft and sympathetic, even though she heard the pain that still lashed through every word. "I need you to accept what is, and to stand with me as we take what we have, together, and make the best of it."

She recoiled from his hand, knowing she could not allow him to touch her. She'd shatter into small, jagged pieces if he touched her. He had already touched her this morning, as he had just reminded her. She had believed she'd found happiness this morning, but it had been a false happiness. While she had been moving toward a new life, her beloved cousin had been moving ever farther away from her, out of her reach, living the bare-bones existence of the Lenni-Lenape, on the run from her own people. How could she, Bryna, have even dared to dream of her own happiness, when Brighid was still out there . . . somewhere . . . lost to them all?

"No," she pronounced with quiet venom, her teeth bared as her all-consuming grief flashed into an intense, uncontrollable disgust directed toward herself and everything and everyone around her. "Don't you come near me. And don't you dare try to chide me as if I'm no more than a willful, hysterical child. I hate you for not understanding. I hate having come here a fatherless child. I hate the savages who destroyed my family and stole my cousin. I hate every inch of this brutal, backward land. And if you ever touch me again, Dominick Crown, I will kill you! Do you understand? *Do you understand!*"

"Whether she wants it or nay, my friend, this woman is the Bright Fire. She cannot help the pain she causes, for she is only the messenger," Bryna heard Lokwelend say across the yawning distance that divided his way of life from her own. She bit back a scream of frustration and bent her head once more, to hide her face and her tears behind a thick curtain of hair, unwilling to look at either the Indian or her husband. "Her heart is good, but she has known too many sorrows. Like any injured wild thing, she strikes out in her agony, unable to tell friend from foe. She has much yet to learn of life. As does my son. Let us hope neither one of them—nor any of us, my friend—are destroyed by the lessons this life holds in store for us all."

Unwilling to hear Dominick's quiet, rational response to Lokwelend's description of her, Bryna got to her feet and ran from both men. She ran from the truths they had been trying to tell her. Her rapidly fleeing feet helped her to escape the angry, hurtful words she had flung at them. Swiftly, blindly, she fled from the happiness she had glimpsed so briefly only a short while ago.

She stumbled into the thick tangle of trees, praying a compassionate Virgin would help her find the path she and Philip had taken earlier. She ran through the dense undergrowth and the snagging branches of young saplings, her hair and gown catching on twigs, her feet cut by sharp stones her tear-washed eyes hid from view.

She ran on, like a young deer racing from the arrow that might find its vulnerable heart, her lungs near to bursting, until she reached the sloping grass and gardens of Pleasant Hill. Until she was upstairs, in her own bedchamber, hiding behind the door she had locked with fumbling fingers.

Until she could run no more.

And still the echoes of Dominick's words found her: *I need you to accept what is, and to stand with me as we take what we have together, and make the best of it.*

"It has been a week, my dear, love-flummoxed Uncle," Philip commented as he and Dominick walked in the gardens after dinner, pointedly gazing up at the curtained windows that marked Bryna's bedchamber, the slowly setting sun glinting golden on the glass panes. "Talks to me, talks to everybody. Smiles. Does whatever it is she does in the gardens, mucking about in the dirt. She's a pleasant little thing, actually. But the moment you show your face, she disappears. I know patience is touted to be a virtue and all that drivel, but I would have thought even a patient man would have put a stop to such nonsense by now. After all, it's not your fault this Brighid person refused to be a good girl and come home."

"Bryna believes her cousin does want to come home," Dominick said, looking at his half nephew and wondering if he looked as silly as the young man, the two of them dressed all in their silks and satins, strolling through what was nothing but a pathetic outpost of English civilization surrounded by a primeval forest filled with few friends and myriad foes. "And I believe she has decided that I am a coward. Among my other failings. This patience you speak of, I'm convinced, is yet another one."

Philip raised one well-sculpted eyebrow. "And? Are you, Dominick? A coward, that is? I wouldn't have thought so. Until now, of course. After all, she's only one small woman."

"Who has been on her best behavior around you, I imagine," Dominick returned, smiling ruefully, "or else you wouldn't say that. Lokwelend calls her the Bright Fire, and has announced that she is the herald, bringing the destruction of the Lenape with her all the way from England, which is where she and her father took ship to Philadelphia. Bryna has been very clear on that head, the one time I dared to tease her about it. Nothing bad ever comes out of Ireland, you understand, unless it is an Englishman carrying away booty from an Irish family."

"Yes, Bryna did make a point of informing me that she is Irish, by surname and birth. But she suffers my lowly English presence. Perhaps that's because I volunteered to go Brighid hunting—the moment misplaced, recalcitrant Irish maidens are in season, of course. Lokwelend, however, talked me out of the venture the moment he explained precisely what scalping entails. Seems you were right, and my blond hair would be a trophy any Indian would do his utmost to possess. Strange fellow, Lokwelend. Talks like some bloody oracle for all his heathen appearance, what with his dreams, and his raging on about grass not being allowed to grow on the warpath. Which brings me to my next question. Will there be a war? Lokwelend talks as if it's a foregone conclusion."

Dominick rubbed at the back of his neck, looking off toward the setting sun, and the wilderness that stretched beyond the mountains. "That seems to be the general consensus. Benjamin Rudolph told me today that the expected contingent of soldiers will arrive in New Eden tomorrow from Lancaster, bringing two cannon with them to help fortify Fort Deshler. I'm thinking of sending Bryna to Philadelphia. And you, too, Philip. I can't have you in danger."

"How condescendingly considerate of you, Dominick," Philip drawled, obviously angered. "Goodness yes, get the bothersome halfling Crown out from underfoot. Not that I'll go. I'd rather stay for the show, if you don't mind. Although I imagine it might be best to send Bryna and the other women to safety."

"Yes. If I thought the road to Philadelphia was still safe. Other than the fort, Pleasant Hill is the most secure building in the area. And don't glare at me as if I'd just told you your cravat is ugly. You are the all-important scion of the Crown family, Philip. Think about it. If you lose your hair, I'm left to be the marquess when your dear father is either shot in a duel or breathes his last in some debtors' prison. The prospect of usurping what is to be your title does not bring me any great joy, I assure you."

"Ouch! That would hurt, wouldn't it, now that you've turned your back on all of us?" Philip took out a large, lace-edged handkerchief and pressed it to the corners of his mouth. "So you're never going to return, are you, to take the reins of stewardship in hand and otherwise sacrifice yourself to the greater glory of our ancestral estate? Can't say as I blame you. I think I'll enjoy telling my grandfather how happy and prosperous you are. Who knows? The news might just choke him."

Dominick continued to walk along the central path of the gardens, his hands clasped behind his back, wishing he could forget the past week the way he still wished he could forever banish his more unpleasant memories of Playden Court. "Now, there's a sight I never thought I'd see," he said after a moment, motioning with his head to where Lokwelend and Lucas sat beside each other on a stone bench, apparently lost in conversation.

"Bryna tells me the Indian is a savage, spouting about the Great Spirit and whatever, although he passes himself off as a Christian," Philip said, stopping on the path as the two men watched Lucas peel off his spectacles and hand them to the Lenape. "She also made me promise never to share this knowledge with Lucas, or else the man would doubtless refuse to leave the cellars."

"Lokwelend is more the Christian than any man I've ever met, Philip," Dominick said, trying not to laugh as Lokwelend put on the spectacles, then visibly jumped as he looked toward him, as if seeing his friend for the first time. "The Lenape are an ancient race, and they've survived because of their intelligence, their great heart, their magnificent sense of fair play. 'Our honor is our law,' Lokwelend has told me, and the Lenape are, indeed, honorable men, known by all the other tribes as the peacemakers, the revered grandfathers of their race."

"Really? They take scalps and sell them, Dominick. I'd barely call that civilized."

Dominick smiled. "Let me tell you about scalping, Philip, if I may. It took the *shawanuk* to make scalping into a profit-making enterprise. The Lenape only took the hair of their enemies as proof of their own victories. It would have been a rare thing to scalp an old person or a small child, for gray hair is no fair trophy, as they have great respect for their elders, and children are considered to be the gift and responsibility of the entire tribe. And, although taking scalps during time of war is a custom, there are certain rules."

Philip's lips twitched appreciatively. *"Rules,* you say? Truly? I cannot imagine what those would be."

"Neither could I, but they do make sense. For instance, no Indian would deny his enemy a trophy by plucking out his hair. However, just to keep things honest, many do remove all hair except for a central scalp lock, keeping an unscrupulous enemy from cutting his prize into two or more pieces and claiming to have felled more in battle than he actually has."

"Interesting." Philip looked at Lokwelend, who was standing now, holding the spectacles to his face as he turned this way and that, looking toward the horizon. "Although I believe I prefer our way of collecting our enemies' flags, personally. Now, what say we join the gentlemen. Deems seems convulsed in laughter, so it should prove amusing."

"Itah! Wulelemileu, Crown!" Lokwelend pronounced as Dominick and Philip turned down the side path and joined the other two men. "I say, my friends, that it is wonderful! I look through big glass, such as that in your house, and nothing changes. But I look through these small circles of glass, and the world becomes new for me. I see the deer in the meadow, when for so long I have seen only the grasshopper at my feet."

Dominick smiled. "We'll have to see about getting you some spectacles of your own, Lokwelend. It is good to see the deer, or else your arrow will do no more than find its home in a distant tree, leaving you hungry."

The Indian sobered. "If only I could see peace in the distance, my friend. Instead I see clearly only in my dreams. I see *chelook schwánnakwak:* many white people. I see rifles of a size never seen. Big and black. *Peelháequon:* they thunder. I see *Ilau*—a great war captain—his body strong and hard inside a scarlet coat. But he is *kpítscheu:* foolish. He is death, my friends. And he is coming this way."

"Told you," Philip whispered in an aside to Dominick. "A bloody oracle. He's got to be talking about the cannon, and that new lieutenant you heard is coming here. How does he *do* that? Rather makes my skin crawl, for all you say he's your friend."

"I have seen you, too, little Crown," Lokwelend continued, returning the spectacles to Lucas, who was standing by very quietly, frowning as only the melancholy Lucas could frown. "You are silly and vain, still too young to know of your power, of what is important to your heart. You will learn much of life as you grow older. When the Night Fire comes, and before. Much of this that you will learn, you will not want to know."

"Oh, well, that tears it!" Philip exclaimed, reaching into his pocket for a cheroot and then sticking it, unlit, into a corner of his mouth, holding it tight between his teeth. "Tonight, Uncle, I'm shaving my head. Sounds as if I'm to be around for a bit, learning my lessons, but it doesn't hurt to be careful, don't you think?"

"Be young, little Crown, not foolish," Lokwelend warned, his tone more sympathetic than censuring as he looked at Philip. "It is not yet your time. It is Crown's time, and I speak now only to him. *Miwelendammauwineen n'tschannauchsowagannéna, elgiqui niluna miwelendammauwenk nik tschetschanilawequéngik.* This is your prayer to your Lord, is it not, friend Crown? 'Forgive us our faults, the same as we who are here mutually forgive them who have injured us.' I have forgiven Pematalli, even in his absence from me, even as he has taken Kolachuisen from me, for his fault lies in his love for our people. It is easy to forgive, when the hurts arise from love. Now it is time for you to do this. For the Bright Fire to do this."

"You are wise, my friend," Dominick said, holding out his arm so that he and Lokwelend grasped each other's wrists and held fast. "Easier healed the pain that rises from love, than that which finds its voice in hate." And then he smiled. "But it is the flinging of cooking pots that I fear, and not her words. I cannot count on her aim always being off."

Lokwelend laughed out loud at this nonsense, easing the moment, for which Dominick was grateful. For the Indian had struck too close to the bone. Bryna's anger had risen from her love. Her love for Brighid, and her seemingly misplaced love for her husband, who had so badly disappointed her.

As his love for his fiery wife had allowed his own anger to rise, when she had repudiated him, when her words had forced him to slap her in order to cut off her rising hysteria. And then had come his silent pain and unexpected fury when she had warned him never to touch her again, as if his touch was an anathema to her.

That fury was still there, hidden beneath a purposely calm exterior—although Lokwelend had doubtless seen through the facade, as always.

Dominick was a patient man, a dubious virtue for which his father had cursed him and because of which his brother had attempted, over and over again, to bait him into any foolish, impulsive act. But he was also a proud man, and Lokwelend had seen that pride, had immediately recognized that the verbal blows Bryna had dealt him had injured that pride almost as much as they had wounded his heart.

If Bryna was successful in locking herself away in her bedchamber whenever he was in the house, it was not only because she willed it, but because Dominick allowed it. Dominick knew that. He was sure Bryna knew that, too, and she was deliberately pushing him, as his father had done, as Giles had done. Goading him into taking some sort of action. The action she wanted, romantic young girl that she was, could only be for him to mount a rescue of her cousin, in order to prove his love for his wife.

The girl in her longed for a knight-errant, a man who would tie her favor to his sleeve and go off to slay dragons for her. But Dominick felt sure the woman in Bryna knew any such action to be impossible, especially now, when he was needed here at Pleasant Hill, as the war clouds gathered over the mountains.

Dominick had spent this past week waiting for the woman in Bryna to come to grips with more of the realities of life in New Eden. He also had spent that week tamping down his own pride and anger, having been seen as a coward by his wife even as he had been termed a disappointment by his father.

Words wounded, even as did arrows and bullets. But love heals. Forgiveness heals. Time heals. Dominick would not defend himself because that would only mean more words. People would believe what they wished to believe. Bryna, he prayed, would come to the truth on her own, without any urging from him.

And tomorrow, Dominick felt sure, his patience of this past week would be rewarded, even as the last of his quietly stubborn, injured pride would fade beneath the bright sun of Bryna's smile when he told her, not with words but with his deeds, how dear she had become to his heart.

*A man so dirty, if you flung him
against the wall, he'd stick.*
— *Irish Saying*

CHAPTER 13

❧❧❧

BRYNA SAT ON THE EDGE OF HER BED, HER FEET DANGLING A
full foot off the floor. She was stewing inside like a pot
moved to the edge of the fire so that its contents dropped
from a rolling boil to enjoy a long, drawn-out simmer,
wondering how she could get herself out of this bitter-
tasting imbroglio she had dropped herself into a full seven
days ago.

It had all seemed so clear to her at the time she initiated
her strategy of keeping clear of Dominick and had drawn
her personal battle lines between him and herself, setting up
the remainder of Pleasant Hill's residents as neutral territory.

After her first, roiling anger had subsided, after her initial
grief and frustration had reduced themselves to a reluctant
understanding of what could and could not be done, she
had been left in the untenable position of knowing she had
to apologize to her husband for her behavior without losing
any more of her own dignity. Or, to term it more simply, she
had to discover some way to take the ingredients she had

brought to the stew and turn them into something palatable enough to her immense pride that she could then serve it up at the truce table.

A cup of abject groveling, mixed with a pinch of tears and flavored with a sprig of sweet rosemary seemed the most direct recipe.

And if there were anyone in her family left alive or able to speak, they would have one and all explained to Dominick that he would never eat from that particular plate of humble pie. For Bryna Cassidy had a good, true, and loving heart—but she'd rather starve than grovel.

But Dominick should know that! If he cared for her at all, he should know that!

Why didn't he *do* something? What did it take to make the man react? Exactly how angry did he have to become before that deeply buried, quiet anger erupted and catapulted him into action?

Yes, he had slapped her. But that hadn't been in anger. She knew that. He had done what any sane person would have done when confronted with her wildly hysterical outburst. The anger she had seen in his dark eyes before she'd run away had been directed more toward himself than at her.

Which had only served to make her angrier, for the man should have been *furious* with her. Furious because she had insulted his friend Lokwelend. She had also insulted Dominick's estate, his dream, what he perceived to be his new country. That she had challenged his manhood as well meant nothing to him, she was sure, because Dominick Crown knew who he was, had always known who he was. The slings and arrows she had flung at him might have stung for a moment, but they could not make him bleed.

If only she knew who *she* was! The easy answers were just that—easy. Simple. She was Bryna Cassidy Crown of Pleasant Hill, New Eden, the colony of Pennsylvania. But she was also Bryna Cassidy Crown, orphan. Misplaced person. A woman who longed for a new life but who had as yet to reconcile herself with the life she had left behind her or accept the differences between the two. She was a woman learning that the world definitely did not turn to her order, and would not always yield to her will.

It was a bitter pill to swallow, and her throat still hurt from the pain of choking back her need to take the world, shake it, and make it right. But she had learned. She would continue to learn. She had to.

Lokwelend had said that Brighid was a woman, when Bryna had always seen her younger cousin as a child. But if Brighid was now a woman, accepting of her new role in life, what was Bryna? Was she a woman, too, or still a child? Was she a young girl or a wife? Brave, or incredibly foolish?

How weary she was of being called the Bright Fire, as if everything terrible that might happen in the future could all be traced to her advent into the community. If Lokwelend was right, Dominick should close every door he'd opened between the two of them, keep everyone from her, and she should take herself off, back across the ocean, in order to keep those she loved safe.

Those she loved?

And who did she love? Mary Catherine, surely. And Lucretia, and Alice, and Lucas. She was angry with Brighid, extremely angry, but she loved her as well, even now that she had decided that her cousin had not been lying—that she truly had left her old life behind her in favor of a future with the Lenape. Lucretia had told her that Silky Wattson had fought for years to return to her captors, only stopping when her mind had broken under the strain and her heart had left her, so that now all she did was drink, and give the shell that was her body to anyone who would put down the blunt for a dram.

Which left Bryna with the question as to her feelings for Dominick. Did she love him? Just as important—did he love her? Since that day at Lokwelend's, that at first wonderful, then awful day, Dominick had not taken so much as one step in her direction. As if he didn't care. As if her actions did not touch him, did not hurt him.

Was it possible he no longer wanted her, no longer desired her? What would it take to get him angry enough to allow her to save face by being forced to behave once more as his wife? He knew her. He knew she was stubborn, that she wouldn't grovel, hadn't been born to grovel. Knowing all of that, didn't he have any faith that she could change, that she could see her mistakes and learn from them—even as he had to understand that, stubbornly Irish to her very core, she'd never, ever openly *admit* to them?

If he did love her, *really* loved her, he'd get angry. He'd bluster and shout and take her decision from her, take the first step back to the brief happiness they had shared and then build on it, saving her pride and winning her love forever.

And if he didn't do all of these things soon, she really didn't know what she would do!

Bryna's morose, self-pitying, endless circle of reverie was broken by the sound of some small commotion taking place outside. She drifted into the hallway to walk to the window at the front of the house, just at the head of the stairway, to see if she could discover what was going on, only to see both the wagon and a rather small but fairly elegant black carriage sitting in the drive.

"Well, I'll be damned!" she exclaimed, thinking Henry Turner had outdone himself in building such a fine carriage, then frowning as she realized that the entire household was outside, appearing ready for a trip to New Eden. A trip they were taking, obviously, without her!

"Fetch your bonnet, wife."

Bryna whirled around, clutching the stair railing for support, to see Dominick standing before her, dressed as if prepared to take a drive in one of London's finest parks. His black hair was drawn back sleekly in a queue, his dark blue coat throwing his white linen into startling relief against his deeply tanned skin. She had never seen him so handsome, so appealing, and it required every bit of her strength not to throw herself into his arms, blessing him for having taken the first step she had been too stubborn and silly to take on her own.

"The devil I will, Dominick Crown!" she told him instead, dredging up her flagging store of bravado and tilting her chin in defiance even as her heart raced, delighted that he had at last come to her, quiet demand in his voice. She had done it! She had brought him to anger. Anger deep and wide and high enough for him to react. And to love. Love deep and wide and high enough to allow her to pretend she had been the winner in their weeklong feud.

How could she ever have believed she couldn't count on him to save her?

He turned on his heels and strode down the hallway and into her bedchamber, reappearing a few moments later with her best bonnet in his hand—which was where it remained only for as long as it took him to jam it down on her head and roughly tie the ribbons beneath her still-raised chin.

Bryna could barely restrain her smile as she glowered at him. "You're a beast and a heathen, Dominick Crown, and I wouldn't cross the street with you to have dinner with the king. Besides which, I told you never to touch me."

She raised her hands to begin untying her bonnet strings, which left her totally defenseless when Dominick swooped down on her without another word. He lifted her up and over his shoulder—her head hanging halfway down his back, her knees captured between his strong arms and his broad chest. He descended the staircase with such dizzying speed that her teeth rattled inside her head.

"Put me down, you idiot! Put me down!" she demanded as he crossed the foyer and carried her out onto the drive.

"You want down, I'll give you down," Dominick told her, and her eyes grew wide as she felt herself being propelled backwards into the carriage.

Philip, who had been holding open the door, saluted her smartly as she was laid sprawling inelegantly on the thin velvet squabs, saying, "Fine morning for a drive, don't you think, dear Aunt?"

"Don't call me that!" Bryna told him for what had to be the hundredth time since Philip had come to Pleasant Hill. "I'm younger than you, for pity's sake, and I won't have it! Dominick Crown—get yourself into this carriage and sit here with Mary Kate and me! Philip—you grinning jackanapes—take so much as a single step in this direction and I'll have your guts for garters! Go ride in the wagon with

Alice, as she, impressionable young girl that she is, seems to find you pretty."

So saying, and with the smile of a woman more than a little pleased with herself and her wonderful, considerate, pride-saving husband, she held out her hand to Dominick as the carriage door slammed closed and a widely grinning Lucas gave the horses the office to start.

Once they had arrived in New Eden, Dominick and Bryna went off on their own, leaving the others to wander about the small village, Philip holding on to Alice's hand to give her courage to face her mother even as he promised to treat Mary Catherine to a large paper twist filled with licorice from the glass jar on Truda Rudolph's counter.

Lucas and Lucretia disappeared into the nearly completed building that would soon hold Crown's Inn and Stores, probably to inspect the construction, Bryna thought as Dominick directed her down the packed-dirt street to where more than two dozen men and women were gathered together, listening to someone Bryna still could not see.

"What's going on?" she asked Dominick, who had sat quietly beside her throughout the drive into New Eden, allowing her to jabber at Mary Catherine, who communicated so well by means of facial expression and hand signals that Bryna rarely remembered that the child did not speak. No, that wasn't true. Bryna would never forget. But she would do her best to learn to accept what she could not yet change. If she had learned nothing else in this past week, she had learned that. "Is there a meeting of some sort going on? I hadn't realized there was some specific reason for coming into the village. I think I even see April Turner and Henrietta there, at the edge of the crowd."

"Some troops have been sent here to bolster the few soldiers already at Fort Deshler," Dominick told her, lengthening his strides somewhat, so that she had to give an occasional skip to keep up with him. "They were to arrive either late last night or early this morning. We've also now got two cannon, and our very own lieutenant, who has been sent here to head up the civilian militia."

Bryna felt her spirits brighten even more. "Why, that's wonderful, Dominick, isn't it? With a show of English force, perhaps the Indians will bypass New Eden if they ever dare to come this way. Oh, what a relief!"

"Is it, Bryna?" Dominick asked, speaking quietly now that they were nearing the crowd. "The Lenape may just take it as a challenge, you know. Especially if the peaceful Indians living in our midst don't soon receive better treatment from the authorities. Now, let's just listen a bit, and hope for the best, all right?"

"Gloomy-gus," Bryna teased him, but quietly, as someone was speaking, addressing the crowd from where he stood on an upturned barrel. "As my own father was fair enough to say, it takes an Irishman to find a cloud behind every rainbow."

And then, as Dominick led her to one side of the crowd, where she would have a clear view of the red-coated soldiers and their lieutenant, Bryna lost all her good humor, staring stonily, unbelievingly, at Lieutenant Renton Frey, her fellow passenger on the *Eagle*.

". . . and so I say to you, ladies and gentlemen," Renton Frey was saying, his right hand stuck into the front of his jacket as if he might be posing for a statue to be struck in his honor at any moment, "I have come here to shelter you beneath the blanket of His Royal Majesty's protection. In turn, you are hereby ordered to give me your complete cooperation. All able-bodied male subjects of the Crown are to assemble here tomorrow, rifles and powder at the ready, to begin drilling for the coming confrontation with the savages. The women will provide meals for the men and otherwise occupy themselves in good works. You will find that I am a hard man, but a fair one. Those over the age of fifty and the infirm are excused."

Frey stopped speaking as many in the crowd began to murmur back and forth between themselves, giving Bryna time to study the man she had only this week told herself she must promise to forget. He was tall and blondly handsome in a vapid sort of way. She had scarcely been able to avoid him for the space of the voyage, although she had done her best to steer clear of his immense good opinion of himself and his willingness to pat himself on the back every time he opened his mouth. He had changed little during the months that had passed since her father's death, his cheeks slightly fuller perhaps, as if he was eating better here in the colonies than he had on the *Eagle*. Eating better, and drinking better, she supposed, watching as Jonah Newton handed a pewter mug up to the man.

She squeezed Dominick's hand, attempting to gain his attention as he bent his head to listen to Elijah Kester, who was loudly lamenting the fact that the lieutenant had informed him it was the smithy's duty to shoe the troops' horses without charge. "Can we leave here, Dominick?" she asked, longing to get away before the crowd dispersed and Renton Frey could see her. She needed some time to think, time to calm her jangled nerves. "Please, Dominick?" she asked again, knowing she was close to begging.

"In a moment, Bryna," Dominick answered, then looked up as Frey banged his empty mug against the barrel of his rifle, effectively quieting the crowd.

"As I have already said, as a representative of His Royal Majesty, I expect your full cooperation. Furthermore, I will brook no further coddling of savages, such as I bore witness to this morning. No one will sell them knives, rifles, or any tools of war. No one will house them, feed them, clothe them, or in any way give comfort to our common enemy except to trade with them for those articles which benefit us. Any who dares disobey these orders will face me, and a possible charge of treason!"

"Ha! You hear that, Crown?" Jonah Newton, who seemed to have rediscovered his spine thanks to its proximity to Renton Frey, a visible symbol of authority, pushed back a few members of the crowd and then pointed toward Dominick. "What about him, Lieutenant? This one—standing right here in all his fancy riggings. He'd be a English subject, damn me if he ain't. Ask him if he's part of the militia, why don't you? And ask him about his Indian ways, and let him tell you about his Indian friends while you're about it. What say you, Dominick Crown?"

"Oh, God," Bryna breathed as many in the crowd began to mumble and nod their heads. Her own fears were forgotten as she stepped closer to Dominick, instinctively moving to protect him with her own insignificant presence.

Which was totally unnecessary, of course.

Dominick took a step forward, acknowledged Newton with a barely perceptible inclination of his head, then turned to Frey. "Good day to you, Lieutenant," he said, extending his hand, so that the soldier had to hop down from his pedestal in order to accept the proffered greeting. "Please allow me to introduce myself. I am Lord Dominick Crown, late of Playden Court, Sussex. I believe I detected a note of Sussex in your voice as well, sir, so that I take even greater pleasure in welcoming you to New Eden."

"Th-thank you, your lordship," Lieutenant Frey stammered, clearly taken aback to find an English peer here, on the edge of the wilderness. "Indeed, yes. I hail from Chiddingly, actually. My God, sir, did you say Playden Court? That would make you——"

"The second son of the Marquess of Playden. Yes, Lieutenant, I know. And as is the way of second sons, I have struck out on my own, off to see the world and all that. I do hope I might extend the hospitality of my home to you at some near date. For dinner, perhaps?"

A ripple of amazement went through the crowd as Dominick's complete identity was repeated from mouth to mouth, and Bryna bit her tongue while attempting to disappear behind a rather large German-speaking farmer, wishing herself back at Pleasant Hill, and wishing Renton Frey on the far side of the moon.

But she wasn't going to escape, which she knew the moment Dominick put out his arm to her, asking her to join him so that the lieutenant could be properly introduced to his lordship's wife, Lady Dominick.

The welcoming smile—as well as the subservient attitude he had been showing—disappeared as Renton Frey espied her for the first time, and he narrowed his eyes for a moment before mouthing the single, silent condemnation: "You!"

Bryna laced her left arm through Dominick's, instinctively seeking his quiet strength. She held out her right hand, smiling until she believed her cheeks would crack. "No need for introductions, my love. Lieutenant Frey and I have already met. Isn't that correct, Lieutenant? We were shipmates, as a matter of fact. What a surprise—delightful, I'm sure—to see you again. I had thought you were to be stationed in Lancaster, Lieutenant." *And I have planned to personally see you eternally posted in the farthest reaches of hell,* she added inside her head.

She had to hand it to the man. He had not betrayed himself aboard the *Eagle,* and he did not betray himself now, still leaving her with only her suspicions, and nothing she could point to and say: "There's your proof! He's the one. He did it!"

Frey hesitated no more than a moment before bowing over Bryna's hand, then, his spine as rigid as a poker inside his scarlet uniform jacket, said, "How delightful to see you also, my lady. Again, my sincere condolences on the loss of your father. He was a most engaging man, truly."

"Really, Lieutenant?" Bryna dared, for she could dare anything now that Dominick, her quiet giant, was by her side. She could dare anything but to give voice to her suspicions, which she had held inside her for too long, and which, if spoken now, could only serve to put Dominick in danger. "I would have thought you might harbor some disenchantment, seeing as how Papa went to his watery grave weighted down with quite a goodly measure of your blunt. Still playing at cards, Lieutenant Frey, or have you given it up for games played for lesser stakes, such as ducks and drakes?"

"Milady jests, my lord," Frey said, his laugh sounding thin, and forced. "But pleasant as this is, I fear I must return to Fort Deshler with my men, as there is much for me to do there. Oh, and of course, you are exempted from duty with the civilian militia. I could hardly issue drilling instruction to the son of a marquess, now could I?"

Dominick took out a large white handkerchief and pressed it to a corner of his mouth, acting more the English fop than the English gentleman. "How good of you to understand, Lieutenant," he drawled, so that Bryna longed to pluck the handkerchief from his hand and stuff it in her mouth, to keep from laughing aloud—which could be her only alternative to screaming. "My store of powder and munitions is at your disposal—as much as I can spare. If it should come to that."

"Oh, it will, my lord," Frey pronounced, his smoky gray eyes narrowed to slits. "One way or another, we are bound to see open warfare, as it is the only true means to rid our land of these heathens."

"Our land, Lieutenant?" Dominick repeated. "Yes. Yes, it is, isn't it. Given, bought, or stolen, it is our land. Good day, Lieutenant." With a last look to Jonah Newton, who appeared decidedly uncomfortable and not a little angry, Dominick escorted Bryna out of the crowd. They walked, arm in arm, back up the dusty street. His lordship and his lady, taking the early summer air.

"What are we going to do?" Bryna asked as soon as they were out of earshot, hoping Dominick would forget that she and Frey had met before, on the *Eagle,* and not question her about the man. "Newton as good as called you a coward, you know. I wanted to box his ears, or worse! Thank God Philip says the matters of Polly Rosebud and Giles are closed issues, or else you couldn't have used your title to keep you out of the militia. Oh, I know Newton thinks you're a coward—or too good to serve cheek by jowl with the likes of him—but I know you want nothing to do with warfare the way Lieutenant Frey seems bent on waging it. That is right, isn't it?"

"Do you doubt my courage, Bryna?" Dominick asked, frowning down at her. "No. I don't think you do. But you're right. The militia are so untrained, they'll be shooting each other in the back as they fire wildly into the trees, and the soldiers will bravely march into battle in a straight line, making themselves easy targets because their commanders refuse to acknowledge that the face of war changed the moment we set foot in this country. Another war with the Indians isn't the answer. I've tried to tell them, more than once, but no one is listening. They're too caught up in their fear, and their hatred, to understand that a truce is our only true way to peace."

"But if it does come to a war? What then?"

Dominick closed his eyes for a moment, then looked down at her, his expression solemn. "Then I will fight with my own people, to preserve the way of life we've founded here. To keep safe all I hold dear. I have no other choice. Just, I believe, as Pematalli has no choice. And both sides will lose. Now, wife, you are to please tell me all you know about our intense Lieutenant Renton Frey. I doubt he'll soon have an invitation to Pleasant Hill, as long as you are my hostess."

"Oh, dear," Bryna said brightly, while hoping she could conceal most of what she felt toward the lieutenant, "and I had so hoped I'd disguised my dislike for the gentleman. Very well, Dominick, I'll tell you what I know, which is what my father told me." She took a deep breath, then launched into a recitation of the peculiarities that made up the lieutenant. "Our Lieutenant Frey touches his left ear when he is lying—which you might have noticed him doing as he announced how thrilled he was to see me again. He shifts his eyes down and to the right when he is about to do something mean, like kick at a cabin boy. He wears a small, French-made, single-shot pistol at the back of his waist, and carries a knife in his right boot, although he wouldn't use either unless your back was turned to him. Oh, yes, and when he's bluffing at cards, he wipes the side of his right index finger across the bottom of his nose—like this."

Dominick let out a bark of laughter. "My God, Bryna, but I would have enjoyed meeting your father! Is that all I should know, or can you tell me what our heavily armed lieutenant prefers for breakfast?"

"No," Bryna answered, feeling the subject safely behind her, which was where it belonged. Renton Frey was her problem, not Dominick's. She knew her husband was slow to anger, but learning what she suspected about Renton Frey would be all he'd need to fly into one of his cold furies—so that he could end up in real trouble. "I have no idea what he eats, nor do I care. Shall we go see the new building? You and your laborers must have been working at a frenzied pace, to have it so nearly completed."

"Well, with the planting done, and with no wife to accompany me on an evening stroll through the gardens, I had nothing better to do," Dominick told her, so that she directed a quick jab to his midsection, punishing him for bringing up her recent horrid mood. "Wounded to the quick!" he exclaimed, teasing her. "I can see that the words 'I'm sorry, Dominick,' will never pass those lips of yours. I imagine I shall just have to content myself with the fact that you've come to your senses and have forgiven me for having taken so long to realize that all you wanted from me was to be tossed over my shoulder and dragged back into my life. You do want to be back in my life, don't you, Bryna?"

"Another man might have come to me on his knees and then given me pearls," Bryna told him as they climbed the wide steps to the new building. "But then, another man would have had those pearls flung back in his face, wouldn't he? Oh, Dominick, I've been a fool. A selfish child, throwing tantrums when she can't get what she wants. But no more, I promise. It won't be easy, and I'm sure I'll have lapses that send you screaming into the night—but I have spent a long week looking at myself, and I don't ever want to see myself that way again. You don't need another child at Pleasant Hill. You need a woman. So, yes. If you'll have me—I most definitely want to be back in your life."

He cupped her cheek in one large hand, gently rubbing his thumb across the single tear that had slid down the smooth skin. "A very pretty speech, Bryna, and, just as I had suspected, without the words 'I'm sorry' appearing in it a single time. Which leaves me to tell you how sorry I am. Sorry about Brighid. Sorry I had to slap you. And you're not a child, Bryna Crown. You're more woman than I probably deserve."

Bryna shook her head slowly, blinking away what promised to be a near deluge of happy tears. "You do have a way about you, Dominick Crown, although I can think of a better place for you to be telling me these things. Is there any reason for the two of us to be standing here while I turn into a watering pot for everyone to see?"

"Well, now that you mention it, there is one small thing I'd like to do before we . . ." Dominick began, a most mysterious smile lighting his handsome features as he handed her his handkerchief—then frowned and turned away as April Turner called out both their names. Bryna turned as well, still dabbing at her eyes, to see the wheelwright's wife standing below them in the dirt-packed street, holding her child and wearing a worried frown.

"Oh, dear. I didn't want to bother you none," April said, her face flushing an embarrassed pink.

"It's all right, April," Bryna told her. "What's wrong?"

"I'm that sorry, but seeing as how you have truck with those Indians, and have some of them living with you and all, I think you should know. My lord, my lady," she added, as if suddenly remembering Dominick's earlier declaration, and dropped into an awkward curtsy.

Bryna frowned as she descended the steps, to take Henrietta from the other woman's arms and press a kiss against the infant's dimpled fingers. "Please, April, no titles, as we're a long way from England and that sort of formality, and just the thought of being curtsied to makes me feel silly in the extreme. Dominick only trotted his title out to shut up Newton. Now, please, won't you tell us what's bothering you?"

April looked nervously toward Dominick, still seeming to struggle with the knowledge that the man was an English lord. "Well—well, it's the new lieutenant. He's mean, you see. That is, he's no meaner than Rudolph and Newton and some of the others, but he's wearing that there red coat, so what he says is law, right?"

"Unfortunately, yes," Dominick said as he looked down the street, to where Lieutenant Frey was on horseback, and ordering his men to fall into step behind him for their march back to Fort Deshler. "What did he do, April?"

"It was early this morning it happened. I was in with

Truda Rudolph," the young woman continued. "I came to pick up a bit of tea Henry promised he'd bring me last night, except he never came home, you see, being here with Rudolph and all the other men, waiting on the lieutenant and his men to show up. And then this squaw and her two little ones came in, wanting to trade a few skins for some supplies."

April turned her head away from them for a moment, as if unwilling to continue, then went on, "She wanted a knife, you see. A skinning knife, like we use on deer and such, and the lieutenant told her she couldn't have it. Said it was an instrument of insurrection, whatever that is. He slapped her face with the back of his hand, and kicked her, then threw her out into the street. The men all went outside after her, even my Henry, sorry as I am to say it, laughing, and spitting on her. She had a baby strapped to her back—and they threw her into the street!"

April lowered her eyes once more. "Anyways, I thought you should know, and I didn't have no one else to tell."

"Ignorant bastards!" Bryna heard Dominick mumble under his breath before he thanked April and the young woman moved away, as if suddenly realizing her husband might see her and understand what she'd been doing. Bryna wanted to weep for her, for all of them.

"Bryna," Dominick said after a long silence, looking toward Rudolph's, "you asked if there would be a war, and April Turner has just given you the answer. Today, and for many, many long days and nights to come, I'm afraid I will be ashamed to be a white man."

Dominick's simple eloquence brought new tears to Bryna's eyes, but she could find nothing to say to him. For he was right. She had met Lokwelend, and he was twice the man Renton Frey pretended to be. Five times the gentleman. And a gentle man. A good man. A man whose only mistake had been to be born here, in the land her race had claimed as its own.

"I'd like to go home now, please," she said at last. She felt once more embarrassed over her actions of the past week, the hateful words she had flung at Lokwelend that were so selfish and petty, especially now, in the midst of the very real problems that surrounded them, the injustices that were to come.

Dominick bent and kissed her cheek. "Not yet. We have something to do first, if you don't mind. You see," he went on quietly, so that she hung on his every word, "there was an Irish priest in Lancaster when Lieutenant Frey was assigned to Fort Deshler. He took the opportunity to travel here under their protection. He'll be moving on, later today, with some of the troops that are continuing toward another settlement to our north. I've arranged, if you don't mind, for him to marry us before he leaves. If you're willing. If not," he ended, his face now lit in an unholy grin, "I could always fling you over my shoulder one more time, and drag you to him."

"A priest?" Bryna's bottom lip began to tremble. "Oh, Dominick. A priest! Where is he?"

To answer her, Dominick opened the double doors to the new building and offered her his arm. She took two trembling steps forward, crossing the threshold, to see that everyone was gathered inside the first room to her right; everyone she loved.

Lucretia came forward, her smile wide and white in her dark face, and handed Bryna a small bouquet of flowers that must have come from the gardens at Pleasant Hill. Bryna took them with trembling fingers, then allowed herself to be enveloped in the woman's quick embrace.

Philip stood at the far side of the room, just to the right of a small, wizened old man with a shiny pate surrounded by a perfect circle of snow white hair. The priest smiled at her kindly while Philip, looking rather pale, maintained a most stiff and serious pose.

Off to Bryna's left, Alice Rudolph stood with Mary Catherine by her side, Lucas hovering behind them, his spectacles in his hand, already wiping at his eyes with a large handkerchief.

As Bryna moved forward on Dominick's strong arm, tears streaming down her cheeks, Alice began to sing a simple hymn. Her angelic voice started out quietly, then rose to a clear, true soprano, even as Mary Catherine awkwardly accompanied her on the flute Lokwelend had given her.

The sharp smell of newly cut wood mingled with that of the two tall vases of spring flowers standing on the rough floor on either side of the priest.

Alice's voice filled the room, sweet and true and innocently beautiful.

If Mary Catherine missed a note or two on her flute, Bryna never noticed.

All she saw was the priest, his arms spread wide, welcoming her into his presence, into the Lord's presence, inviting both her and Dominick into the holy sacrament of marriage. All the hurt and pain in her past, all the trials she would face in the future, melted away as she stopped in front of the priest and gazed into Dominick's eyes, seeing the promise and the sweet, enduring peace reflected in their depths.

Before the priest could recite the words of the church over them, Dominick leaned down and whispered softly, his tone that of a friend and lover as well as a husband, "I promise you, Bryna. As long as I'm living, you will never be alone."

And then, from somewhere far, far away, she could have sworn she heard something else. Her father's voice, floating somewhere high above her. He called her his darling, and then he crooned to her in his beloved, well-remembered brogue, "It's liking this boyo, I am, Brynnie, love. So let it go. Let me go. I'll rest easy enough now, here with your sweet mother. Let it go, *aingeal,* and be happy."

Released from her promise, although she'd only made it to herself, by herself, Bryna lifted her eyes to Dominick and prepared to make a vow.

Bryna lay on the high, wide bed, replete and smiling, blissfully tired as dusk began to settle over the skies above Pleasant Hill, but not in the mood to sleep.

For the first few weeks Bryna had resided in the great stone house, she had done her best to avoid Dominick's bedchamber, for the most part pretending that it did not exist. After that, she had begun finding excuses to slip inside the room, delivering vases of flowers, flicking a cloth across the nonexistent dust on the dark mahogany furniture, smoothing the already pristine spread and then testing the firmness of the mattress with her fingertips.

The chamber, and its contents, had held an endless fascination for her. The bow and quiver propped against the side of a tall mahogany chest whose top drawers were a full six inches above her head. The silver brushes Lucas lined up so neatly on the dressing table concealed behind a screen in another corner. The portrait of a smiling young woman and her raven-haired son, obviously that of Erin Roarke Crown and her child, Dominick.

But always, when Bryna had dared to enter the room, she had done so with her heart pounding as if she were a thief entering without permission, so that her visits had been furtive, and short-lived.

But not tonight. Definitely not tonight. Not after the quick, fervent lovemaking that had followed their arrival home from their marriage ceremony that afternoon. Now this was her room as well as his. As it should have been a long time ago, if only she hadn't been so stubborn.

Dominick groaned quietly in his sleep, and Bryna leaned over to lightly trace the strong muscles of his back with a single fingertip. She felt heat rushing into her cheeks as she saw the thin, reddened lines her nails had etched on his skin in her earlier passion. She had a few bruises of her own, she knew, although she could not remember inflicting or receiving any "wounds" during their energetic bout of lovemaking.

She had discovered, to her delight and surprise, that she was very vocal in the midst of passion, having quickly banished any maidenly inhibitions that may have remained after their initial coming together on the bank of the creek beside Lokwelend's log house.

Now she allowed the satin coverlet to slip to the floor, leaving her naked except for the long fall of flamelike hair that hung down past her shoulders. "Dominick," she whispered softly as she bent beside his ear. "Is it sleeping your whole wedding day away you'll be, or are you up for a bit o' frolicking before the sun sets?"

In answer, her husband shoved his arms farther into the mound of pillows just above his head and turned away from her playful breath blowing into his ear.

"Oh, ignore me, will you?" she persisted, straddling his back at the waist so that she could lean forward, her full lips pursed, and blow in his other ear. She touched the tip of her tongue to his velvety soft earlobe, then bit down on the sensitive skin until he came fully awake, nearly bucking her off him and onto the floor before he realized what he was doing. A heartbeat later, she was on her back on the mattress, her wrists held above her head.

"You insatiable little minx!" Dominick grinned down at her even as she raised her hips against him and saw immediate passion flaring in his dark eyes. "Can't a man even take a moment's rest without having you sneaking up on him like some crafty Indian and then swooping down to attack?"

"Not in this bedchamber, no," she answered truthfully, keeping her hips moving in a slow, enticing rotation that had his hardness trapped between her soft stomach and the inward flare of her pelvis, a marvelously sensitive spot, she had already discovered, one that also served to give him pleasure. "Not when you've already warned me that, come the morning, you'll be out and about again, leaving your poor bride alone for an entire day, with only her memories to sustain her."

She raised her hips a last time and held them hard against him. "That being said—would you be considering gifting that poor deserted bride with yet another fond memory to ease her through her day?"

"Keep on pushing yourself against me like that, wife," Dominick warned, dipping his head to press his mouth against her throat, "and you might end up with more to remember than you bargained for." So saying, he levered himself away from her, breaking all contact with her save for his hands, which still held her arms captive above her head.

"Oh, really?" Bryna struggled to raise her hips once more, but his hands and carefully confining legs kept her effectively pinned down, denying them both what they wanted while, she couldn't help noticing, giving Dominick a clear view of her openly yearning body. Good Lord, but she was a hoyden! She'd never known she was a hoyden. The thought made her smile.

"You've a mean streak in you, Dominick Crown," she told him as he bent to plant a kiss on her left breast before he moved his attention, and his clever tongue, to her right breast . . . where he lingered, laving her slowly even as he watched her face intently.

She felt the beast coiling in her stomach, bringing with it an already familiar and most welcome hunger that gripped her with a ravenous appetite that demanded immediate satisfaction. "Dominick," she whispered hoarsely, catching her bottom lip between her teeth as she struggled to raise herself to him. "For the love of Heaven—touch me!"

But he ignored her pleas, both physically and verbally expressed, and continued to concentrate his attention on her breasts, her skin taut because of the position of her arms, her every nerve ending alive to each new sensation his lips, teeth, and tongue so expertly evoked. Her throat went dry with longing. Her heart pounded in her chest even as the sweet, throbbing ache between her legs became nearly unbearable. "Dominick! Damn you to the darkest reaches of Hades! Take me now or leave me, but for the love of Heaven, do *something* to make this stop!"

He lifted his head, smiling into her eyes even as he lowered himself between her legs, legs she eagerly spread wide to welcome him. She could not suppress a sob as he slid inside her, filling her. She raised her legs to cross them over him nearly at his waist, her teeth clenched as she willed him closer, deeper.

Still, he didn't take her. He didn't plunge into her, again and again, faster and deeper, the way he had done before;

losing control until he buried himself in her body and she held him, soothing him as his muscles convulsed and he momentarily lost the ability to breathe.

No. Not this time. This time he was the one in control. It was he who called the tune and she who was about to pay the piper. She knew it, knew it as well as she knew it was more than time she placed her full trust in him, even as she placed control of her body completely into his hands.

But it was so hard. So hard. She thrashed her head from side to side, fighting the sensations that rocketed through her, denying herself release until she could anchor her arms around him.

But it was no use. She couldn't fight what was coming. Couldn't stop it. Didn't want to stop it. She wasn't in control, and he knew it. He knew how much she longed to be in control, how she feared allowing another, even him, to direct her path for her, to be in charge of her ultimate destination.

Her entire being centered in that most dark and mysterious part of her, a part of her that responded without her command, then took her past control, beyond thought, outside the limits of her strong personality and stronger will, making her vulnerable to a raw, primitive power that, once unleashed, was impossible to recapture.

And here it was. Here it came. Tearing at the gates, demanding to be let out. With her eyes wide open, with Dominick watching her every reaction, she gave up the unequal fight and allowed her last defenses to fall, gave herself over to be conquered. By Dominick. By that secret part of herself that proved her vulnerable, proved her human, proved her dependent on another human being for her happiness.

"Oh God." Her voice was low, reedy, tinged with awe and the last, ragged remnants of a slowly dying fear of loving, just to lose, so that, at long last, she could tell him what was in her heart. "Dear God, Dominick, I need you in my life. I need you so much."

"As I need you in mine, Bryna," Dominick said as he released her hands and they held each other, held each other tightly, each one proving that, without the other, they were no longer whole.

"Say it again, Dominick," Bryna murmured into the hollow just below his collarbone, then lifted her head to smile up at him through happy tears. "Tell me again what you told me just before we said our vows."

He rolled over onto his back, taking her along with him, so that her long curls slid forward as she leaned down toward him, sealing them both inside a flame-hot cocoon.

His voice was husky as he did as she had bid. "As I promised you before God, Bryna Cassidy Crown—as long as I'm living, you'll never be alone again."

BOOK THREE

To Begin Again

*One must therefore be a fox to recognize traps,
and a lion to frighten wolves.*
—Machiavelli

And Heaven had wanted one immortal song.
— Dryden

CHAPTER 14

DOMINICK STOOD ON THE CREST OF A LOFTY HILL OVERLOOKING Indian Creek in the distance, his hands gripping the barrel of his upturned long rifle as he contemplated the scene that spread below him and reached out on three sides to the green horizons of primeval forest.

Was there any greater pleasure, any deeper satisfaction for a man, than to stand on a hill and survey his own land? To see the wheel of his own sawmill turning as water rushed through the millrace, powering the saws? To listen to the breeze as it rustled through head-high rows of growing corn, making the long green leaves sing? To breathe in the heavy sweetness of a wheat field, to glory in its light golden color below a cloudless, vividly blue late summer sky?

Lokwclend had said that no man can own the earth. "Who causes the grass to grow?" the Indian had asked Dominick one day as they sat outside the log house beside the creek, smoking from the same long pipe. "Can you make the grass to grow, Crown? That which grows out of the earth has been given to us all. The bird, the butterfly, are for us all to share. When you eat of the bear, or the deer, you eat what was common to us all before you took it as a hunter. Possess what you think to possess. Build your walls, your fences. Still, you own nothing. What we have, Crown, are all gifts from the Great Spirit, and no more yours than mine."

Lokwelend lived this Lenape philosophy. He thanked the deer he had just killed for the gift of meat he was to eat, the hide he was to wear. His respect for the land, for every living creature, impressed Dominick even as it confused him. For Dominick did believe that he owned this land. He had cleared away the trees, planted the seeds, tended the crops. He fenced in his fields, fenced out the world. That was the way of civilization.

It had never been the way of the Lenni-Lenape.

But the Lenape were learning. Their once generous capacity to share had been curtailed by the enormity of the losses they had incurred. They had held out the hand of brotherhood, of comradeship, and the *shawanuk* had taken it, then demanded more. Always more. Until the holy places had been taken. The ancient hunting grounds had been plowed into cornfields. And still the *shawanuk* wanted more. More. Always more.

Land the Lenape had shared freely with their white fathers now ran red with the blood of both races. News of isolated raids to the north, to the west, in the wilderness beyond the mountains, had filtered through to New Eden as the spring had disappeared into late summer and the crops grew tall in the softly rolling fields of Pleasant Hill.

When would this war that was not a war at last reach into New Eden's small, benighted community? What would be its cost? How many would die? And for what?

Each day that Lieutenant Renton Frey and his men set out on patrol across the valley, the prospect of open warfare became more inevitable. The English presence could no longer be denied, so that the authority of the troops would, sooner or later, have to be challenged by the Lenape who remained in the area. Lenape who were being treated as less than human, without rights of their own; cheated at the trading stores, spat upon on the streets, their women in danger of rape or worse if they were caught alone, without a man to protect them.

Lieutenant Frey kept order by way of intimidation, replacing Lenape unhappiness with hostility, Lenape resignation with belligerence, Lenape lingering hope with ever-growing anxiety and resentment. All through the summer the kettle had heated, its contents slowly rising to the boiling point. In the very air, even here, high on his own hill, on his own land, Dominick felt the heat. Smelled the fear.

Just yesterday, Lokwelend had told him and Philip a story he'd heard from a Lenape passing through the area, a young brave who'd stopped to give Lokwelend news of Pematalli and Kolachuisen, who had not returned to Pleasant Hill after Pematalli's condemnation of his father.

"I tell you this as it was told to me," Lokwelend had said to Dominick and Philip as they sat together in the gardens, watching night fall over the land. "A young brave went to sleep in a meadow near this place you call Heidelberg, and woke to find his horse gone. He went upon a search for the animal, and found him tied inside the fence of a *shawanuk*. When he confronted the man, saying that the horse was his, the man told him to produce a paper to prove his claim, as the horse had been in the man's meadow, so that he had the right to call it his own. When the brave could not produce a paper of ownership, the man said again that he would not give back the horse unless he had something to read that showed him proof. He told the brave to go away at once, to leave him alone."

Dominick had shaken his head, knowing that no Lenape had ever possessed a bill of sale. Indians did not trade in this manner, their word being their bond. The man who'd taken the horse, then demanded a written proof of purchase, had to have known this as well. Lokwelend's story was just another in a long litany of injustices done to the Lenape by the people who would view them as inferiors.

"The brave was angry," Lokwelend had gone on in his low, guttural voice, "but he was not without an answer for the man. He picked up a piece of burnt wood from the fire and drew a picture on the man's own front door. This pictured showed the man, on his knees, his face wearing a vision of horror, with the brave standing above him, a knife in his hand, in the act of taking his scalp. 'There,' the brave then said to the man. 'You asked me to give you something you can read. Can you read this, *shawanuk?*' The man replied that he could, and quickly gave back the horse which he had stolen during the night. The brave went on his way, satisfied, and the *shawanuk* kept his hair.''

Philip had laughed, Dominick remembered, finding the story amusing, but he and Lokwelend had exchanged solemn looks, seeing beyond the mere story, to the deeper meaning. This was how wars began. With a single incident, a confrontation that ends, not peacefully, but with the first loss of temper, the first swing of the knife, the first shot from a hastily leveled rifle. And on the day that such a thing happened, the whole world as they knew it would explode.

All the ingredients of war were coming closer. The discontent, the anger. Closer. The menace, the fear, the intolerance. Closer. The inevitable.

When? When would it come? How long before sweet reason and justice failed to halt the first blow?

"Dominick? Are you going to stand there all the afternoon long, admiring your own prosperity? Look—I've unloaded the basket Lucretia packed for us. I do believe the woman thinks I should be eating enough to keep an army marching for a week. Dominick?"

He took a deep breath, letting it out on a silent sigh. He and Bryna were seldom alone, and there would be plenty of time for thinking once she was gone. He smiled deliberately, hiding his somber mood as he returned to the blanket and sat down beside his wife. "I can understand Lucretia's reasoning, pet," he said, shaking his head to reject the piece of cold chicken Bryna was offering him. If he had any appetite at all, it was for the woman sitting beside him on the blanket. "After all, I was present last night when you were stealing forkfuls of pie from Philip's plate after he'd announced he couldn't swallow another bite."

"Wretch!" Bryna pronounced, grinning as she laid the

plate aside and leaned her back against the tree trunk, her expression blissful as she sought and found a more comfortable position. "It is a sin to waste food, you know. Didn't your mother teach you that, boyo? Besides, it was peach pie. My favorite."

Dominick reached out a hand, running it over the growing bulge of Bryna's stomach. "I imagine it is his favorite as well," he said, experiencing again the joy, the absolute wonder, of knowing that his child slept just there, inside the body of his wife. Soon, he knew, he would be able to feel the baby kick, announcing his presence and his impatience to be out and about, getting on with the business of life.

Bryna rested her hand on top of Dominick's, drawing it up so that he could cup one full breast. Her body was blossoming, coming into full flower, from the new heaviness in her breasts to the enticing lushness of her more rounded hips, the life-affirming swell of her belly. The seeds of spring were all maturing, growing more ripe every day, from the corn, to the squash, to the beans, to the wheat—to the seed of life that had, according to Bryna, been sown that first day beside the creek, as Bryna had confronted him in his sorrow over the loss of his mother; goading him back into life.

Soon it would be October, and the harvest would begin, keeping him busy from dawn to beyond dusk. Keeping him away from this woman, who never questioned, never complained, even as the aroma of summer squash sent her running for the nearest basin, or when the humid, stifling heat of August bore down on her as she worked in the gardens, refusing to give an inch to the new demands her body was placing on her.

She spent three days a week in New Eden, ordering supplies for Crown Inn and Stores, overseeing the placement of clean linens on the inn beds, checking delivered stock against the carefully prepared inventory sheets she worked over in his study, her bottom lip caught between her teeth as she figured, and planned, and counted. Bryna Cassidy Crown might have the heart of an Irishwoman, but she had the soul of an English shopkeeper.

Slowly, insidiously, and then with a sudden explosion of

passion and desire, Bryna had become his life. His reason to rise each morning, the siren call that lured him back to Pleasant Hill each evening. Yet, unlike this land he had tamed and cultivated and fenced in, she was not his possession. As Lokwelend had said, she was a gift of the Great Spirit. She was his Bright Fire, giving light and warmth and meaning to his own existence. How he would miss her.

Dominick moved his hand slightly as, at the same time, he maneuvered himself closer, cupping Bryna's breast even as she pushed away from the tree, to lie fully on the blanket and turn toward him, her smile welcoming, her silvery eyes glinting fairy green with mischief.

"You do have a penchant for misbehaving out-of-doors, don't you?" she asked, freeing her hair from its pins even as she nipped at his ear, showing him by both word and deed that she was not averse to whatever naughtiness he might have in mind. "Have you considered that we might be discovered?"

"No one would dare," he grumbled into the sweet-smelling cleft between her breasts as he unloosed the laces holding the bodice of her emerald green gown over the white lawn chemise that tied just as conveniently. In a moment, her breasts were free, the milky white skin so in contrast to the warm, fiery curls cascading over her shoulders, tangling around his fingers. "Christ, but you're beautiful. You grow more beautiful every day."

"His lordship flatters me," Bryna responded cheekily, reaching for the buttons of his shirt, opening them one by one before slipping her fingers inside, to trace butterfly-light circles on his chest, his taut belly. "But will you still think so as February nears, and I've grown as heavy and round as Lucretia's new cooking pot?"

"Even when you waddle like the ducks in the pond back at Playden Court, and Philip and I have to use a winch to get you up from the dining table," Dominick teased, sucking in his breath as she opened the buttons of his breeches and her hand searched lower, finding him . . . finding him ready for her . . . finding him as eager for her as he had been from the first, would be until he could no longer draw breath. Until he was dead. And beyond.

Their clothing slipped away, along with all Dominick's thoughts of anything but the moment. All that was real was this small slice of time, and the soft breeze smelling of late summer, of growing dreams, blossoming hopes, a world awash in possibilities and promise.

He kissed her smiling mouth, drinking from her, drawing out her sweetness, swallowing her encouraging sighs.

He kissed her breasts, suckling at them the way his child would soon be nourished by them, as she lifted herself to him, using her hands to help mold her fullness to his mouth; feeling her nipples harden, reveling in the knowledge that he had aroused her.

He kissed her stomach, partly in passion, partly in awe, humbled by both the miracle of her and the miracle of life.

And then, as if by unspoken agreement, the passion swept over them both, and Bryna pushed him away, coming to her knees, straddling him, staring down into his eyes, her own full of the desire she had learned to enjoy without embarrassment or reserve.

She settled herself over him even as he supported her, then threw back her head as he lifted his hands to her breasts, cupping them, molding them, rubbing her nipples between thumb and forefinger, his ministrations calling forth mewing whimpers of pleasure from her even as she began to rock, rhythmically, against his aroused manhood.

She was the Bright Fire again, the wanton lover who burned him with her heat, singed his very soul with her passion, engulfed him totally in the flames of her desire. He raised himself up toward her, pressing kisses against her breasts even as she leaned against him, bracing her hands on the ground behind his head, enveloping them both in the living curtain of flame that was her long, vibrant hair.

Neither spoke, nor did they close their eyes as, together, in total communion, watching each other as the blaze built, they willingly succumbed to the intense conflagration that threatened to burn them both into cinders.

Afterwards, the fires of passion banked, Dominick held

Bryna in his arms, cradling her against him as she struggled to regain her breath, as he struggled to remember to breathe at all. He stroked her hair, kissed her temple, hugged her close as she took one last, possessive nip at his chest with her sharp little teeth, laughing quietly as she scolded him for making a soon-to-be mother into a wanton.

It was only after they were dressed once more, two plates of half-eaten food between them, that he took a deep breath, remembering once more why he had brought her here today, and said quietly, "We must talk, Bryna."

She hesitated, a plump chicken leg half-raised to her already opened mouth, then replaced the meat on the plate with more force than aim. "Oh, dear. You're wearing your serious face all of a sudden, I see. Well, if you're going to tell me that I mustn't ride into New Eden anymore, I am not going to listen," she told him, her chin already beginning to tilt upward, signaling an onset of one of her totally Irish belligerent moods he was secretly grateful she had never quite conquered.

"Bryna—" he began, only to have her cut him off.

"No, Dominick, I won't hear it! Truda Rudolph is weeping and gnashing her teeth as customers pass her door and make their way to us instead, and I refuse to give up a single moment of my enjoyment of her despair. Not while I can still climb up onto a wagon seat!"

Dominick used his own serviette to wipe at Bryna's chin, which showed only a faint trace of the butter in which Lucretia had cooked the chicken—but he longed to touch her, and would use any excuse to get what he wanted. Besides, if she tried to hit him, he wanted to be ready to catch her wrist before she could crash her small fist into his nose. "This isn't about going into New Eden. I want you to go to Philadelphia. Tomorrow, Bryna."

Her eyes grew so wide, he could see the whites all around her wonderful silvery irises. "What!" She pushed his hand away, as if suddenly unwilling to have him touch her. "Philadelphia? Why? And what do you mean—you want *me* to go? Wouldn't you be going as well?"

Dominick sat up on the blanket, crossing his legs in front of him. "No. I have to stay here. I've got to take care of the house, the crops, the outbuildings. We'll begin harvesting in another few weeks. But I want you to go to Philadelphia. You, and Mary Kate, and Alice, and Lucretia—even Lucas. I already talked it over with Philip several times, and he has finally agreed to chaperon you on the road. He's young, I know, but he's competent. I trust him to keep you safe."

Bryna looked at him for a long time, and as it had been from the first, he could read her emotions in her face. First had come surprise. Then question, followed by understanding, which had quickly changed to anger and, lastly, a resolution to be as stubborn as she knew how to be until she got her own way. "The devil you say, Dominick. Have it all planned out, do you? Well, much as it pains me to discommode you, I won't go."

He smiled, believing her statement to be as predictable as it was superfluous. "Bryna—" he began, just to have her cut him off yet again. If he had learned nothing else from their infrequent arguments, it was that he should feel fortunate each time she allowed him to complete a sentence.

"No! I won't! This is because of what I've been hearing in New Eden, isn't it? Oh, you think you're protecting me, hiding the truth from me, but I know, Dominick Crown. I *know*. And I haven't forgotten. Lucky as we've been all the summer long, we're not assured that a war party won't arrive on our doorsteps tomorrow. It's coming closer now, isn't it, this attack we've all been dreading? I had thought, for a time, that New Eden would be spared, but it's a false hope. You want to send us away because you believe we're in danger. Well, damn you, Dominick Crown. *Damn* you for a bloody liar!"

"Damn me? I want you safe. Only you could condemn me for that. Think, Bryna! I have to have you safe. I didn't send you away before because I wasn't comfortable that the King's Highway was secure, and then because I'm a selfish fool. I wanted you here, with me. But some of Frey's troops will be leaving for Philadelphia tomorrow, for reasons only those in command understand, and I've decided that I can't be selfish anymore. I've got to know you and Mary Kate are out of harm's way. Can't you understand that?"

Bryna blinked back tears as she answered him. "Oh, yes. I understand. You want to have your mind free to fight, and not be worried about a houseful of women. You want to spend your days and nights protecting possessions, not people. Land, not lives. You want me out of the way so that you can save your precious Pleasant Hill!"

"Well, now that you've made all my arguments for me . . ." Dominick said, trying for humor, only to break off abruptly as he ducked his head, narrowly escaping being conked by the chicken leg Bryna hurled at him in her fury. "Bryna," he warned quietly, feeling himself beginning to grow very angry at her unreasonable response to his very commonsensible arrangements. "Think of our baby."

"I *am* thinking of our baby, Dominick!" she exclaimed, reaching into the basket, obviously on the hunt for another weapon to toss at the man she had, only minutes earlier, in the heat of passion, told she would desire for all time.

Hefting an apple in her hand, she declared flatly: "I know you're angry with me, that you are probably more angry than you've ever been before. I'm smart enough to realize that I should shut up this instant, as you don't believe you can be pushed any farther. I've seen your temper a time or two, Dominick, but I can't care about that now, no matter how much I've come to respect it. I can't think about that quiet anger, or run from you until I discover a way to make you understand. You asked me to think, Dominick. I *am* thinking! I am thinking that our baby needs his father. I can shoot, Dominick. I can help. But if you send me away, if you send me to Philadelphia . . ."

She put down the apple, tears spilling over onto her cheeks, all her own anger seemingly gone, to be replaced by a deep, palpable sorrow. "I can't do it, Dominick. I can't be away from you. No matter how frightened I am, and I'll admit to being terrified by the thought of an attack, I would be more frightened without you. I can't be safe in Philadelphia while you're here, under attack, maybe even wounded, maybe even . . . maybe even . . ."

Dominick put out his hand to her, feeling himself torn in two by her words, her tears. "Bryna, I—"

"No! Don't say anything yet—not until you've heard everything I have to say! *You're* my life, Dominick. My whole life. Don't you understand that? I know we've never said the words, but haven't I shown you how I feel? For the first time, I know how my mother felt, how my aunt Eileen felt. Nothing and no one can be more important, not even our own child. I can't go. Please—don't make me! I'd rather die here with you than live without you. You promised me you'd never let me be alone again. You *promised* me. Dominick, please don't tell me that was a lie."

She sat very still then, her untamed hair a fiery halo lit by a slowly setting sun, her eyes shining with tears that broke his heart, her expression that of a woman reeling at the prospect of a soul-shattering loss. She was as indomitable as she was frightened, as resolute as she had been from the moment he'd first met her. And he loved her so very, very much.

I must be mad, Dominick thought as he drew Bryna into his arms, promising her that he wouldn't send her away, promising her that he would keep her safe, that he would keep everyone safe. *I must be mad.*

Bryna was careful to be on her best behavior for an entire week. She didn't go into New Eden at all, because she knew Dominick worried about her being out on the roadway with only Philip to protect her. She canceled her planned excursion to the East Meadow, where sweet berries ripe for the picking grew along the split-rail fence, and put off a planned visit to the former Cassidy farm to gather up the last of her relatives' belongings before a small contingent of troops could take over the rooms inside the barn.

Half of Lieutenant Frey's troops had indeed departed for Philadelphia, but they had been replaced only three days later with fresh troops sent to New Eden from Easton. Frey,

Bryna had learned, had suffered some insubordination in the ranks, probably brought on by his continued harsh treatment of the local Lenape as well as his appointment of Benjamin Rudolph and Jonah Newton as titular heads of the locally recruited militia.

Frey's men had been trained to fight, to protect—not to harass, not to spend their days watching as their lieutenant badgered old Lenape men already defeated by life and delighted his audience of Rudolph and Newton by ordering his troops to level their rifles at women and children, frightening them into near insensibility.

Dominick had told Bryna that it was only a matter of time before Frey was cashiered, as rumors already abounded that he had deserted his wife and left a mountain of debt behind him in England, volunteering for duty here in the colonies as a way to hide from his crimes. And it had been Dominick, Lucas had told her, who had been the one who had written to the colonel headquartered in Philadelphia, detailing Frey's incompetence and cruelties, so that she understood why her husband had been openly disappointed when the new troops had arrived with orders to report to the lieutenant.

Which, Bryna thought as she balanced herself on the wagon seat, was probably why Dominick had offered the use of the former Cassidy farm as headquarters for the new troops. Keeping them as separate from their lieutenant as possible might help alleviate some of the tension that Frey's actions had brought to the valley. Here, on the farm, they could train and become familiar with the terrain—and be exposed to Dominick's own opinions on how best to deal with the Lenape in the area.

Frey had taken Dominick up on his offer, slyly inserting that it was the least his lordship could do, as the man seemed curiously reluctant to lift his own rifle in defense of his countrymen. Still, Frey had insisted that he be allowed to use the land as a training ground for his civilian militia as well. He had demanded full use of the barn to store weapons, and had gone so far as to command everyone connected with the militia to meet at the farm this very morning, prepared to spend the day drilling and engaging in target shooting meant to improve the aim of men still more accustomed to plowing fields than firing rifles.

Dominick couldn't refuse without losing the chance to have trained troops residing on his property, close by Pleasant Hill if an attack should come. At the same time, he also couldn't deny Bryna's request that she and the other women of his household be a part of the group of wives who would prepare food for the men without worrying about a small mutiny in his own "ranks."

Bryna smiled secretively as she thought about how very good she had been, how obedient, so that to deny her the treat of being able to see April Turner and the other women could only seem petty on his part. And they would have a wonderful day!

Mary Catherine, dressed in one of her favorite gowns, a pure white creation that flattered her sun-kissed complexion and vibrant red hair, sat in the back of the wagon now, playing a tune on her flute, the lively music reflecting her childish good mood. Her tantrums had grown fewer and more widely spaced. Bryna worked with her daily, trying to coax her into saying something, anything, that would show that there was some hope she would one day speak again. So far, all she had overheard was Mary Catherine's rusty humming as she rocked Miss Arabella Thistlewaite in her small arms, but the child lapsed into stony silence immediately if anyone approached.

Alice, no longer afraid to see her parents, sat beside the child, tucking Mary Catherine's collar down neatly and occasionally pulling up the hem of her own gown to look at her new half boots, which had been specially made by the shoemaker. The sole of the left, on Bryna's orders, was a good two inches thicker than that of the right in order to minimize the young girl's limp. The half boots had bolstered Alice's self-confidence no end, so that she was on her way to the farm with her cheeks flushed prettily, eager to see young Willie Traxell, who had shyly asked if she was coming to the "party" today.

Lucretia was also in the wagon, holding her hands out

protectively each time the wheels found another rut, to guard the baskets of food she had risen at five that morning to prepare for the men. By the time Bryna had awakened, the entire house had been saturated with the luscious aromas of fresh-baked breads, fruit-filled pies, and the corn cakes the woman had carefully slapped into shape with her large, pink-palmed hands before allowing Mary Catherine to place a thumbprint in the center of each one.

Only Lucas was a reluctant participant in the plans for the day, caught between being the only living soul left in the stoutly shuttered Pleasant Hill and spending the day watching a gaggle of rude, boisterous louts drinking up all the beer he and Lokwelend had brewed in the springhouse.

Bryna looked to her left, past Lucas's frowning face, and smiled as she caught Dominick's eye as he rode beside the wagon on his huge bay mare. Her husband was dressed in his comfortable deerskins, the collar of the pale blue shirt she had sewn for him visible above his fringed jacket. Tied snugly around his waist was the multicolored sash she had fashioned for him herself.

He looked so at home in these clothes, much more so than Philip, who was wearing deerskins for the first time, and obviously still debating whether he was comfortable or conspicuous.

Yet, for all Philip's uneasiness, he seemed determined to become a part of New Eden. He had received a letter from his grandfather just three days ago, a terse communication demanding he return to Playden Court at once. He had read it to Dominick and Bryna at the dinner table before wadding it into a ball and asking Lucas to please dispose of it in the bucket where all the slops for the hogs were stored. "Let others of my age and position trip around Italy and Greece for years, gazing at ruins," he had told them, winking at Bryna. "I much prefer seeing the beginning, and not the end, of a civilization."

The only one missing from their small party was Lokwelend, who had stood on the front steps of Pleasant Hill, both Gilhooley and a rifle by his side, waving them on their way before moving off in his familiar, relaxed lope for a day in the woods. He would much rather hunt rabbits, he'd told Dominick as he assisted Bryna onto the wagon seat, than spend the day being one, which might be the case if one of the militia saw him carrying a basket of Lucretia's food and mistook him for thirty war-painted warriors.

Bryna refused to think of such things now, about the threat that hung over all their heads, preferring to concentrate on the festivities ahead, and on seeing April and Henrietta. She looked forward to watching as Alice flirted with her Willie, and perhaps having the chance for a dance or two with her husband when Samuel Clark brought out his fiddle after dinner and played for them.

The broad, open expanse in front of the Cassidy barn was already populated by more than four dozen people by the time Lucas pulled the wagon into the clearing. Children chased each other, giggling and pretending to be wild Indians, while mothers stood in small groups, gossiping, or fussed over babies lying on blankets under the trees. Both confused-looking farmers and brightly clad red-coated troops marched up and down in formation, the militia looking more like a drunken snake as Benjamin Rudolph barked out orders and Newton Frey stood with a mug in his hand, cursing all of them for dolts and drunkards.

"And a fine time will be had by all," Dominick whispered as he helped Bryna alight from the wagon. He lifted her hand for a kiss, then reached behind her to take hold of Mary Catherine and swing her high above his head before putting her down and giving her backside a playful swat as she scampered off to join in the fun.

"Why, my lord," Bryna shot back, "are you disappointed, then? Perhaps you would rather be at Court, bowing and primping and eating from silver plate?"

"I'd rather be upstairs with you at Pleasant Hill, locked in our rooms, my dear lady wife, spending the day wrapped around you, the two of us—"

"Lord Dominick! How good of you to grace us with your presence!"

Bryna could feel Dominick stiffening as Lieutenant Frey joined them, his smile wide, although it did not reach his slate gray eyes. She watched as the man tugged at his left ear, proving his lie. He wasn't at all happy to see Dominick. He probably wished her husband at the bottom of the deepest ocean. Where, she was all but sure but could never prove, he had sent her father two nights before the *Eagle* docked in Philadelphia.

The Devil's own spawn, that's what her father had called Renton Frey, and Bryna believed more in that statement with every passing day. Not that she'd say anything to Dominick—not about anything she might think about Lieutenant Renton Frey. That was all behind her now. All voicing her suspicions could do now would be to place her husband in danger.

"Lieutenant," Dominick said shortly, turning to offer his hand to the man. "Bryna, why don't you go with Lucretia and show her where she might put her baskets. And I believe I see April Turner waving to you from over there."

Bryna was reluctant to leave her husband's side, especially as Lieutenant Frey was looking Dominick up and down, his smile bordering closely on snide as he took in the deerskin leggings, the moccasins. "In a minute, Dominick," she told him, staring at the lieutenant, just daring him to say anything.

Which turned out to be a total waste of time, as the lieutenant immediately proved, saying, "I have yet to see this savage you harbor on your property, my lord, although I have often observed his influence. Your rather strange clothing, the rumors I've heard as to your coddling of Lenape trash, your unwillingness to pledge your rifle to His Royal Majesty's service. I can only wonder if you have not so much offered your land to my men as you have presented it as a sort of bribe meant to keep you safe from an investigation concerning your loyalty."

"And does all this wondering keep you awake nights, Lieutenant," Dominick responded, "or are you just happiest sitting in Rudolph's common room to all hours, drinking and gaming? When you aren't waving your authority about by bullying helpless women and children, that is."

Frey's eyes narrowed dangerously, and Bryna instinctively pressed a protective hand to her belly. "You're the one, aren't you? High-and-mighty Lord Dominick Crown. You're the one who wrote to my commanding officer, crying and whimpering about how unfair I am, what a bloody bully I am. But it didn't work, did it, my lord? I was allowed to send away the malcontents and obtain new troops who have already seen action and are eager to fight again. And fight, we will, my lord, the first moment we are given provocation—and then we'll rid this countryside of these heathens once and for all. Including your own personal savage. You can rest assured of *that!*"

With a razor-sharp salute that was more insulting than proper, the lieutenant cleanly turned on his heels and strode off, returning to his men.

"That man positively makes my teeth ache," Bryna said, laying a hand on Dominick's arm, "for all he'd never think to attack you save with his mouth or from the rear, when your back was turned."

"Although he does seem to be gaining confidence in his own conscquence, doesn't he?" Dominick asked as they walked up the hill, arm in arm, to a vantage point in front of the barn where others had gathered to watch the drilling. "And he has just explained his actions of these past months. He's being deliberately provocative, hoping to cause an incident that will send the Lenape down on our heads, wanting blood, just so that he has an excuse to exterminate them."

"Can he really hurt Lokwelend?"

"He can think about it," Dominick told her. "But he knows I have his commandant's ear, so I doubt that he'd be that stupid. Besides, I'd kill the bastard without flinching if he or his troops so much as looked in Lokwelend's direction, and he knows that, too. And now, wife, why don't you go sce how much little Henrietta has grown while I chase Jonah Newton and his friends out of the barn. The damned fool has gonc in there with his pipe. The man is not only an idiot, he's a menace."

Bryna spent the next two hours with the women of New Eden, smiling weakly as, one by one, they described the agonies of childbed to her, speaking of breech births and of prolonged labors and even of poor Hilde Traxell, who "near died of childbed fever with her last, you know. Never been quite the same since, and won't let poor Johann near her, lest he put another baby in her and kill her outright."

She helped Lucretia serve food, and braided Mary Catherine's long hair into two thick coils when the child came to her, flushed and overheated from playing with the other children.

She ignored Truda Rudolph's deliberately loud laments as to how she and her "Benjie" were being worn to a frazzle, trying their best to keep their heads above water because "that bastard Crown and his high-nosed bitch" stole their custom as well as their beloved daughter.

She watched indulgently as Alice and young Willie Traxell walked past side by side, their blond hair bright in the warm sunlight, their fingers brushing, not saying anything, but a world of words in their young eyes. *Poor Philip,* she thought, smiling, *it would appear you've been replaced in Alice's affections.*

At last the troops were released from their drilling, and the militia collapsed in untidy heaps on the grass, to be served mugs of beer and plates of food by their wives. Bryna sat on a thick blanket beside her husband, comfortable in the shade thrown by the huge barn her uncle had built, and laughed as Philip allowed the infant Henrietta to tug on his aristocratic nose and stick her drool-wet fingers into his mouth. "Making another conquest, are you, Philip?" she asked, laughing all the more when the young man grimaced and pulled a face at her.

"I keep trying to remember that your nephew will one day be the Marquess of Playden, Dominick," Bryna said as Philip lifted Henrietta high into the air, the child kicking and squealing in delight, "but he makes it difficult. I believe we may have to boost him onto a ship with a rifle in his back in order to ever get him to leave."

"Yes. He does seem to be happy here, doesn't he, repeatedly putting off his plans to tour all of the colonies?"

Dominick pulled up a handful of sweet grass and let it slip through his fingers, caught by the breeze that had begun to stiffen as the morning had slid into late afternoon. "We'll have rain before long. Have you had enough of socializing, pet, or are you waiting for the fiddle playing to begin? I could do with a dance or two, I believe, even if we do get a bit damp on the ride home."

Bryna opened her mouth to answer, only to be cut off by the sound of a woman's shrill scream. The metallic clicking of dozens of rifles being cocked in anticipation of an immediate attack had barely had time to be recognized for what it was when another female voice cried out: "Fire! *Fire!*"

Bryna turned to look in the direction everyone was suddenly pointing, even as Dominick leapt to his feet and began coolly issuing orders for the women to find their children and the men to grab anything they could, blankets, cloths from the tables, their uniform jackets—anything — and follow him as he ran toward the barn.

Smoke appeared just inside the main doors to the building, and flames fed by the stiff breeze already licked around the outside of the loft window. The loft, home to remnants of last year's straw, and dry as tinder, seemed to turn into a solid block of flames in an instant, so that they had to enter the barn to fight the blaze. Dominick and Philip raced inside at the head of the mass of shouting men even as Lieutenant Frey ordered his troops to remain where they were, as the barn was already as good as lost.

"Bloody coward!" Bryna exploded angrily, then wasted no more time on the man as she hiked up her skirts and began searching for Mary Catherine, who had to be frightened out of her wits by all the excitement. Did nothing good ever come from her visits to this place? "Lucas!" she called out, seeing the servant standing beside Lucretia, looking as helpless as a child himself as he held his smashed spectacles in his hands, his face screwed up as he tried to focus on the sound of her voice.

Bryna tugged on his sleeve, shouting to be heard above

the screams of mothers calling to their children, the crackle and pop of the fire, the shouts of the men. "Lucas! Where is Mary Kate? Have you seen her?"

"My lady?" Lucas held up his hand to show her the damage his spectacles had sustained, then shook his head. "I got knocked down by that Newton fellow as he ran out of the barn just before someone saw the fire. Broke my spectacles, my lady. I can't see much of anything!"

"I ain't seen her neither, ma'am," Lucretia said, wringing her hands. "And her not able to call out to us, neither. Poor baby! But she must be close hereabouts, for she's not the kind to wander. Found her once, earlier on, in the barn and scooted her out. But she wouldn't go back in there, would she?"

Terror, swift and cold, chilled Bryna to her marrow. "Oh, God. Oh, sweet Jesus! Mary Kate! *Mary Kate!*" Picking up her skirts once more, Bryna made one more circle of the women and children huddled some distance from the fire, nearly blinded by her tears and the smoke that rolled down the hill at her, propelled by a twisting wind the heat of the fire had created on its own.

"I thought I saw her going into the barn," April Turner said, touching Bryna's shoulder in obvious sympathy. "Alice and her young man disappeared inside a little bit ago, probably to be alone, you know. Mary Catherine must have followed after them. You should look for Alice."

"Yes, yes, of course! She's with Alice! Thank you, April!" Bryna set off once more, calling for Alice, feeling as if entire hours had passed even though she knew it had only been a few minutes since that first warning scream.

But Alice was nowhere to be found.

Braving the crush of soot-blackened men who were, one by one, abandoning the fight to save the barn, Bryna threaded her way back up the hill, still calling for Alice and Mary Catherine.

And then she saw it. She saw it in the hands of the young boy who had been teasing Mary Catherine earlier in the day, pulling at her pigtails and tormenting her in the way only little boys can do. The boy was looking toward the barn, his expression one of guilt and fear, tears running down his pale cheeks—and he was holding Mary Catherine's flute.

"Sweet Virgin—*no!*" Without thought, without another moment's hesitation, Bryna ran into the inferno, holding a hand to her mouth as she then turned to her right and fumbled with the latch to the door that opened into the onetime home of the Cassidy family.

The fire hadn't reached this far as yet, but the smoke had, so that Bryna could barely see six inches in front of her. "Mary Kate!" she called out, coughing as she sucked in smoke, then called out again. "Mary Kate! Mary Kate, where are you? *Answer me!*"

She was totally disoriented, unable to remember where Eileen Cassidy's bed was, which wall it sat against. All she could do was drop to her hands and knees in an attempt to avoid the worst of the smoke, and keep calling her cousin's name, all the while knowing the child couldn't answer her.

Mary Catherine didn't have her flute. She had lost her voice the day her mother had died. She had been silent as a wee mummy, hiding beneath the bed until Dominick had discovered her, doing as her mother had told her. Not moving. Not making a sound so that nobody could find her.

Never again making a sound. *Yes!* Yes, that was it! Why hadn't she realized it before now?

"Mary Kate! Listen to me!" Bryna put down her head, gasping for breath, then called out once more. "You were a good girl, Mary Kate. A good, good girl! You didn't talk. You didn't make a sound. Just like Mama wanted. But now you must talk! Mama wants you to talk again. Mama wants you to talk so you'll be safe. Talk to me, Mary Kate! *Tell me where you are!*"

Bryna pressed her hands to her mouth, stifling her sobs, hearing roof beams beginning, one by one, to crash onto the stout ceiling above her. They were running out of time. The silence that had kept Mary Catherine safe was now going to be the death of her. The death of both of them, for Bryna wouldn't leave her. Couldn't leave her.

"Bryna—for the love of God, where are you! *Bryna!*"

"I'm here! Dominick! I'm here!" Bryna cried out, reaching up a hand to him, hoping he was behind her. It sounded as if he was behind her. The smoke was so thick. The heat so overpowering.

She felt him take her hand, roughly pulling her to her feet, and she began to fight him like a mad thing. She had to stay here. She had to find Mary Catherine. "No! Mary Kate's in here, Dominick! Under the bed. I'm sure of it. I just can't find the bed! Mary Kate! Mary Kate! Mama wants you to *talk!*"

"Mama? *Mama!*"

"Dominick! Did you hear that!"

"I didn't hear anything," he answered, shoving her toward the door and into Philip's waiting arms. "Take her the hell out of here!" he ordered sharply.

Bryna inhaled on a sob, reeling with both her exhaustion and the hope that she was not just dreaming the sound of Mary Catherine's voice. "Dominick, no! I *heard* her! She's in here! She's under the bed! I know I heard her!"

Philip lifted Bryna into his arms and ran with her as fire fell like rain from the loft above their heads, ran with her out of the burning barn, depositing her on the ground and then dropping down beside her.

She fought to rise again, to race back into the barn, but Philip held her fast. Her whole world was inside that burning building, and she couldn't even pray. Couldn't find the words. She screamed Dominick's name, Mary Catherine's name, over and over again—but only silently, inside her head, for she was now coughing so hard, she began to retch.

She was going to lose it all. Again. Oh, dear God, not again!

The sound of another crashing beam brought a whimpering sob to her lips and she raised her head and rubbed at her stinging eyes, trying to see her husband, once more fighting for Philip to release her arms so that she could run back into the burning building.

"There he is!" someone cried out, and a loud cheer went up as Dominick appeared as if out of a living wall of flame,

Mary Kate's small form clutched in a fierce, protective embrace. "He's got her!"

Bryna held out trembling arms, and Dominick tenderly placed Mary Catherine's limp body in them, wiping at the child's blackened face with the equally blackened skirt of her once pristine white gown. For long moments Bryna believed the child to be dead, but then she began to cough, and retch, clearing her lungs of smoke.

"Sweet Christ, thank you," Bryna whispered, hugging the child to her, rocking her as if she were an infant, showering her small face with kisses. She held the crying child for long minutes, not reacting even as a loud, long crescendo signaled the complete collapse of the interior of the barn her uncle had built with his own two hands. Only its two stone end walls remained, blackened and empty as the fire slowly smothered itself and a thick plume of sooty smoke rose toward the sky.

She gazed up at Dominick, feeling the first drops of rain on her face, not knowing whether to cry or to laugh, her emotions tangled between fear at what had almost happened and joy that he and Mary Catherine were both safe. She looked around her, noticing that Philip was no longer beside her, that no one was near, and that there was no more shouting, but only an eerie quiet broken by the sizzle of raindrops against the smoldering ruins.

"Dominick? What's wrong?" His eyes were so sad, his expression so grim behind a mask of soot, that Bryna didn't try to keep hold of Mary Catherine when Lucretia finally took the child from her, to begin washing her little face with a wet cloth.

Dominick dropped to his haunches beside her. He took her hand, squeezing it tightly, then looked to his left, to where a dozen people stood silent while Hilde and Johann Traxell knelt on the ground, holding each other as they wept over the crumpled body of their oldest son, Willie.

"Oh, sweet Mary, no," Bryna breathed softly, looking to Dominick so that he could tell her that Alice was safe, that at least Alice was just fine. Just fine.

But Dominick remained silent as he gathered Bryna

against his chest, attempting to shield her face as a stone-faced Philip Crown slowly walked over to where the Traxells mourned their son. A large bundle was gently cradled in his arms.

Before Bryna fainted, before a merciful God could give her shelter behind a concealing veil of darkness, she saw the horribly burned arm that swung limply as Philip reverently bent to put his burden down . . . and recognized the thick-soled half boot visible below the hem of the blanket.

*Envy is a pain of mind that
successful men cause their neighbors.*
— Onasander

CHAPTER 15

NEW EDEN TRULY WAS A BEAUTIFUL PLACE. GREEN AND LUSH AS
Ireland. The sky high and wide and deeply blue. Almost as
blue as the memory of Alice Rudolph's eyes. The clouds,
nearly as white as the little gown Mary Catherine had worn
the day of the fire. The birdsong bright and cheery, the smell
of the air, fresh, clean, the acrid stink of smoke washed away
by two solid days and nights of rain.

And Bryna Cassidy Crown, walking alone in the Pleasant
Hill gardens as the sun reflected off small droplets still
clinging to leaves, to crushed stone, loved every rock, every
tall, nodding wildflower visible in the near distance, every
blade of grass, every bird, every tree. In her pain, she loved
it. In her happiness, in her sorrow, whether she took of this
land or it took from her, she loved this place.

And now she was destroying it. Destroying everything she
touched, everything and everyone she loved.

Because she was the Bright Fire. Lokwelend had been
wrong. She had not come to conquer, but to destroy.

In her stubbornness, she had sent Lokwelend and

Pematalli off on a fruitless search for Brighid, which had cost Lokwelend his children.

That same stubbornness, that selfish pigheadedness, had now cost the lives of young Willie Traxell and poor, sweet Alice. If she had only done as Dominick had asked, Alice would have been safe in Philadelphia, not being laid to rest this afternoon, never to live out the promise of her youth. Willie Traxell would not have been in that barn at all, attempting to steal a few precious minutes alone with a pretty young girl.

Mary Catherine had nearly perished in the fire as well. Philip had been injured, a livid burn across his back where a falling beam had hit him a glancing blow as he fought the blaze. Dominick had burns on both hands, his blistered skin paining him so much that, although he did not complain, he moaned in his sleep, his rest disturbed by both his scorched flesh and the nightmares that caused him to wake, suddenly, calling out, "Bryna! Where are you? *Answer me!*"

For a day and a night, Bryna had believed she would even lose her baby, so sick was she from the smoke she had ingested; her body racked by incessant coughing, violent bouts of nausea and vomiting. Dominick had held her head in his bandaged hands, supporting her as she leaned over a chamber pot . . . crying and retching and coughing until she could not find the strength to stand on her own . . . so racked with guilt that she hadn't spoken a word, not to anyone, since seeing Alice's body being laid on the grass . . .

"Itah!"

Bryna closed her eyes, not wishing to turn around. Not wishing to see Lokwelend. Not wishing him to see her, or the guilt in her eyes. She knew now what *Itah* meant. *Good be to you.* But there was no good, not anymore. Didn't Lokwelend know that? He should. He was the one who had seen it, seen the truth long ago, in his dream of her.

"You carry the world on your shoulders, Bright Fire," Lokwelend said, tipping up her chin with one long, dark finger, so that she had no choice but to look at him, see his face painted black for Alice in the Lenape ritual of mourning. No choice but to see her own sadness reflected in his all-knowing eyes. He held such majesty in his bearing, in his ornamental dress, the beadwork on his fringed jacket, the eagle feathers that dressed his long, iron gray hair. To Bryna, in this instant, he seemed as regal as any English king, as powerful as any ancient god of lore.

But even he, in all his wisdom, all his majesty, couldn't help her. Not this time. Not now. "It's my fault, Lokwelend. It's all my fault."

"We thought as much. Crown has come to me in his concern. He has told me of your sadness. But this world of sorrows must be shared. The burden is too heavy for one so young. You must lay a portion of it down, for it is not yours alone to carry. We are none of us without blame, for we are all born without the answers, and must spend our lives in seeking them, often down the wrong paths."

Bryna felt her chin begin to tremble, the Lenape's gentle sympathy bringing her to tears that were already too close to the surface. "I was stupid! I didn't know—I didn't understand. But you at least knew there would be a tragedy, didn't you, Lokwelend? You were the one who said it would come to this. That I was the herald of terrible things to come. That—that things could end badly."

"This is true, Bright Fire. I saw the smoke, the fire. I heard the cries of the dying, the tears of those left behind. It is begun. Worse is yet to come. But I was wrong to think that you would be the cause of all that has happened, all that will happen. You have brought the trouble with you, but you are not the trouble. Only if you falter, Bright Fire, only if you give in to sorrow, to despair, can you hurt Crown, hurt yourself, hurt the child you carry beneath your heart."

Bryna shook her head, unable to understand. "How can you be so kind? It's because of me that Pematalli left, taking your daughter with him. If I hadn't demanded that someone be sent to search for Brighid, Pematalli wouldn't have seen what he saw beyond the mountains. He wouldn't have said those terrible things to you."

Lokwelend held up his hand, and Bryna fell silent.

"Pematalli does what Pematalli must do," he told her as, together, they walked along the paths through the gardens. "If he had stayed, the result would have been the same. It is not in my son to believe that there is no future for the young Lenape except to move west, always west, until the Lenape are once more facing the sunset over the water. I have no fear for Pematalli, as his spirit is strong and he has freely chosen his path. He is Pematalli, which means Always There. And so he will ever be, Bright Fire. This, too, I have seen in my dreams. No matter how the *shawanuk* try, no matter how many brave Lenape die or are forever scattered to the four winds, Always There will endure as a symbol of our ancient people. This will be the legacy of my son."

Bryna stood on tiptoe and kissed the old Indian's cheek. "You must be the wisest man in the world, Lokwelend. I only wish I had your patience, your belief. But Alice is dead. Willie Traxell is dead. Smoke and fire, Lokwelend. Just as you said. Smoke and fire. It may have been Jonah Newton's pipe, his or one of his cronies', as Dominick suspects, but it was my fault."

"You did not cause the fire to start, as you did not make this Jonah Newton a fool or place the two young ones inside the barn. This was their choice, their destiny. As I have said, we all are born unknowing, and sometimes take wrong paths on our way to knowledge. I was wrong. I did not read my dreams correctly. Only lately has all become clear to me. You are the herald, yes, but another will be the instrument of destruction. You brought Walks With Death with you from your far country, Bright Fire, and that is all you have done. I did not at first see him, but now he is here. Now it is clear. And now it begins."

Bryna shook her head, trying to understand. "He? I don't think I—*Frey!*" She felt a quickening in her belly, as if her unborn child had started at the sound of the lieutenant's name. "He was on the *Eagle* with Papa and me. Lokwelend, is that what you're saying? That Renton Frey is the one who will cause all the troubles you've seen?"

"He is Walks With Death, Bright Fire, as you know but cannot prove, for his evil has already touched your life, before he ever set foot on this land. You hate him even as you fear him."

Bryna blinked back tears. "Then you know, Lokwelend? I've thought so from the first, but how do you *know?* I was alone when the ship docked, with no one to listen, no one to care. Nothing would have changed that. So I came here, to tell my uncle Daniel, to gain his help, and found that I had lost even more. God, if I could only prove—"

"The proof comes in looking at him. Death hangs from him like rotted flesh. His poison, like that of the root of the mayapple, destroys all who eat of it. His evil lays barren the ground on which he treads. You came to us to conquer, yes, but to conquer our hearts. And you have done so. He comes to kill. Women will weep and rend their clothing. Children will see their fathers fall, and perish with them. The long houses will empty, and be burned to the ground. The world as I know it will end. I have seen all this, Bright Fire, and I cannot change it. But you must endure, for in you lies the hope."

Bryna's head was spinning as she struggled to take in all that the old Indian told her. "But *how*, Lokwelend? How will I do this? Are you saying that it is up to me to destroy Frey?"

"We will speak of this no more, Bright Fire," the Indian interrupted, pointing back down the path, to show her that Dominick was approaching and would soon be within earshot. "And you will not tell Crown. Without this proof you spoke of, he could do nothing, and that would pain him, for he would feel he has failed you. But if you were to know for certain, Crown would have to think of his honor and slay Walks With Death. This could be the end of him as well, as *shawanuk* laws do not allow for revenge, leaving that to their God. You have conquered Crown's heart, and made it your own. You carry within you the seeds of tomorrow. Protect what is your own, Bright Fire, and let the dead rest with the dead. You cannot change what is past, or what is coming."

Bryna looked down the path, at her husband who was dressed so somberly, a wide black band pinned to the sleeve of his dark jacket, his expression caught between sorrow and concern. He looked old as time, as young and vulnerable as a child. And her heart squeezed tight in pain, in love.

Everything in its time. Isn't that what Lokwelend had been saying? And now it was time. Time to take her husband's hand and begin the long walk to the Cassidy farm behind the wagon bearing Alice Rudolph's mortal remains. It was time once again to put the past away . . . time to let the dead rest with the dead . . . and for the rest of them to get on with this strange business of living.

"Stay with us, Lokwelend," she begged quietly before Dominick came within earshot. "No matter what happens, please stay with us. We'll need your calm counsel."

"I will stay for you, and for Pematalli. I will stay until it is over, as that is my destiny," he answered calmly. "Then I will go."

Alice's funeral had been over for hours when Mary Catherine appeared in the gardens just at twilight, holding Miss Arabella Thistlewaite tight in her thin arms. She approached Bryna and pressed her small, solemn face against her skirts. Bryna reached down to brush a stray lock of hair back from the child's cheek, unable to find the words to comfort her, to ease the aching loneliness Alice's death had left in the child's life, in all their lives.

She had hoped that she hadn't been mistaken. She'd prayed that some small good could have come out of the tragedy that day at the barn. That God had taken, yes, but would give something in return. But Mary Catherine hadn't spoken a word since Bryna had sworn she'd heard the child call out for her mama.

She had to have imagined it, hoped so hard to hear it that she had believed the child had understood, and had answered her.

Dominick had made her promise not to push the child, not to press her to talk, and Bryna fought the impulse to prod at her now, knowing that this was not the time to look for miracles. The miracle, their heavenly gift, if there was one to be found in all of this, was that they hadn't buried Mary Catherine today beside her family.

At least now Bryna felt sure she knew why Mary Catherine didn't speak. Eileen must have made her promise not to, believing the child's silence might keep her safe as she lay hidden under the bed. By remaining silent, Mary Catherine was only obeying her beloved mother's final order, keeping her last promise. With this new knowledge, this possible reason to guide her, Bryna hoped she would one day be able to convince Mary Catherine that her mother had released her from that promise.

Bryna kept her arm around the child's shoulders as she walked to a nearby bench. They both sat down, facing the view of trees and sky and the slowly setting sun. How Alice had loved to watch the sun set.

Slowly, silently, Bryna began to cry. For still there were no words. There couldn't be any words. Only this silent communion between woman and child, sitting here together, mourning the loss of their dear friend.

Bryna allowed the tears to flow unchecked down her face, not wanting to move in order to reach in her pocket and retrieve her handkerchief, not wanting Mary Catherine to know she was crying.

But after a few minutes, she felt the doll being laid into her arms, a gift from the child obviously meant to ease her grief. A deep sigh escaped Bryna's lips as she clutched the doll against her breast, rocking slowly back and forth. She closed her eyes against the pain racking her, until she felt Mary Catherine's fingers gently wiping at her tears.

"Don't cry, Brynnie," the child said quietly, leaning into Bryna's breasts, pressing her head beside the doll's. "Don't cry."

Bryna lowered her face into the child's warm curls and sobbed.

"Five handkerchiefs, red. Five blue. Six aprons, plain. Twelve silver thimbles. A half dozen large tin funnels. Do you have that, Dominick? Good. And now, to the foodstuffs. Two sacks brown sugar candy. Three sacks white. Is there licorice? I specially ordered licorice, as Mary Kate is so partial to it."

Dominick looked around him, to the boxes that littered the floor and counters, finally seeing Mary Catherine standing off by herself in a corner, a finger to her lips, urging him to silence. She had one hand behind her back, and there was a suspicious bulge in her left cheek.

"I think you can rest assured that the licorice is around here somewhere, pet," Dominick said, winking at the child. Mary Catherine grinned, then turned on her heels and ran out into the sunshine, her small hand drawn into a fist around what had to be at least a half dozen more of her special candies.

She didn't say much, their little Mary Catherine, having grown so accustomed to communicating without words, but he was sure she'd be chattering like a magpie before the first winter snow. Bryna, his wife of the strong will and brave heart, had gotten the world to turn for her again. Nothing would take the hurt of losing Alice from any of them, but Dominick thanked God every day for the gift of Mary Catherine's voice, which seemed to have given Bryna the will to move on.

He smiled at his wife now as she looked up from her list, blowing at a long, curling strand of vibrant red hair that had somehow fallen loose from the twisted topknot meant to keep her cool in the heat of this unusually hot, humid early October day. "Now," he teased, "if we're done checking to make sure everything's here and we haven't been roundly cheated by Mr. Hunsicker, perhaps you'll pay the poor man and let him be on his way?"

"I would never accuse our friend of being even the slightest bit dishonest, Dominick," she told him, rising from her chair and going behind the counter, to pick up the pouch holding Mr. Hunsicker's payment. "However, I have to be sure my order is complete. It's a long time between deliveries, and I don't like to disappoint our customers."

She smiled brightly as she held out the pouch and Mr. Hunsicker took it, doffing his hat to her as he prepared to leave—probably to go no farther than the common room located on the other side of the hallway. "Thank you, kind sir, for being so prompt with my deliveries. I know the ladies of New Eden will be delighted with the fine selection of buttons you have brought me, just as their husbands will appreciate the pigtail tobacco. Now, here's my list for your next delivery. Six weeks from today, I believe, Mr. Hunsicker? No longer!"

Mr. Hunsicker's head bobbed up and down like a cork tied to a line just bitten on by a six-pound catfish. "Yes, ma'am, yes, ma'am!" he agreed, hefting the pouch a time or two, then sticking it in his pocket. "Seein' as how you're m'best customer this side of Easton, ma'am, I wouldn't wish to disappoint you. You sure you ain't wantin' any of them fine feathers, ma'am? Got me white ones, blue ones, even those ostrich ones. Ladies in Philadelphia are snatchin' them up fast as I can get 'em. For their hats, you know. I've got a whole box outside, in one of m'wagons."

"Thank you, no. Strange as it may seem, there just isn't much call for ostrich feathers here in New Eden," Bryna said, smiling at Dominick as they shared in the private joke. Mr. Hunsicker had been trying to foist those same ostrich feathers on her on each of his last three visits. "But please don't give up, Mr. Hunsicker. Civilization may reach us any time now. Why, just last week Elijah Kester's wife publicly berated poor old Samuel Clark for spitting in the street."

Dominick laughed as Mr. Hunsicker shook his large head as he retreated across the hall to the tavern side of the building, obviously knowing he had been bested again by the little Irish lady with the soul of a penny-pinching English shopkeeper.

"I suppose, as long as you've given permission for Harold to leave the store and go to the taproom, where he is undoubtedly drinking up all our profits, I'm the one who is going to have to put all of this away?"

"Harold works hard for us, both here in the store and in the taproom. We're lucky to have him."

"Of course we are. I go down on my knees each night, thanking God for our grand employee. Why, the man is a prince among men—as long as someone watches him every moment," Dominick answered brightly as Bryna returned to her chair, picking up the small white gown she had been embroidering in neat little stitches. She had been sewing almost constantly these past weeks, her hands never idle, her brain never unoccupied by lists of chores or plans for the house, her gardens—anything, he supposed, that would keep her from thinking about Alice. About what had happened to Alice.

Like Lokwelend, whose Lenape culture forbade those of any sensibility from mentioning the names of the deceased for fear of upsetting those who loved them, whenever it became impossible to avoid speaking of the dead girl, Bryna now referred to her as Beautiful Song, a sad smile lighting her face each time she said the words.

And in the evenings, before the sun finally set behind the mountains, Bryna often sat in the gardens with Lokwelend. They kept their backs to the house, the two of them gazing out toward the west, lost in their own thoughts, the unspoken communion between the old Indian and the young woman eloquent beyond words. Their compatibility was eerie, that's what it was, but Dominick refused to interject himself into their growing friendship, knowing that Bryna had chosen her own way to heal, and her own physician.

All Dominick could do was wait, and watch, and pray that, with time, Bryna would be his again. Which was why he was here today, knee-deep in the role of shopkeeper's apprentice, when he had a thousand things to do back at Pleasant Hill. He wouldn't be anywhere else.

"Put everything away? Nonsense," Bryna told Dominick now, taking up her needle. "I think we should leave everything just as it is. The pots mixed with bolts of linen, the candlesticks cheek by jowl with those fine gentlemen's hats, the fishing hooks and Dutch quills sharing—"

"I believe I comprehend the idea, Bryna, thank you," Dominick said, picking up a large crate and carrying it over to the floor-to-ceiling shelves, to begin unloading varying sizes of glass jars the women of New Eden would use to store vegetables for the winter.

"I could do all of that, you know," Bryna said rather pettishly. Dominick turned around, unsurprised to see his wife's bottom lip thrust forth in a pout. It had been three weeks since Alice's funeral and her own illness, and he knew he had been treating Bryna as if she were made of the most delicate crystal. But he couldn't help himself.

She *was* delicate. And precious, so very precious to him. More precious to him than all of Pleasant Hill, all of Playden Court, and all of the crown jewels of England together. She had frightened him with her illness after the fire, when he had thought for the space of a day and a night that he might lose her. No matter how Lokwelend assured him that she was growing stronger every day, he could not forget the panic he had felt when he had taken a break from fighting the fire only to have Lucretia tell him that Miss Bryna had run into the burning barn.

And so, as he had been doing for these last three weeks, he lied. "I told you, pet. There is nothing for me to do right now at Pleasant Hill. The corn won't grow any faster if I stare at it all day, and the laborers are all competent men. Besides, like you, I rather enjoy these days here in the village, counting our customers as they grow to rely on us more and more, and ignore Truda Rudolph. If it weren't for Newton and Traxell and a few of the others, along with Frey and his men, all of them drinking everything but ink as they warm Benjamin's chairs, the Rudolphs would have been forced to close long since. Not that I want any of them here, you understand."

"And not that they'd come," Bryna answered, frowning. "Philip says that Walks—that Lieutenant Frey is telling anyone who will listen that Lord Dominick Crown is a coward and a near-traitor, and more than half-Indian into the bargain. If we don't stop encouraging the Lenape to trade here, we may end up losing the custom of everyone in New Eden, no matter how good our stock or how unreasonably low our prices. But that isn't the point. What I do worry about is what Lieutenant Frey might do if—"

Dominick placed the last jar on the shelf and threw the carton onto the floor, the sound of wood hitting on wood echoing throughout the store. "Bryna, we've been over this and over this. Before we came here, the Lenape were self-sufficient. We gave them our God, our tools, our customs, our way of life. Now they're dependent on us. I don't like it, Lokwelend doesn't like it, but it's a fact. The hunting grounds have been plowed under, the animals have disappeared—damn it all, there's barely a beaver left on this side of the mountains. Our trouble, if it comes, will come from beyond the mountains, from the Indians closer to the frontier. The Lenape who live here aren't going to attack us. They need us too much. And since when do you care what Lieutenant Frey thinks of any of us? I thought you couldn't stand the man."

Bryna avoided Dominick's eyes, a sure sign that what he would hear next would have little to do with the truth. "I don't care what he thinks, really. But he could be dangerous. He could insist that you join the militia. He could make you a part of the horrible things he's doing to the Lenape."

"He could try," Dominick said quietly, pushing boxes and barrels to one side as he crossed to Bryna's chair, holding out his hands to her. "That's enough doom and gloom for one morning, wife. And enough shopkeeping as well. I'm all for a stroll, if you don't mind. The work will wait for us."

Bryna laid down her sewing and allowed Dominick to take her hands. "Well, I did want to stop in on Mr. Quimby, to see if Lucas's new shoes are ready. It should cheer him no end if they are, perhaps even making him forget for a few moments that his new spectacles won't arrive for at least another two weeks. He feels quite lost without them."

"Yes," Dominick agreed, calling for Harold to watch out for customers before pushing open the door leading to the dirt street that was the main thoroughfare through New Eden. "But he has developed the most distinctive squint, reminding me of one of the headmasters of my checkered youth, as a matter of fact."

"Someday you must tell me more of this checkered youth of yours, Dominick. Unless my sensibilities would be too shocked by such tales, that is." Bryna leaned on his arm as they began walking along the otherwise deserted street, her head tipped against his shoulder, and he wondered, not for the first time, if he was depriving her by keeping her here in New Eden, when she could easily be the Toast of London.

"Do you ever think of London, Bryna?" he asked now, guiding her around a fresh deposit made by one of the horses that shared the street with the pedestrians as they neared Rudolph's Inn and Stores. "Do you ever miss the balls, the theaters—the ostrich feathers?"

"Finding things to worry about again, are you?" she asked, smiling up at him. "As I've never been to a ball, I can't say that I miss the experience, although I did enjoy the theater the few times Papa took me there. And, if you'll recall, Dominick, I can have ostrich feathers whenever I want, which would, I believe, make Mr. Hunsicker the happiest of men."

Dominick smiled down at her, only to be brought up short when she suddenly halted in her tracks, her face going oddly pale for a moment before hot color raced into her cheeks. "What is it? Has our son delivered yet another kick when you least expected it?"

She started forward once more, clinging more tightly to his arm with both hands, her eyes concentrated on the ground in front of her feet. "It's Lieutenant Frey," she whispered fiercely. "He was standing behind Rudolph's window, watching us, and smiling like a cat with canary feathers sticking out of the corner of his mouth. Come on, Dominick. Let's just keep walking."

"Bryna, this has got to stop," Dominick told her, even as Lieutenant Frey, Benjamin and Truda Rudolph, as well as the ever-present Jonah Newton, stepped out onto the street. "I don't like these people any more than you do, and would never want them sticking their legs beneath my dining table, but I refuse to act as if we're somehow *afraid* of them."

"A wise man doesn't poke sticks at rattlesnakes," Bryna told him quietly. "Snakes are powerful warriors, and we shouldn't give them any reason to declare war on us. Trouble will come soon enough, on its own."

"I think I hear Lokwelend's voice in that speech somewhere," Dominick said, deliberately keeping his tone light. "But it might be a good idea."

Then he watched as Lieutenant Frey, resplendent in his scarlet coat and bagwig, his sword at his waist, his hands on his hips and looking extremely satisfied with himself, descended to block the pathway of packed dirt between the building and the puddles in the roadway.

"Good day, Lieutenant," Dominick announced, his voice ringing out clearly as he then extended his greetings to cover the innkeeper and his wife, although he ignored the grinning Newton, who seemed to more easily summon his courage in numbers. In fact, all four appeared entirely too pleased with themselves, as if they had been hovering at Rudolph's window, just waiting for him to come along so that they could pounce like rats on a piece of cheese. Or rattlesnakes, prepared to strike at any vulnerable ankle. "I do believe you're blocking the way, Lieutenant, or were you hoping we'd join you for a mug of ale?"

"Hardly. Rather, I consider this a fortunate coincidence, as we—" he motioned up at the Rudolphs and Newton "—were only now discussing you. So, as you're here now, saving me a trip to your estate, a word with you, my lord, if I may."

Dominick swore silently, and wished Bryna back at Pleasant Hill. He closed his mouth on any hint of sarcasm and merely inclined his head, encouraging the lieutenant to speak.

Frey took another step forward, totally ignoring Bryna. He loosed the first three buttons of his jacket, slipped a hand inside, and extracted a folded sheet of paper. "I've been given the authority to act as I best see fit by permission of my superiors in Philadelphia. Therefore, I have just this morning written up a proclamation concerning trade with the hostiles."

"Hostiles, is it, Frey?" Dominick shook his head, already knowing he was not going to like what he heard next. "Would those hostiles be the women and children and the few old men and Christian Indians who you've been doing your best to bully? Please, go on. You've certainly captured my interest."

Frey looked at the ground for a moment before raising his gaze to Dominick's face. "You would be wise to be very interested, my lord. As of this moment, it is a crime against the Crown to trade, barter, sell, or in any other way give aid and comfort to the savages. A crime punishable by hanging, you understand. Men and women both."

He replaced the paper inside his jacket. Only then did he turn to Bryna, bowing to her smartly. "The usual defense of pleading one's belly will be honored, of course, as *we* are not the savages here. But the sentence will still be carried out after the condemned has whelped. I do hope this warning is sufficiently clear, my lady, my lord?"

"Oh, they knows, all right, Lieutenant!" Newton called out, hanging around one of the wooden posts on the narrow porch as he leered down at Bryna, looking every inch the hyena she had once termed him. Dominick could feel her trembling beside him, whether with anger or fear, he didn't know. "Paradin' around here all rigged out like a bleedin' lord one day, lookin' worse than a painted savage the next. Keepin' that old Indian on his land. Won't join up with the militia—like he's too good for the likes of the rest of us. Him and his high-nosed bitch both!"

"They stole my baby!" Truda Rudolph chimed in loudly, pointing an accusing finger in Dominick's direction. "They stole her and then they made her into a slave like that there nigger they keep—and then they kilt her! My baby! My only sweet child! My poor, poor Alice!" The woman burst into raucous sobs, burying her head against her husband's shoulder for a moment before taking a dry-eyed, smiling peek at Bryna and Dominick.

Dominick opened his mouth to speak, but Bryna beat him to it.

"A pity you don't have a larger audience, you witch, as that was quite the performance. How dare you use your daughter's death that way?" She took a single step forward, then halted, biting her bottom lip as she looked up at

Dominick. "I'm sorry," she said quietly. "I shouldn't have said anything. Neither of us should say anything. Please, let's just go back to the store."

Dominick appreciated her warning, not that he had planned to say another word. That's what Frey wanted, what they all wanted. That's why they were goading him. Pushing at him. They wanted him to lose his temper. They wanted him to challenge one of them, take a swing at one of them, do anything that could end with himself arrested and clapped in irons, locked away from Pleasant Hill. Away from Bryna.

He'd rather be branded a coward than leave his wife unprotected. It would do no good to mention that he'd had to chase Jonah Newton out of the barn because the man had gone inside with a lit pipe, that the idiot had probably gone back into the barn with his friends again later, carrying that same lit pipe. It would do no good to deny that he had either abducted or abused Alice Rudolph. But that didn't mean he was about to turn tail and run. Not for Bryna. Not for any reason at all.

"First we'll get Lucas's new shoes, pet," he told her, ready to stare down Renton Frey until the man moved out of the way.

Benjamin Rudolph stepped to the end of the porch, his gap-toothed grin more than a little sickening as he took his turn in this small battle of insults. "Running away, are you? What's the matter, Crown? Finally find somethin' all your money can't buy, did you? Like a *backbone?*"

"Yi-ee! Stung him proper with that one, Benjie!" Truda Rudolph chortled as she and Jonah Newton hung on each other, both convulsed in mirth. Benjamin stepped back from the edge of the porch, pulled up his breeches around his large belly, and threw back his shoulders as if he'd just accomplished some great feat.

Out of the corners of his eyes, Dominick saw that Lieutenant Frey's hand was on the hilt of his sword, the man ready to strike out if Dominick, who was unarmed, made so much as a single move toward him or anyone on the porch. Thanks to Bryna, he also knew that Frey carried a small pistol at the back of his waistband, and a knife in his boot.

Dominick longed to throw himself into a bone-crushing brawl, breaking heads and teeth and shutting their foul mouths. The way he had shut his brother Giles's mouth all those years ago. But he was a patient man. Justice could wait for another day, when Bryna wasn't there to be caught up in that justice.

"We'll get Lucas's shoes on Saturday," Dominick said evenly, turning Bryna about and beginning to retrace their steps to the store. They had only traveled a few yards before Benjamin Rudolph's booming voice slammed into their backs.

"Where you goin', Crown? You turning tail on us? You gonna let your *lady* here think you're nothing but a big-talkin' coward?"

Dominick kept walking back the way they had come, Bryna still silent beside him, a warning hand on his forearm.

But the fools wouldn't let it alone. Like dogs tearing at a cornered fox, they kept ripping at Dominick, laughing and hooting and stamping their feet in their triumph. Until Jonah Newton took up where Benjamin Rudolph had left off, in an obvious final attempt to push Dominick past the point of rational thought.

"Some wife!" Newton called after them. "The lieutenant here told us all about her, didn't he, Benjie? About how her and that cardsharper papa shared a room on the *Eagle,* all cozy like. About how the bloody Irisher used her to trick honest men into losin' most of their blunt to his thievin' ways. Then she tipped herself over on her back for the rest of it. Even the lieutenant had a poke at her a time or two, till he figured out the fancy little cunt most probably had the pox."

Dominick heard Bryna's impassioned *"No!"* as if from a great distance as he turned and charged back the way he had come. He had responded without thinking, all his better judgment flown to the four winds at this insult to his wife.

He took the lieutenant out of it first, slamming into him

with the full weight of his body, the two of them crashing to the ground in a heap. Frey's sword fell, useless, out of his reach. Taking hold of the neckcloth around Frey's throat, Dominick held him a good six inches off the ground as he straddled him, rapidly plowing his right fist into the lieutenant's face three, four, five times, before loosing his grip on the unconscious man and letting his head fall back into a muddy puddle.

Benjamin Rudolph obliged Dominick by coming down the steps and into the street, the two huge hams that were his hands already drawn into fists. "I've been waitin' a long time for this, you Indian-lovin' bastard!" he gritted out, winding up for a punch.

Benjamin Rudolph outweighed Dominick by four stone or more. He was a good three inches taller. Which didn't mean a thing to Dominick, who just lowered his head, gave a short, guttural growl, and ran full tilt into the man's corpulent midsection. He pushed him backwards until the innkeeper's spine sharply collided with the edge of the porch. Rudolph's breath left him in a whoosh, and Dominick finished him with a blow to the right ear that sent the man down like a rock. Or a boulder, as Rudolph was much larger than a mere rock.

Dominick quickly looked up to where Newton had been, fully prepared to tear the man into very small pieces, just to see him standing there quite alone, Truda Rudolph having disappeared. Newton's hands were raised beside his head, his mouth hanging open in fright as he stared, bug-eyed, across the dirt street.

"And it's a fine day this, isn't it, Mr. Kester? A fine day for a wee bit of rat shooting?" Bryna called out in a broad brogue from somewhere behind him, so that Dominick turned around, looking at her in disbelief. His wife was standing in front of the smithy, breathing hard, a pistol held out in front of her in both hands. There was an evil-looking rifle in Elijah Kester's hands as he stood beside her, its barrel pointing straight at Jonah Newton's quivering belly.

"Dominick, I can see that Mary Kate is already on her way to the wagon, bright child that she is, so it's taking ourselves off home now, I believe we'll be. Unless," she continued, pausing slightly every few words to catch her breath, "you'd be thinking you'd first like to pummel the village idiot there into flinders. In which case . . ." She paused once more, smiled brightly, and ended, "In which case, Dominick, I suppose I can wait."

She sliced Dominick a quick look as she advanced across the street, her smile weak but rather triumphant. "Just don't be too long in making up your mind. I think I may be about to lose my temper and fire this pistol. I'll aim for his ear, but we both know how terrible my aim can be. I might shoot him straight in between the eyes simply by mistake."

Newton dropped to his knees, his hands still raised above his head, crying. "It wasn't me! It wasn't me! Frey told me what to say! I swear, I *swear!*"

Dominick couldn't help it. Out of breath, with his head ringing to beat the devil after its collision with Rudolph's belly, and his right hand throbbing, he threw back his head and laughed out loud at the sight of his small, increasingly pregnant, most belligerently beautiful Irish wife.

"I think you can put down the pistol now, pet, as Elijah has everything well in hand. Would you give me a moment?" he then asked as Benjamin Rudolph vomited into the dirt and Lieutenant Frey groggily got to his feet, his bagwig dripping mud, a hand raised to his cheek as he gingerly opened and closed his mouth, as if checking to be sure his jaw still worked.

"Lieutenant?" Dominick inquired, as Elijah Kester remained at the door of his smithy, his rifle now standing at his side. Dominick bent to pick up Frey's sword and then held it out to him. "I do hope you're all right. Nasty spill the lieutenant took down those steps, wasn't it, Elijah?" he called out loudly, so that the smithy grinned.

"Saw it all, Mr. Crown, that I did. Took a terrible fall," Elijah confirmed affably. "And so I'll say to any who ask me what happened here today."

"There you have it, Lieutenant," Dominick said as the blacksmith waved and went back to his work. "You've made a multitude of friends here in New Eden. All that drilling for the local militia, forcing these people to provide for you and your men out of their own pockets, keeping the Lenape away from the village so that we've lost all their trade. Yes, a multitude of friends. Oh, and you really must insist that Rudolph here sees to it that those boards are more securely fastened. Once he can stand on his own again, that is."

Frey looked at Dominick for long moments, then cast his gaze in both directions along the street—seeing several other people were now watching them, more than a few of them having a good laugh at his expense. "Get out of here. Get the bloody hell out of here!" he shouted, wincing as he quickly brought both hands to his jaw. "And remember what I said, Crown. Trade with the savages again, and I'll have you hanged! I'm going to clear every last hostile out of this valley, if I have to do it over your dead body!"

Frey turned in a full circle, looking to each of the persons watching the events taking place in front of Rudolph's Inn and Stores. "And that goes for anyone else who gives aid and comfort to the enemy!" Then he bent down and scooped up something that had fallen to the ground during the short, violent exchange that had left him lying on his consequence in the mud.

It was over.

Dominick wanted Bryna away from the area now, before any more damage could be done. He turned to her, ready to take the pistol and escort her to the wagon, then stopped as her stunned expression told him something else was wrong. Had Frey gone for his knife?

He whirled about, ready for another fight, to see the lieutenant about to stuff a rather distinctive dark green leather purse back inside his jacket. He looked back to his wife, asking quietly, "What is it? He's not going to try anything else. Not now that we've got an audience."

Bryna handed Dominick the pistol, still staring at Frey, then turned away, her shoulders slumped, her entire posture the picture of exhaustion and defeat. "It's nothing," she said, her voice small, curiously flat. "Nothing. Please, let's go. I want to go home now, Dominick. I'm tired. I just want to go home."

Dominick swept her up in his arms, ready to carry her to the wagon, afraid she was about to collapse, then looked back one last time at Lieutenant Renton Frey.

The man was still standing there, looking straight at Bryna, swinging the deep green purse in front of him by its thin leather strap. His lip was bleeding from Dominick's punch and the skin below one eye was already beginning to swell. His scarlet coat was thick with mud. His bagwig sat tilted on his head, showing the shortly cropped blond hair beneath.

And he was smiling.

*Endure, my heart: you once endured
something even more dreadful.*
— *Homer*

CHAPTER 16

❧

"GET IT, GILHOOLEY! GET IT!" SHOUTING ENCOURAGEMENT TO the large dog, Mary Catherine threw the stick, then chased after it along with the animal, the two of them collapsing to the ground together, engaging in a playful tug-of-war Gilhooley allowed the child to win. Mary Catherine's childish giggles filled the air, bringing cheer to the two friends who watched her carefree play.

"The young heal quickly, both in their minds and in their hearts," Lokwelend said, sitting beside Bryna on the blanket she had placed on the grass in her favorite spot behind the house. "They forget the pain and look only forward. We could learn much from them."

Bryna shook her head, her smile sad as she placed the last few stitches in the hem she was sewing. "You're being cryptic again, aren't you, Lokwelend? How have you said it? 'I wipe the tears from your eyes, and place your aching heart, which bears you down to one side, in its proper position. I have, for love of you, covered yonder grave with

fresh earth; I have raked leaves, and planted trees thereon.'
Isn't that what you told me?"

"Yes. That is our way of saying that it is time to heal, that
happiness is still here, waiting, if only you look for it. The
child knows this, and so must you."

"Dom'nick! Dom'nick!" Mary Catherine cried out suddenly in obvious delight, and Bryna turned to see her
husband riding toward them on his large bay mare, not
stopping on the drive, but only bringing the horse to a halt
once he had reached the tree, dismounting in one clean
motion. "Dom'nick! Do you want to play with Gilhooley,
too?"

"Not now, love. Go into the house and stay with Lucretia," Dominick answered shortly.

Bryna looked at him quizzically. "Do as Dominick says,
darling," she said quickly, kissing the child's forehead and
then gently shooing her away. "What is it? What's wrong?"

Dominick took up the hand Bryna held out to him,
squeezing it, hard. "It's happening," he said without pream-
ble, his features drawn tight, his chest rising and falling
quickly, as if he had just run a long way. "That damn fool
Frey has gone and done it! This time there is no avoiding a
war."

"Sweet Jesus, Mary, and Joseph," Bryna whispered,
instinctively placing her other hand on her stomach, as if to
protect the child growing inside her. "What did you hear?
What did Frey do?"

Dominick looked at Bryna as if gauging her ability to
handle what he might tell her, then sighed. "You might as
well hear it all, pet, although none of it is pretty, or says
much for our governor and his troops."

"Yes. I want to hear everything, Dominick," she told him.
She needed to know the worst so that she could prepare for
the unthinkable.

"I don't have to tell you what happened late this past
winter," he began after a moment, "as God knows you're
aware of the last raids to come to New Eden. But since then,
thanks both to what is happening on the frontier and to
Frey's incompetent behavior, the prospect for another raid

has been becoming more and more inevitable. But there are things you don't know, things I haven't told you. Nearly two months ago, one of the soldiers came to me to complain about Frey. It seems he and this soldier were on patrol, searching for a lost rifle or some such thing, when they saw three Indians in the distance. Frey immediately shot one of them, but the other two ran away."

Dominick looked at Lokwelend. "Frey scalped the Indian he'd shot, and then demanded that the soldier take the scalp to Philadelphia, to sell it, and bring the money back to him. Instead, the soldier, disgusted by what had happened, came to me for help."

Lokwelend nodded, making a guttural sound low in his throat. "I have heard this, Crown."

Bryna was instantly angry. "Well, I haven't! Honestly, Dominick, if we're to have secrets from each other—" She broke off, lifting a hand to her mouth to stop her words. What was she saying? Of course they had secrets from each other. Terrible secrets, all of them involving the same terrible man. "I-I'm sorry, darling. Please, tell me the rest."

"There's nothing much else to tell. I wrote to Frey's superior in Philadelphia, but the man chose to transfer the troops that were unhappy, and leave Frey here. Idiocy seems to be the order of the day when it comes to dealing with English authority—or so I thought at the time. Let's go into the house. I think I need a drink before I tell you the rest."

Dominick helped Bryna to her feet as Lokwelend folded the blanket, passed it to Dominick, and began walking away from them. "No, my friend. I did not ask you to leave us. Please, come inside."

The Lenape shook his head. "I do not wish to hear more, Crown. I can see in your face that the killing has begun, and that is more than I wish to know. I cannot fight with you against my own people. I cannot lift my arm against you, my brother. I am an old woman now, as Pematalli has said, and I go where old women go, into the forest, to hide. *Itah!* May we meet again in harmony."

He turned to leave and Bryna called after him, hoping to change his mind. "Lokwelend—please!"

"Let him go, Bryna. Lokwelend is between two worlds," Dominick said quietly. He turned her toward the house. "As he can't divide his loyalties, he has long since told me this is what he would do if it ever came to open war."

"And it's open war, Dominick?" Bryna asked as they stepped inside his study and she sat on the couch, watching as he poured himself a glass of wine. "Because of what Frey did? But you said yourself that what you told me about happened months ago."

"Yes, Bryna, I know," Dominick said, seating himself on the edge of his desk, his long frame clothed in his usual deerskins, his entire posture one of someone relaxed, yet poised for immediate action should it became necessary. "There's more, unfortunately. In August, just thirty miles to our north, a Christian Indian named Zachary—a man who preached against violence—his wife, children, and another woman were murdered, put to the sword by troops after being allowed to take shelter with them for the night."

Bryna couldn't understand. "But, why, Dominick? What had they done?"

He swallowed the last of his wine then, and in a deliberate act of violence she barely recognized in him, threw the glass into the fireplace, where it shattered against the andirons. "They existed, Bryna. That was all the crime the soldiers needed." He rubbed his hand across his forehead, then sighed. "I'm sorry. Did I mention that, once again, Frey was the man in charge of these troops? In a few short months he has managed to make himself one of the most hated men in the colony, which is why it's so dangerous to us all that he is quartered in New Eden. He'll be the first target, if the Lenape come. *When* the Lenape come."

Bryna looked down into her lap, surprised to see that she was still holding the small infant gown, unsurprised to see that she had somehow torn it in two. "What happened today, Dominick?" Her own voice sounded thin to her, and very far away, barely audible above the roar of her own blood hurtfully pounding in her ears.

He stood and began to pace the room, reminding her of a lion she had seen caged in London. Back and forth. Back and forth. Energy bound by four walls, anger enclosed in a small space, power poised to explode.

"Frey was begging for a fight after the way I—the way you and Elijah and I—embarrassed him yesterday. Harold told me that he ordered us closed down for the day after we left New Eden," he explained, finally stopping to look at her as he spoke. "But then Frey allowed two Indian families to enter Rudolph's last night. He allowed them to trade their furs and beads and seed corn. He insisted Rudolph give them rooms for the night."

"Like that other family," Bryna whispered. "Like that man—Zachary."

"Exactly. This morning, as the families were gathering their goods, Frey ordered them away at gunpoint, leaving those goods behind, then followed after them later with a few of the civilian militia. Rudolph, Newton, a few others. I doubt you need to know all their names. I understand that at least two or three of the Indians escaped, but five women and children are dead. Put to the sword as they pleaded for their lives, then scalped."

"Do I—did either of these families trade with us?" Bryna closed her eyes, feeling tears burning behind her lids. With her eyes closed, she could see the young Indian children who had come into her store over the past months, giggling as they stuffed their mouths with licorice, their mothers, with infants strapped to their backs, looking longingly at the pretty buttons Bryna kept in a dish on the counter. "Why? Why would he do that? Just for the scalps?"

"Why? Because he wants a war, Bryna. He was sent here with *orders* to start one. That's why the soldiers who disagreed with his tactics were replaced. Frey's a cold-blooded killer, Bryna. He *enjoys* it. And he needs to impress his commander in Philadelphia or else be cashiered for the miserable bastard that he is. Oh, yes. They picked the right man for the job."

Bryna still didn't understand. Or perhaps she did, but she didn't want to believe what she was hearing. "Frey's commanders *want* a war? With all of us here—with all the children? Why? Dominick, why?"

Dominick rubbed at his forehead, looking weary as well as angry. "It's fairly simple, actually, once you get past the ugliness of it, the callousness of it. After years of unimpeded western growth, the frontier is shrinking. It has been shrinking ever since last year, with settlers falling back to this side of the mountains because of attacking war parties. The Indians have decided that the *shawannakwak* have enough land now, and won't give or sell us any more—won't allow us to take any more."

Bryna laid the ruined gown beside her on the couch, and waited for Dominick to continue.

"If New Eden falls," he added slowly, as if measuring his words, "if Allen's Town or Bethlehem or any more of the settlements in this part of the colony fall, the frontier will soon be backed up all the way to Philadelphia. Fort Pitt is already all but surrounded by hostiles, and is doomed to destruction if we are forced to withdraw. The English command, along with the land brokers, want the Lenape completely out of the Pennsylvania colony, relocated in the Ohio territories—and they don't much care how that end is accomplished."

"I find it difficult to believe risking the possible deaths of many of the settlers is part and parcel of any plan to secure the colony," Bryna said, knowing she was simply mouthing words, for her husband's arguments all made a strange, tragic sort of sense.

"Really? Think about it, Bryna. One good massacre of settlers, reported in the Philadelphia newspapers, will rally the entire colony behind any plan to relocate the Lenape. It was bad enough for Frey to do what he's done while away from New Eden, out on patrol, away from any of the towns, but now he's deliberately soiled his own nest. It's New Eden that will become the target for Lenape revenge, and the settlers of New Eden who will pay the price."

"When? When, Dominick?"

He ran a hand through his hair, closing his eyes as he seemed to consider her question. "The braves who escaped must have gotten back to whatever tribe they're traveling with by now. I don't know, Bryna. Tonight? Tomorrow?

Next week? I just don't know. But you're safe here, and you're not to leave this house, do you understand? Philip stayed behind, in New Eden, to close and lock the store, the inn, and then he's riding to all of the closest families, warning them to get to Fort Deshler. If anyone listens to him. I stopped at two farms on my way home—at Micah Jennings's place, and at Peter Moore's—telling them they could take refuge here, at Pleasant Hill, and nobody listened to me."

He sat down beside Bryna and gathered her into his arms. "Philip will be home before dark, and then we'll all be together, and safe. Oh, sweet Christ! I should have figured this out earlier, should have been able to put all the pieces together. You shouldn't be here, Bryna. You shouldn't be here."

"I wouldn't be anywhere else, Dominick," she told him, laying her head against his shoulder, breathing in the scent of his male flesh, resolving to be brave, no matter what happened in the next few hours, the next few days. "I wouldn't be anywhere else."

Philip didn't come.

Darkness fell inside Pleasant Hill long before dusk, all the stout wooden shutters shut tight as Dominick and some of the men from the estate manned the gun slots cut into those shutters on all four sides of the house. Silently they watched the tree line for any sight of an advancing enemy.

A dozen families, all of Dominick's tenant farmers and laborers and anyone else who asked, sheltered behind the strong stone walls, settled in and prepared to wait out the raid. They, too, waited, praying no one manning the gun slots would announce that there was a plume of smoke rising over the trees in the direction of their own houses.

Dominick had vowed as he'd buried the Cassidys, the O'Reillys, that he would never again feel the guilt of having lived through a raid only because no war party would attack his carefully planned fortress. Because it wasn't enough to be safe himself; he had to know that others were as well. He knew, thanks to Lokwelend, that a war party on the hunt, their number usually not more than two dozen or so braves, was like a pack of wolves—moving quickly, striking swiftly, searching out the weakest, the least protected, and avoiding any stronger, superior enemies.

Dominick had built Pleasant Hill with defense as his architect. No shrubberies were closer than fifty yards of the foundation. The house sat on a rise, surrounded by closely scythed lawns, forcing any enemy to cross that open expanse, completely visible to anyone watching through the gun slots, before reaching those locked inside the imposing stone walls.

The cellars were stocked with foodstuffs, and the freshwater spring ran through troughs cut into the basement floor. It would be possible for Dominick and his temporary occupants to withstand a siege lasting several months, if necessary. In another age, there would have been a moat, a drawbridge, a flat roof suitable for launching boiling pitch down on an attacking enemy. If there was any safety to be had in all of New Eden, it was at Fort Deshler, and within the ornately furnished drawing room of Pleasant Hill.

Yes, they'd be safe here. Safe, while all of hell exploded around them.

Lucretia lit candles while Bryna held Mary Catherine, singing her lullabies as Gilhooley lay at her feet, seeming to know that he had no other mission than to guard the child, the young woman, who meant so much to his master.

Lucas wandered about the rooms on the ground floor of the solid stone mansion, safe inside its two-foot-thick walls, fretting over Philip's continued absence, betraying the affection he had grown to hold for the smiling, cheerful young man who was the son of Polly Rosebud's attacker.

Darkness fell all over Pleasant Hill, the land lit with only a slight sliver of moon, most of the stars hidden behind a light covering of swiftly moving clouds that cast strange, frightening shadows over the lawns. The birds had gone to their resting places more than an hour ago, leaving the air empty, devoid of sound.

And still Philip didn't come.

Mary Catherine fell asleep, and Lucretia lifted her out of

Bryna's clinging arms, depositing her on a small cot Lucas had fixed for her in a corner of the drawing room, away from the doors, away from the shuttered windows. In all the bedchambers, in the formal dining room, women and children slept, crowded into beds or huddled beneath blankets spread on the carpets.

Outside, an owl screeched as it swooped down over the lawns, and moments later a small animal shrieked in pain as the nocturnal hunter closed its sharp talons, piercing living flesh.

The tall clock in the foyer rang out the hour of ten, and then eleven.

And still Philip didn't come.

"You could be out looking for him, if it weren't that Mary Catherine and I were here," Bryna said at last, pressing her head against Dominick's shoulder as he kept his vigil at one of the gun slots overlooking the main drive.

"He may have decided to stay at the store," Dominick said, turning away from the gun slot long enough to kiss Bryna on the forehead. "There's a goodly supply of guns and powder, remember, something no one would like to see falling into the wrong hands. Perhaps he thought he'd be more useful there, with Harold."

"Yes. Yes, of course. He's at the store," Bryna agreed. "And he has probably eaten himself halfway through the sugarplums by now."

"Why don't you go lie down, Bryna? You look tired. Lucretia brought blankets and pillows from upstairs and has been asleep for hours."

"All right," Bryna said as Dominick motioned for another man to take his place at the gun slot. "If that's what you want. I am a little tired."

Bryna lay down on one of the couches while Dominick knelt to pull a light blanket over her. "Go to sleep now," he said, tracing the line of her cheek with a single finger.

"I love you, Dominick Crown," Bryna told him quietly, taking his hand and pressing a kiss against his palm. "It's not just being here, being safe. It's not just having a family again, not being alone. I love you. I—I just thought you should know."

"I've known for a long time, my darling Bryna," he responded just as quietly, for she had made her declaration in a roomful of sleepy yet not unobservant people. "Just as I have prayed you've known how much I love you."

Bryna smiled, happy tears making her eyes shine brightly. "A true pair of googeens. We certainly took long enough to say the words, didn't we, darling?"

"We'll have the rest of our lives to say the words, Bryna, over and over again. And I promise you, we're both going to live for a long, long time."

"I'll hold you to that promise, Dominick," Bryna answered with a watery smile, then reluctantly allowed him to go back to his post.

The candles began to burn down, and Lucas replaced them, one by one. The tall clock struck out the hours of two, of three. Of four. Of five.

The first light of predawn began sending its fingers along the trees and grass of Pleasant Hill; a small brightening appeared beyond the gun slots, heralding the beginning of yet another day.

Bryna lay on the couch, not having spoken a word in hours, although she'd never slept, and watched Dominick watching the drive. They would begin another day of watching, of waiting.

And still Philip did not come.

Mary Catherine was the first to see the smoke.

Standing on a stool in the drawing room, peeking out to see how the world outside was faring without her, she tilted her head first to one side, then to the other, before announcing rather calmly, "The barn is burning again. But I won't hide this time, Bryna. I promise."

Dominick deserted his own post and ran across the room, pulling the child out of the way as he threw open the shutter for a better look. Smoke rose high above the treetops, curling up toward the sky. About a mile's distance, he decided. At least the waiting was over. It had begun. "That's Peter Moore's farm," he informed Bryna, who had come to stand beside him.

"Oh, no! Dominick—they have three children at that farm. Do you think they finally believed you and went to Fort Deshler?"

"I don't know. God! I don't know." Dominick picked up his rifle and headed for the foyer along with the other men, throwing open the front door and stepping out onto the porch. "Look—over there." He used his rifle to point toward the tree line to his left. "There's more smoke, just starting to rise above the trees. That would be Micah Jennings's farm. Sweet Christ, they're moving fast. But not, I think, in our direction. It looks more as if they're coming directly from New Eden, and heading toward the river."

He looked more to his right, straining to see into the distance, knowing he couldn't see all the way to New Eden, which lay three miles away, and on the other side of a large hill. "I don't think I see any more smoke, but I can't be sure."

"Philip." Bryna's voice was a benediction, a whisper of hope when hope was all any of them had to cling to.

Dominick slid an arm around his wife's shoulders, raising his eyes toward the rapidly brightening sky as he offered up a silent prayer for his nephew, his friend. "He's all right, Bryna. He has to be all right."

Even before the words were entirely out of his mouth, Bryna broke free from his grasp and ran down the steps, only stopping at the edge of the drive. "Philip! Oh, Dominick, go help him! It's Philip!"

Dominick looked at Bryna, then beyond her and to the edge of the trees to the right of the drive. He saw Philip, his deerskins torn and bloody, slowly making his way toward them, a bundled blanket in his arms. Beside him was April Turner, stumbling as she tried to keep walking, her face contorted in an agony of fear and exhaustion, her clothing ripped and stuck with burrs.

"Get back inside, Bryna," Dominick commanded as he and the men raced past her toward the two weary people.

He quickly scooped April Turner into his arms as Philip broke into a limping trot, no one speaking a word until Lucas had shut and bolted the door behind them, sealing them all safely inside the thick walls of Pleasant Hill once more.

"The baby! Is she all right?" Bryna raced ahead, into the drawing room, Philip following close behind. As if to answer her question, Henrietta began to wail piteously. Lucretia quickly took her from Philip's arms and unwrapped the blanket, so that the child could breathe freely. "Dominick, put April here, right here on the couch. My God, Philip—what happened?"

The room became cluttered with people, everyone rushing to see April Turner, to hear the news, to shout questions at Philip.

"Did you see my house?" one asked. "Did they take my horses?"

"Damnable savages!" another swore, holding his sobbing wife close. "It's back to Philadelphia for us, once this is over!"

"Close the shutters," Dominick ordered Johnny Hooper, the young laborer who had spent the night in the kitchens, watching the back of the house. "And man that gun slot. Everyone else—please clear this room! Go back to your posts! Philip? You look like you need a drink—and a doctor."

"It's not my blood, thank God," Philip said, collapsing into a chair. He looked just as handsome beneath his dirt as he had appeared that first day he'd arrived at Pleasant Hill, only no longer quite so young. "I killed three of them before the rest ran off, would you believe it? Two with gunshots. One was much more personal, however. He just kept running toward us before I could reload, his face all painted, yelling at the top of his lungs as he launched himself at me. Thank God I had my knife. Damme, Dominick, I'll hear those screams for a long time, see that savage's face in my nightmares. Is it over now? The Lenape way of war is not an experience I'm in much of a hurry to repeat."

"I don't know," Dominick answered. "I think they're probably gone, having done as much damage as they could. But I don't know."

"Please—give me my baby," April Turner implored, holding out her arms toward her daughter. "I—I really need to hold her."

"Yes, Lucretia. Give Henrietta to her mother," Bryna said, suddenly clearheaded. "Then you might go into the kitchens, brew us all some tea, and ask some of the ladies to help prepare breakfast for us all. Although I do believe, Lucas, you might search out some brandy for Master Philip."

"Bring the whole damn decanter, Deems, if you will," Philip called after the man, then collapsed his head against the back of the chair, his smile rueful. "Christ on a crutch, Dominick, what a night! Did you ever hear the Lenape war whoop? Chills a man right to his marrow, it does."

Dominick waited until Philip had drunk down half the snifter of brandy Lucas had brought him before asking, once more, exactly what had happened.

"I did as you told me, Dominick, and rode farm to farm, telling everyone to go to Fort Deshler. It was probably a waste of time, as nobody seemed to believe me. Although I see you've got all of your people here," he said, then waited as Lucas refilled his glass. "Then I went back to New Eden, just to check on Harold one last time. I saw Henry Turner going into Rudolph's—there was a jolly large bunch of laughing men eagerly swallowing down all the watered ale Rudolph was handing out to celebrate their *victory* over the hostiles—all those poor souls they massacred. Ignorant bastards. Anyway, I decided it might be best to go check on Mrs. Turner before I came home."

"He saved our lives, Mr. Crown, mine and Henrietta's both," April interrupted, looking to Philip as if the young man were personally responsible for hanging out the sun that morning. "He waited with me for a while, waited on Henry, and when Henry never did come home, he said he'd spend the night, seeing as how it was already past dark. I couldn't see any reason for him to do that, but Henry weren't coming, and I didn't much like the idea of staying there alone with just the baby."

She bent her head and kissed the child's brow, then went on, her voice low and still wavering with fright, "The . . . the savages came at us in the middle of the night, a couple of hours afore dawn . . . yelling and hollering and . . . and . . . they were so *ugly* . . . their bodies all painted and . . ."

April buried her face against her daughter's small form and began to sob, rocking back and forth as she sat on the couch, clearly overcome by her experience.

"Mrs. Turner's right, Dominick," Philip said, smiling at Bryna as she wiped at his cheeks with a clean, wet cloth, then pressed a kiss against his brow. "A Lenape at peace is an odd, but endearing fellow. A Lenape at war is a most formidable sight. Nothing like our own dear Lokwelend, I assure you. As I was killing the last one, my knife in the side of his throat, he was still trying to bite off my ear. Sorry, Bryna—I shouldn't be saying this in front of you ladies, I know, but I did have a hell of a time! Never killed a man before, you know, although one does tend to learn quickly when someone is trying to fillet you. Anyway, we waited for about an hour, to be sure they weren't coming back, and then we headed out, through the trees, taking the straightest path to Pleasant Hill."

He looked around the room, smiling at little Henrietta Turner, who was now clapping her hands as Mary Catherine played on her flute. "And it has never looked more welcoming! Deems—do you think there is anything yet ready to eat in this great, lovely fortress my so intelligent uncle has built, or am I going to have to drink my breakfast?"

"I'll give you an hour to eat and get yourself together again, Philip," Dominick told him, "and then I want to ride into New Eden. We'll take the wagon, in case there are any other people who might want to take refuge here, at Pleasant Hill. Although I think the worst is over, at least for now."

"Will—will you look for Henry? I'm that worried about him," April said.

Dominick caught Bryna's gaze for a moment, seeing in

their gray-green depths the same answer he longed to give April Turner. "I'll make sure Philip tells him you and Henrietta are here, and safe." *And then,* he thought, watching a small smile curve Bryna's lips as she read his mind, *I'll stand back and watch while Philip pummels the stupid, drunken son of a bitch into the ground.*

*When sorrows come, they come
not single spies, but in battalions.*
— *William Shakespeare*

CHAPTER 17

SLOWLY THE MYRIAD STORIES WERE PIECED TOGETHER AS
Dominick learned what had happened as he had kept his
all-night vigil from the relative safety of Pleasant Hill. With
Philip and some of the men from New Eden all sharing their
stories, he patched together information that shed light on
the particulars of the raid.

First to die had been Ceallach Hart, out before dawn to
borrow coals from a neighbor to light her morning fire.
She'd been tomahawked on the roadway leading into the
village, probably to keep her from raising an alarm throughout New Eden. Her husband and seven children had slept
on not twenty yards away, inside the house, unharmed and
unaware.

But Dominick had been right—Rudolph's had been the
main target, and the Lenape, obviously familiar with the
inn, had for the most part selected their victims beforehand. Only after the main objective had been realized had
they attacked any of the farms on their way out of the area,
probably never to return.

The Lenape had scalped Ceallach Hart, left her body in plain sight on the roadway, and gone on to Rudolph's Inn and Stores. There had been, Elijah Kester said, at least twenty braves in the war party, their nearly bare bodies slick with bear grease; signs of the tortoise, the deer, the bear, painted on their cheeks; their foreheads stained red with the color of war.

They had probably hidden themselves in the trees behind the inn. Once there, they had waited patiently until first light, when one of the soldiers opened the back door, on his way outside to relieve himself in the bushes.

The soldier's scream as the tomahawk slammed into his chest had roused the household of drunken soldiers and militia who stumbled about clumsily, muzzy-headed, attempting to locate their weapons. One soldier raced to the open door, probably intent on pulling the body of his wounded comrade clear so that the door could be shut. He, too, fell, his body now also blocking the door.

This, according to Kester, had been all the Lenape needed, and several of them hastened to storm the breach, five or more of them actually able to enter the inn, where the combat was hand to hand, and fierce.

Benjamin Rudolph had leaped from his bedroom window on the second floor, still clad in his nightshirt, and run into the trees. His body was found hours later, more than a mile from the inn, hacked to pieces, his scalp gone. Indeed, only the innkeeper's torn, bloodied nightshirt and gap-toothed death grimace rendered the body recognizable.

Four of the soldiers had died; three shot, one tomahawked. Two of the militia were gravely injured and not expected to survive the day.

Jonah Newton, like Rudolph, had received swift but very personal attention from the Lenape, somewhere outside the vision of Elijah Kester and others who stayed safe inside their houses, cringing at the sound of the tanner's blood-freezing screams. When, around noon, a few of the men hauled Newton's waterlogged body from the well where it had been thrown, it was to see that his nose was gone. As were his hands. And his heart.

Later, Elijah Kester, in his matter-of-fact way, told Philip he believed Newton's heart had been the last to be removed.

The blacksmith, a large man of few words, had ordered the men to drop the body back into the well, which was boarded shut later that same day, hopelessly fouled. Mrs. Newton, already back at work at the tannery, did not ask them to retrieve it for a more formal interment.

Truda Rudolph's had been the only body Dominick and Philip had seen when first they drove the wagon down the packed dirt street in New Eden a full four hours after the raid. She was still lying half on, half off the front porch, as if caught from behind as she attempted to escape the carnage, her skull split to the chin. Someone said one of the village dogs had made off with her brains.

The war party had separated after being routed from the inn by Frey's troops, a few of them attempting to break into April Turner's house, more of them traveling in a near straight line leading to the river, killing and burning as they went. Two of the Moore children had perished along with their father, and Micah and Susan Jennings and their five children were all dead.

In all, in the space of a few short hours, twenty-three people had died. Some burned alive inside their houses. Some hacked to death as they tried to flee. Some escaping into the trees, only to be run down and scalped.

Several children were still believed missing, carried off across the river in the way Brighid Cassidy had been carried off, either to be sold to another tribe as slaves or taken to replace the Lenape who had died in the most recent attack by Frey and his men.

Lieutenant Renton Frey, however, hadn't so much as cut himself shaving as he'd ordered his men to regroup in preparation of launching an offensive against any Lenape found within a ten-mile radius of New Eden.

But that had been his second order of the day. The first was to send one of his soldiers to Philadelphia bearing a written report of the massacre to be delivered to his commanding officer, and another, a personal account of both the tragedy and the lieutenant's heroic conduct in repelling the savages, to be given to the *Philadelphia Gazette*.

Not that Dominick planned to tell Bryna everything that he and Philip had learned on their visit to New Eden, or all that they had seen as they traveled the narrow roadways with Elijah Kester and a dozen other men, their rifles at the ready, identifying and burying the dead.

Dominick was bone-weary as he climbed the steps to Pleasant Hill while a pink-edged dusk settled over the valley. He nearly broke down as Bryna ran out to greet him, throwing her arms around him and kissing his neck, his cheeks, clearly overjoyed and relieved to have him home safe.

"You might kiss me, too, if you think of it," Philip said, coming up the steps behind Dominick, Gilhooley tangling in his legs, barking and wagging his tail in near ecstasy. "Not you, you daft animal! Mary Catherine! Come on out here, love. Where's a kiss for your cousin Philip?"

"We've been nearly out of our minds with worry. We have baths ready for both of you," Bryna said, not relinquishing her hold on Dominick as they walked inside, Lucas quickly barring the door behind them. "Lucretia has food waiting, and Henry Turner came to retrieve April and the baby a full hour ago. He says they'll all be going to Fort Deshler while we wait for more troops to arrive, as he wouldn't want to *bother* us. He wasn't injured at all, except for a very painful-looking bruised eye. Would that be your doing, Philip? If so, please allow me to extend my congratulations. Now, please—I have to know everything. The Moores, the Jennings family. Are they all right?"

Dominick caught Philip looking at him out of the corners of his eyes. The two of them had helped gather up the bodies and, because of the continuing danger, been part of a burial party that had wrapped those same bodies in bedsheets and hastily interred them before moving on to the next farm, to the next scene of death and destruction.

"Dominick, don't think to hide things from me," Bryna warned tersely. "Remember, bad news doesn't improve if it's fed to the listener slowly."

"Let's go upstairs, pet," he said, slipping an arm around her shoulders. "You may want the truth, but Mary Catherine doesn't have to hear any of this quite yet."

They talked for an hour, Bryna crying softly as he told her of the deaths, shaking her head as, one by one, she asked about the children by name. "I feel almost guilty, being safe behind these walls. If only they'd listened to you and Philip. But now what, Dominick?" she asked at last, watching him as he dried himself after his bath. "What happens now? Will there be more raids?"

He slipped his bare arms into his dressing gown, tying the sash tightly at his waist before sitting on the edge of the bed, beside Bryna. "I don't think so, pet, although we'll still keep guard tonight. Frey's got the bit firmly between his teeth now, and the Lenape who did this are on the run and moving fast. One of Frey's men found the spot where they crossed the river, at a place called Indian Falls. He's given orders to have all the local Indians, Christian and otherwise, rounded up to be transported to Philadelphia—just as though everything had already been planned, which you and I know it most probably was. From there, I would imagine they'll be moved west, herded like sheep on their way to Ohio."

"Lokwelend? Not Lokwelend."

Dominick avoided her eyes. "I don't know. Damn it, Bryna, I just don't know. No Indian is safe here anymore, not after today."

He closed his eyes, a flash of memory showing him a vision of little Maria Jennings as he had last seen her alive, laughing as she ran with Mary Catherine on the grounds of the Cassidy farm the day of the fire. It was a vision that quickly turned to how young Maria had looked late this afternoon, lying sprawled on her back in her father's apple orchard, her hair gone, her sightless eyes staring up at the sun.

"Bloody savages! By God, Bryna, I want to kill them myself!" He held his hands out in front of him, looked at his spread fingers, then slowly closed them into fists, his knuckles turning white, his nails digging into his palms. "With my own hands. I want to kill them all. I'm as much a savage as the worst of them!"

She laid her head against his shoulder, her arms spanning his waist. "Hush, darling, hush. It's all right. I felt the same when I first heard about my family, when I first saw Lokwelend and Pematalli. All you can feel now is the pain, and the hate. And none of it makes any sense. It makes no sense at all."

Dominick stood up, then bent and kissed her hair as she also rose, hugging her close, his emotions very close to the surface, making it difficult for him to talk. He looked toward the window, at the darkness outside. "It's getting late. I don't think I want anything to eat, Bryna. I believe I just want to go to bed, with you beside me. I want to hold you. I want to know that we're together. That we'll always be together."

He remained beside the bed, watching silently as Bryna turned down the covers. He didn't say a word as she untied the satin laces of her dressing gown and let it slip to the floor, her sheer cotton night rail made nearly transparent by the brace of candles that rested on the small chest beside her. She stood in front of him, silent, as she untied the sash of his dressing gown and pushed the burgundy silk from his shoulders, so that it dropped to the floor beside hers.

He looked down for a moment, past his own nakedness, his own vulnerability, seeing the twin spills of soft white cotton and burgundy silk at his feet.

Purity and savagery.

Innocence and blood.

He closed his eyes, even as Bryna slid her arms around his waist, pressing her lips against his bare chest.

He didn't resist as she indicated that she wanted him to lie down on the bed, only drawing her with him as he lay back on the clean-smelling sheets, allowing himself to relax against the soft pillows.

He kept his eyes closed as she kissed him, as she stroked his skin, as she caressed him with her hands, her mouth, her soft words of love, her promises of forever.

Her every touch was cleansing, smoothing away the rough

edges of his anger, his grief, the unspeakable horrors he had seen. Her every whispered endearment brought him slowly back from the edge of darkness, back to life, back to the business of living, and to a thankful reverence of the tomorrows that still awaited them.

The events of the past night and day would never fully leave him. Not the waiting. Not the horror. Not even the sure feeling that it could all have been avoided, if only men used reason rather than force; if only men behaved as the brothers they were surely born to be. Cain and Abel. Dominick and Giles. The white man and the red man. Would they ever learn? Would they ever, ever learn?

"I love you, Dominick Crown," Bryna said quietly, pressing her lips to the tear that had run, unnoticed, down his cheek, squeezed from between his closed eyelids. "I will love you forever."

He refused to give voice to the sob that lay buried deep in his chest. He only took his wife in his arms, capturing her mouth with his own as, in a reaction as old as time, they consummated their love in a reaffirmation of life itself.

I must be either very brave or exceedingly foolish, Bryna thought as she lay beside a sleeping Dominick—once more dressed in his deerskins so that he would be ready if an attack should come—wondering why she wasn't demanding that he pack her up and take her back across the ocean on the very next ship leaving Philadelphia. Take them all to the peaceful, rolling hills of Ireland, or even the sweet, lush meadows of Sussex, where savages didn't attack in the night, where children played on the green, where men only walked their fields with guns if they were out hunting down a bird for dinner.

What was she doing here? What were any of them doing here? All of New Eden had been set out as a sacrificial lamb, purposely served up to receive the brunt of the Lenape anger so that the government could wage war against them with impunity. The Moores, the Jenningses, the Crowns, all of them had been nothing more than pawns in the dangerous chess game the government was playing in order to expand their territory, in order to line the already deep pockets of the land speculators, in order to keep the great English empire growing, always growing.

Wasn't Ireland enough for them?

Her head hurt. She was thinking too much, and none of her thoughts were making any sense. Bryna eased herself from the bed, moving quietly so as not to wake Dominick, and slid her feet into slippers before picking up her dressing gown and tying it at her throat. She made her way in the darkness, her only light coming from the nearly dead fire in the hearth, and opened the door into the hallway.

Once at the bottom of the stairs, she hesitated in the foyer, waiting as the tall clock struck the hour of one, then placed her fingertips against the small portrait of Queen Charlotte. "And how are you doing, Your Royal Majesty? Have you held your husband in your arms tonight, feeling the grief in his every pore? Have you ever felt that, without you, without hiding your own fears, your own sorrows, you might be forced to watch your husband turn away from all he knows, all he believes, and become a prisoner of the hate that surrounds us all?"

She sighed, blinking back tears. "What will you tell your child about the world he will someday be born into, Your Royal Majesty? Will you tell him of its beauty? Or will you warn him of its pain? Is life so very different for a queen than it is for other women?"

"Out there! On the lawns! *Indians!*"

Bryna froze in place for a moment, a single heartbeat in time, before running in the direction of Lucas's voice. She entered the drawing room just as he slid his rifle through one of the gun slots—and just as Philip withdrew his own rifle from another gun slot and threw himself toward the servant, shouting, *"No! Don't shoot!"*

Philip pulled Lucas away, so that the smaller man fell to the floor, then threw open the shutters and pressed his hands against the window frame. "Oh, Christ, Deems, you nearsighted baboon—you nearly shot Lokwelend!"

"Lokwelend? Philip, are you sure?" Her dear friend, her

cherished companion. He had come back to her! Her mentor, her savior when life had seemed impossible to understand, her guide through that dark place in her mind when happiness had only been a memory. Bryna turned back the way she had come, racing for the front door even as Dominick bounded down the stairs in his bare feet, his long hair flying free, a rifle in his hand. "What happened? Are we under attack?"

"Lokwelend's out there! He's come back!" Bryna called over her shoulder, already working to unlock the door.

Lucas was right behind her, near to sobbing in fright even as he held a lantern high above his head, so that they could better make their way through the darkness outside. "I didn't know, my lady! I couldn't see clearly without my spectacles! Something was moving, and I was sure it was savages come to murder us. Oh, my lady! I almost shot him!"

"It's all right, Lucas," Bryna assured him, smiling as she peered into the darkness for her first sight of the Indian. "I've nearly shot him myself, remember? Lokwelend will forgive you." Where was he? She had been so worried about him, so fearful that Renton Frey and his men would have found him, and killed him. "There," she ordered, "swing your lantern over that way. I think he's kneeling on the ground. Oh, sweet Mary, he must be injured! Dominick, can you see him?"

"I see him. Go back in the house, Bryna. We'll take care of this."

But she ignored him, racing toward a darker splotch in the already dark night, lights from the lanterns some of the other men had brought outside with them now enabling her to make out the outlines of not one, but two figures on the ground. "Lucas! Bring your lantern this way!" And then she stopped, at last realizing what she was seeing. "Oh, God, Dominick," she breathed quietly, swaying where she stood, her eyes already stinging with tears. "Oh, dear sweet and merciful God."

Dominick was beside Bryna as she dropped to her knees

on the dew-wet grass. Neither of them spoke as Lokwelend sat cross-legged on the grass and looked up at them, his son, Pematalli, cradled in his arms.

"Lokwelend—" Bryna put out her hand, wanting to offer her help, even as she saw how Pematalli's head lay limp against the crook of his father's arm, saw the wounds in the young man's chest, his throat. In the soft, golden glow of the lanterns, for all his size, for all the fierce images drawn on his cheeks, the pair of vivid scarlet painted handprints on his chest, the boy looked as young and innocent as Mary Catherine.

The men whispered among themselves for a few moments, passing the word of Lokwelend's identity from one to the other, then fell silent as the old Indian began to speak.

"Pematalli came to me in the forest, to the place by the cliff, where he knows me to go to pray. He was unwilling to make war on the white fathers without his own father's blessing. I gave this to him, as he was my son, and could not be made into a woman, as the *Mengwe,* the Iroquois, once made us into women, as the white fathers have made me into a woman. So full of anger was Pematalli, so full of hate. He made sacrifices. As I watched, he painted his body with the images of our people, seeking strength and courage for the battle that would come."

"Pematalli took part in the raid? He took part in the killing?"

Bryna sliced a quick, angry look toward Dominick, who had asked the question, barely able to see him through her tears. How could he ask such questions now—with Lokwelend's only son lying dead in front of them?

"My son saw his life disappearing, saw all our lives disappearing. He felt the fear, the anger, the hatred." Lokwelend looked up at Dominick, his dark eyes inexpressibly sad. "Fear such as Pematalli's has discharged more than one rifle, my friend, on both sides. Anger and hatred have swung many war clubs, unsheathed many knives. Have you not felt this same fear, this same anger, this same hatred—toward us? I look into your eyes, and see your answer. Yes, my son has killed this day, taken many scalps.

And he has died a warrior. As he wished to do. As he was meant to do. There is nothing left now between us, Crown. Nothing more than the grief we hold for our dead. This is why I have come, and this is what I have to tell you. It is over, my friend. It is finished."

Bryna watched, her hands pressed flat to her mouth, as her dear friend struggled to rise with his son in his arms. The boy's limbs hung limply. His feet swung low, his head thrown back over his father's forearm, as Lokwelend gripped him at the shoulders and knees. His father cradled Pematalli like a baby, like what he was, what he had been— a well-loved child.

"Don't go, Lokwelend," she begged quietly as Dominick helped her to her feet. "Walks With Death has given orders to arrest any Indians in the area. You're not safe in the forest, but we can hide you here at Pleasant Hill until the worst is over, until—" Her voice faltered as she realized that Lokwelend would not be welcome anywhere in New Eden. Not now. Perhaps not ever again. His home was gone. His son was gone. His way of life was gone. Lokwelend was right. It was finished.

She turned to Dominick, grabbing on to his arm. "Do something, Dominick!" she yelled at him, demanding a miracle she knew he could not perform. "This isn't fair! This isn't right!"

But Dominick ignored her outburst. "As you say, Lokwelend, it is done. May we be present at the burial, my friend? It is right that Crown honors the warrior."

Bryna turned away in disgust, in exasperation mixed with grief. This was no time for formal Lenape ceremony, for pretty speeches. A boy was dead! That once innocent, smiling boy she had seen that first day here at Pleasant Hill. *Dead!*

"I wish to give my friend Pematalli gifts to take with him on his journey," she heard Dominick continue. "Tobacco, for his pipe. A dressed deerskin, for moccasins. My women will weep for him, and bring food to the place where he rests, each day for twenty days and one, until he has found his way to his new place of residence."

Lokwelend inclined his head only slightly, saying, "It is good that you wish to so honor my son. We will meet tomorrow, beside the log house where Pematalli grew to be a man, and we will then take him to his place of burial at the cliff where he and I last met. I will go now."

"Dominick! You can't let Lokwelend carry Pematalli all the way back to the creek," Bryna implored him. She felt helpless, completely without control over a situation that had no way of improving, of reverting back to that moment before Renton Frey had arrived and begun the madness that had brought the world crashing down around their shoulders once again. "Not by himself. Please—go with him. Help him."

"No," Philip said firmly, stepping forward, his posture very straight, his shoulders squared. "I'll go with him. And so will Deems. Won't you, Deems? Dominick, you'd better take Bryna back into the house. She's shaking like a cat in a wet sack."

Lokwelend looked at Philip for long moments, then nodded. "Yes, little Crown. You may come with us. It is fitting that my son have a warrior by his side."

"You've grown up today, haven't you, Philip?" Dominick asked quietly, pulling Bryna close against his side, as if to warm her with the heat from his body as one by one, the still silent, hovering men turned and went back to the house. "Learned many of those lessons Lokwelend said you wouldn't want to learn. About war. About death. About forgiveness. I only thank God you're still alive to learn more."

"Yes, I've had several lessons today, actually," Philip agreed, looking down at Pematalli's face, then raising his eyes to Dominick, so that Bryna sucked in her breath at the sight of the naked pain visible in their clear blue depths. "And I've learned a lot. More than you can know."

Bryna allowed Dominick to lead her back toward the house, pausing every few steps to turn and look behind her, watching as Lucas led the way toward the trees, holding the lantern high, with Lokwelend and Philip following him.

The last time she turned around, Philip had taken Lokwelend's heavy burden from him, and was walking tall, his shoulder-length blond hair visible in the light from the lantern, his spine arched back to balance out the weight of Pematalli's body. Lokwelend had laid his arm around Lucas's shoulders, as if suddenly finding himself in need of some support.

"I'll never understand this, Dominick," Bryna said, watching as the trio of men disappeared into the darkness under the trees. "I'll never understand any of it."

Dominick was silent for a long time, until they were back in the house and walking, arm in arm, up the stairs to their bedchamber. "You saw how Pematalli was dressed, didn't you, Bryna? Nothing more than a breechclout to cover his body, nothing to protect him from injury. The Lenape have only weapons to kill, and no shields or armor or helmets to guard against the weapons of their enemies. Pematalli had his hair in a scalplock, to provide his enemy with a trophy if he should kill him in battle. You aren't the only one who doesn't understand. I'll never understand how the Lenape can show such respect for their enemies. I'll never understand how they can kill one child, yet take another with them and adopt him as their own. I'll never understand how they can love the land and yet not claim any part of it for themselves."

He stopped beside the bed and laid his hands on Bryna's shoulders. "And I'll never understand how Lokwelend can love his son, and not want to murder the man who has killed that son. You saw Philip's face, didn't you, Bryna? I'm sure Lokwelend saw it too, and realized the truth. Philip had never seen Pematalli before tonight—and yet he recognized him. He recognized the face of the man who tried to kill him, the man that he killed."

Bryna wiped at her tear-wet cheeks. "You saw that, too? I had hoped I was wrong, but . . . ." Her voice trailed away as she allowed Dominick to lift her into bed, and she watched as he used the hem of his dressing gown to dry her feet. "I'm so confused, Dominick. My heart is breaking for all the people who have died in this madness. It's breaking for my family, for the families that died today, for Lokwelend. For Philip. It's breaking for all of us."

"Don't think about it anymore tonight." Dominick bent to kiss her forehead, then pulled the covers over her. "I love you, Bryna Cassidy Crown. Now, try to get some sleep."

He turned away from her, and she grabbed at his sleeve as he bent to pick up his moccasins. "You're not coming to bed? Where are you going?"

"I'm going downstairs to uncork a bottle and wait for Philip," he told her. "We'll probably uncork more than a few of them before the night is over, while we sit and talk, and try to tell ourselves we're not hypocrites. For at the bottom of it, Bryna, sorry as I am for Lokwelend's loss, I can't say that I regret Pematalli's death."

"I know, Dominick," Bryna said, grateful he understood her own jumbled feelings, then sighed, turning her face in to the pillows. "I know."

Beware the fury of a patient man.
Dryden

CHAPTER 18

IT FELT GOOD TO BE OUT-OF-DOORS AGAIN, WALKING IN THE sunlight of the early November days, spending time with Mary Catherine in the gardens, teaching her the names of the last of the fall flowers, helping Lucretia to gather herbs to dry for the coming winter as the first frost would slide into the valley soon. All around Pleasant Hill, the trees were turning gold, and red, and a most glorious orange. The harvest was nearly complete, the stock brought into the East Meadow in preparation for winter.

The heavy velvet draperies were back in place at the windows, windows that had not been shuttered in many a long day. The rooms smelled of beeswax and Lucretia's apple tarts, and the air rang with Mary Catherine's sweet laughter as she rode on the toes of Philip's shoes, learning how to dance as Dominick played for them in the music room. There were no longer rifles and shot and powder standing at the ready beside each window. Dominick had planted a dozen oak trees at the front of the house, lining one side of the drive.

How very easy it seemed to forget.

They had buried Pematalli, and Lokwelend had left that same day, heading west, over the mountains, to be with his daughter. Settlers were coming into New Eden, some having drawn back from the western frontier, but more of them arriving from the East, secure in the knowledge that no hostile Lenape were left in the area. They were all "safe as houses" now, as Elijah Kester's wife had said, or at least as safe as anyone in Philadelphia.

Even Lieutenant Frey was gone, having been put in charge of escorting the local Indians to Philadelphia, and then on to Lancaster, where they were being held until they could be moved to the West. Bryna had never told Dominick of her suspicions about Frey having murdered her father, and she was glad she had not, as it would serve no good purpose. As Lokwelend had told her, both in words and by his own example, she must learn to let the dead rest with the dead.

Dominick was busy again, building. Always building. Crown's Inn and Stores was being expanded, even as a German couple had come to purchase Rudolph's building, the two establishments easily existing side by side, as the number of travelers through New Eden seemed to grow each day, all of them needing a place to rest for the night, all of them requiring supplies before they moved on.

Only once did Bryna give in to her emotions, feeling all the old anger rising as Dominick had told her that he had bought the Jennings and Moore farms and installed two tenant farmers and their families, adding even more land to his already sprawling estate.

"There are times, Dominick Crown, when I can really hate you!" she had exploded, bursting into tears and running for their bedchamber, locking the door behind her.

She had known that she was being silly, and womanish, but blamed her weakness on her blossoming pregnancy when Dominick had come to her, as he nearly always came to her, to apologize for being a practical man.

"I've also bought the Werley farm this morning, as they've decided to move west to be with their daughter,"

Dominick had told her as they lay together on their high, wide bed, having settled their argument in a most pleasant manner. "I hadn't realized it, but Pematalli is buried on the fringes of that land, and not on our own. It's not good farmland, not with the cliff so near to it, so I'll never put it under cultivation, but I just felt better having it in our possession. I think Lokwelend would want it that way, don't you?"

"I doubt it matters who holds the land, Dominick," Bryna had told him honestly. "Pematalli means Always There, or so Lokwelend has said. That's why he buried him where he did, near the edge of the cliff, so that Pematalli's spirit can keep watch over the valley of his grandfathers. Do you think Lokwelend will ever come back, Dominick? Or was he right, and only Pematalli will be left, to always remind us all that the Lenni-Lenape once made their home here?"

Dominick hadn't had an answer for her, and she hadn't expected one.

Throughout the remainder of October, Bryna and Lucretia had done as was the Lenape custom, carrying a small pot of food to Pematalli's grave every day for three weeks after the burial. They always found the uneaten pot from the previous day waiting for them, but Bryna was unwilling to curtail the ritual out of respect for the absent Lokwelend.

Bryna came to consider that trip to the grave as a part of her day. It had become a small, welcome comfort to her. In the quiet hours she spent there, surrounded by trees and birdsong and grass and open sky, the river lying far below her, she had found her first real peace since the raid. She also knew that, with winter coming soon, and with her pregnancy keeping her closer to the house, she might not be able to go back to the grave again before spring.

Leaving Lucretia in charge as Mary Catherine napped on the couch in the drawing room, Bryna set out for the grave shortly after lunch. She took a half dozen fishhooks with her, in case Pematalli's spirit came by for a visit and was in the mood to drop a line in the creek beside the log house where he and his father had spent many a day on the banks, lifting out catfish and tickling trout. She didn't feel in the least silly doing this, having decided that, if her father could have believed in leprechauns and fairies, there was no reason not to believe that Always There could not avail himself of a fishhook or a pot of stew now and then.

Bryna drew the horses to a halt on the narrow dirt track at the base of the hill and spent a moment just sitting on the wagon seat, surprised, as always, at how peaceful it always seemed in this place, how quiet. But not at all the site for a house, or for stock, not with the cliff so close, so dangerous. Not a place for farming, either, as it was rocky and steep, the only really flat area of land being that where Pematalli had been buried. "As poor a land as ever a crow flew over." That's what her uncle Daniel would have said. But in its way, it was also quite beautiful. Lokwelend had chosen well.

Bryna climbed down from the wagon and gauged the steepness of the rise to the top of the hill. Her back began to ache just at the thought of the effort it would take to climb it. No, Pematalli would have to do without his fishhooks until the spring, for in the past week she had somehow slipped past her hill-climbing days. "It's a wise woman who knows what she can and cannot do, Bryna Crown," she told herself, turning around, ready to mount the wagon seat once more.

"No, please, dear lady—stay where you are. Stay just where you are. Oh, except that you might be so kind as to put up your hands, seeing as how I'm holding a pistol at your back."

"Frey." Bryna whispered the lieutenant's name even as she slowly turned around in time to see him step out from behind a tree, a pistol pointed in her direction. "Dominick will murder you for this."

"Really? I rather don't think so," Frey said almost affably, looking strangely sinister in his dark broadcloth coat and breeches, his scarlet uniform gone. "Now keep your mouth shut before I lose my temper. I've been hiding in the woods for days, watching, waiting for you to let me close enough to grab. You see, believe it or not—worthless Irish bitch that you are—I have finally found a use for you.

Your dolt of a husband will pay a goodly sum to have you back."

Frey's eyes narrowed and Bryna remained silent, waiting for what would happen next. She was being kidnapped, that much was already certain. But where would he take her? How would he contact Dominick to demand her ransom?

The lieutenant smiled yet again as he took a folded paper from his belt. He opened it with one hand and placed it on the wagon seat, then picked up a rock and placed it on top as a paperweight. "You always did underestimate me, you know, you and your loose-lipped father both. Now start walking." He indicated the direction with a movement of the pistol. "Over there, into those trees. And if you can't keep up, you fat sow, I'll gut you where you fall and then tell Crown where he can find the body. After he pays me, of course."

Bryna stood her ground. "Pay you? He'll hang a piece of you on every tree from here in to New Eden!" she told him, lowering her hands, sure he wouldn't shoot her. From what he'd just told her, he needed her alive in order to have bargaining power with her husband. "Dominick said you'd be cashiered sooner or later. From the look of you, I'd say he was right."

Bryna winced involuntarily as Frey pressed the barrel of his pistol into the center of her breasts. A moment later, she felt the loop of rough hempen rope he slipped over her head. "That's another thing I never liked about you, bitch. You talk too much." The rope went taut as he gave it a vicious tug, so that, even with her hands still free, she had no choice but to follow him as he moved off toward the trees. "Now, come on—I want to be on our way before we lose the daylight."

Holding on to the rope so that it wouldn't choke her, Bryna followed after him, careful to drag her left foot slightly every few feet as they moved cross-country, the back of her neck soon growing raw as he continued to tug on the rope.

She and Lokwelend had spoken of many things in those long nights after Alice's death. They had spoken of life, and mysteries, and more earthly things—like how the creek talks, if only you listen, and how to read the weather in the clouds . . . and how to lay a path through an unmarked territory.

Bryna blocked her mind to the pain, to her fears. She drew on the lessons she had learned. And she kept walking. Brushing against a low-hanging branch to dislodge a small shower of nearly ready-to-fall leaves. Scattering a few loose pebbles with the toe of her half boot. Careful to tread on any soft clump of moss. Dropping her store of fishhooks, one every several hundred yards or so, until, with only a single fishhook left, and with a pain in her side so sharp she could barely breathe, she stepped out into a clearing and saw Lokwelend's abandoned log house.

"This is good enough. I've been here for days, biding my time, although I couldn't risk a fire. Not that anyone would think to look for me here. As I remember from the schooling of my long-ago and unlamented youth, it is rare to find this year's birds in last year's nests."

Bryna smiled, then quickly hid her pleasure as she was hustled along toward the log house. Renton Frey wasn't a stupid man, she decided, slipping the remaining fishhook into her pocket. But he wasn't particularly smart, either.

"You're a real founding father, aren't you, Dominick? Do you think the grateful citizens of New Eden will make you lord high mayor?"

Dominick shifted slightly on the comfortable Lenape-style saddle and looked at his nephew. No. His friend. "Don't exaggerate. All I did today was offer lumber for a school and the first year's wages for a teacher. New Eden is never going to rival Allen's Town, Philip, but that doesn't mean we can ignore the necessities. The school can also double as a church, for a while at least."

"Oh, by all means, yes," Philip agreed, grinning. "And then, once the school is established, you can put your energies to the building of proper roads—after you've laid out plans for the development of streets, that is. There could be squares, and a park, and—"

"Shouldn't you be making plans to begin your tour of the colonies, Philip?" Dominick interrupted, unable to hold back a smile as he looked into Philip's laughing eyes as they continued along the road to Pleasant Hill at a leisurely pace. "Or you could simply go home. After all, your father must be pining for the sight of his heir by now, if only so that he can try out any number of plans he must have formulated in your absence—each one of them designed to free you of some of your inheritance. Perhaps a pudding-faced heiress who'd bring even more money into Giles's pocket?"

"That was low, dear Uncle, low! But I'll take your not-so-subtle hint and change the subject. You were deep in conversation with the estimable Elijah Kester when I looked into the common room from my place behind the counter, weighing up sugar for Mrs. Kester like the good shopkeeper you've encouraged me to become. Which will keep me safe from pudding-faced heiresses, by the way, as I can scarcely go to the altar smelling of the shop, no matter what my prospects." Philip screwed up his face comically, then added, "By God, I imagine I should be grateful, come to think of it, as the last thing I want is to be caught in the parson's mousetrap."

"There's a lot to be said for marriage, Philip," Dominick pointed out, thinking of Bryna, who was at home, waiting for him. He had a gift for her, tucked into his shirt: a fine pair of silver shoe buckles he'd bought from Mr. Hunsicker just that morning. He wanted to buy her pearls, and diamonds, and he would, next spring, when they traveled to Philadelphia. The wonderful thing about Bryna—one of the many wonderful things about his wife—was that she would be as delighted with the buckles as she would be with the pearls. Not that she ever asked for anything for herself. Not Bryna. It had, however, been at her request that he had made arrangements for the school. Which was another reason he loved her.

Philip leaned forward in his saddle and looked over at Dominick, shaking his head. "You're doing it again, you know."

"Doing what?" They were nearly back to Pleasant Hill,

and Dominick was anxious to be shed of Philip so that he could be alone with Bryna.

"Grinning," Philip said shortly. "You grin a lot lately—most often when you're thinking of Bryna. You are thinking of her, aren't you? Don't you consider it in the least odd to be so thoroughly infatuated with one's own wife? I know you've been away from home for a long time, so perhaps I should remind you that it's not at all fashionable."

"Neither, I imagine, is toppling you from your horse and boxing your ears," Dominick replied easily, "but I may just do it anyway. Now, do you want to hear what Kester told me, or do you have anything else you want to say on the subject of my unfashionably happy marriage?"

Philip held up his hands as if in surrender. "I'll be good, Uncle, I promise. Please, tell me all the gossip. Did someone steal a pig? Or perhaps one of the local matrons was seen winking at Mr. Hunsicker in hopes of talking him out of one of his ostrich feathers?"

"Nothing so earthshaking as that, Philip. Kester told me that Lieutenant Frey has been cashiered. It seems his superiors have decided that the man was more of a liability than they could afford. Public opinion, as fickle here as anywhere, is now turning back in favor of the Lenape."

"Does that mean they won't be shipping the survivors off to the West?"

Dominick shook his head. "No. They're already on their way to the Wyoming Valley. But if Lokwelend were ever to return to Pleasant Hill, he would most probably be left alone. The threat of attack is over, Philip, and the government has decided it will look better if they turn a blind eye to the few Indians who remain in the area. According to Kester, several have already come back to Bethlehem."

"And Frey's gone," Philip said reflectively. "I wonder where he's gone *to*. Back to England, I suppose."

"I doubt it," Dominick told him. "He'll probably head straight for Philadelphia and hire himself out to a land broker wanting to clear the Indians from territories closer to Fort Pitt. The man has all the attributes of an agitator, and is not lacking in ambition. I'm just thankful he's gone, and I know Bryna will be overjoyed."

"You're probably right. I only wish I could have been there to see you knock him down. According to Bryna, you're a handy one with your fives. I—"

Dominick reined his horse to a stop and lifted a hand to silence his nephew.

"What is it?" Philip whispered as Dominick laid a hand on the butt of his rifle. "What do you see?"

"I don't see anything," Dominick answered quietly, urging his horse forward slowly as he strained to see around the next bend in the roadway. "I hear it. Somebody's coming, and coming fast."

Just then a horse and rider rounded the bend, and Dominick saw Lucas Deems in the saddle, holding on to the reins with both hands and looking as if he might topple to the ground at any moment. The servant saw them at once and began sawing on the reins, digging his heels into the horse's sides as he yelled at it—pleaded with it—to stop. Philip urged his own mount into a turn, allowed Lucas to come up alongside of him, and made a grab at the reins, finally slowing the horse and stopping it a good twenty yards beyond Dominick.

"What is it, Lucas?" Dominick asked, dismounting himself, even as the servant slid to the ground, his knees nearly buckling as his feet made contact with the packed dirt. "What's wrong? Is it Bryna? Is something wrong with Bryna? For God's sake, man, take a breath and answer me."

Lucas swallowed hard, his Adam's apple bobbing up and down, then rushed into speech. "She took the wagon out to the grave, sir," he said, pulling a large white handkerchief from his pocket and wiping his forehead with it. "But that was more than three hours ago. Lucretia . . . Lucretia sent me to find you, sure something's wrong. The horses ran away with her, or perhaps she twisted her ankle climbing that hill . . . I'm sorry, sir," Lucas ended, collapsing into the dirt. "I don't ride, you know. I have to sit down."

"I'm going after Bryna," Dominick told Philip as he

mounted the bay in one fluid movement. "Get Lucas to the house and have one of the men ride for Billie Kester. Bryna's probably fallen asleep beneath a tree, but Lucretia could be right. She might need some nursing."

"But—"

"Not now, Philip." Dominick turned the mare and urged her into an immediate gallop, retracing his way back down the road until he came to the narrow turnoff leading to the Werley farm. He didn't think, couldn't think. He just wanted to find his wife. His mind was a near blank as he rounded a curve a half mile along the road and saw the abandoned wagon, the horses standing idle in their traces, and the piece of paper pinned to the seat.

And he knew. He felt a cold fist of fear twisting in the center of his gut as he tossed the small rock to the ground and picked up the paper. God help him, he knew. He should have ended it long ago. Now Bryna and his child were paying for his mistake.

He read the note quickly, for it contained only a few lines, and he was already fairly certain as to what it said. Renton Frey had his wife, had Bryna, and he would return her—for a fee. "This is no more than unfinished business. Behave like a gentleman, my lord, and I will behave like a gentleman also," Frey had written. "A gentleman of means, of course." The last line of the note bore the instruction that Dominick was to simply follow "his nose," which would lead him to where Frey waited, ready to discuss terms for Bryna's safe release.

Follow his nose? What the devil did *that* mean? Dismounting, Dominick walked the roadway first on one side of the wagon, then on the other, careful where he stepped, looking for some sign that his wife had been there. And then he saw it, glinting in the sunlight that sliced down through the tall trees. He bent down and picked up the small metal fishhook, already looking into the underbrush beside the road, leading away from the hill.

His mind no longer blank, but concentrated, in the way of the hunter, he set off, leading his horse, following the easily read signs. His heart beat slow and steady, his movements were quiet and precise, his emotions stayed locked tight behind a steely determination to find his wife. To rescue her. To see her safe.

And then, once Bryna was all right, once he had her back, he would put an end to this. He would do what he should have done long since. He would kill Lieutenant Renton Frey.

Without pity. Without remorse. Even without anger. The way he would step on a bug.

"I fail to see why you're spending your time looking out that window," Bryna said, wishing the ropes that now tied her hands and bound her to a chair weren't quite so tight. Not that she'd complain, because her discomfort would only delight Frey. "You can't expect Dominick to come here with money if you haven't so much as sent him an invitation."

"On the contrary, bitch. I've sent him two, the fire outside being one of them. The other would be all those bent twigs and the like that you were so gracious as to supply, so that a blind man could follow us here."

"You—you knew what I was doing?" Bryna fought to keep the nervousness from her voice. She had thought she was being so brilliant! But had she really played directly into Frey's hands? How long would she keep underestimating this vile excuse for a man?

Frey looked away from the window for a moment, to grin at Bryna in a way that made her long to throttle him. "Oh dear, and you thought I was stupid, didn't you? So sorry to disappoint. Yes, bitch. I knew what you were doing. I even left your hands free so that you could do it better, seeing as how that belly of yours kept you from trying to run away. Now shut up, if you please. Your husband should be along any moment now, and I want to be sure to see him before he sees me. That way, maybe I won't have to shoot him."

Antagonizing Frey might not be the best idea, considering her circumstances, but it appealed to Bryna and she decided to indulge herself. "What happened, Lieutenant? Was your last round of killing too much for your keepers? That is why you're not in uniform, isn't it? You've been used, haven't you, like any Judas, and now they've cast you out, neglecting to even give you your thirty pieces of silver."

"I told you to shut up!" Frey barked out, turning away from the window once more.

Bryna smiled, keeping her eyes on the man, so that he didn't look away, which was just what she wanted. "Falling is easier than rising, isn't it, Frey? That's what my father always told me. You took a nice climb there for a while, fair-haired boy that you were, but you didn't really think you'd get all the way up the mountain, did you? Did you think you were going to be one of them? That they'd welcome you into their little circle of power? Oh, no. You've fallen all the way down, haven't you? Because they knew, these masters of yours. They knew who you are, what you are. A hyena. A jackal."

"If so, I'm going to be a rich jackal," Frey told her, his smile more congenial than evil, which made it doubly difficult for Bryna to keep looking at him. "And speaking of purses, I saw you looking at mine that day in New Eden. I've often wondered why you never told your husband about it. Or maybe you did? The man's such a bloody coward, though, that he wouldn't have dared to confront me. No, not Lord Dominick Crown. He'd just write another bloody letter."

Frey pulled the green purse from his pocket and waved it at Bryna. "It is a pretty thing, isn't it? I took an immediate fancy to it, and your father didn't need it anymore, or its contents. You haven't asked yet how he died. Do you want to know, bitch? Or are you afraid to ask?"

Bryna refused to flinch. "I would imagine you *bored* him to death," she said, involuntarily closing her eyes as Frey's control snapped and he ran across the room, raised his hand, then sent his palm crashing against her cheek. She felt a trickle of blood at the corner of her mouth where her lip had split.

"Why am I not surprised that you'd hit a woman?" she asked, smiling up at him through the pain. "I should expect nothing less from a pig than a grunt."

Frey shoved his hand into Bryna's hair and pulled, so that her head was thrown back as he lowered his face to within an inch of hers. "I'd slice your throat for you now, but I wouldn't want to do Crown a favor. Better you live to murder him by inches with that Irish mouth of yours. I only kill for money—or if I don't get it."

"Mark me again, Frey, and Dominick won't give you a bent farthing, unless he uses it to carve out your spleen."

He raised his hand, to hit her again, only for them both to freeze like statues as a shot rang out, splitting the tension like a knife ripping through silk.

"Frey! It's Crown. I want to see my wife!"

"Dominick," Bryna breathed gratefully as Frey let go of her hair and raced back to the window, cursing under his breath. "Dominick! I'm here!" she cried.

"Stay where you are, Crown!" Frey warned, sliding the barrel of his rifle over the window frame. "Take another step and I'll put a hole straight through you."

Bryna hastily tried to wipe away the blood on her face by rubbing her chin against her shoulder. She began to cry, silently, truly frightened for the first time; not for herself, but for Dominick. Frey was like a cocked pistol. Any small jostle might set him off. "Do what he says, Dominick. He hasn't hurt me."

"You mentioned a gentlemanly exchange, Lieutenant, and I am agreeable to that. Now put down your weapon— I'm coming in," she heard Dominick say, his voice low and tight, so that she knew he was angry. Very, very angry. And very much in control, thank God! "I know you want money. Shoot me and you'll never see a cent. Frey—put down that rifle!"

Frey withdrew the rifle from the window and propped it against the wall. He picked up a pistol from the table, and pointed it at Bryna as he peered out the window once more. "No farther than the threshold, Crown, I'm warning you! You can take a look at the merchandise, but that's all. Do anything else and I'll kill you both and cut my losses. I haven't forgotten that day in New Eden, you know, how you attacked me when I was off guard."

Bryna held her breath as the door slowly opened and Dominick entered silently, his moccasins making no sound as he stepped into the room. She shifted her eyes to her left, to where Frey had moved to stand behind the opened door, wordlessly letting him know where the man was. "Do what he says, Dominick," she told him, appalled to see that he was not armed. "He won't hurt me if you do what he wants. He only kills for money—or if he doesn't get it. The lieutenant is a man of honor, in his own twisted way. Isn't that right, Lieutenant?"

Frey stepped out from behind the door. "I don't know how you stand her, Crown," he remarked with a grin, lifting the pistol slightly to motion that Dominick should remain where he was. "Just like her father—without enough sense to keep her mouth shut. He made the mistake of telling me he was going to the captain of the *Eagle* to report that I was fuzzing the cards. Did you ever hear of anything so unremittingly stupid? I'm only glad I thought to check his pockets before I tossed him overboard, as it seems he'd been holding out on me. I thought I'd taken all his blunt at the table, but he had a whole other purse tucked in his waistcoat. A lovely green purse. Isn't that right, *my lady?*"

"My uncle's patent money," Bryna said dully, looking at Dominick intensely, aware that he, too, remembered the green purse she'd seen that day in New Eden. "I suspected from the beginning that my father's death hadn't been an accident, even told the captain so, not that he believed me. I was all alone, and there was nothing I could do. And I couldn't even be sure myself," she explained quickly, "not until I saw the purse. I didn't tell you because you'd want to kill Frey for me, and I didn't want you to do anything in the heat of temper. By then, I'd just wanted Frey gone—out of our lives. Let the dead rest with the dead, that's what Lokwelend said. But he was wrong. I was wrong. Please, Dominick, forgive me."

"It's all right, Bryna," Dominick told her, his tone gentle, so that she relaxed slightly, which was ridiculous, as they were no closer to safety than they had been a moment earlier. He turned to Frey. "So. What now, Lieutenant? Am

I to trust you not to harm my wife while I go to Pleasant Hill and bring you all the money I have, at which point you'll release us both? Each of us trusting in the other's honor, of course."

Frey smiled, a truly evil smile for such a handsome man. "Naturally, Crown. I have full trust in *your* honor, as you must have in mine. After all, we're both gentlemen. You, through birth, and me, thanks to all the lovely money I shall soon have."

"Have my wife outside in twenty minutes, Frey," Dominick said, taking one last, long look at Bryna. "I'll hold up the pouch, open it to show you I'm not trying to trick you, then toss it to you once my wife is halfway between this cabin and the trees. Agreed?"

"Not really, no," Frey responded, his smile seemingly frozen to his face. "A few more conditions, if you don't mind. I'll need a horse. Yours, I believe, as I've noticed how sound the bay is. Your wife will fetch the horse to me, and the pouch, and *then* we will be finished. And you're to come alone, which I'm sure you already know. No quibbling, Crown. I'm really in no mood to quibble."

Dominick looked at Bryna again, so that she mouthed the words "I love you," then closed her eyes.

When she opened her eyes again he was gone, and she and Frey were alone in the cabin once more. He put down the pistol and began leisurely gathering up his belongings, folding each article of clothing precisely, rolling them all up neatly inside a blanket, and then placing them just outside the door, ready for his escape.

Bryna didn't say a word as he untied her from the chair, then re-bound her hands in front of her. She didn't speak as he pulled her to her feet, guiding her toward the door, none too gently pushing her out into the fading sunlight and the rapidly falling temperature of the November day. She refused to react when he told her that it had been a "pleasure, a distinct pleasure," doing business with an English gentleman. "Or a coward, which seems a more fitting description for the man," he added, so that she had to bite her tongue to keep from responding to his taunt.

Dominick must have raced his mount through the trees all the way to Pleasant Hill, for he was back at the edge of the clearing in less than twenty minutes, dismounting from the large bay mare, a canvas bag in his hand. "I'll tie the bag to the reins, Frey," he said even as he was doing it, then began slowly walking the horse to the center of the clearing.

"Leave the horse there, and step back where you were," Frey called out, only releasing Bryna's elbow when Dominick had done what he said. Not taking her eyes off her husband, she walked to where the bay waited, taking up the reins and leading the horse to Frey, who now had a pistol in his right hand, a rifle in his left. "Open the pouch and let me see inside," he ordered, excitement evident in his voice. Not cool at all. Not calm. He was a man in sight of his victory, already congratulating himself on his brilliance, and he could barely contain his glee.

"Open it yourself, you bloody Englisher," Bryna told him, already moving away, knowing she was gambling, but relying on her father's teachings on the behavior of their fellow humans. A fool who believes himself a winner rarely has time for anything else but counting his booty. "I'm weary of this whole sordid business, frankly, and I'm going home now to my dinner."

Mere moments later, only vaguely aware of the sound of hoofbeats as Frey rode off, she was in Dominick's arms, and being carried into the shelter of the trees. "Are you all right?" he was asking her even as Philip appeared from her left, holding his rifle.

"I had a clear shot at him, Dominick," Philip complained. "Why didn't you let me drop him?"

"Because I'm an honorable man, Philip," Dominick said, untying Bryna's hands and accepting the kiss she reached up to press on his cheek. "I made a bargain, and I stuck to it. To do anything else would have put Bryna in danger. Please take her back to the house now so that everyone knows she's all right."

All of Bryna's fears came rushing back. "But, Dominick, where are you going? Surely you aren't going after Frey? It's over, darling. This time it's truly over. Let him go."

He bent and kissed her on the lips, then accepted the reins of Philip's horse. "Not this time, Bryna. Go with Philip."

"I said no!" Bryna could see the cold fury in his eyes, the determination in his rigid posture, and she began to tremble. She grabbed at his arm, trying to make him understand. "He's not worth it, Dominick! Please! We're safe now. He'll never come back." She tried to hold on to him as he mounted the horse, then hung on to the bridle, still unwilling to give up. "Damn you, Dominick Crown—I refuse to let you go!"

"Philip. Your rifle, if you please," Dominick said tightly, catching the weapon with one hand as his nephew tossed it up to him. "And my knife."

Bryna held on to the bridle for long moments as Dominick slipped the knife into the plain blue sash around his waist. She looked up into her husband's face, seeing the quiet resolve there, sensing the cold fury he must have held in check since first discovering what Frey had done. Arguing would do her no good, no good at all. Not argument, not tears, not temper. Nothing. Not this time. Stifling a sob, she released the bridle and settled for a threat. "You had better come home to me, Dominick Crown, or I'll haunt you through eternity, I swear it!"

"Might I believe that's some sort of Irish blessing? Very touching, I suppose." Philip took Bryna's arm and guided her to the side of the narrow path, motioning for Dominick to go ahead.

"We'll have another talk about the joys of matrimony when you return, Uncle," he called after him. "I think I still must be missing something."

Dominick fought to block out the memory of Bryna's cut lip as he followed the progress of the large bay mare through the underbrush, knowing he had to think with his wits, not his emotions. It was nearly dark now, and he had never lost Frey's trail, but preferred to hang back, keeping his distance until the man stopped for the night. Until he was sitting at his ease beside his campfire, engrossed in counting his ill-gotten money, secure in his belief that Lord Dominick Crown was both a gentleman and a coward, and already tucked up at home, his wife tending to his bruised consequence.

Underestimating Dominick Crown had been Giles's mistake, and their father's mistake. Now it was Renton Frey's turn to learn the folly of believing himself the stronger man, impervious to attack.

As dusk neared, and a horseman's progress necessarily slowed, Dominick dismounted and tied Philip's mount to a nearby tree. He set off again on foot, leaving the rifle behind. He stopped occasionally to look for signs, the way Lokwelend had taught him, then moved on, quietly, careful not to disturb the birds or other small animals that might start up, giving him away.

For another hour, and then two, he moved southeast, always to the southeast, cross-country, in the direction of Philadelphia, so far away. It was only after the sun had fully set, as stars began to shine high above in the night-dark sky, that he halted, dropping to his haunches as he smelled the smoke of a campfire.

Frey.

With his rifle, his pistols. And with a French-made one-shot pistol tucked at his waist behind his back; a knife slipped inside his right boot.

Lokwelend's teachings came to him, quietly whispering in his ear. *Always know your enemy. Always know his strengths, his weaknesses. And have no weaknesses of your own.*

Dominick moved to his left, following the sound of a small stream of gurgling water. He didn't stop until he was crouched alongside the muddy bank, his gaze following the path of the water, knowing that Frey must be camped just around the next bend.

He pulled the leather strip from his tied-back hair, letting its weight fall free to his shoulders, then retied the strip around his forehead, pulling the leather taut. He dipped the fingers of both hands into the soft, black soil and pulled streaks down his cheeks, down the center bridge of his nose.

His heart beating slowly, with a calm and certainty born of years of self-control only rarely unleashed, he laid down his knife, loosened his sash, and removed his jacket, his shirt. Pushing his palms into the wet soil at the edge of the stream once more, he lifted mud-caked hands and pressed imprints of those opened hands on either side of his chest. Pematalli's mark. For Dominick's revenge would be his, and Bryna's, and that of the innocent families who had died to feed Frey's ambition. But it would also be Lokwelend's revenge.

He was ready.

The blade of his knife clamped between his teeth, Dominick moved off, into the trees, his body bent low over his knees, his progress without sound, swift and fluid and without hesitation. He stopped only when he saw the outline of Frey's body, his back turned to him as he sat in front of his campfire, counting the gold coins Dominick had paid for the release of his wife.

The man was greedy, confident, and more than a little bit of a fool. Killing him would be simple. Dominick could come up behind him, unnoticed, and slit his throat with ease.

But that was not Dominick Crown's way.

His plan was already set in his mind. First he had to separate Frey from his weapons, and for that he needed the element of surprise. Crouching low, his muscles tensed for action, he gripped the knife in his right hand and slowly counted to ten. Then he drew in a deep breath and let it out in a loud, piercing war whoop, the sort Philip had said could freeze a man's blood in a twinkling.

And then everything happened at once. Frey leapt to his feet even as Dominick vaulted forward into the small clearing, somersaulting through the campfire and landing on his feet, his crouched body positioned to separate Frey from his rifle, which was propped against a nearby rock.

"Crown!" Frey looked, shook his head, then looked again. His former fear seemed to flee as he threw back his head and laughed. "I always knew you were nothing but a bloody savage. Painted on a little courage, I see. Well, now what?"

"Now, Lieutenant," Dominick said, spreading his arms slightly in preparation of a fight, "you're going to reach behind your back—with your left hand, thank you—and remove that little toy you carry. That's it. Gently—now throw it over here, into the water."

Frey was still smiling, except he no longer appeared amused, but feral, his lips drawn back over his teeth. There was a soft splash when the pistol hit the surface of the stream. "Your bitch wife told you about that, didn't she? I never did like her, or her cardsharping father. What now, Crown? Are you going to ask me to turn my back, so that you can stab me like the coward you are? Or are you done playing the Indian?"

Dominick never took his eyes off Frey, but already he knew every inch of the clearing, the way the campfire was to his right, the steep bank leading down to the stream to his rear. "No, I'm not yet quite done, Lieutenant," he said calmly, mentally pacing off the distance between himself and the other man. "We're going to perform a small experiment, you and I. Take that knife out of your boot. Slowly, Frey, slowly. Using only two fingers."

The knife dangled between the fingers of the lieutenant's right hand. "You actually intend to fight me? Would you mind if I removed my jacket?"

"Lay down the knife first, if you please."

Frey did as he was told. Moving slowly, he stripped off his jacket and rolled up his shirtsleeves, then quickly dropped into a crouch himself, the knife retrieved and clasped across his palm. He held both his arms extended, his entire posture showing that he was no stranger to this sort of hand-to-hand combat. His eyes shifted side to side, as if hopeful of spying out some other weapon, some additional means of defense. A frown gathered between his eyes. A worried frown.

"You understand now, don't you, Lieutenant? No defenses, no hidden weapons. Here we are, Frey. Just two men, facing each other in the middle of nowhere. No names, no ranks, no titles. Warriors, Frey, like the Lenape. Stripped of all the trappings of our English civilization, and about to find out which is the better man."

"You really mean this, don't you? You're insane," Frey said, then cleared his throat. The man seemed to have trouble finding his voice. "Insane!"

Dominick gave a slight inclination of his head. "That's entirely possible, I suppose. At your pleasure, Lieutenant."

"I'll have your hair, Crown, and your heart as well!" Frey shouted, sending the birds out of the treetops. "And I'll send them both back to the Irish bitch in a *box!*"

With that, Frey launched himself against Dominick like a madman, obviously putting his faith in the element of surprise, sending the two of them hurtling backward into the stream.

They hit the water with a mighty splash, Frey having the upper hand. For a moment. Then it was Dominick who found his footing and rose out of the stream, only to have Frey trip him, sending him back beneath the water once more. The trashing roused an owl high above them and he flew away, flapping his wings angrily in his agitation.

An arm broke the surface of the water. A knife blade glinted in the firelight, then plunged swiftly downward, into unprotected flesh.

There was a scream. A terrible, hideous scream. Then silence, only silence, as blood dark as the night sky stained the water.

A candle burned in every window on each of the three floors of Pleasant Hill. The panes of the fanlight above the front door glittered in welcome in front of the brightly lit chandelier in the foyer. Curling white smoke drifted from each of the four chimneys, sending the smell of woodsmoke out into the starry November night.

Mary Catherine had been asleep in her bed for hours, her flute tucked under her pillow, as always, Miss Arabella Thistlewaite clutched tightly in her arms.

Lucas Deems remained in the kitchens with Lucretia, the two of them polishing silver, for want of anything else to do, and both loath to go to their beds even though the tall clock in the foyer had just struck out the hour of three.

Philip Crown sat in the study, his feet propped on his

uncle's desk, sipping brandy and alternately cursing and praying, depending on the moment.

At this particular moment, he was praying.

Bryna Cassidy Crown, bathed and fed and dressed in her nightclothes, stood at the open window in her bedchamber, a warm shawl pulled close around her shoulders, looking down at the empty drive, alternately praying and cursing, depending on the moment.

At this particular moment, she was cursing.

A lone horseman astride a large bay mare appeared at the bottom of the drive, leading a second, riderless horse. His upper body was bare, his shoulders only slightly bowed. Long hair blackened by the night hung loose to those shoulders, and a brightly colored sash was tied around a knife gash in his upper arm.

He reined the horse to a halt, remaining still for long moments, looking up toward the great stone house, watching the many lights splinter into brilliant stars as he viewed them through tear-bright eyes. Listening closely, he thought he could actually hear Bryna calling out his name.

He shook his head, smiled, and urged his mount forward.

Dominick Crown was going home. To where his whole world waited.

KASEY MICHAELS

Kasey Michaels has enchanted millions with
her exquisite Regency romances. Now she
embarks on a bold new journey, exploring
the wilds of colonial America while weaving
an unforgettable romantic adventure...

THE HOMECOMING

And look for the second book in the series

THE UNTAMED
Coming mid-October 1996

POCKET
B O O K S

Available from Pocket Books

1209

POCKET BOOKS
PROUDLY PRESENTS

THE UNTAMED
Kasey Michaels

Coming soon from
Pocket Books

The following is a preview of
The Untamed . . .

The sun shone down brightly as Philip Crown, Earl of Ashford and reluctant savior of damsels in distress, guided his mount along the dusty groove of a footpath leading toward a small encampment of teepees and rude tents outside the gates of mighty Fort Pitt.

"This is where they're keeping the returned captives, Lokwelend?" he asked of his companion, the elderly Lenni-Lenape who rode beside him, holding the lead rope of the extra mount they had brought with them from New Eden. "Hardly seems fitting, unless they're all lousy with lice or some such thing."

Lokwelend grunted. The Indian grunted a lot, Philip had decided. At least he had for the past three weeks, the time it had taken for the two men to cross nearly from one end of the Colony of Pennsylvania to the other. When he wasn't quoting long dead Greeks and Romans, which Philip alternately saw as a splendid joke and as one that wore thin very quickly when it was only the two of them traveling through the wilderness between outposts.

"To your people, Little Crown, the captives are White Indians, Lenape, no matter what the color of their skins," Lokwelend said now. "These people did not come here willingly, and the whites inside the fort fear them as enemies. The Night Fire might not agree to go with us. As I always thought, we may have made a long trip for nothing."

Philip smiled, shaking his head. "You think so, do you? And would you be willing to be the one who says as much to my dear Aunt Bryna when we return to Pleasant Hill without her cousin, now that she has hope Brighid may have been found at last? Wasn't having her shoot at you once enough for you? Why, the way I heard the story told, Bryna singed your feathers and came within a whisker of blowing your head right off. That was before she learned to love you or my Uncle Dominick, of course."

"You have too long a memory for so young a man," Lokwelend answered as the soldier he had spoken to earlier motioned for them to approach. "Here, they are lining up the captives for our inspection. Like cattle at a sale. Nipawi Gischuch will not thank you for this humiliation. If she is even here."

"It would please me immensely, Lokwelend, if you would stop referring to Brighid Cassidy by that name."

Lokwelend grunted, again, then shrugged eloquently. Sometimes Philip couldn't decide between considering the Indian as a Greek oracle or as a damned Frenchman, speaking more with his gestures than his mouth. "It is who she is, Little Crown. She is the Night Fire, just as her cousin is the Bright Fire. Such it will always be. A name cannot change what is inside."

Philip gave up the argument. He only dismounted while Lokwelend, who could recognize Brighid Cassidy, got on with the business of identifying the girl so that they could all go inside the fort and find a wet bottle and dry beds.

The captives had been herded into a ragged single line along the pathway, standing with their heads bowed, their posture defeated. Philip flinched in reflected embarrassment at his government's treatment of his fellow human beings. Like cattle at a sale . . .

These, Philip knew, were the last known Lenape captives; the men, women, and children who had fled Pennsylvania with their captors five years before, having formed new bonds, new relationships with the Indians that superseded those they had left behind. There were young mothers standing in the dust, children sitting at their feet. A redheaded man dressed all in deerskins was chained to a wagon wheel, obviously not overjoyed to have been returned to the "civilized" world. And behind them, standing just outside the tents and teepees, were Indians, young and old. They were already weeping and pulling at their hair and clothing, sure that this time, with this new inspection, their particular loved ones were about to be separated from them forever.

Some of the captives had been living with the Lenape for more than ten years: long enough for a young child to forget his natural parents and far too long to conceive of a separation from their adopted families. Many had married into the tribe that had captured them and were content in their new lives. White Indians, as Lokwelend had said they were called.

Returning the captives and their half-white children had seemed a plausible, even laudable idea when the last treaty had been signed and the edict had come down from the government. Seeing it in practice made Philip uncomfortable.

Lokwelend's warning that he would not be greeted with effusive thanks for "rescuing" Brighid Cassidy sounded more logical now. His mission seemed less noble than when he had agreed to— how had he said it? Oh, yes, he remembered. He had volunteered "to go Brighid hunting, the moment misplaced, recalcitrant Irish maidens are in season, of course."

For the five years since making that promise to Bryna Cassidy Crown, Philip had traveled throughout the colonies, even returned to England for a few months, his offer more than half-forgotten. Until the long arm of the government had reached out and found the last of its once-loyal subjects and demanded they be brought home.

Philip had been visiting at Pleasant Hill once more at the time of the news, and Bryna hadn't hesitated a moment to remind him of his promise. Dominick couldn't leave—not with Bryna once more with child and all the responsibilities he had at his estate and in the town of New Eden, where he remained its most prominent citizen.

That left Philip to make good on his promise. Philip would be the one who got to ride on horseback across the width of the Colony with the grunting, shrugging, bear grease–smelling, Greek-quoting Lokwelend, who swore he could recognize Brighid Cassidy no matter how many years had passed.

The sound of weeping brought Philip back to the moment at hand. "Let's get this over with, Lokwelend," he urged quietly, "before the soldiers decide to silence a few mouths with their rifle butts." He accepted and held the reins of all three horses as the Indian began walking down the line, looking intently into each young woman's face.

Lokwelend had known Brighid Cassidy when her family first came from Ireland to settle in New Eden. It had been Lokwelend who, at Bryna Cassidy Crown's request, had searched for the girl several months after her capture by a raiding war party. And it had been Lokwelend who had found Brighid, then left her behind with her new Lenape family, returning to New Eden empty-handed.

No more than a third of the way down the line, Lokwelend halted in front of a particular young woman, saying quietly, *"Itah!* Good be to you, Nipawi Gischuch. When last we met you told me of your wish to remain with your new family. I had promised the Bright Fire only that I would find you, and so I left you, as you asked, without breaking my word. The Bright Fire learns quickly and was more pointed in her request this time. She wants the sister of her heart to come home. As her friend, and as the friend of Crown, I could not refuse her. Forgive me."

Then he stepped back a pace and pointed to the young woman as he stared levelly at Philip, his dark eyes silently imploring the younger man to measure his words well. "This is she, Little Crown. Before you stands the Night Fire, the one you call Brighid Cassidy."

"Are you sure?" Philip leaned forward slightly to get a better look at the girl. This proved to be rather difficult since she kept her head bowed, refusing to acknowledge his presence just as she had ignored Lokwelend.

Her hands were bound in front of her, unlike those of the other women, as if this one particular woman might be dangerous if untied. Her skin, what he could see of it, was as dark as either heredity or the elements could make it, and it glowed from the usual Lenape application of sunflower oil meant to keep her safe from sunburn while working in the fields. Her black hair, slick with bear grease that could tame any tendency to curl, hung nearly to her waist in thick, long braids.

Tall and slim, she wore a fringed, deerskin wrap-skirt that fell to her knees over deerskin leggings and soft-soled moccasins, and a man's blue cotton shirt was tied at her waist with a striped length of material. Colored beads decorated her clothing, a band of beads sewn to a thin strip of leather encircled her forehead. She looked about as Irish, as white, as Lokwelend, clad in a kilt, would appear Scottish.

Philip, a tall, broad-shouldered English peer with shoulder-length hair the color of liquid sunlight, a man dressed in comfortable deerskins yet carrying an English walking stick—and not for a moment considering his own confusing appearance—laughed out loud. Then, speaking in the slightly amused, cultured tones of London, so unusual an occurrence here in the middle of a wilderness, he said advisedly, "Time to reach into your pouch and pull out those spectacles of yours, Lokwelend. Look at her. That's no white woman."

"You want this one?" the soldier interrupted, walking up to the young woman. "Be glad to get shed of her, if you do. We had to tie her up after she bit Corporal Manton. Damn near took off his ear, as a matter of fact. Here, I'll give you a better look-see."

So saying, the soldier grabbed at the girl's braids and roughly pulled back her head. Suddenly Philip, his good humor quickly leaving him, found himself looking into a pair of angry yet excruciatingly lovely aquamarine eyes, their whites startling against deeply tanned skin. "God's teeth, I don't believe it," he swore quietly as something tightened deep in his gut. "Those Cassidy eyes. So many ways to be green."

Brighid Cassidy looked at him for a long while, her aquamarine gaze unwavering, rudely assessing, and infinitely hostile. Then she turned her back to him, exposing the wooden cradleboard strapped to her shoulders, and the sleeping child tied to the board.

"This is my son, Tasukamend. In your language he is known as The Blameless One. And this," she continued in her odd Irish brogue that carried a hint of Lenape gruffness, "is my mother-in-law, Lapawin." A small, wizened raisin of a Lenape woman scurried to her side. "Her son, my husband, is dead. Killed by the white man. Move me one step from this place without both Tasukamend and Lapawin by my side, *Geptschat,* and it's a sharp knife I'll be taking to your gullet first time you turn your back. Is it understanding me you are?"

Philip was nonplused for a moment, but only for a moment. *"Geptschat?"* he asked, leaning on his walking stick as he turned to Lokwelend. "That, if memory serves, would be the Lenape word for *fool,* would it not?"

Lokwelend smiled, then reached forward to untie Brighid Cassidy's hands. "We'll need a wagon, Little Crown," he said unnecessarily as Lapawin broke into loud sobs, obviously believing she was about to be left behind.

Brighid put an arm around her mother-in-law's thin shoulders as the soldier walked away, and whispered something in her ear which seemed to silence the woman. She then smiled at Philip, displaying straight teeth as brilliantly ivory as the whites of her eyes. "And a cow, Little Crown. We must have milk for Tasukamend, as I have gone dry with shock and the cow we brought with us must remain with the other mothers. I'll be wanting us on our way before nightfall, I will. Once we're out of sight of the fort, you can let us go, and we'll be making our way back to our own people."

"The devil you will!" Philip exclaimed, wondering what great sin he had committed to find himself saddled with this trio of impossible charges—one too old, one too young, and one too exotically and belligerently beautiful. "We're leaving before nightfall, all right, but we'll be traveling east, all the way back to Pleasant Hill and your cousin."

Brighid lifted her chin a fraction. "Very well, Little Crown. I hadn't really believed otherwise. But I warn you now, I will do my level best to make every step of that trip a living hell for you."

"Yes. I'll just wager you might," Philip said dryly. He took one last look at those amazing aquamarine eyes before deftly swinging the ebony walking stick up and onto his shoulder, turning smartly on his heels, and heading for the fort. *I've got to make Lokwelend stop calling me Little Crown,* he decided as he walked. *The girl finds the name entirely too amusing.*

Brighid sat quietly on the uncomfortable wagon seat, refusing to cry as the man called Philip Crown sat beside her and guided the lurching, dipping wagon along the rutted dirt roadway. Crying would do her no good. Besides, Lapawin had been doing enough weeping for the three of them. For the past two hours the old woman had keened and howled. She had wept so long and so hard that she now snored in exhaustion in the back of the rudely jolting wagon, a sleeping Tasukamend beside her.

But Brighid refused to cry. She was going back. Against her will and contrary to her wishes, she was going back. While the remainder of her tribe, as unwelcome in Ohio as they had been in Pennsylvania, moved once more to the West. Every turn of the wagon wheels made the distance between them greater, until that distance would open into a wide, deep chasm she could never cross.

All of her friends, gone. Her family, scattered. Wingenund, her dear friend and sister, buried beside the White River. Wulapen's body lying somewhere she'd never know, unprotected from the ravages of wild animals, his bones bleaching in the sun, his hair hanging on some Iroquois belt or in an English trading post. She didn't know who had killed him, who to hate. Instead, she hated everyone.

She had no one now, no one save Lapawin and Tasukamend. She'd had a mother, once. A father. Two wonderful brothers. She'd had a sister. But they, too, were all gone from her. Gone these five long years. Lokwelend had told her this not four months after the raid that had swept her from New Eden and into a new, frightening, and ultimately welcoming world.

Until that moment so long ago when Lokwelend told her Brighid had believed all of her family to be dead. She'd had no other choice but to accept their deaths, since she could remember little more than playing with her baby sister, Mary Catherine, as her father moved to the doorway of their small living quarters. Of the raid itself, of what had happened after her father reached the doorway, she remembered nothing.

It had been Wingenund who had nursed her back from a serious head injury during those first days. Wingenund who had explained that their captors had cut a path of death and destruction through New Eden, sold their captives to Lapawin and other Lenape a week later, and then moved on. All Brighid had left of her family were happy memories and, thanks to Lokwelend, the comforting knowledge that young Mary Catherine was still alive, safe, and living with her cousin, Bryna, in the glory that was Pleasant Hill.

Brighid could have gone back then. Home, to Mary Catherine. To her cousin Bryna. Home, to the memories that eluded her yet filled her with some nebulous and crippling fear, as if recovering her memory of the raid held more danger than it did answers. Home, to taint Mary Catherine with her presence as a woman captive. Whether she was gone four months or five years, she was assumed to have been violated by savage, dirty Indians—so that she was tainted, less a woman, and a definite embarrassment to her family and her community.

With Lapawin and Wingenund, Brighid had felt safe; safe from her hidden memories. She had felt loved. And she had felt *necessary.* If Mary Catherine had needed her, Brighid would have gone back. But she would not go back only to humiliate the child with the stigma of her "soiled" presence.

No, there had been no reason to go back five years ago. There was less than no reason for her return now. Better to starve with the ragged remnants of her small tribe as they moved ever westward than to return to New Eden, where she would soon outwear her welcome and taint Mary Catherine's future. Better to die with her people than return to a place where she could never belong. And if it weren't for Tasukamend and Lapawin, who depended on her, she would have found a way to escape long before Philip Crown could come and get her.

For she had no future now. Nobody wanted a woman of one and twenty who had lived with "savages" for more than five years. No one wanted a half-breed child, especially a man-child, and she would never give up Tasukamend. Bryna would say she wanted her but, after the thrill of the reunion of the two cousins, what would there be for either of them? Not when she was Nipawi Gischuch, wife of Wulapen. Not when she bore such hatred of the white man in her heart.

"This won't work, you know," she said flatly as the roadway widened, signaling their approach to some small frontier hamlet. It was rapidly growing fully dark, when only the moon and Lokwelend would be able to guide them. "They won't let me in their inns, and I wouldn't stay there if they did. I'd suffocate beneath a roof, I swear it."

Philip Crown turned his head toward her, his smile so naturally pleasant that she longed to bite off his nose. "You'll stay where I put you, Miss Cassidy, and like it. And while I'll admit that you and your small company don't smell especially wonderful, I'll wager that my money will be as good at the upcoming inn as it was on my way out here."

Brighid looked him up and down, then sniffed. "And you smell even less appealing. You smell English to the marrow. Little Crown is a suitable name, I'm thinking, as you're no more than half the Dominick Crown I remember. What are you then, the toad-eating relative? Playing fetch and carry at a rich woman's whims? That's what our Bryna is now, isn't she? A rich woman? Rich Bryna Crown, of Pleasant Hill. Never lived with the chickens, our Bryna didn't, even when her nimble-fingered, card-sharping Da had not a feather of his own to fly with."

"This is how you talk about a woman who has done everything but move Heaven and Hell to get you back? God, but you're a pleasant little bitch, aren't you?" Philip remarked, nodding to Lokwelend as the Indian spurred his horse into a fast trot, taking him ahead of the wagon to guide the way. "I suppose telling you that I am actually Philip Crown, Earl of Ashford, and sole male heir to the Marquess of Playden and the Sussex estate called Playden Court—along with several other properties whose names and locations I won't bore you with right now—would do no more than convince you that I am a liar as well as a toad-eating poor relative?"

Brighid looked at him for long, assessing moments, taking in his clothing, his accent, his infuriating good humor. "A bloody Earl, is it?" she commented at last. "Well, of course you are." She then rolled her eyes exaggeratedly and spoke to the darkening sky. "And isn't that just like Cousin Bryna? Sending off a madman to fetch a fool! For it's a fool I must be to still be sitting here beside this poor deluded fellow who thinks himself to be such a mass of grandeur."

She then watched, astonished, as Philip Crown threw back his head and laughed out loud, clearly amused rather than insulted by her intentional sarcasm. "Oh, lady! Bryna won't be able to deny I've brought her the right Brighid Cassidy," he said when he'd recovered his composure. "In your own way, you're going to be every inch the handful your cousin is, and more, aren't you? And if I turn my back on you between here and Pleasant Hill, I'll deserve that knife in my gullet, I swear to God, I will!"

Look for
The Untamed
Wherever Paperback Books Are Sold
Coming soon
from Pocket Books